Just One Look

Joanne Kukanza Easley

Red Boots Press | Texas

Publisher-Red Boots Press

Cover Design-Erin Cronin Pearson

Author Photo-Spunky Cloud Photography

ISBN: 979-8-9867133-4-2

Library of Congress Control Number: 2022915797

Contents

Just One Look is dedicated to the kids of Kenton Avenue who shared my childhood on the southside of Chicago.

Chapter One

FIRST LOVE-CHICAGO 1965

I fell in love at thirteen, full-blown, knock your socks off, lifetime commitment, soul mate love.

The adult consensus: impossible. Teenage girls flailed in a stew of hormones and drama and knew nothing about love.

But they were wrong—at least about me and John. The first glimpse of him seared my optic nerve and imprinted him in my heart.

One look—and he struck me boy-blind.

My friend Sandy banged on the kitchen door that steamy August day in 1965, calling for me in the typical neighborhood fashion. "Yo, Dani!"

I flung open the screen door.

"Sheba ran off again." Sandy's face glistened with tears. "Please help me catch her. My parents are real pissed. They said they're gonna take her to the pound if I can't keep her home."

"Never! We'll find her. But you gotta do something about her. If she gets hit by a car...well, you don't even want to think about that." I stepped outside. "Which way did she go?"

"Not sure." Sandy sniffed and wiped her eyes with the back of her dirty hands. "I'll hop the fence and look on Kolmar. Can you head to the turnaround and see if you spot her on 77th?"

"Okay. Let's go."

We ran off in different directions. I made it to the corner in record time. My parents wouldn't let me have a dog, no matter how much I begged, so Sheba, Sandy's little mutt, was important to me. I spotted her fifty yards away but knew better than to call to her. Already, I was sweating and short of breath. I bent over and gripped my knees, taking a moment to recover.

Sheba stopped at a fence to visit a spaniel, sniffing, touching noses through the chain-link, and marking the concrete driveway. Approaching on tiptoes, I closed in on the wily dog. When I got within lunging distance, she took off again.

Diesel fumes from a moving van idling at the curb two houses down hung in the heavy air. A guy who looked a little older than me lounged on the front steps, watching me run after Sheba. When I dove for the dog, and she slipped out of my fingers, he grinned and said, "You missed."

I swiped my arm across my perspiring face and grumbled, "You *could* help me."

He stood and jogged down the stairs. "Name's John."

I didn't respond.

John made some moves on the crafty dog, finally making a flying tackle to catch her. Impressive. He handed the little runaway to me and scratched her ears. He looked me up and down, raised an eyebrow, saluted with two fingers. "You take care of her now."

Was that a Southern drawl?

"She's not mine." To meet his eyes, I had to look up. He was over six feet, maybe six-two or three. Most of the boys my age came to my collarbone. His direct stare made me nervous. I'd never had such a cute guy, an older guy, speak to me. My tummy swirled, and my face burned. Words fled. Holding the escape artist to my chest, I started walking backward, staring at him—taking a mental photograph—dark wavy hair, deep brown eyes, and that one-sided smile. Then he winked, and I turned and hustled away.

I knew he was watching me and couldn't stop myself from glancing back at him. "I'm Dani." Burying my face in Sheba's sweet neck, I murmured, "Let him look."

The next day, Sandy told me John's family had moved to Chicago from Tennessee. He was starting sophomore year. Two years older than me, but because I skipped a grade, I'd be entering high school in a few weeks. When Sandy said he'd asked about me in the neighborhood, I erupted with joy. Never having had a boyfriend, I prayed John would be mine.

Of course, I tried to talk to Sandy about the possibility, but she just giggled. "C'mon, let's go hunt for snakes!"

That summer, like every summer since we were seven, Sandy and I spent the days hopping fences, climbing trees, roaming the empty lots, and taking clandestine dips in neighbors' pools. Those days would soon be over for me, but I had a feeling my friend was stuck on tomboy.

Now that I knew where John lived, I found myself strolling down 77th Place several times a day. I convinced Sandy we should train Sheba to walk on a leash, so she'd get more exercise and wouldn't want to run away. Sandy probably saw right through my excuse to parade past his house, but she was my best friend and humored me. My plan failed—I never caught sight of him.

One night a week later, I was sitting on the curb watching a game of running bases. The pitcher was smoking fast and the catcher skilled, so most of the players were called out. I had given up the game that summer, although I was pretty quick and was usually called safe. I thought about how my life would change in a few days when I entered Bogan High School for the first time, a year younger than most freshmen. St. Bede's was in the rearview, and I flat refused to attend Queen of Peace. No more nuns, at least at school. Sunday Mass was non-negotiable. So many things in my life were that way. For instance, my mother hadn't consulted me about clothes, which I thought was unfair. Didn't most high school girls pick out their own clothes?

I heard someone call my name. The deep soft drawl was like honey, exotic to my Southside Chicago sensibilities. I didn't have to turn around to see John because his face was seared into the synapses of my brain. Since the day he caught Sheba, I hadn't stopped thinking about him. But faced with the physical fact of him, I was paralyzed.

"It *is* Dani, right?" His voice sounded amused.

Recovering my wits, I swiveled to face him. "Yeah."

The left side of his mouth lifted, and his eyebrows formed an inverted V as he studied me. "So, I hear you're a freshie."

Feeling like a fool sitting on the ground, I rose. "Yeah." Brilliant. "I hear you're from Tennessee. Your accent is cool."

He threw back his head and laughed. "Cain't take any credit for how I talk. Been doin' it like this my whole life."

I laughed too. "I guess that's right. Never thought of that. What's Tennessee like?"

He brushed his hair back. "Well, it ain't flat like here. Land's not all cut up into tiny little squares and all paved over. More trees." He shrugged.

"Sounds nice." I relaxed a little. Hard to believe I was having an actual conversation with John—or any boy, for that matter.

Out of the corner of my eye, I saw the porch light flash. My mom yelled from the side door, "Dani, time to come in!"

How embarrassing. I wanted to sink into the sidewalk.

"You better go." He gave me that funny little two-fingered salute and sauntered away. When he got to the end of our yard, he turned back. "Catch you later, Dani."

I was ready to be caught.

I turned to Paige, my younger sister, for advice. That may seem weird, but Paige was my go-to person for social advice. Maybe I had a high IQ, but Paige received all the social skills. I was shy. Paige was not. She was popular. She'd already kissed a number of boys—a huge number—even kept a list with their names, scored them from zero to ten. Her list contained over fifty boys from the seventh grade all the way up to high school sophomores. I wondered if she'd done more than kiss, even though she was twelve. Paige and I were less than a year apart. If we were Irish, we'd be called Irish twins, but the Mareks were Hungarian to the core.

Paige was in our room, sorting through a jumble of discarded clothes—probably everything she'd worn in the last week. Paige was a slob. I was not. Sharing a room was a daily ordeal. I closed the door, so we'd have privacy, then spilled the story of meeting John.

"Well, it's about time you got yourself a boyfriend."

"Come on, Paige, don't give me grief. Just tell me what to do."

She turned to me with her blue eyes wide. "Ever seen a James Bond movie?"

"Only all of them," I shot back.

"Did you watch the kissing scenes?"

"Duh." I'd have to tolerate her attitude if I wanted help.

"Then why do you have questions?" She sniffed a t-shirt, screwed up her face, and threw it in the dirty clothes pile.

"I've never kissed a boy." As I admitted this to my younger sister, heat rose from my neck to my cheeks. I hated to blush.

"I know. It's pathetic." Her mouth turned down.

"I've seen your famous list. I know you go to all the make-out parties. Can you take me to one, so I can practice?"

Paige laughed and put her finger on her chin, looking me up and down. "Friday night there's a party at Andy's. His parents are out of town, so it'll be boss. But I'm going to pick out your outfit and fix your hair. God knows you need the help."

I swallowed my response, knowing I couldn't alienate her.

"And I'll let you use my makeup."

"You have makeup?" What else didn't I know about my sister?

"Shh, not so loud. Mom will hear. I lifted some from Kresge's."

"Holy crap!"

Maybe I was a little jealous of Paige's ease with people. It didn't help Mom called her a "social butterfly." I was no butterfly, more like a hermit crab. I spent a lot of time alone reading, or exploring the prairie with Sandy, my only friend. She was an outcast, like me. I thought it might be because her mom was the only woman on our block to have a job. Moms didn't work outside the home in my neighborhood. Mrs. Wilkins was the subject of much gossip at the morning coffee klatches. Perhaps the other moms were envious, given their perpetual griping about the kids and housework and their cumulative intake of Miltown.

Friday night, Paige wrapped my straight brown hair around pink hot rollers, poking my scalp with the metal clips. Good luck, I thought. Nothing could make my hair keep a curl.

Pulling away, I yelped, "Ouch!"

"Shut up and hold still. You'll thank me later."

Once my head was covered in the torture devices, she tore through our closet, looking for a cool top to go with my new hip-huggers. She held up a white eyelet crop top with three tiers of ruffles.

I gasped. "Where did you get that? I saw one just like it in Lerner's window." I snatched it from her, held it to my chest, and looked in the mirror. "Okay, I'll try it."

"Yeah, no-brainer." She didn't reveal where she got the top, and I didn't push it.

I sat on the side of the bed while Paige released my tresses, then bent forward as she brushed my hair. Straightening up so she could style it, I urged her to hurry. It seemed like she took forever.

"Okay. Check it out."

I got up, gazed in the mirror, and was stunned at my image. How did she get my hair to do that? The style was full and bouncy and worthy of the cover of *Sixteen* magazine. She sprayed a cloud of Aqua Net that almost choked me. When the mist cleared, I had to admit I looked pretty good. The hip-huggers and crop top made me look like one of the dancers on *Shindig* or *Hullabaloo*.

"Where's the makeup?" I whispered.

She lifted her mattress and pulled out mascara, blue eye shadow, eyeliner, blush, and lipstick. With a satisfied smile, she tucked it all into a tiny shoulder bag. "Not in the house. We'll go in the alley to put it on."

"Smart thinking." Not something I said to her often. We hugged. "Thanks, sis."

She pulled away and said, "No problem. When we get to the party, follow my lead. I'll hook you up with a great kisser."

Andy's basement was packed with all the cool kids from St. Bede's, Stevenson, and a few high schoolers from Bogan. The Rolling Stones played on the Hi-Fi, and the lights were dim. Strands of Christmas bulbs draped across the low ceiling and a lava lamp on the bar provided the only illumination.

My eyes adjusted to the gloom, and I saw couples in clinches on the ratty old couches, mashed up against the walls, on beanbag chairs. Lots of lip action. I gulped and hoped the half- gallon of Listerine I'd gargled with worked as advertised.

Shouting from outside drowned out "Satisfaction," and heavy footfalls clattered down the stairs. Eddie and the two Mikes, the coolest guys in St. Bede's parish, made an entrance. When I saw John bringing up the rear, I just about fainted.

He scanned the room and noticed me right away. Strode over. The left side of his mouth turned up in that half-smile I saw in my dreams. "Hey, Dani."

I nodded. My lips moved, but I don't think my "hey" was audible.

Paige appeared out of the shadows, dragging Joe Carey by the hand. "Dani, meet Joe. Joe, meet Dani."

Joe took one look at John and pulled away from Paige. "Later," he said as he backed off.

Paige gave John a sidelong glance, then turned to me. Her mouth hung open, then she mouthed, "Wow." She faced John and said, "I'm outta here."

We watched Paige melt into the crowd.

John lifted his chin. "Who's the blond chick?"

"My sister Paige."

"Sister? You don't look nothin' alike."

I shrugged. "Nope." I fell silent, at a loss for what to say.

He bailed me out. "So, you like make-out parties?"

Oh, God. My mouth opened and closed. "Um, I don't know. This is my first one."

He laughed. "Really?" He grasped my hand and drew me close.

A screech of the record player's needle cut off the Stones, and someone put on an oldie, Doris Troy singing "Just One Look." Her pure, yet sultry voice embedded the lyrics in my consciousness. It became our song.

When his lips touched mine, the tummy swirling I'd experienced when I first saw him returned, along with new, indescribable sensations. I moaned, and he backed me up to the wall, still kissing. I never wanted this to stop. By the end of the night, my lips were swollen with overuse, and my heart belonged to John. He walked me home, holding my hand.

"So, how did you like your first make-out party? Guess you'll be going to all of 'em now."

Stopping dead in my tracks, I gulped. I gazed up at him and saw him holding his laughter in. "Nope. I learned everything I need to know tonight." Taking a risk, I continued. "With you."

John looked at his shoes, then met my eyes. After a moment, he said, "I was hopin' you'd say that." He grasped my hands and pulled me to him. Another luscious kiss. "I want you to be my girl."

I think I squealed. How embarrassing. Then I didn't care because I couldn't remember ever being this happy. All too soon, we reached my house. I didn't want to go in, but there was Mom with the old porch light trick. Feeling transformed, ethereal, I floated into the house.

My mother asked, "Where's Paige?"

I shrugged and glided up the stairs. In the bathroom, I stared at the image in the mirror, touching my lips that still tingled. There was a red chafed ring around my mouth. My eyes looked older and wiser—or something. I felt like a woman—initiated into the club. Now the song by the Shangri-Las from last year made sense. All I wanted to do was give John a great big kiss.

The first day of high school was the worst. I tried to convince myself my mother didn't really hate me when she insisted I wear a below-the-knee, bright yellow, full-skirted shirtdress with ruffles down the front and three-quarter sleeves.

"I bought it especially for you. Yellow works beautifully with your coloring," she cajoled. Mom's fashion sense stopped developing in the '40s. I threw a fit, threatened to stay home or go to school in my slip, but she prevailed.

Somehow, I didn't believe Mom would ever foist such a fashion blunder on Paige. And I doubted Paige would cave to Mom's pleas and wear it. My sister not only didn't resemble me—we had nothing in common except our parents, and sometimes I questioned even that association. I was tall, dark-haired with hazel eyes. How could the same parents produce me and curly-haired, blond, blue-eyed Paige? I couldn't help comparing my spare bosom to Paige's gigantic breasts. After years of fruitless waiting for my elegant ballet-dancer mother to rescue me from these Marek people, I'd given up and accepted what it said on my birth certificate.

That day, I learned the meaning of "laughingstock." Finger pointing, chortles, elbow nudges, catcalls, ironic whistles, and outright laughter followed me through the halls of Bogan. The only saving grace was I didn't see John. After my last class, I ran home in tears. Bursting through the door, I shrieked at my mother. "Everybody made fun of me in this crap dress. I hate you!"

Mom gasped and tears sprang to her eyes. I spun, stormed up to my room, and ripped the yellow rag from my body. Balling it up, I threw it downstairs, watching it fall like a lemon-colored parachute.

The only positive thing that came from my humiliation was I was allowed to choose my own clothes from then on. I never found out what Mom did with that horrid dress, but I never saw it again.

After the yellow dress incident, I distanced myself from my family, preferring the company of John's—the Nagys. They welcomed me into their home and hearts without reservation. John worked afternoons at his father's car repair business, so I spent much of my free time after school at the garage. Mr. Nagy was quiet and focused on his business, hoping to make it a success. He was older than my dad by several years. His family fled Hungary in 1939, when the government started "getting cozy with the Nazis and the Fascists," as he often said. They settled in Knoxville, Tennessee, where Mr. Nagy and his brother started a car repair shop. When Mr. Nagy was drafted, he served in the Pacific Theater. He grumbled, "I wanted to kill those fucking Nazis but only bagged me some Japs."

John never said why they moved to Chicago, but I was grateful they had. Mr. Nagy called me "little grease-monkey girl," although I never touched a tool or peered under a hood. The smell of motor oil and hot metal became as familiar as the kolaches John's mom baked.

Mrs. Nagy still had a thick Hungarian accent, much more pronounced than that of her husband. She made me feel loved and accepted. *Lánya*, she called me, and I did feel like her daughter.

John's older brother Chuck graduated high school just before their move. He shared John's same dark good looks, down to the expressive, mobile eyebrows, but he was only five-foot nine—my height. He had diabetes and wasn't in danger of being called up in the war. Chuck worked six days a week at the garage, opening in the morning and closing at night. I wondered if he thought his illness diminished him in his father's eyes, and if that was the reason for his dedication. The small refrigerator in the garage office held his insulin as well as their lunches.

No one I knew had diabetes. The Nagys, who were very involved in Chuck's care, taught me a lot about it. Mrs. Nagy told me Chuck's life got a whole lot easier with disposable insulin syringes. Before that innovation came on the market, he had to boil glass syringes. Recently, new test strips to check sugar in the urine became available. Chuck was meticulous in monitoring his condition and, with what I learned about the complications of diabetes, this was of paramount importance. All the Nagys were invested in having Chuck live the best life possible.

When I compared my chaotic home life to theirs, I started to question our family dynamic: two girls close in age but not in heart, and two insufferable and adored younger brothers. A house divided.

My mother knew something was up because I was seldom at home, and Sandy stopped coming by. No doubt the nosy-neighbor grapevine had been buzzing about me. One afternoon, Mom cut me off at the door on my way out to see John after school.

"Where do you think you're going, young lady?"

"Out."

"No, you're not."

"Why?"

She frowned and pointed to the kitchen table. "Sit down. I want to hear about this boy you've been seeing."

We sat. She lit one of her Viceroys. I swallowed a smile, thinking about the first time Paige and I stole a couple of her "cigs" and lit up down in the turnaround.

Paige had taken a huge drag and fallen flat on her back. "Hot damn! What a rush."

I couldn't believe her reaction. Did she hit her head? "Rush? You passed out."

She hopped to her feet. "No, I didn't. My head was spinning, that's all. I feel great." Paige inhaled another big mouthful of smoke. This time, she remained vertical. "See?"

I took a timid puff and choked, coughing until my eyes streamed. Paige thought that was hilarious.

We continued to snag a Viceroy when we could. My sister seemed to enjoy smoking, while I only wanted the sophistication and glamour, like in the movies, but without the smelly, acrid reality. Maybe I'd get one of those cigarette holders like Audrey Hepburn in Breakfast at Tiffany's. I wouldn't even have to light up, just gesture grandly with the holder. Then I cringed at the visuals of Cruella de Vil and Phyllis Diller—not the look I wanted.

Mom's stern voice jolted me out of the memory. "Well, Danielle, what about this boy?"

Full first name, not a good sign. "Who ratted me out? Mrs. Perkins? Mrs. Kretchmer? Mrs. Bronkowski?"

"Nope. Mrs. Garrity, not that it matters." She exhaled a cloud of smoke and squinted. "Who is he?"

"His name is John. John Nagy. His family moved here from Tennessee this summer. He lives down 77th Place." I told her what she wanted to know but couldn't wait for interrogation to end.

"So, you've been to his house?"

"Yep."

"Were his parents home?" Mom sent me a piercing look as she stubbed out her cigarette.

I rolled my eyes. "Yep."

"I want you to bring him here to meet me and your father."

My voice rose about three octaves. "Oh, my God! You can't be serious."

"Your father is concerned. Invite this John over for dessert on Friday, so your father can look him in the eye and decide if you can see him."

I jumped up. "What is this, a dictatorship?"

"We're your parents. So, yeah, a dictatorship. Friday night after dinner."

"Fine!"

I dashed for the door and raced toward the Nagy garage on Cicero. Would John come to meet my family? I'd met his folks, so I sure hoped he would.

Why was I subjected to this scrutiny? Because I was the eldest? My rulers needed to pay more attention to their smoking, kissaholic, shoplifting daughter. It sucked being the oldest one. I had to be the example for the younger children.

I'd heard that my whole life, as long as I could remember.

My mind traveled back to a prime example, the haircut incident, when Paige was six. She cut the ponytail off my Barbie, a present for my seventh birthday. Walking into our room, I found her sitting on the floor with scissors in one hand and my shorn Barbie in the other. The doll's auburn ponytail lay in a curl, like a dead caterpillar.

"Barbie got a haircut." Paige beamed at me.

"You brat," I screamed. Paige hollered for Mom. I yanked Barbie from her hand and drew back my fist to slug her. My mother rushed in, grabbed me in a bear hug, and said, "No hitting! Danielle, you have to be an example for your sister."

I glared at my mom, feeling the tears well. "What about *her*? She wrecked my birthday present. Who is she an example for?" I ran outside with the stupid doll. When I reached the vacant lot, I dug a hole with my hands and buried the thing. That day I became friends with Sandy, who was busy building a fort at the base of an oak tree. Together, we created a serviceable hideout using some discarded tin panels and boards, and I never played with a doll again.

That night, I lay awake plotting my revenge against Paige.

A few days later, scissors tucked up my sleeve, I snuck up behind the little monster who was coloring at the table in our room. I pushed her off the chair and sat on her. Paige screamed in my face, but I wasn't deterred. I cut her curly blond hair, chopping it off in random clumps. "Paige got a haircut, Paige got a haircut," I chanted over and over.

Before I could finish, Mom charged into our room. She shrieked, "Her beautiful curls!"

Knowing I'd better stop, I tossed away the scissors and stood. "I was just following Paige's example." Got my face smacked and no TV for a week.

The perils of being the firstborn child never ended.

When I arrived at the garage, all three Nagy men had their heads under the hood of a '57 Chevy. When they finished studying whatever they were studying, I said "Hi," and asked if I could talk to John. "Privately."

His dad wiped his hands on a shop towel. "Go ahead. I gotta order parts for this bucket of bolts." Chuck followed him into the back office.

"Privately?" John grinned. "Okay. What's up?"

"My parents. They're so lame."

He shrugged. "Parents are parents. If you're under their roof, they're the boss. What's the problem?"

"Well, they want to meet you, for one thing."

"Okay. What's the other things?"

"Oh. Okay? You'll come over?" I was astonished and happy he'd agreed.

"Sure. Why not? You met my parents. So, what else?"

"Nothing else, actually. I-I wasn't sure what you'd say."

"Come here." He held out his arms, and I leaned into him, inhaling motor oil and Jade East.

"Dani, you worry about the craziest things. I was wondering if you didn't want me to meet them for some reason."

His reaction made me feel so stupid. "Can you be there Friday after dinner? At seven?"

"Yep. I'll be there."

Friday night dinner was the usual. Fish sticks, tater tots, and soggy, overcooked canned green beans, Wonder Bread (helps build strong bodies twelve ways) and butter. My mother was crazy about butter. We never ate margarine. My annoying little brothers—Phil, eight, and Joe, five—kicked each other under the table. My dad talked about the White Sox and Phil's Little League game on Saturday. Paige and Mom chatted about Dr. Ben Casey, their shared TV idol. I felt left out—the usual.

It was my night to clear the table, and Paige's night to wash the dishes. There would be time to run upstairs and get ready for John. Earlier, I'd made a chocolate cake for dessert and placed it as far as possible from the edge of the counter to keep Phil and Joe's grubby hands from digging into it.

"When do we get some cake?" Phil demanded, always the instigator. Joe repeated most of what came out of Phil's mouth and followed him around like the puppy I never had.

"Yeah, I want cake. When do we get some cake?" Joe pounded the table with his little fists. So obnoxious.

"You two have to wait a few minutes. We're saving it for when John gets here. Mom, make sure they don't wreck the cake while I run upstairs."

I dashed to the bathroom to brush my teeth and comb my hair. It was almost seven.

John arrived right on time. He wore black pants, a white shirt, and a tie. He carried a bouquet of peonies. I hadn't thought my opinion of him could get any higher, but it did that night. I'd never seen him in a tie, not even at church. And the peonies. I knew they were from his yard, his mom's pride and joy. I never expected him to try so hard to please my parents. Although my heart soared, as it did each time I saw him, I feared what indignities my family might visit on him.

"Hello, Mr. and Mrs. Marek. These are for you, ma'am." John handed the peonies to Mom, who gasped and sank her nose into the magenta blossoms.

"Thank you, young man." My mother loved getting flowers.

Dad stepped forward and shook John's hand. "You from the Nagy family that has the garage on Cicero?"

"Yes, sir."

"I hear good things. Have a seat."

So far, my parents hadn't ruined my life. I exhaled, feeling a little less stressed.

"Hi, John. Wow, you went all out with the tie," Paige teased.

John laughed. "Have to make a good impression."

Heat rose from my neck to my face. "I baked a cake for you. Let's have dessert."

My brothers succumbed to a giggling fit. When I brought the dessert to the table, I discovered the cause of their mirth: one side of the cake had been scraped almost clean of frosting and small finger holes marred the surface.

I glared at them. "Well, boys, I see you've already marked your slices. I'm just glad there's a little left for everybody else." Being the good example I was, I resisted the urge to smack them.

John politely answered every question my parents threw at him. My dad cracked a smile now and then as they talked cars and baseball. My mother, however, seemed thoughtful and not convinced. She glanced from John to me with her mouth set in a thin line. I believed she feared I'd found true love. If so, she was right.

After the cake, Mom ushered the boys upstairs with their typical foot-dragging and whining; my dad followed with the *Chicago Daily News*, grumbling about American planes shot down in Vietnam. Paige, ever the opportunist, slunk out for some unknown destination.

Alone at last, John and I sat in the living room, talking about his plans to buy an Indian motorcycle to restore.

"The hoods all ride Harleys, and they're cool and all, but I like the Indian. A true classic. I'm talkin' about the bikes constructed before 1953, when the company went out of business. They made some British imports until about 1960, but they ain't the real thing."

"You know so much about cars and motorcycles." I loved hearing John's voice, although he could be speaking Martian for all I knew.

"Thought about gettin' you a sidecar so you can ride in comfort, but you cain't go over forty-five miles an hour with one of those. It'd take a month to get to Tennessee."

"Tennessee?"

"Sure. I wanna take you to see the hills of Tennessee."

Soft footfalls and giggling came from the stairs—my bratty brothers snooping.

I jumped to my feet and climbed a few steps. "You two go to bed. Quit spying on us!"

Phil and Joe ran back to their room, laughing and making kissing sounds. What monsters!

John and I talked until ten. After leaving the house through the kitchen door, we stopped and kissed on the stoop. Wishing I could go home with him, I watched him walk down the street.

When I stopped in to say good night to my parents, who were in bed watching the news, they glanced at each other. Dad nodded. Mom said, "John seems like a nice boy. You have our permission to see him. Just bring him around once in a while."

"Okay." Before they could pile on more conditions, I turned to leave. There was no doubt I wasn't meant to hear what came next.

Dad chuckled. "Puppy love. Be over in a week."

Mom answered, "I'm not so sure. I'll say a novena to Mary for this crush to end—quick."

Aglow with love as I was, my freshman year passed in a flash. Because I was taking honors classes and John took shop, we never had a class together. We met before homeroom each day and held hands while he walked me to Room 232. I couldn't help but notice the envious looks directed at me by the other girls. I didn't think much of it until one day, while changing classes, I was shoved in the back by what felt like a linebacker from the Bears. Catching myself before I landed on my knees, I whirled around to face the wrath of a bovine, hatchet-faced senior whose younger sister Darla had made it known she liked John.

Mr. Bryan, the vice-principal, who happened to be monitoring the stairwell, apparently heard the commotion and probably saved my life. Hatchet-face was easily double my weight and towered over me. She was almost as tall as Mr. Bryan, whom I despised, as did the entire student body. But that day, he was my hero. I smirked as he grabbed the beast's elbow and escorted her to the office. She snarled, and my smile evaporated. I'd better watch my back.

With many of my friends attending Queen of Peace for high school, I felt a bit untethered at Bogan, but my social life revolved around John. There was no room in my life for anyone else.

I worried about the tough girls taking John away from me. The group of girls who hung out with the hoods were reputed to be fast. They ratted their hair, lacquered it to the firmness of a football helmet, wore heavy eyeliner swooping into wings, and chewed gum as if their very lives depended on it. Another way to spot a member of this bunch was by their legs, encased in black hose—usually with runs, which they treated with an application of clear nail polish.

John didn't hang out with the hoods. But because of his dad's repair shop, he encountered them when they brought their hot rods and cycles in for service. A few times, Hatchet-face's sister Darla showed up at the garage with her latest conquest. She glared at me as she tried to flirt with John. He ignored her, acted as if she didn't exist. Our bond was so strong, I never doubted he'd remain true to me. When school ended in June, we were inseparable and committed to one another.

Our perfect path stretched in front of me—I could see it, touch it, taste it—a beautiful journey that would take me to a wedding and a future with the love of my life.

Chapter Two

STONE IN LOVE 1966-1968

The summer of 1966 was blissful in our corner of the planet. Being in love enveloped me, and rose-colored glasses didn't begin to characterize the way I experienced life.

My corner of the planet was a post-World-War II GI Bill neighborhood, close-knit and a virtual melting pot of ethnicities, but not of race. Chicago remained a racially segregated town, with a distinct "color line" the grownups whispered about as it kept creeping closer to the southwestern edge of the city. My dad often said before the war Chicago was a patchwork of ethnic neighborhoods. "I could tell by somebody's address if they was a Polack or a Mick." Dad never minced his words. National origin was of paramount importance to his generation.

Our postage-stamp-sized city lots were dotted with small bungalows where Greeks, Italians, Jews, Lithuanians, Polish, German, Irish, Hungarians, and others lived together in ostensible harmony. However, there was an undercurrent of the past because even the kids were aware of their neighbor's ethnic identity and certain of their own tribe's superiority.

Most of the couples began procreating right after buying their homes, as if they were competing in the fertility Olympics. We kids numbered over sixty on a single city block, and we segregated ourselves by age and grade level. For instance, it was beneath a fourth grader to play with a third grader.

With the need for space in their burgeoning households, several families added onto the back of their homes, obliterating their already tiny backyards. Three years earlier, my mom had inherited some money from her great-aunt, and our family built up, adding a second story with three bedrooms and a bathroom my mother decreed the "girls' bathroom." Although I still had to share a room with Paige, not sharing a bathroom with my dad, Phil, and Joe was heavenly.

My father was the ultimate authority—my mother content to let him take the reins. Family dinners—mandatory—revolved around my father. Three topics of conversation dominated: baseball, the Chicago police force to which my father belonged, and the Vietnam war.

We subscribed to the *Chicago Tribune*, the morning newspaper and the *Chicago Daily News*, the afternoon broadsheet. My mom usually got to the afternoon paper first and scanned it for coupons and human-interest stories, especially tragic ones. I dubbed her Morbidia the Crepehanger, a name that made me laugh and made her angry.

Some of my fondest memories center on the Fourth of July. Each year, the neighborhood celebrated with a block party. Just about all the dads were veterans of WWII or Korea. My father was too young for WWII. To my mother's relief, he snagged a 3-A paternity deferment during the Korean War because she was pregnant with me. Dad fulfilled his patriotic duty in the Illinois Guard.

Courtesy of the cops in the neighborhood—including my dad—Kenton Avenue was blocked off on each end with official sky-blue city barricades. Each family lugged grills, picnic tables, and coolers into the street. An area was set aside for curb ball and fast pitch. The aroma of hot dogs, burgers, and various ethnic sausages filled the air. Cans of Miller High-Life, Pabst, Old Style, and Hamm's beer were popped.

Mr. Garrity said, "We won't be needing a church key no more, not with these new ring tabs."

Mr. Bronkowski, who won a Purple Heart in Korea and wore a black patch over his left eye—or where his eye used to be—raised his Hamm's in a toast. "To progress and good old-fashioned American ingenuity."

My dad replied, "To the greatest country in the world, the U S of A."

Mr. Kretchmer bellowed, "I'll drink to that!"

Radios were tuned to the Sox game. We were Southsiders, and most of us had no love for the Northside team, the Cubs. But Sandy's family were die-hard Cubs fans, and their radio blared the play-by-play. If I heard the name Ernie Banks once, I heard it from her lips a thousand times. This year the Sox were leading the Yankees at Yankee Stadium, while the Cubs were busy losing to the Pirates at Wrigley. All was right in the world except at the Wilkins' picnic table.

Sandy and I no longer ran together. She'd just finished eighth grade while I was going to be a sophomore. My life was so different from our shared tomboy days. She still had skinned knees. I had a manicure and a boyfriend.

John and I grabbed cups of lemonade and sat on our front stoop, away from the noise and activity.

"I'm savin' up for a car," John said.

"Cool. What kind?" I put down my cup and moved closer.

"Not sure yet. Maybe a Mustang." He thought a moment. "Maybe a Mopar, they make some fine cars."

"What about the Indian? And Tennessee?"

He put his arm around me. "The Indian, someday, doll. But now I'm thinkin' about a car first. We can ride to Tennessee in a car too."

"Do you miss it? Tennessee, I mean."

"A little." He glanced at me. "There's one thing Tennessee doesn't have. Dani Marek."

My eyes misted. I leaned into him, floating on happiness.

"Besides the hills and the trees, I miss my friend, Noah. He was like my brother. When he was real little, his dad died in Korea. Growing up, you couldn't keep us apart. Haven't found a Noah here in Chicago. Y'all got your hoods and your jocks and your brains, but no one like him."

"Tell me about him," I murmured into his neck.

"After his dad died, him and his mom moved in with his aunt and uncle, right down the road from us. His uncle is a vet and raises Border Terriers. Man, we used to have a blast running the woods with his dog Fred." John reached for my hand. "Noah was the smartest kid in class, but he never bragged about it. A good guy. And the best catcher at our school."

Phil and Joe came running up, sweaty and dirty from playing running bases.

"Hot dogs are ready," Phil announced. "Dad said get 'em while they're hot."

"Yep, hot hot dogs," Joe echoed.

I rolled my eyes. One of these days Joe might discover he wasn't an extra appendage on Phil.

John pulled me to my feet. The boys tagged after us.

"John, will ya pitch for us? Huh? Will ya? After the hot dogs?" Phil walked next to John, pulling on his shirt, generally making himself a nuisance.

"Sure, kid. After we eat, I'll throw a few for you."

"All right." Phil ran ahead, with Joe trailing him, trying to keep up.

Dad served up the hot dogs. John filled his plate and dug in. "This potato salad is very good, Mrs. Marek."

Mom beamed at him, then frowned at me when I refused to take a bun and took only a tiny spoon of the potato salad.

"Where's Paige?" Mom craned her neck, looking around at the neighbors' tables.

"Down the block at the Hennessey's." I didn't add that she was with her latest boyfriend, Brian.

Umpteen cans of Hamm's beer—from the land of sky-blue waters—were raised when the Sox shut out the Yankees in the first game 5-0. The Sox dads cheered, but I caught a few words that worried me. Mr. Bronkowski: "Things looking bad in Southeast Asia." Mr. Garrity: "We woulda kicked their commie asses by now and been home for dinner." My dad, glancing at Phil and Joe: "Too many of our boys dying."

Those rose-colored glasses slipped a bit.

That fall, school chugged along. I kept my grades up; it was easy for me. John barely skated by in his academic classes, but he was the star of auto shop.

I continued to hang out at the garage after school. But on Fridays, I learned to bake Hungarian pastries with Mrs. Nagy. Rétes was my favorite.

Well, it was John's favorite, so I was eager to learn how to make the Hungarian strudel, which was quite the production.

Mrs. Nagy, the woman I hoped would be my future mother-in-law, heated up water to just lukewarm. Then she added salt and vinegar to it. She sieved pastry flour onto a huge marble slab, added egg and butter, then started mixing with her hands. I followed her directions, slowly adding the water mixture while she constantly kneaded the dough until bubbles formed on its surface.

"Look, Dani, the dough is soft. It should never stick to your hand, or the marble. Now I make two loaves, cover with butter, and put in oven to rise. No heat."

"It sure is a lot of work. My mom bakes from a box. Betty Crocker or Duncan Hines, whatever's on sale."

Mrs. Nagy rinsed her hands. "Yes, American food." She scrunched up her nose. "Cans and boxes. This is how we cook in the old country."

"How long do we wait?"

Mrs. Nagy waved her hand in a sideways motion. "About one hour for dough to double. I will show you some photographs of Hungary and from when John was a baby."

"Okay. I'd love to see them."

Mrs. Nagy left the kitchen and, after a few minutes, came back with a carton. Inside were several albums. One held yellowed photographs of Hungary. Szentendre, the town where Mr. and Mrs. Nagy were born, nestled on the Danube, north of Budapest. It was difficult to discern much from the faded black and white photos. Of course, I was more interested in seeing John as a child. The album of family pictures revealed John was cute as a baby and a little boy. But now he was even more handsome than Rowdy Yates on *Rawhide*.

The hour passed quickly. I loved the stories Mrs. Nagy shared: John was a good baby, rarely crying; he walked early, at eight months. I cherished those little nuggets and wondered if our children would take after me or John. In Biology, I'd learned because I had blond, blue-eyed parents and siblings, there was a one-in-four chance I could have a fair baby, but I hoped our offspring would be dark like us.

We spread a cloth on the kitchen table and Mrs. Nagy sprinkled pastry flour all over it. I'd never seen anything like this.

"Get me the pans from the oven, please. And hand me the rolling pin."

As promised, the dough had doubled in size. Mrs. Nagy rolled it flat. "Work the dough, *Lánya*. Like this." She demonstrated, walking around the kitchen table, spreading the dough with the back of her hand, stretching the puffy concoction until it was translucent, paper thin. "Now the dough will rest, and so will I. Sit a minute."

"Can I make you some tea, Mrs. Nagy?"

"Yes, thank you, darling."

While we drank tea and rested like the dough, Mrs. Nagy told me she'd prepared cottage cheese filling and poppy seed filling. "We make two rétesek, one of each."

"Which is John's favorite?"

"Poppy seed." Naturally, I worked on the poppy seed.

We returned to our task, spreading butter over the pastry, and folding it using the tablecloth. More butter on each fold. My mother would love this. After we got the correct size, we spread the fillings. Mrs. Nagy showed me how to roll up the rétes with the help of the tablecloth.

"More butter on top, then put in buttered baking pan."

More butter? My mother would be in heaven.

The delicacy baked at 375 degrees until golden. We looked at more photographs and chatted about Hungarian food while the loaves cooled, then cut our strudels on the diagonal and sprinkled them with powdered sugar.

The three Nagy men came home from work to the aroma of baking. Mrs. Nagy spent so much time baking on Fridays Mr. Nagy thoughtfully brought dinner home those nights. He carried in a big red and white barrel of Kentucky Fried Chicken.

John's smile when he saw me—and the poppy seed strudel—made all the effort worthwhile. My mission in life was to please him, but I wondered how I'd fit in all the baking when I had my dream job in fashion marketing after I graduated college.

The holidays came, and I was devastated to learn the Nagys were going to Tennessee to visit family for Christmas. I begged my parents to let me go with them but ran into a united front of refusal. I cried for a week and wouldn't speak to them, but their decision stood.

John came over the night before the Nagys were leaving. "I'll be back before you know it. Open your present before I go." He held out a tiny box wrapped in gold-glittered paper and a fancy bow.

I groaned. "I haven't wrapped yours yet."

"Don't worry. Give it to me when I get back."

"No! It'll only take me a minute. I want to give it to you now."

I ran upstairs and raided the closet where Mom kept the wrapping paper. Chose the prettiest paper but did a sloppy rushed job. No time to attempt a bow.

John was waiting at the bottom of the stairs. We exchanged gifts and a kiss.

I'd bought him The Kinks' new album *Face to Face*. John loved all the British rock bands, something we had in common.

He bought me an opal necklace on a delicate white-gold chain. It must have decimated his car savings.

I kissed him goodbye and knew I'd be counting the days, the hours, the minutes until he returned.

Going steady—the most important social rank—usually didn't last long in high school. John and I were the exception. Our relationship never faltered. We were happy together, and the eponymous song by The Turtles became my new favorite in the spring of 1967.

Music changed that year. The Brits were still rocking, but American artists surged in popularity. WLS and WCFL played the music from Monterey Pop. Janis Joplin gave me goose bumps with her raw wailing. Such pain and passion. Jimi Hendrix and The Doors records appeared in my collection, although The Stones still held top billing on my charts.

As the war invaded our living room on the television, it was hard to escape from it. My parents combed the *Trib* and *Sun Times* for the latest developments. Yet, my little piece of the planet hummed along, oblivious. For obvious reasons, I didn't want to think about the war.

Our block party that Fourth of July 1967 didn't differ materially from last year's festivities, except for the weather. It was overcast with a chilly north wind, and the temperature never got out of the sixties. But we were a hardy bunch on Kenton Avenue, and nothing was going to prevent the dads from grilling. Sweatshirts were dug out of winter storage. Beer was still consumed, although Mr. Garrity carried a pint of whiskey in his jacket pocket.

Same menu. Same ballgames. The Sox were at the top of the rankings and beat the Baltimore Orioles at Comiskey. The Cubs were busy losing to the Atlanta Braves. At least they weren't embarrassing themselves in front of the home crowd. They lost the doubleheader. The taunts from the Sox dads directed at Sandy's dad were brutal. "Get Ernie a wheelchair, he's an old man." Mr. Wilkins took the gibes good-naturedly, but Sandy looked angry, scowling as she stalked away to join a game of fast pitch.

Phil and Joe spent the day running with their friends and didn't bug John, which was a blessing. I had him all to myself. Paige was down the street with her new boyfriend, Russell Kovac. She hadn't found that elusive perfect pair of lips and was still searching for the ultimate kiss. When I realized I'd finally beaten Paige at something, I couldn't hide my smile.

John and I took a walk as the sun was setting. We slipped into the alley. Under cover of darkness, we held each other. I kissed him like I was drowning, and he could resuscitate me.

Our community was dealt a shock in December. Mr. Wilkins died of a massive heart attack. Worried brows on the moms as they urged their husbands to get more exercise and searched for low calorie recipes in *Good Housekeeping* magazine. But Mrs. Wilkins didn't have a need for any of that. She was well-positioned to take care of her family because she already worked.

John and I attended the wake at the funeral home. Mrs. Wilkins, a slender blond, clutched a handkerchief, but she stood bravely, greeting her friends and neighbors. Sandy's eyes were puffy and bloodshot. She'd been close to her dad.

I hugged Mrs. Wilkins and told her how sorry I was for her loss, hoping I said the right words. As we walked away, I squeezed John's hand and whispered, "So sad. I can't imagine losing my dad. Mr. Wilkins wasn't even forty."

John squeezed back. "I know. Very sad."

My eyes stung with tears. "I'll be right back." As I turned the corner to the hallway, searching for the ladies' room, I saw something that shocked me. Sandy, holding hands with Beth Lawton, faces close. Were they about to *kiss*? Oh my God. I realized Sandy batted for the other team. It explained some things and made me wonder about others.

Sandy and Beth jumped apart; both looked stricken. Faces pale, mouths open. There was no way to ignore this. They knew I saw them. I recalled the years Sandy and I spent playing together, remembered we had been best friends since second grade until—John. Although we didn't hang out together anymore, we had a history and a bond.

I stepped toward them. "I'm so sorry, Sandy. Your dad was a great guy, even if he was a Cub's fan. I'll pray for you and your mom."

"Thanks." Sandy stammered, "Let me ex-explain."

Patting her shoulder, I asked, "Explain what?"

Beth and Sandy both exhaled with relief. They understood I'd keep their secret.

Christmas was better that year. John's family remained in Chicago, and their Tennessee relatives came to visit. I had hoped to meet Noah, but he couldn't make the trip because he had to work at the boarding kennels for the busy holiday. I had a glimpse of how the holidays would go when John and I were married, a careful dance of pleasing both families. Christmas Eve at my house. Christmas dinner with his family.

With the house full of John's uncles and their wives and offspring, John and I took advantage of the chaos and snuck down to the basement. We lay on the couch in the dark and kissed until I felt like I was on another plane of existence. John unhooked my bra, and I pulled it off through my sleeves, a practiced routine. I wanted to consummate our love, and there was no doubt John was ready and willing.

He moaned. "Dani, I'm dyin' here. Can we?"

I breathed him in. "Yes."

The light came on. Busted by the cousins coming downstairs to play ping pong. I jumped up from the couch, shoving my bra down the back of my skirt. Wide eyes and giggles from the troupe of John's younger cousins, knowing grins from the older ones. My face burned.

John put his finger to his lips and winked at the kids. He took my hand and tugged. "We better head to your house for dessert."

Upstairs in the bathroom, I put my bra on, contemplating love interrupted. The issue was now on the table, and I felt a sense of inevitability: we'd go all the way soon. That night was the closest we'd ever come to doing it. The only thing stopping us was the lack of a secure place, what with my busy household and Mrs. Nagy rarely leaving the house. Stolen moments of deep desire left us breathless and frustrated. It had to end.

We bundled up and walked to my house for dessert. When we entered the kitchen, Phil and Joe were standing at the counter about to ravage the pumpkin and chocolate pecan pies. I rushed to save the desserts. "Where's Mom?"

Phil said, "She's in her room. I think she's crying."

"Yep. She's mad at Dad," Joe added.

"Why? And where's Dad?"

Phil shrugged. "I dunno."

"Be right back. I'll get dessert in a minute. Go play with your toys. John, make sure they don't touch the pies!" I raced upstairs. The door to my parents' room was closed. I knocked and turned the knob. Locked. "Mom, it's Dani. Let me in."

I heard soft halting footsteps, then Mom opened the door. There was no doubt she'd been crying.

Stepping in the room, I asked, "What happened?"

Mom shook her head. "Oh, not a big deal. Your dad got me another thoughtful gift. An iron. I almost lined it at his head. He got huffy and left."

"Jesus. I'm sorry. Come on down, and we'll have dessert. Where's Paige?"

"She's at Aaron's house. She promised to be home for dessert too."

We returned to the kitchen. John sat at the table talking to my brothers. Paige and Aaron Goldstein drifted in as Mom was squirting whipped cream on the pies. "Where's Dad?" Paige asked.

"Out." Mom's clipped voice offered no room for more questions.

With everyone gathered at the table, conversation fizzled. All eyes stared at the festive Christmas plates. I picked at a tiny piece of pumpkin. John had a slice of each flavor. Two pieces of chocolate pecan pie disappeared in record time from Phil's plate. Joe's selection was obscured by a mountain of whipped cream. The white stuff circled his mouth, and a dollop decorated his nose.

I handed Joe a napkin. "Did you sink your face into your plate or shoot the whipped cream in your mouth from the can?"

Paige and Aaron sat together holding hands and feeding each other little bites of pie. I gave him another week or two before she found a better pair of lips.

Mom sat quietly, chain-smoking, shoulders slumped. A sliver of pumpkin sat untouched in front of her.

While John and Aaron helped Mom clean the kitchen, I pulled Paige aside. "Dad gave Mom an iron for Christmas."

Paige frowned. "What a shitty gift!"

"Yeah. Mom started crying, and he left. Where would he go on Christmas night?"

"Good question."

Mom sent the boys to bed. Paige said goodbye to Aaron with a fairly short and chaste kiss and clomped upstairs in her white go-go boots. After Mom put the leftover pie in the fridge, she followed, her head drooping and her step slow.

John and I had the living room to ourselves. I hoped Phil and Joe were asleep. After a day of setting up their train set and playing slot cars, they should be.

John and I exchanged gifts. He always took care wrapping my presents. Each beribboned package sported a bow. I, on the other hand, used whatever paper I could find and never included ribbons or bows. I opened his gifts, a gold bracelet with a heart engraved *Dani and John 4ever* and Oh! de London cologne. Yardley from London—the coolest.

I gave him The Door's album *Strange Days* and a bottle of Jade East.

The new year brought uneasiness that spread like a pool of spilled milk. Some revolutions start slow; others happen overnight. The antiwar movement nibbled at the corners of our neighborhood like a stealthy rat. Cohesion slipped away. Longer hair on the boys, a tie-dyed t-shirt here, a peace sign flashed there—even on my block.

There was a small cadre of hippies that year at school. Beads, headbands. Not my thing. When Martin Luther King was assassinated on April 4th, riots and lootings took over the country. The west side of Chicago was hard hit, with many businesses on Roosevelt Road destroyed. The damage occurred only a few miles from our neighborhood. Woodlawn, on the south side and even closer, also saw protests. Mom sat at the kitchen table, reading the newspapers and smoking, worried because the unrest was close to Dad's station. My dad brought home dire reports about the fires, thirty-six in the span of six hours. Firefighters were stretched to the limit. Mayor Daley imposed a curfew, closed some streets, and called in the Illinois National Guard.

After a whispered discussion with mom, Dad made a decree. "You girls are not, repeat not, allowed to take the bus out of this neighborhood until further notice."

Paige was angry because she liked to take the Archer Express downtown to WLS on Saturdays to get the Silver Dollar Survey and autographs from the singers who visited their studio. I didn't much care because all I needed was right around the corner on 77th Place.

The student antiwar demonstrations spread at colleges around the country but didn't affect my daily life. Stubbornly and determinedly, I closed my mind to the idea of John going to war.

Then on June 5th, Bobby Kennedy was assassinated, and I had to wonder what was happening to our country. I remembered five years earlier when John F. Kennedy was assassinated. I was eleven and clearly recalled being sent home from St. Bede's. Grief gripped the nation once again.

John graduated and went to work full time for his dad. Instead of going home after school, I made a beeline to the garage. My mother didn't seem to notice or care; she had other things on her mind.

When school ended for the summer, I was still a virgin—barely—and that was an issue. John and I had been together three years. We knew we were headed toward marriage, and our passion for each other made it hard to stop our increasingly urgent make-out sessions. Besides lacking a venue for lovemaking, I was kind of scared of the physical act.

Once again, I turned to Paige for advice. She continued to slash her way through the male population in our neighborhood, and I wondered if there was a single unkissed-by-Paige boy in the city. Except John. She kept her lips away from him.

"Of course John wants to fuck you. Are you an idiot?" She sat on her bed, flipping through *Glamour* magazine.

"Nice. I didn't say the 'f word.' And you know I'm not an idiot."

She glanced at me for a second before returning to her reading, mumbling, "You're an idiot about some things."

"Okay, potty mouth, has any one of your numerous boyfriends f-f-had sex with you?"

"Can't even say it. You're such a prude." Paige laughed and jumped up, lifting the corner of her mattress.

My mouth fell open when I saw the calendar, pen, and thermometer. And a strip of foil squares. I hoped she was careful; she wasn't very good at math. The rhythm method. The Holy Roman Catholic Apostolic method of birth control. And the forbidden back-up method, rubbers. I was actually impressed she was so well prepared.

The rhythm method was the eighth sacrament. I'd heard my mom talking with her friends at their morning coffee klatches. The main subjects were their children's foibles, the next Tupperware party, and the rhythm method. Whispering about who used condoms in defiance of the Church, who got a new prescription for tranquilizers. I'd been in many kitchens on our street, and most of the glass knick-knack shelves abutting the metal kitchen cabinets displayed a bottle of little white pills—Miltown. I'd seen the ads in the women's magazines and heard Mick Jagger singing about "Mother's Little Helper" with sardonic energy. Mrs. Wilkins, Sandy's mom, the only one in our neighborhood who worked, didn't have a bottle of Miltown. Even then, I sensed a connection between Miltown and contraception—or its failure.

When I recovered my ability to speak, I said, "Oh, my God! It's Tim Finnegan, isn't it? You went all the way." My mouth was hanging open.

"Yep. At Maple Lake, a couple months ago." Her smug smile was hard to take.

"Why didn't you tell me?"

Paige shrugged. "Why should I?"

That comment summed up her side of our relationship. I tried to push my hurt aside because I needed her advice.

Paige's new boyfriend, Tim Finnegan of the notorious Finnegan family, was one of nine boys—all out-of-control hell-raisers. Either the rhythm method failed, or his parents kept trying to have a girl.

"Well. Another milestone in life. Paige wins again." Even as I spat the words at her, I hated my antipathy.

I recalled another of Paige's firsts—the day she got her period at the age of eleven, four years ago and almost a year before I got mine.

Sandy and I were hot on the trail of a garter snake in the prairie on the next block. I had to pee—bad timing. Unlike the boys, I didn't pee out in the open. I hated to leave and promised Sandy I'd run fast and be right back.

At home, when I dashed out of the bathroom, I ran smack into my mom.

"There you are. I need to talk to you. Now!" She pointed down the hallway. Paige was already in my parents' room, sitting on the bed. Mom closed the door. "Sit down, Danielle. We need to talk."

The first thing that crossed my mind was one of the nosy moms in the neighborhood had seen me sneaking into the Garrity's swimming pool, but Paige wasn't involved in that. The second thing was Mom had counted her Viceroys.

I kept my mouth shut, tried to project an air of innocence—eyes wide. Paige scooted over and patted the space next to her. For some reason she appeared quite pleased with herself. Did she rat me out? No, if she had, she wouldn't hang around. Something else was going on.

My mom looked nervous. She didn't sit, just paced back and forth, wringing her hands. Maybe she needed a cigarette, or another Miltown. "All right. You need to pay attention to this. Both of you." She bit her lip, then blurted, "Okay, do you know where babies come from?"

Paige giggled.

I bit my tongue, so I didn't crack up. "Sure, you told us God buries a seed under your heart, and it grows into a baby."

Mom's face got red. "Somehow I doubt you believe that." She glared at me.

My sister fell back on the bed, laughing so hard she couldn't remain upright.

I'd known where babies came from since I was seven and Sharon Elmont spilled the beans. While we were on the day camp bus on the way to Wonder Lake, she held court. "My mother told me the truth—the guy sticks his wiener in you and that's how you get a baby." Several of the younger girls, first graders, started to cry. One of them wailed, "You're a liar. That's disgusting." Because I was a little older, they turned to me, "Is it true, Dani?"

"'Course not. Sharon's crazy as a bedbug. Looney Tunes." My belly felt tight and my skin tingled. I knew Sharon was right. Sometimes the truth, no matter how bizarre, has a ring to it that can't be denied. I couldn't imagine the guy I'd ever let do that to me. For sure, it wasn't anyone I knew. Then I realized we'd probably have to be naked. I wished Sharon had kept her big fat mouth shut.

My mother's voice rose, and I snapped back to her lecture. Mom's eyes blazed with tears. She was obviously having great difficulty telling us things we already knew. "I have a feeling you both know very well where babies come from."

"Duh." Paige giggled again.

"Yeah, Mom. Is that all? I gotta go." I stood and took a step toward the door.

Mom stormed up to me. "Sit down! I'm not done." She drew a deep breath. "Today, Paige became a woman." She made the pronouncement as if heralding the Second Coming of Christ. Oh, the drama. She definitely needed another Miltown.

While my mother droned on about belts and pads, I gaped at my little eleven-year-old sister. That summer, she'd sprouted little buds on her chest and, as I looked closer, I noticed the buds had bloomed.

Brought back to the topic of Paige's newly revealed sex life by her laughter, I took in her question. "I win *again*. What does that mean? Are you keeping score?"

I studied no-longer-a-virgin Paige, and she seemed genuinely puzzled by my animosity. Then I realized I was engaged in a one-sided rivalry. She wasn't competing with me. That was my faulty perception. Paige and I were simply different. She took after Mom, and I took after some unknown ancestor. I sighed and let go of my bitterness. "Sorry for sounding bitchy. I came to ask for advice, and it looks like I came to the right place."

Paige grinned. "Yes, you did." She swept a pile of clothes from her bed to the floor. "Come sit down. I'll tell you all about it."

After our conversation, I took a walk. So much to process. I learned it didn't hurt *that* much. The first time was awkward, but it got better. A lot better. Paige let me use her calendar and thermometer. She used a blue pen, and I wrote in black. She even gave me a couple of rubbers. We were Catholic but not stupid. I knew the moment of truth was near.

That year, over the objections of my parents, I skipped the 4th of July block party and went to Rainbow Beach with John. Last summer, millions of dead alewives washed up onshore and ruined the beaches. Word had it the beaches were okay, so we convinced Chuck to drive us. He had a '48 Dodge, a hunk of junk with the split backseat cover and the wire frame poking me in the rear, but it got us there. Chuck brought his girlfriend, Debbie. I hadn't met her before. She reminded me of Annette Funicello with her big bouffant black hair and huge boobs.

John slathered Coppertone on my back, and we lay in the sun until we couldn't, then we plunged into the chilly water of Lake Michigan. He held me close in chest-deep water, and I wrapped my legs around him. That was a mistake. He moaned and pulled me close. I buried my face in his shoulder, feeling his erection pressing against me. I wanted him just as bad as he wanted me. A wave washed over our heads, ending the moment. I came up sputtering and swam back to shore. John waited a few minutes before following.

We dried off and packed our things in silence. John cleared his throat. "Dani, my parents are goin' out of town next week for a wedding. In Tennessee."

I stared at him. "Okay. Yes." At last, we had a place.

John didn't answer or smile, just returned my gaze. He took my hand and kissed it.

On the drive back, we held hands. I put my head on his shoulder and almost dozed off after the day in the sun. Chuck turned on the radio. "Jumpin' Jack Flash" ended, and the deejay announced the baseball scores. The Cubs split their double-header with the Phillies, and the Sox lost at Baltimore. An arrow of regret passed through me for missing the annual block party, a moment of nostalgia that quickly ended. I had other things on my mind.

That week crawled by. John's parents finally left for their nephew's wedding. Chuck stayed behind to run the garage. Because he stayed late every night, and John left at five, we had a clear path in the evening, until eight or so. We agreed to do the deed the next afternoon.

I soaked in a lavender bubble bath for two hours, my mind running through scenarios of lovemaking that relied on James Bond movies. With wrinkled toes and fingers, I dried off and spritzed Oh! de London just about everywhere on my body and dressed in a tank top and bell-bottoms. I left the house with the rubbers Paige gave me in a beaded shoulder bag. John and I hadn't discussed particulars, but I wanted to be prepared, even though the calendar said it was safe. I walked to his house in a daze. Scared, excited, an emotional mess.

John opened the door, and for a moment, we stared at each other. Then he grinned and grasped my hand.

My voice shook as I said, "Take me to your boudoir." Why did I say that? Was it from a movie? A book? So stupid.

"My boo-what?"

"Your bedroom." My face was hot. I looked at my feet.

He gently tilted my chin up, gazed into my eyes. "Are you sure?"

I could only nod.

We lay on the bed and kissed until I wanted, needed more. Feeling bold, I pulled my tank top over my head. He took off his shirt. Our alley-way fumbles and stolen moments in the back room of the garage didn't allow for undressing. A fleeting thought passed through my mind: who is this mythical man I'll allow to put his wiener in me? I burst out laughing.

John sat up and stared at me. His furrowed brow told me he was puzzled by my sudden mirth. "This is funny? I thought it was kinda sexy. Sorta hopin' you would too."

"I do. Really. But I just had a blast from the past that cracked me up."

"Now?" He groaned. "Okay, I gotta hear this. Hope it's a short story." He brushed his hair back.

"When I was seven, I learned where babies come from. I remember being horrified and wondered what guy I'd ever let put his wiener in me. Now I know!" I laughed, laughed until tears rolled down my face.

John grinned his lopsided grin. "Well, doll, don't take this the wrong way, but I used to wonder what girl I'd ever *want* to put my wiener in, since back then I thought y'all had cooties." He fell back next to me. "Now I know." He reached for my hand.

We lay there until the hilarity passed. The laughter eased my nervousness.

John rolled onto his side and pulled me to him. We kissed, and our passion reignited. The rest of our clothes came off, and I wasn't even embarrassed. He whispered, "I love you." Then we finished what we started.

On the walk home that evening, we were silent. I reflected that making love with your one true love was what made you a woman, not getting your period. Gazing up at the stars, I imagined the life John and I would share.

We'd move to Tennessee and start a family. Thoughts of college and a career evaporated. I thought my family was a good model, at least in theory—two boys and two girls—not in any particular order, although I often wondered what it would be like to have big brothers. For sure, being the eldest sucked for a girl. My parents hadn't let up on their scrutiny of me, while Paige, in my opinion, was allowed free rein.

When John kissed me good night, I clung to him like a stubborn vine, not wanting to part.

Hippies descended on Chicago for the Democrat convention at the end of the summer. Although the protests were spread throughout the city, the riots seemed far away from our neighborhood. The convention was held at the International Amphitheatre on South Halsted. But there were also riots on the north side in Lincoln Park and downtown at Grant Park. My memories of Grant Park were of the Buckingham Fountain's colorful light show on a summer night when Dad drove us to see the sights downtown. Mom bought us ice cream from a Good Humor truck, and we watched with wonder. Hard to reconcile that idyllic image with the news footage of tear gas, running and screaming kids, and billy-club wielding police.

My dad said the protesters were "agitators brought in from out of town." He spat out the words, "Yippies and SDS. Students for a Democratic Society? Students, my ass. Society? They wouldn't recognize society if it bit 'em in the ass!" We were thankful he wasn't caught up in the streets because he was the desk sergeant at the Chicago Lawn station. All the cops were on twelve-hour shifts. He brought home stories of the bravery of the police and the disrespect of the hippies. "Up against the wall, motherfuckers. I'll give them motherfucker. They can take their LSD crap and shove it. Buncha bums. Don't you ever let me catch you with none of those damned love beads, Dani."

Perhaps he should have worried more about Paige. One evening, when he got off duty after his shift, Paige was out in the driveway busily tying all his undershirts into knots and dipping them in purple, blue, or green buckets of dye. Every last one of his undershirts branded him a hippie.

Because it was Paige, he let it slide. He stepped in the kitchen and yelled, "Ellen, I need some undershirts. You know the kind I like. Try Goldblatt's. I don't want you driving over to Sears on Western. Too dangerous."

After the convention, the hippies sort of fizzled out, with only three hundred showing up for the SDS Days of Rage in October. The activists had expected 10,000. Dad said, "They got a little taste of good police work at the damned convention. I'm not surprised they chickened out."

That Christmas, I was released from family bondage and spent both Christmas Eve and Christmas Day with John's family. Over traditional Hungarian fish soup, we talked about Tennessee.

"You will love Knoxville, *Lánya*." Mrs. Nagy beamed at me.

Chuck nodded. "Knoxville is much smaller than Chicago, but so much nicer. Who needs all the tall buildings?"

"Chicago is good for business. Don't forget that." Mr. Nagy's shop was flourishing with three full-time employees.

The roast turkey with chestnut stuffing and giblet gravy was delicious. Moist, unlike my mother's dry, stringy turkey. And Mrs. Nagy created delicious vegetable dishes my mother could only dream about. As I envisioned the array of soggy canned vegetables that punctuated our meals at home, I shuddered.

"The pictures from your trip this summer really made me want to visit. Someday." Three heads swiveled to look at me, then John.

He grinned and ducked his head. "We'll have to see. I'd like to see my buddy Noah. Not in winter, that's for sure. And I gotta get some wheels first."

"Wheels? What wheels?" Mrs. Nagy asked.

"He means a car, Mom." Chuck laughed and scooped more broccoli casserole onto his plate.

That was the first year I opened presents with the Nagy family. I bought everyone a gift. Mrs. Nagy loved her Evening in Paris cologne. I had the feeling she wasn't spoiled much by the three men in her life. Mr. Nagy received a pair of leather-palmed, knit gloves. Since Chuck was a big music fan, I bought him the Rascals' greatest hits album, *Time Peace*. John appreciated the Bulova Accutron watch, the most expensive thing I'd ever purchased.

The Nagys gave me a real cashmere sweater in soft blue. I hugged them both. Chuck gave us tickets to see Led Zeppelin with Jethro Tull opening at the Kinetic Playground for February. I didn't know much about the bands, but Chuck said they were very cool.

While Chuck picked up all the wrapping paper strewn about the floor, John left the room for a moment and came back with a gigantic box wrapped in silver paper printed with snowflakes. Mrs. Nagy clapped her hands. "Yes, yes, a big, big present."

"Open it, doll." John sat beside me on the couch.

I pulled off the ribbon and bow and placed them over John's head. Then I popped the tape and opened the box. Inside was another box wrapped the same. When I opened that one, there was another box inside it. With each new box, my excitement grew. He'd gone to a lot of trouble, and I started to suspect this was no ordinary gift. I was right. Inside the last box was a tiny velvet jeweler's box. Ring-sized. My heart was pounding so hard, I thought it might escape through my chest. Gasping, I picked up the box and opened it. There it was—a white-gold band with a clever twisted setting that held a tiny diamond.

"It's a promise ring. I promise to marry you, Danielle Marek. Will you marry me?"

My vision blurred. "Yes. Yes, I promise."

I was overwhelmed, by the ring, and the warm, loving acceptance from John's family. Chuck clapped and whistled. Mrs. Nagy brushed a tear from her eye. Mr. Nagy said, "Soon you will be our daughter, little grease-monkey girl."

My joy was short-lived. When I showed my parents the ring and told them I was engaged—well, pre-engaged, they threw a fit.

"You're sixteen years old, Danielle," my father roared, his face as red as his plaid robe.

"Uh, Dad, I turned seventeen. Weeks ago. Guess you didn't notice."

My mother, her angry face shiny with cold cream, arms folded over her chest, wore that tatty chenille bathrobe she'd had since I could remember. She shook her head, so her pink foam rollers bounced. "Sixteen, seventeen, you're too young."

"How old were you when you got married? Eighteen. Don't tell me I'm too young! We're in love, and we're getting married."

I grabbed my Fingerhut catalog and stormed off to bed. There were several more items I needed to add to the list for my hope chest.

As I climbed the stairs, Dad grumbled, "This ain't no crush."

"I'll say another novena. This time I'm going straight to the top—God Almighty himself," Mom proclaimed.

Chapter Three

BAD MOON RISING 1969

My family shattered in 1969. I should have seen it coming, but I didn't. I was too wrapped up in planning my future with John.

That night in late April, Mom and Dad barely spoke at dinner. The atmosphere was so tense, even Phil and Joe picked up on it. Eating their burnt meatloaf, undercooked roasted potatoes, and soggy carrots silently, without looking up. No fights. No fidgeting. No giggle fits.

Paige studied my parents. She kicked me under the table, and when I kicked back and glared at her, she gestured at Mom as if to say something's up.

"Duh," I whispered.

Dad cleared his throat, and we all turned to him. "Ellen, do you want to tell them?"

"Oh, no, no, no." Mom glowered at him. "This is all on you. Go right ahead."

I knew immediately. Divorce. Our lives would never be the same.

Dad shoved his plate aside and wiped his mouth with his napkin. "Fine."

Mom sat back and shredded her paper napkin, perhaps visualizing doing the same to my father. Phil elbowed Joe. "Uh-oh." Joe put his thumb in his mouth. He was nine and hadn't sucked his thumb since he was five. I felt bad for him.

"Kids, your mother and I have decided to take some time apart."

Paige blurted, "Just say it, Dad. You're getting a divorce!"

Dad winced. "We haven't decided—"

"We haven't?" Mom pushed away from the table and stood. "Like I'm gonna stay with a cheater. Leave! Go to your whore!" Mom rushed from the room, and we all jumped when the door to my parents' bedroom slammed.

Joe's thumb popped out of his mouth. He wailed, "No!" and started to cry. Phil, for once, didn't call him a baby. He took Joe's hand and dragged him out of the kitchen. The television blared from the living room.

Paige and I stayed at the table. My sister's face twisted in anger, eyes blazing with tears. "You suck, Dad!" Paige screamed. She would normally get her face smacked for such impertinence, but he didn't make a move toward her.

Wondering how he could do this to our family, I stared at my father. My opinion of his character plummeted. I couldn't even speak to him. Leaving my half-eaten dinner, I got up and walked over to John's house.

Divorce was rare in our neighborhood. As far as I knew, only one family two blocks over had split up. They moved away, so I had no clue about the details. What would happen to us? Would we stay in the house, go to the same school? It wasn't so bad for me. I'd be graduating high school in two months. My future as Mrs. John Nagy was set.

John was out in the driveway waxing his dad's car. I told him what happened.

He hugged me and said, "I'd never cheat on you, Dani."

I believed him.

Our family split along the gender fault line. Dad rented a two-bedroom apartment in a building that went up a year ago on 79th Street, around the corner and down two blocks from our family home, which Mom kept. The apartments were an anomaly in our single-family-home neighborhood, but providential because we'd all be able to remain at our schools. To my surprise, the boys departed to live with Dad. I wasn't privy to the fight that must have ensued to decide that, but Mom would have to get a job, and that could be why she agreed. Paige and I got our own rooms, which was great, despite the circumstances.

Funny thing, I had a suspicion my parents still got together for sex. Paige didn't think so, but someone was keeping a satisfied smile on my mother's face. The simplest answer was often correct.

Paige said the best thing about the divorce was there were no more arguments over the television. No more baseball, basketball, football, hockey, or (gag) golf.

"I'll never miss *Laugh-In* or *Love, American Style,* or *The Mod Squad* again," Paige enthused. She and Mom lived for their TV shows.

I felt bad I didn't see my brothers very often, but they were so much younger our lives didn't intersect. Besides, I was wrapped up in my love cocoon.

Unbelievably, Dad moved his girlfriend Ginger into his apartment. Mom just shrugged. "Who cares? He needs help with the boys." I couldn't believe my father chose that blowzy, gum-popping, peroxide blonde over my mother.

Paige and I were equally appalled at Dad's choice. I asked, "Does she have any other clothes besides pedal-pushers and tank tops?" Ginger dressed like a teenager, and she was no teenager. "And those wedge sandals! And the ankle bracelet!"

My sister smirked. "Dad says she's got a heart of gold. You know what that means, right?"

"She's nice?"

"Close, but no cigar. That's what they say about hookers." Paige looked pleased as she imparted that nugget of information.

"No! You can't be serious."

Paige challenged me. "Where did he meet her?"

"No clue," I confessed.

"Maybe he booked her? Or spotted her in the lock-up at the station and liked what he saw?"

"Don't you ever say that to Mom. It would destroy her."

Paige rolled her eyes. "No, it won't. Actually, Mom's the one who suggested it to me. She's tougher than you think. And now she's screwing the guy across the street who lost his wife, she's a happy camper."

I thought my eyes would pop out of my skull. "I assumed she was in a good mood because she's still getting it on with Dad."

Paige patted me on the shoulder. "You're such a child, Dani."

We carried on the traditional Fourth of July party as if Dad didn't exist. With John's help, Mom set up our grill in the blazing heat. To say it wasn't the same was an understatement. Mom burned the hot dogs. She wasn't good with the grill. Her potato salad seemed to be missing something—something vital. For dessert, there was a store-bought cake, which wasn't necessarily a bad thing.

Phil and Joe came over for the day. Mom's eyes watered when she hugged them. They squirmed away and ran off, jumped right into a game of curb ball. John and I had to drag them back to eat. After bolting down a few bites of food, Paige announced she was leaving to watch her new boyfriend's band play a gig.

"What new boyfriend? What happened to Tim?" Was Mom finally paying attention to the many loves of Paige? Did she think she had to be both mother and father now Dad had moved out? My sister wouldn't like that.

"I needed some space." Paige shrugged. "Too intense."

"What the heck does that mean?" Mom frowned. "Just be home by ten."

Paige's bottom lip protruded. "Ten? Jesus." She hurried off before Mom could tell her not to take the name of the Lord in vain.

John and I ate our hot dogs and potato salad and kept Mom company. I wanted to split early but felt sorry for her. She looked a little wilted and sad—and sweaty—in the 94-degree heat.

Glancing over to the Bronkowski's table, I saw Dad's former friends enjoying their Hamm's, cheering on the Sox. Did they miss him? Mom was casting longing looks at one particular guy in the knot of men. Paige was right. Mom was getting it on with our widowed neighbor. Apparently, she was trying to keep the affair secret.

Impossible to get away from the ballgames pouring out of the portable radios. The Sox split a doubleheader with the California Angels. The Cubs beat the Cards in St. Louis. They were at the top of the rankings, the Sox near the bottom. I noticed there wasn't a Wilkins table this year. No one to celebrate the Cubs' win.

I spotted Sandy and Beth coming toward us with Sheba. Because the dog was now leash-trained and walked every day, she stopped running away. I convinced John to go over to say hello. Beth fidgeted, obviously uncomfortable with the situation. Sandy was Sandy, smiling, happy that her beloved Cubs won.

Remembering the role she played the day I met my true love, I knelt and hugged Sheba, whispering sweet words to her. John rubbed Sheba's ears. "Hi there, little one."

"We better get going," Beth said.

I stood. "Sure. And we've got to help Mom clean up. See you later."

Sandy and Beth walked away. John took my hand, and we headed back to our table. After hauling the trash and the grill and table back to our yard, John and I slipped away and borrowed his dad's car. We drove out to Maple Lake. John spread a quilt in a shady grove, well off the beaten path, and we added the heat of our lovemaking to the heat of the day.

As soon as I graduated, I landed a job at Lerner's. I still planned to get my business degree at DePaul, so I needed to save up. To my everlasting disappointment, I missed out on a National Merit Scholarship by one lousy question, according to my guidance counselor. At least I got a nice certificate worth the paper it was printed on. My dad made too much money to qualify for any income-based financial aid. How could a cop with four kids make too much money? Because Dad was contributing to two households and Mom's check was barely keeping us in groceries and clothes, I'd get no help with tuition from my parents.

In the fall, I'd probably sign up for a course at Bogan Junior College. But the classes were held in trailers in the parking lot of the A&P—visible from the windows of the high school. It sure wouldn't feel like college. At least I could get a couple of core classes under my belt at a lower cost.

No one in my family had ever gone past high school, and I was determined to be the first to graduate college, despite the lack of money. That way if anything happened to John—God forbid—I'd have the ability to get a decent job. My mother was forced into a boring job in a boring office, answering the telephone and typing up forms. That would never happen to me. The only examples of working women I had were from Doris Day movies set in New York City and Sandy's mom. Before her husband died, her banking career was prime conversational fodder at the coffee-drinking, Miltown-taking morning gossip sessions, gossip sessions my mother no longer attended. Now, Mom was forced by circumstances into what she disparaged Sandy's mom for—having a job.

John and I wanted to get married next year, but the overhang of the Vietnam War prevented us from making plans. I didn't tell him, but I thought about getting pregnant so he wouldn't get drafted. But if I did, I wouldn't be able to go to college. The rhythm method and rubbers were successful so far.

College. So glad I wasn't going away to school, where it seemed the kids were protesting more than they went to class. That was mostly on the east and west coasts, at least from what I saw on the news. I had absorbed my parents' newspaper-reading habit, devouring both the morning and evening papers. The world got crazier by the week. There was good crazy, like Neil Armstrong and Buzz Aldrin walking on the moon. The moon! We finally one-upped the Russkies.

Then there was bad crazy. That summer, Senator Edward M. Kennedy caused the death of a young woman, Mary Jo Kopechne. He drove his car off a bridge into a pond at Chappaquiddick, Massachusetts. Then he got out and slunk home to bed, leaving her to die. He pled guilty to leaving the scene of a fatal accident and got a two-month suspended sentence. I was horrified and couldn't help but compare him to his two dead brothers. How was he allowed to remain in the Senate?

My mother was all over that story. "Such a pretty girl. And a good Catholic. A college graduate too. Her parents must be devastated. She was their only child. Don't have just one child, Danielle, promise me, promise me."

I stared at her hand trembling as she brought her cigarette to her mouth.

More bad crazy. Murders in California by a group called the Manson Family. That story made me shiver and brought to mind the murders of eight nursing students two summers ago, right in Chicago. Richard Speck and Charles Manson—twin faces of evil. Morbidia, or Mom as she liked to be called, obsessed on both stories, so much so, I began to avoid her. I didn't want to be dragged into her psychodrama. But I couldn't help thinking: Was the world going crazy, or had it always been so, and I was just starting to notice?

The radio was alive with talk about a music festival called Woodstock. Oval blue stickers with a white bird on a guitar neck appeared everywhere. All the kids wanted to go: the jocks, the preppies, and the hoods. And, of course, the tiny band of hippies.

Paige became a full-blown hippie that summer. Since she'd dumped Tim Finnegan, she was dating some guy from Tommy More Parish who had a band. I guessed she'd run through and devastated every boy in St. Bede's and had to expand her hunting grounds.

At Mom's insistence, we finally met Jeff. Mom was really pissed when Paige took off on the Fourth to see his band play and laid down an ultimatum—bring him home. Jeff Tobin had dark brown hair longer than mine, perfectly straight, parted in the middle. He was pretty cute, despite the hair. Tall. He sang and played bass. He came by in his VW van, covered with peace signs, butterflies, doves, and flowers, to pick up Paige. My father would have had a cow if he saw that. But Dad was wrapped up in his squeeze, and we rarely saw him.

Paige flounced into the kitchen one afternoon as I was about to leave for my job at Lerner's. Her blond hair a halo, a beaded headband across her forehead. She wore a tie-dyed tank top and a tiered skirt. No bra. No shoes. Total hippie.

"Can you loan me and Jeff some gas money? We need some bread if we're gonna make it to Woodstock."

"Are you kidding me? I make a dollar five an hour. No cash to spare. I'm saving up for a set of dishes. And I have to buy sheets and towels." I was one of Fingerhut's best customers, although half my paycheck went right back to Lerner's. My wardrobe was killer. Still, I managed to save a few dollars toward tuition—very few.

"Already a sell-out to the establishment? Pathetic, man." She drew a box in the air with her fingers. "You're such a square. Why do ya wanna be someone's old lady when you're seventeen?" She must have forgiven me because she flashed me the peace sign as she bopped out the door.

No one in my neighborhood actually made it to Yasgur's farm in Bethel, New York, not even Paige and Jeff. Lots of kids turned hippie that summer, two years after the famous Summer of Love. The Midwest was slow to catch on to trends.

The Chicago Seven faced trial in October. They were the out-of-town troublemakers who came to our city to protest the previous summer at the Democrat convention. I could only imagine what my father was saying about the defendants.

The war was all over the evening news. I didn't watch much; the newspaper's reporting was enough to cause nightmares. That summer, *Life* magazine printed the pictures of the week's dead in Vietnam. My mother kept that issue on the kitchen table in a pile with all the other depressing news she collected and couldn't get enough of. One afternoon, I rifled through the stack. On the bottom was a yellowed *Trib* article with the gallery of the dead from the 1958 Our Lady of Angels school fire. Almost eleven years ago. She needed to make a scrapbook for her tragedies. I dropped the mountain of misfortunes back in place, but hesitantly picked up the June 27th issue of *Life.* I studied the 242 pictures, trying to imagine how the families coped with the death of their sons, and broke down in tears. Was I turning into my mother?

Several of my classmates planned to enlist after graduation; some of the guys who graduated with John had already shipped out. A few had already lost their lives.

John was torn between his patriotic duty and his desire to be with me. He told me, "By the time they draft me, the war will be over. Cain't go on forever."

Oh, how I wanted to believe him.

Then I read troops were being withdrawn from Vietnam. Nixon announced a new policy, "Vietnamization." Sounded good to me. Let the South Vietnamese fight the Commies themselves.

Thinking the war would end soon, I started planning my wedding. St. Bede's for the ceremony, obviously. Then I'd have to start checking out banquet halls. Menus, price per person, family-style, or individual service. Would my father pay for the reception? Would peonies be in season? I longed to have one of those cakes with a built-in fountain and colored lights, but that would be expensive. Print shops to look at invitation styles. My mind reeled with all the details I needed to work out. Honeymoon, a no-brainer. Tennessee.

Since graduating last year, John worked full time with his dad and brother at the garage. Now that I was employed, we couldn't spend as much time together. One evening he called me at work and asked me to stop by his house on the way home. "Got something to show you."

"Is it something you've shown me before?" I giggled and felt my face flush.

He laughed. "No. Something else. Can you run by?"

Intrigued, I said, "Sure. I'll be there after the store closes. Love you."

"Me too."

When I arrived at the Nagys, John and his parents were in the kitchen eating ice cream. I declined a bowl, had to watch my figure.

John scooped out the last of his treat, rinsed his bowl, and held out a cloth napkin. "Turn around."

"You're going to blindfold me?"

Mrs. Nagy clapped her hands. "*Lánya*, you will like surprise."

Mr. Nagy continued to eat his ice cream, but he smiled and nodded.

I allowed the blindfold. John took my hand and led me out the back door. Around the edges of the thick fabric, I glimpsed the driveway, lit bright as daylight.

John whispered in my ear, "Ready, doll?" He untied the napkin and, like a TV host, threw his arm to the side and stepped back. The car was gorgeous. John's new pride and joy. A 1966 silver Oldsmobile 442, with four on the floor, four-barrel carburetor and dual exhausts. He explained that was why they called it a 442. He'd worked for his dad at his auto shop since he was thirteen and saved $10.00 a week. At last, he collected enough money to buy the car from a guy who was shipping out to Vietnam.

At night, after the stores closed, he taught me to drive stick in Ford City parking lot. It took a while before I could shift without jerking the car or grinding the gears.

John was so patient with me. "Babe, reverse is up top, farthest to the left. Find neutral, push sideways, past first. Then up."

Crunch. Grind. "Oops."

"No. Here, I'll show you. When we get to my house, I'll draw you a diagram." He shook his head, maybe a little frustrated, but he never raised his voice or gave up on me.

Now that we had wheels, most nights we parked at Marquette Park along the drive circling the lagoon, a popular spot for making out. Many cars filled with couples lined the road. It wasn't ideal for lovemaking because the cops patrolled the area. I shuddered to think about getting busted by someone from my dad's precinct.

The bucket seats forced us to scramble into the back. Other nights we went to the Double Drive-In. John parked in the last row, as far away from the other cars as he could. We never saw a movie. I was meticulous with the rhythm method. On the risky days, we used a rubber. I was too embarrassed to buy them, but John stepped up.

My job was going well. After only five months, I was promoted to assistant manager and now made $1.35 an hour. The added responsibility included opening the store some days and closing on others. I loved fashion and was more certain than ever I was going to study marketing when I could afford DePaul.

One evening at work, I heard my name called. I spun around to see Sandy—and Beth Lawton. So, they were still, what, a couple? My mind flashed to the *Time Magazine* cover from a couple weeks earlier, a stylized, multicolored image of a man's face with a superimposed black-and-white sketch of another man. A ribbon across the cover proclaimed: "The Homosexual in America." My mother was horrified and uncharacteristically threw it in the trash. Curious, I retrieved the magazine and read it. The article's focus was on homosexual men, but I was looking at two women who had such a relationship.

"Hi, Sandy, Beth. Shopping for the holidays?"

Sandy giggled. She still hadn't lost that giggle. "No, we saw you through the window and stopped in to say 'hi.'"

"Cool. Well, hi." There didn't seem to be anything else to say. After a few uncomfortable moments of silence, I said, "I better get back to stocking this display."

Beth never made eye contact. A stocky girl known for her devastating serve in volleyball, she had bobbed brown hair and freckles. I never would have noticed her if it weren't for that day at the funeral home. She nodded and started walking backwards, plucking at Sandy's sleeve.

I didn't understand and doubted I ever would. But Sandy, if not her friend, seemed happy. Then it occurred to me Beth might be jealous of me, thinking I was Sandy's ex. After a minute, I laughed. Boy, Beth was wrong. Couldn't she see I wasn't Sandy's type?

The war became more unpopular, even in our patriotic neighborhood. My mother was starting to worry about Phil being drafted. He was only twelve, but the war had been raging in Vietnam for years.

One evening when I got home from work, she was sitting at the kitchen table with an overflowing ashtray. Chain-smoking again. The room reeked of smoke and stale cigarettes.

"Night, Mom." I was starting up the stairs when she spoke.

"I should go to bed. But I can't sleep after watching the news. How long is this damn war going to last?"

I stepped back into the kitchen.

"I'm driving Phil to Canada myself if I have to. And his father better not try to stop me. And if it comes to it, I'll drive Joe too." She stubbed out her cigarette and got up. "Aren't you worried about John?"

"God, Mom, you have to ask? I'm petrified, but I try not to think about it. John says the war will be over soon. There's this new thing, Vietnamization. Our troops are starting to come home. Absolutely, I don't want John to go. But if he's called, he's going. He'd never go to Canada."

Mom hugged me. "He should, Dani. Go to Canada, I mean. But I can see that's not something he'd do. I sure hope he's right about the war ending."

Could it continue forever? The *Chicago Tribune* and the *Daily News* ran stories about battles at home and in Vietnam. My mom continued to subscribe to the papers for the coupons and the tragedy. She and I were the only ones who read them. Paige was too busy searching for the perfect kiss.

The antiwar sentiment spread, and there were countless demonstrations in cities around the country. In late November, Nixon signed an executive order changing the draft into a random selection process. There would be a lottery drawing covering the birth years of 1944-1950, which included John. The worst thing: nineteen-year-olds would be drafted first, a change in the policy of drafting the oldest eligible men. Happy Thanksgiving. So random. For the first time in months, I attended Mass at St. Bede's and prayed for divine intervention. I should have prayed for luck.

There was nothing to do but turn on the TV and learn John's fate. That Monday, December 1st, I joined John's family in their living room. CBS pre-empted *Mayberry RFD* for the drawing. Roger Mudd murmured, "Good evening. Tonight, for the first time in twenty-seven years, the United States has again started a draft lottery." Some gray-haired man with glasses stuck his arm in a bowl of blue capsules, pulled one out, and opened it. The birth date, September 14th, was called out. Then they placed the paper on a board. The announcer read more dates: April 24th, December 30th, and so it went.

It wasn't very long before we learned John's ranking. July 24th was the twenty-third number called.

John jumped to his feet and faced me. "Holy crap! Twenty-three? Dani, that means I'm gonna get called up. Soon." His eyes were wide. I couldn't read him. He looked shocked, but was he *upset*? I thought he might be excited, and that scared me.

Mrs. Nagy held her handkerchief to her face. Mr. Nagy sat stone-faced. Chuck stared at his shoes. The phone rang, but the Nagys sat motionless. I ran to the kitchen to answer.

"May ah speak to John?" asked a man with a soft drawl much like my fiancé's.

"Noah?" I asked.

"Yes, ma'am. Dani?"

"Uh-huh. Yes. Let me get him." I returned to the living room, where John sat next to his mother, his arm around her shoulder. "It's Noah."

John stepped into the kitchen and after a few minutes, came back. He sat beside me on the arm of my chair. "Noah got a twenty-two. We'll both be going soon."

I wrapped my arms around my middle, as if I could protect myself from reality. I studied John's face. His eyes were focused on something I couldn't begin to imagine.

That year, 1969, ended with tragedy and violence. The Altamont Free Concert in Northern California was no peace and love festival. Because of all the violence, The Grateful Dead canceled their appearance. The Rolling Stones were the last act, and chaos descended. A woman was stabbed to death. Three other deaths occurred—two people in a hit-and-run and someone who drowned while on a bad acid trip. The Age of Aquarius was over. Peace, love, and understanding—so much bullshit.

Christmas Eve was sad that year. My father had Paige and me over for dinner with the boys. John and Paige's latest boyfriend Tom Kawaleski weren't invited due to lack of space. I vowed to leave at the first opportunity. My mother was at home alone, unless her boyfriend strolled across the street for a quickie. She was serving dessert at eight. At least John would be there. And Paige's latest.

Ginger was an even worse cook than my mother. I don't know what she did to the roast beef, but I gave up chewing and discreetly spit it out in my napkin when no one was looking.

Worst of all, Ginger served margarine instead of butter.

Phil and Joe were remarkably subdued. They didn't so much as glance at each other during the silent meal. I sort of missed their antics and wondered what their home life was like. They came over for dinner every Wednesday and spent time at Mom's on the weekends, although they spent most of the visit outside with their friends. They never talked much about Dad and Ginger.

Ginger's brittle forced smile faded as her conversational gambits fell flat. I couldn't find a reason to help her out. Paige was kinder. "Ginger, the gravy is delicious."

I glanced at the empty jar of beef gravy on the counter.

At Paige's benevolent words, my father perked up, and his shoulders relaxed.

"Thanks, Paigey." Ginger preened.

Paigey? Did she call Phil "Philly" and Joe "Joey"? Yikes. My mother would flip out.

We exchanged gifts after dinner. I gave Ginger a set of embroidered handkerchiefs. Was that an appropriate gift for the woman who broke up your family? Dad gave me and Paige twenty dollars each in a card. When Paige and I opened Ginger's gifts to us—the same handkerchiefs I gave her—I had to bite my tongue to keep from laughing.

Paige stood and announced, "We've got to get back to Mom's. Thanks for everything." She hugged Dad. I didn't.

As we walked home, I thought back to past Christmases and sighed.

"What?" Paige asked.

"I was thinking of life before Ginger."

"Yeah, I hear ya."

"She called you 'Paigey.' I nearly choked. Thought you'd let her have it. You know how Mom hates that. How did you control yourself?"

"Didn't bother me." Paige shrugged.

"Where did Mom come up with the name Paige anyway? I've never met anyone else with that name."

She squinted at me. "You don't know? I'm named after Janis Paige, a Broadway star. I like it 'cause it's different."

"Hmm. Never heard that story. It's different all right. Anyway, what about Ginger? What does Dad see in her?"

"Who knows? If I had to guess, I'd say the sex is good. So, she's a flake. She makes Dad happy. And I think Mom is happier without Dad."

I stopped, stunned at Paige's insight. "Oh my God! I think you're right. I'll tell you this much, what happened with them will *never* happen to me and John. Never."

Paige twisted her lips. "Don't jinx it."

John and Tom stood on the sidewalk in front of our house. I heard them from three houses away, singing along to "Whole Lotta Love" by Led Zeppelin. Tom never went anywhere without his Silvertone radio. Paige and I cracked up, and they must have heard us because they stopped mid-wail. Robert Plant had nothing to worry about.

"How was dinner, doll?" John asked.

I rolled my eyes. "Ginger is not good in the kitchen."

"I bet she's good in the bedroom," Paige cut in.

We entered the house laughing.

Mom had expanded her menu repertoire. Since she'd been working, she brought home new recipes from her co-workers. Occasionally, something was edible. This year she made peppermint icebox pie. The crust, made from crushed chocolate cookies, was delicious, and the filling wasn't half bad. Cream cheese and Cool Whip along with the peppermint candy. John, Tom, and Paige raved about it, and Mom blushed.

The doorbell rang. I was closest, so I opened it. Standing on our stoop was Mr. Elliott, the guy supposedly banging my mother.

I realized this was a set-up, and Mom thought it was time Paige and I met her...boyfriend, honey, lover? The thought of my parents having sex was bad enough, but now that they'd split, I found it unbearable to contemplate the new relationships.

Mom rushed to take his coat and introduced him as "Ken Elliott, my friend."

John and Tom stood and shook hands with Ken. Paige greeted him with a peace sign.

I smiled. "Hi, Mr. Elliott."

To my embarrassment, I recalled the time Sandy and I picked all the cantaloupes in his garden and smashed them against the back of his house. We gorged ourselves—ate until we were sick. His wife had stormed out of the house, royally pissed, but Mr. Elliott hadn't seemed to be. Maybe he didn't like cantaloupe.

Mr. Elliott insisted we call him "Ken."

"Let me get you a piece of pie, Ken," Paige said.

After dessert, Mom slipped off to her lover's place, for a "nightcap." Paige and I smirked at each other, then she took off with Tom.

As soon as the door closed behind them, John and I ran upstairs to my room. We kissed peppermint kisses and ripped clothes off each other. We rarely got a chance to use a real bed and took full advantage of the luxury. Afterwards, we lay facing each other, my leg slung across his hips, breasts-to-chest to maximize skin contact. Utter happiness. I realized how lucky we were to have found each other.

He grasped my hand, kissed my palm, and placed it on his face. "I love you, Dani Marek."

"I love you, John Nagy."

After cuddling and kissing for several minutes, we reluctantly dressed—in case Mom came back early—and went downstairs.

"Let's open our presents," I said.

We had the living room to ourselves. The scent of the Scotch Pine perfumed the air—each year, my family named our Christmas Tree "Timothy." I made certain I was the only one to drape the tinsel on the boughs. My meticulous placement created a fantasy of reflected light. I rummaged through the stack of albums in the Hi-Fi cabinet and selected Three Dog Night's *Live at the Forum*.

I brought John's gifts to the couch. Last week, he had placed his gifts to me under our tree. For eight days, I wondered what he got me. One box was rectangular and light, probably clothes. The other package was squarish and heavy. This year, I bought John a book about classic cars. *The Racing Fords* by Hans Tanner. Although I couldn't find a book about Oldsmobiles, I did score a 442 t-shirt in a shop in Peacock Alley at Ford City. Even though it was yellow, he absolutely loved it. "Way cool! Anything by Rat's Hole is outta sight."

Rat's Hole? I finally figured out he was referring to the t-shirt brand.

John gave me an iron, and I didn't even *think* about lining it at his head. Instead, I imagined ironing his military uniform, and when he came home from the war, his work clothes. Inside the light rectangular box was a gorgeous leather fringed vest and matching skirt.

"It's beautiful. The color of cinnamon."

"You're my cinnamon girl."

"Neil Young and Crazy Horse. I'll have to think of a name for you." I put my arms around him and, after several kisses, pulled away. "Got it! It's an oldie. Johnny Angel."

Chapter Four

WAR 1970

When we walked in the door of John's house that Friday night in February, his mom and dad were in the kitchen staring at an envelope on the counter.

"John, this came today." His mother's voice shook.

John opened the envelope and scanned the letter quickly. "Yep, it's my report for physical notice." He was calm, at least outwardly. I was hysterical, both inwardly and outwardly. Even though I'd watched the lottery drawing and knew it was coming, the letter was a gut-punch. I covered my face with my hands and wept.

"Come on, Sonia, leave them alone a minute," Mr. Nagy led his wife out of the room. John wrapped me in his arms and stroked my hair. "Hey, hey, honey, you knew I was gonna get called."

I convulsed with sobs. "I-I-I knooooowww!"

He held me until my weeping lessened.

I found a tissue in my pocket. "What happens now?"

"Gotta take a physical. Then I'll get a draft notice."

Of course he passed his physical. Then the draft notice arrived, and I was struck numb. Now it was real. He was told to report to Fort Leonard Wood in Missouri for basic training. Time speeded up. The day of his departure arrived all too soon.

After an early lunch with his family, where the false good cheer seemed like a presence in the room and little food was consumed, John said his goodbyes. I felt like I was in suspended animation as I watched him hug his mother. Her trembling lips and shiny eyes revealed her worry and fear. "*Menj Istennel, fiam.*"

Did John speak Hungarian? I'd never heard him speak it. I knew fiam meant son, but as for the rest, I had no idea.

Mr. Nagy shook John's hand. "I'll miss you, and not just around the garage." His gruff voice betrayed his emotion, although his face was the picture of stoicism.

Chuck clapped John on the shoulder. "Take care, brother. Kick some commie ass for me."

"Count on it." He picked up his bags.

John and I walked outside to the car. I was supposed to drive him to the bus station downtown, but tears blurred my vision. I couldn't stop crying.

"Here, doll. I'll drive." He took the keys and put his bag in the backseat. "Sure gonna miss this car."

"I know. Will you miss me as much?" I couldn't really be jealous of a car, could I? My emotions were so raw.

"You kiddin' me? I love you, and I'll miss you like crazy." He kissed my cheek, backed out of the drive, and proceeded down 77th.

I buried my face in a wad of tissue. I'd brought the box with me and wondered if it would be enough.

Merging onto the Stevenson Expressway, John flipped on the radio. WCFL. A promo for "Chicken Man" came on. "Buck, buck, buck, bu-uuuuck. Chicken-mannnnn!"

In unison we chanted along with the radio, "He's everywhere, he's every-where." John grinned his lopsided grin at me, and I laughed through my tears. The serialized spoof, featuring the shoe salesman/superhero, Benton Harbor, was our favorite. "I'll be sure to tell you about each episode in my letters."

"I'm holdin' you to that."

I didn't want the ride to end, but we reached the bus station twenty minutes later.

He parked on the street and grabbed his gear. We walked to the bus lane together. The cold March wind cut right through my jacket. Some draftees seemed to be alone, hands shoved in pockets, glancing at each other, then down the road at where the bus would appear. Others were engaged in tearful goodbyes with loved ones. Right on time, the bus arrived in a cloud of diesel fumes. The driver opened the luggage compartment and tossed in the bags.

I knew this day would arrive, but still I couldn't believe he was leaving. Clinging to John as if I could make him stay by force of will, I buried my face in his coat. A deep voice called his name, and I gasped. A stern-looking uniformed man looked up from his clipboard when "Nagy, John" didn't immediately answer. "Nagy, John!" he shouted.

"Yo! Nagy here." He bent to kiss me. He had to go. My tears wet his face. He didn't wipe them away.

I studied his face, memorizing him. His eyelashes were wet. I hadn't thought he would cry.

"Remember, I'll get to come home before I ship out. In just a few months. I love you, Dani." He let go of my hand and turned away.

"I love you. Write to me as soon as you can." I'd packed a huge supply of envelopes, writing paper, pens, and stamps for him.

"Promise," he called from the bus steps.

Then he was gone. Standing there, watching the bus pull away, I'd never felt more alone.

I wrote every day. John did too. Basic training got him in the best shape he'd ever been in. He hated the food but ate it anyway. What he wouldn't give for some poppy seed rétes. Sharing the latrine took some getting used to. After basic training, he planned to go airborne. I had no idea what he meant and when I learned, my fear ratcheted to the max. Airborne—the concept was frightening. I knew nothing of the military and hadn't known what type of service was the most dangerous. Now I did. He wrote about advanced infantry training. About trying to get into jump school at Fort Benning and not getting accepted. The army had determined the jungles of Vietnam were not the place for parachutes and the 101st was training for a helicopter war. To qualify for the Air Mobile Badge, John had to rappel from a helicopter—not only once—but several times. There were tests on safety procedures, hand and arm signals, combat assault operations, preparing sling loads, among other technical things. He had to pass them all. He did.

Reading his letters, I took comfort in knowing his hands had held the same paper. Was there a hint of Jade East on the envelope? I studied his words as if I could decipher his inner thoughts. I slept with his letters under my pillow, tried to dream about him. Played mental movies of our lovemaking, ached for him.

My letters were upbeat. I filled him in on Paige's love life. He always got a charge out of her many romances. She was back with Tim Finnegan, a massive surprise because Paige wasn't known for repeats. But he was her first lover, and perhaps that was why. I'd always thought they made a good couple; both had a wicked sense of humor. I told him Ken was now a fixture in our lives. No talk of marriage, but he and Mom spent a lot of time together. Phil was in high school and was going to try out for junior varsity baseball. Joe still worshipped Phil, but now they were in different schools, Joe was expanding his horizons, making friends, on the honor roll.

I learned Fort Campbell was on the Kentucky/Tennessee border, two hundred and forty miles from Knoxville, where John was born. He loved seeing trees and green hills again. He wrote that Noah, his friend, was also assigned to the 101st Airborne. John was happy they'd serve together. Noah planned on becoming a doctor after the war was over. He'd already accumulated sixty hours of undergraduate work in biology before he was drafted. Noah was assigned to the 326th Medical Brigade, which supported John's combat unit—The Screaming Eagles.

Ever since John left, I obsessively read the *Tribune* and watched the evening news. Walter Cronkite somberly related fatality statistics. Nixon announced the war was expanding to Cambodia. What happened to the plan to bring troops home?

On May 4, 1970, four students were shot dead by the Ohio National Guard at Kent State University. I couldn't believe kids their own age shot them. Morbidia saved that day's newspaper, adding it to her macabre collection. She avoided talking with me about the war now that John was headed there. That was fine with me. I decided to pray a rosary each day that the war would end before John completed basic training. Well, I tried to pray. But only fragments from the prayers memorized during my years at St. Bede's floated through my mind, and I couldn't concentrate enough to complete one.

Nixon called student protestors "bums blowing up campuses." Students around the country joined the Moratorium to end the war and closed colleges. The demonstrators attacked and even bombed ROTC buildings on campuses, lashing out at the closest representation of the military they could find. That led to more states calling up their National Guard. The war wasn't raging only in Southeast Asia.

Our neighborhood Fourth of July party went on as it normally did, although in a far from normal world. Mom and Ken hosted and invited the boys. For lack of anything better to do, I spent the day with them. My heart wasn't in celebrating the birth of our nation given the peril John was soon to face defending it. At least that's what the generals said he was doing.

Paige stopped by with Tim. They stayed long enough for a hot dog, then they were off.

Since I last saw him, Phil had a growth spurt and was as tall as I. In the past year, he had really matured. After eating, he left our table to spend time with Mary Ellen Garrity. Joe shrugged when Phil left. "No biggie. Got to get back to my curb ball team."

I was glad he was cool with his older brother going his own way. Because John was at basic training, I was more tuned in to my family than I'd been in years. I felt a pang for the loss of our unity.

My mouth fell open when I spotted Dad and Ginger coming our way, holding hands. Dad stayed away from the block party last year, and I figured he would no longer be attending. They stopped at the Bronkowski table and chatted a moment. Ginger was wearing her summer uniform, pedal-pushers and a low-cut tank top. I had to admire her control as she strolled along in her stilettos. Ankle bracelet, charm bracelet, a necklace—with whatever was on the end of the chain disappearing between her half-exposed breasts—and a gaudy collection of rings on every finger. Good God! Or Good Golly Miss Molly. As she wiggled her way to our table, she literally turned heads.

I glanced at my mother to see how she was reacting to the approaching couple. She turned to Ken, placed her hand on his arm, and giggled like a schoolgirl. I figured she'd never let Dad and Ginger see her pain. That was if she had any.

"Hi, Ellen," Dad said.

Mom spun to face him. "Hello, Stanley." She nodded at Dad's girlfriend. "Ginger." Flat, monotone.

I watched the two couples with interest.

Dad shook hands with Ken. Manly shake, eye contact.

Ginger fidgeted and grabbed my dad's hand as if it were a lifeline. He winced and put his other hand on hers, gently prying away her crimson claws.

No one spoke for several excruciating seconds. With a spurt of generosity, I bailed them out. "Have you eaten, Dad? Ginger, can I get you some lemonade? Something to eat?"

Mom came out of her funk. "Where are my manners? Let me fix you both a plate."

Waving away the offer, Dad said, "Thanks, but we just came to check on the boys. I see Joe, but where's Phil?"

I shared a glance with Mom. She said, "He went down the street to visit a friend."

Dad nodded. "Okay. We're going to dinner. Be back in time to take them to the fireworks."

"I'll have them ready to go. Enjoy your dinner." Mom sounded convincing with her well wishes, but I wondered if she actually meant it.

I knew Mom hadn't forgiven Dad—and probably never would—for his betrayal, but over the past year, she'd dealt with the situation. Having a boyfriend helped. Most of her contact with Dad was on the phone. It had to be hard for her to see him—and Ginger—face to face. I looked forward to our conversation tonight when we'd dissect and critique the hussy's wardrobe and jewelry choices.

The dads gathered with their beer and bemoaned the Sox's season, although they beat the Minnesota Twins that day. No one even mentioned the Cubs. Mrs. Wilkins hadn't set up her grill and table since her husband passed away. I wandered down the street, hearing bits and pieces of conversation.

Jerry Garrity, who had just graduated from Bogan, had hair down to his shoulders and wore a t-shirt with a peace sign. He was waving his arms as he argued with his father about the war. "I filled in the paperwork yesterday. I'm officially a conscientious objector. C. O., Dad. Hell no, I won't go! I *object* to getting fucking killed. And don't give a shit what you think."

Mr. Garrity, eye-popping angry and red-faced, scowled at his firstborn. "No son of mine is going the pansy chicken-shit route. Pack up and get out!" He pointed at the house. Mrs. Garrity, with all the little Garritys, stood there in tears. Phil and Mary Ellen were nowhere to be seen. Probably making out in the alley. I sighed, remembering past Fourth of Julys doing the same thing with John.

Things weren't any happier at the Kretchmer's table. Mrs. Kretchmer wiped her eyes with a tissue. Their son Tommy had just received his draft notice.

I stopped to talk to him. "Hey, Tommy, I heard the news."

He nodded but had nothing to say. He'd always been quiet.

"So, they're drafting guys who got numbers over a hundred already?"

Tommy cleared his throat and said, "Over a hundred? Hell, yeah. I got a hundred fifty-nine. January 2nd. Guess I won't be going to Champaign after all."

"Well, maybe you can when you get back."

"You mean, *if* I get back."

"Don't think like that! My fiancé, John, got a twenty-three and left for basic in March. He's training for airmobile right now, helicopter landings. He'll be home in a few weeks, before he ships out."

"Helicopters, huh? Wow."

"Yeah, sounds scary."

"Sounds far out."

I stared at him. He was serious. "If by far out, you mean dangerous, then, yeah. Good luck, Tommy."

As I walked away, Mr. Kretchmer clapped Tommy on the shoulder. "Proud of you, son."

Most of the dads were proud their sons were going off to war, but the moms and a few of the kids had a different take.

Five long, lonely months since I'd seen John. At last, he was coming home on leave. The night before his arrival, I didn't sleep a wink and gave up at 5 a.m., got out of my tangled sheets, and took a shower. I must have tried on my entire wardrobe before settling on the first outfit I put on, hip-hugger jeans and a paisley halter top.

My sweaty palms slipped on the steering wheel, and my stomach turned flips as I drove the freshly washed 442 to Midway airport to pick up my betrothed. John had two weeks of leave before deployment. How had he changed in the past five months? For sure, his hair would be shorter. No more dark waves. I felt like I was on my way to meet a stranger.

Parking close to the terminal, I tried not to run inside. Didn't want to get sweaty in the August heat. I arrived early and waited at the gate. A half hour later, the plane pulled in. Watching for him to come down the walkway, I spotted several fatigue-wearing men. Then my eyes found John, taller than the others, and my heart soared. Goose bumps. Tummy twirl. His face broke into that lopsided grin I saw in my sleep, and he waved. I rushed forward. He dropped his backpack and swept me into his arms, kissing me. I was in heaven. How I'd missed him! How could I let him leave again in only fourteen days? Rash plans to kidnap him flitted through my mind.

After I returned to earth, I took a step back to study him. "You got taller, I swear. And your hair, it's gonna take me a minute to get used to it. I didn't think I'd like it, but you look very handsome."

"Handsome? I'll take it." He picked up his bag and grasped my hand. We started toward the luggage carousel. "You look beautiful, doll. I showed your picture to the guys, and they didn't think you were real."

I swung around to face him and kissed him some more—I'd have to stock up.

After he picked up a gigantic duffel bag, we hurried to the car. A couple of hippies shouted, "Baby killer."

John ignored them. I was livid and opened my mouth to yell an insult, but John squeezed my hand and shook his head. "Not worth it, babe."

I drove. "My mom's at work and Paige is out with Tim, so we have the place to ourselves for a few hours." I shot him a glance. "Unless you want to swing by to see your mom first."

He put his hand on my thigh and squeezed. "You kiddin' me? Mom can wait, but I can't."

My smile stretched my cheeks, and I hit the gas.

We left his bags in the car and ran to the door. My hand was shaking, and John had to take the key and let us in. He picked me up, carried me inside, and kicked the door closed behind him. I put on the deadbolt while in his arms.

We gazed at each other. My eyes filled, and my breath caught. It was so good to see him, so good to touch him. He put me down, brushed my cheek, and bent to kiss me, leaving me breathless. I grasped his hand and tugged. "Let's go to my room."

"Thought you'd never ask." As we rushed up the stairs, he unbuttoned his shirt.

I hated the wait while he unlaced his boots and took them off. I shed my clothes in record time and scooted under the sheet. My single bed could barely contain us because of its size and our athletics.

Five months. Five months without him. Luckily, I'd just finished my period because there was no waiting to apply a rubber. I was parched for his touch and shouted in ecstasy when he entered me. And when I came, violently, I felt tears on my face.

The first time, we were quick. As we lay facing each other, my leg over his, getting as close as I could, we clutched each other, knowing we would be wrenched apart all too soon. The second time, we were slower. The third time, we were tender.

How had I endured five months without him? He couldn't leave again. "I missed you so much."

"Not as much as I missed you, doll. I can't believe I'm here."

"I can." Wriggling a little, I moaned. "Oooh, my body believes it."

He laughed and kissed me. "We better get dressed. I need to check in with my mom and dad. Tell Chuck about army life."

"Am I invited?"

"You betcha."

The days flew by; it seemed like hours instead of two weeks. I'd taken time off work and my quarter at DePaul hadn't started yet, so I spent every minute with him. Mom worked all day, and Paige, when she was home, didn't care that John and I were holed up in my room.

Two days before he shipped out, John wanted to go to the currency exchange so he could sign the 442 over to me.

"Why bother? You'll be home soon, right?"

He smiled his lopsided smile. "Right. But let me do this anyway."

The night before he left, we had a farewell dinner with his family.

"Let me tell you about communism." Mr. Nagy made a slashing gesture with his fork. "You gotta wipe it out. Once the boot is on your neck, it's over." Mr. Nagy, the most talkative I'd ever heard him, related harrowing stories of how his family suffered under the Nazis before fleeing Hungary in 1939. "Nazis, commies, I don't care what those bastards call themselves. A dictator is a dictator."

Mrs. Nagy widened her eyes. "Language, Miklos."

"They've heard worse. Pass the sausage." When the sausage wasn't forthcoming, he looked up. "Please, Sonia." Humbled, he accepted the platter from his wife.

Chuck asked, "What was that business of going into Cambodia? We're out now, but what the heck?"

John cut up his sausage. "Above my pay grade. I'm just a grunt."

"What is this grunt?" Mrs. Nagy looked from John to Chuck.

"It means a new guy, Mom." John grinned.

The minutes ticked down on John's final hours at home. My stomach ached. I could barely force food into my mouth.

"Nixon said he's drawing down troops. That true?" Chuck asked.

"That's the story. One hundred and fifty thousand this year. We're turning things over to the ARVN—that's South Vietnamese to you civilians. I may not even see action. Probably get off the plane in Nam and right back on."

I perked up hearing that. "From your lips to God's ears."

John winked at me. "Don't worry, doll. I'm in the best division in the entire United States Army. Screaming Eagles, baby!"

Mrs. Nagy stepped into the kitchen and came back with a tall cake on a silver plate.

John threw down his napkin and stood. "Mom, you made Dobos Torte. Thanks. Here, let me help you."

"Sit, my son. For you, anything."

I accepted a slice of the seven-layer cake and picked at it. The confection looked and smelled delicious, chocolate butter cream between each layer, but it might as well have been made of sawdust and motor oil.

All the Nagy men had two pieces of the cake, even Chuck. No one said a word about his diabetes.

"Son, I admire you for doing your patriotic duty. So many good-for-nothing kids running away to Canada. Cowards! Damn hippies. Blowing up colleges."

"Miklos. You'll have a stroke." Mrs. Nagy touched her husband's hand, and he subsided.

"Well, Dad, I just ignore the demonstrations. Have to do my job and trust the generals runnin' the war. I'm sure my tour will be short. Made a bet with Chuck I'll be home for Christmas. One dollar."

"That's a bet I hope I lose. I'd rather have you home safe than make a dollar."

"Glad I'm more valuable to you than a dollar bill," John teased.

Chuck seemed to realize how his statement sounded and cracked up. Everyone laughed except me. Nothing was funny.

I said good night to John's folks and promised to be over for breakfast at eight. John walked me home. When he left, the tears started.

I had to have slept because I woke up at 1 a.m., then 3:30, then at 9:00. Panicked at missing breakfast with the Nagys, I flew to my closet and dressed in a flash. Brushed my teeth, then ran a comb through my hair as I bolted down the stairs. I hustled up the street and around the corner to John's house. He and his family stood around his car. Time to head to the airport.

"I tried calling but didn't get an answer," John said.

"I overslept. Sorry. Were you leaving without me?"

"Not a chance."

I hugged everyone and got in the passenger seat. The tears were already flowing despite my wish not to burden John with my sadness.

The day was hot, hazy, and humid. After dropping him off at Midway, I would be driving the 442 home to my driveway. That simple fact loomed in my mind as momentous.

John concentrated on the road as we turned onto Cicero. "Dani, you won't believe this, but the North Vietnamese call us 'chickenmen,' because of our screaming eagle badge. I learned that from one of the trainers who fought at Hamburger Hill."

Hamburger Hill? Screaming Eagles? A world I couldn't understand.

The drive was too short. Before getting out of the car, John reached under the seat and handed me a beautifully wrapped package. "I betcha I'll be home before Christmas. But just in case..."

"Oh. I didn't get you anything." So thoughtless of me.

"Don't worry. You have four months to shop." He chuckled. "Go on, open it."

I peeled the star-spangled midnight blue paper off and stared at a book with an orange, lime-green, and blue cover. *Love Story*.

"When I went to Ford City, the bookstore window had stacks of the thing." He shrugged and gave me his one-sided smile. "I don't know anything about the book, but I liked the title."

I wiped my eyes. Again. "I do too." I knew I would read that book until it was in tatters.

As I trudged into the airport, my unwilling feet dragged. I didn't want to go in, but each moment with him was precious. No hippies hurling insults today. I couldn't have stood it if they had—not with John on his way to combat. After a few last, desperate kisses, I watched him stride down the boarding ramp to the plane. My heart went with him.

I started DePaul in September. My credits from Bogan Junior College transferred and met some core requirements. That fall I took Accounting 101. To get a business degree, I had to take accounting, economics, and management courses before I got to the stuff I really wanted to study—marketing.

I thought about changing jobs. There was an opening at Gossage Grill, and the thought of the tips was tempting, but Lerner's was good to me, allowing me to adjust my hours according to my class schedule. I received another raise, which was great.

DePaul's Loop campus was located at Jackson and State. I drove in and parked at a city garage a couple of blocks south. Walking fast, I passed Van Buren Street, which was lined with flop houses and rough-looking men sitting on the sidewalk. The south Loop was pretty seedy, and I promised myself I would never take a late afternoon or evening class. At least I felt like an actual college student, although I was going to classes in a high-rise instead of on a leafy green campus with brick buildings—and student demonstrations. No one I saw at DePaul seemed concerned with protesting the war. Sure, there were kids in headbands and peace-sign t-shirts, but my fellow students seemed serious about getting a degree and getting ahead in the world. The black kids with their Afros and dashikis were a new experience for me, but they were cool. I thought back to the talk I heard as a kid of the color line. I didn't understand it then, and I sure didn't understand it now. There was no color line at DePaul.

The first week of class was a revelation. The instructor covered a lot of material in each class. My textbook weighed about twenty pounds and cost a mint. Getting my degree would be slow going because of the cost of books.

The classrooms had stadium seating, and I usually sat near the middle halfway up. A blond guy with short hair wearing jeans and a green army shirt with the name tag ripped off sat next to me the second week. He looked a little older than most of the guys. "Hey. Name's Ron. Who do I have the pleasure of sitting next to?" His wide smile was engaging.

I smiled back. "Dani. Nice to meet you. Can I ask...are you a veteran?"

"What gave me away?"

"Well, the hair and the shirt."

"Got me. Returned from Nam in August. Getting back to my degree. Gotta love the GI Bill."

"My fiancé deployed last month."

"Fiancé? That's too bad." He grinned.

My face felt hot. I hated to blush, to be at a loss for words. I didn't want to deal with a bunch of come-ons at school. At first, I couldn't think of a smart retort. Then I did.

"Too bad for you, I guess." My voice sounded harsh, even to my ears.

Apparently, Ron got the message. He picked up his books and moved to the end of the row.

After that, I maintained an ice princess exterior and avoided eye contact with men. Accounting was boring, but I studied and aced all my tests. The bad thing was that Accounting 102 was my next class.

Driving home from school one Friday in September, singing along to the radio, the DJ cut in and announced Jimi Hendrix was found dead in London. Drugs. Sixteen days later Janis Joplin died. Drugs. What a loss for rock 'n' roll. John would be sad. He was a major fan too. John told me Jimi Hendrix had been in the 101st Airborne. As for drugs, neither of us indulged, although I knew lots of kids who did. And I heard the stories coming out of Vietnam about soldiers taking drugs. Don't let that happen to John, I prayed.

John's optimistic prediction about being home by Christmas was wrong. After he deployed, I visited the Nagys on Friday nights when I wasn't closing at the store. We shared our letters and our hopes he'd be home soon. I spent Christmas Eve with them. Despite the festive decorations and roast turkey, dinner was dismal without John. We had decided not to exchange gifts that year. The only thing we wanted was for John to come home. I didn't stay long.

"*Lánya*, have a blessed Christmas with your family. Please come by next Friday."

"I will. Promise." I hugged all three of them. Being with his family made me feel closer to John. Every time I visited their home, I spent a few minutes in John's room, lying on his bed, touching his Little League trophies, and inhaling his scent on the clothes in the closet. It made me cry, but it comforted me too.

That year, all four of us kids would be at Christmas dinner at Mom's. Dad and Ginger had plans, so the boys would join us.

Paige and Tim came by after eating with the Finnegans. "We're not hungry, Mom," Paige said.

Tim patted his flat stomach. "Stuffed with stuffing. We'll hang with you and have some dessert."

Mom bustled around the kitchen with Ken. They were cute together, bumping into each other, winking, bursting out laughing at whispered jokes. I watched them with envy. Longed for the time when John and I would do the same. The bell rang. Mom spun around with a bright smile. "Can you get it, Dani?"

I opened the door to my brothers. Phil was singing off-key. "I think I love you." He had his earphone in, adding his spin to The Partridge Family hit. I almost laughed. Joe was waving a Hot Wheels in the air making vroom-vroom sounds. Phil had grown since the summer. He topped me by two inches, almost six feet at thirteen. Joe hadn't had his growth spurt yet. The boys stomped snow off their boots and came in with a blast of frigid air.

Mom came over to hug them. "We'll eat in a few minutes."

"Good, I'm starving," Phil's voice had deepened.

"Me too," Joe chimed in. He took several more Hot Wheels out of his pockets before I hung up their coats.

Ken rubbed his hands together in anticipation of carving the first turkey he'd cooked for us. He sharpened the carving knife and approached his victim. "Ah. Nice and moist. The secret is basting. Basting with butter. Then tent it with foil for the first hour. And don't forget to cover the wings and legs in aluminum foil at the same time."

"It looks wonderful, darling." Mom beamed.

Darling? She used to call Dad "darling." Ken didn't have kids of his own and treated the four of us with kindness. He never tried to act like a father, and I respected that.

Ken brought the gigantic platter of turkey to the table while Mom and I carried the side dishes. Joe licked his lips. Earphone still in place, Phil sang, "My Sweet Lord." I cracked up.

"Phil, take that thing out of your ear," Mom scolded. He reluctantly complied, although he drummed a few riffs on the table from some inner tune throughout the meal. Joe brought his Hot Wheels to the table and ran them next to his plate between bites, but Formica was indestructible. Mom didn't even correct him.

Dinner was delicious. Ken was worth keeping around.

When dessert was served, Paige and Tim shared a slice of pumpkin pie. They were seniors and planned on getting jobs at Second City when they graduated next June. I thought they'd be successful. They were both so full of fun.

"Got to split." Paige stood and yanked on Tim's arm. "Party at Tim's cousin's place."

Tim nudged my shoulder. "Wanna come with us, Dani?"

"No. I want to go see that new movie, *Love Story*." My eyes filled, and tears ran down my cheeks. I hadn't thought about John once during dinner and that wasn't acceptable.

"Oh. I'll go with you." Paige took pity on me and sent Tim home. I drove the 442 slowly along the ice-rutted streets. We waited in line at the Evergreen Theatre. The large crowd was mostly girls and women, stomping their feet to keep warm. Having read the book about thirty times, I knew what to expect and brought one of those little tissue packs. I used the whole thing. Paige had to borrow a couple too.

For its entire run, I watched the movie at least once a week, usually alone, although once I convinced my mother to join me. She was as devastated as I by the tragedy. I knew she would be. "Oh my God, I haven't cried over a movie like that since *Charly* or maybe even *Old Yeller*."

In the darkened theater, I sniffled through the movie. It took my mind off my worry about John. Cancer. A totally different fear.

For months, it seemed as if every time I turned on the radio, the theme song from *Love Story* played. Inescapable. Each time I heard Andy Williams croon, "Where do I begin?" I broke down. That winter and spring, I must have gone through a truckload of tissue. And I carried those little packets with me everywhere.

Chapter Five

IT'S TOO LATE 1971

My life was simple. Work, school, wait. Wait for John's letters. Wait for the war to end. I watched Walter Cronkite as if he were an oracle. Troops levels were 280,000, down from almost 500,000. I tried to wrap my head around half a million families living with the fear and dread I did.

In January, President Nixon announced, "The end is in sight." Well, I sure hoped so. Maybe that had something to do with Congress forbidding the use of any U.S. ground forces in Laos or Cambodia. But they were bombing.

The war raged on at home. A group called the Weathermen tried to blow up the Capitol in March. Radicals. My dad would have a thing or two to say about that, but I wouldn't hear it. Since the divorce, I rarely saw him.

The other big news that month was Lieutenant William Calley being convicted of murder for his part in the My Lai massacre. His sentence—life imprisonment. The next day, President Nixon ordered him transferred from Leavenworth to house arrest at Fort Benning.

In April, Vietnam veterans threw away more than 700 medals on the west steps of the U.S. Capitol to protest the Vietnam War. Antiwar organizers claimed 500,000 marched that day in Washington, D. C., making it the largest demonstration since the November 1969 march. Stories appeared about protesters cursing at and spitting on soldiers returning from

Vietnam. On John's leave, we had experienced a taste of that disrespect. When he finally came home, it better not happen again.

Then his letters stopped.

I had dinner at the Nagys on a Sunday in July. They hadn't received any letters from John either.

Mrs. Nagy made her famous Hungarian goulash. *Gulyás* was the national dish of Hungary. I learned that when I first shared a meal with the family. Hard to believe that was nearly six years ago. Mrs. Nagy—I just couldn't bring myself to call her Sonia although she asked me to—used only real Hungarian paprika from the Kalocsa region. John used to buy it for her at a little shop in Brighton Park. She simmered the beef dish for hours, then served the stew with crusty bread and cucumber salad.

"What do you think it means, not getting letters?" I broke off a piece of bread and crumbled it to pieces without taking a bite.

Mr. Nagy said, "I don't know what to think. Could be they're behind with the mail."

"It's the government. Who knows?" Chuck shook his head. "Nixon said the end was in sight months ago. The marines have all left."

I took a sip of water. "The *Trib* said support for the war is falling. I see it on the news every day. And now veterans are protesting. That's what bothers me the most."

Mrs. Nagy patted my hand. "It is very sad, those young men throwing away medals. I don't understand them."

"Me neither." I sighed.

Chuck followed the news even closer than I did. "Congress has called for an end to the war, first time in history. Of course, Nixon can just ignore them. And what's up with those Pentagon Papers? Sounds like treason to me."

I gave up trying to eat. "I can't even think about that. All I care about is John coming home." Who could I call to find out why the letters had stopped?

Mr. Nagy and Chuck discussed the newspapers printing government secrets. I excused myself and went to John's room. After I closed the door, I couldn't stop the tears. I didn't know what I'd do if I didn't hear from him soon.

On Saturday, August 14th, 1971, I woke early. For some reason, I startled awake. I dressed, then went downstairs to make a cup of instant coffee. Before I could fill the kettle, the phone rang. Glancing at the clock, I wondered who was calling at 7:05 a.m.

I picked up on the second ring.

Chuck's voice. "Can you come over?"

I froze. After a moment, I said, "What's wrong?"

His voice broke. "Just come."

I dropped the receiver on my foot. Didn't even react to the pain, just bent to retrieve it. I felt like I was moving through gelatin as I watched my hand replacing the receiver. My stomach sank like a stone. My mouth, dry as the desert.

I knew.

I ran out of the house barefoot, not bothering to put on shoes. Light rain was falling, the sky dark with clouds, the air heavy with humidity. My chest heaved with the effort of crying and breathing. Running down the block, my tears diluted by the rain, I blubbered to a God I never visited anymore. "Please God, not dead, not dead, not dead."

A green sedan with a military logo sat at the curb. Several concerned faces peeked out windows. The next-door neighbor woman stood at her screen door, her hand covering her mouth. I ran up the front steps of John's house and pounded on the door.

An officer opened the door, and I flew past him to the living room. Mr. Nagy sat beside his wife on the couch, motionless, face slack. Mrs. Nagy, bent at the waist, sobbed into a sodden mass of tissues. I sank to my knees and patted her arm. My grief matched hers.

"*Ez nem lehet igaz. Nem, nem, nem...*" she shrieked. She didn't seem to realize I was there.

The chaplain sat in a chair across from my no-longer-to-be mother-in-law, reading aloud from his Bible. Chuck stood in the corner, head down, pinching the bridge of his nose. He moaned and left the room.

I wiped my face with my arm. The officer who answered the door handed me a box of tissue. Mr. Nagy sat like a rock, staring straight ahead.

"*Egy hiba*, Miklos. *Egy hiba*." Mrs. Nagy sat up and grabbed her husband's shoulder.

"No, Sonia, no mistake."

"My boy is dead!" She noticed my presence at last. "*Lánya*, our John…"

Mrs. Nagy's wailing gradually decreased in volume, and her sobs became less frequent. I went to the kitchen and got a glass of water for her. When I came back, she was wiping her eyes and looking at some papers the officer had given her. She stared at the glass of water as if she didn't know what it was. I put it on the end table and knelt at her feet. She said, "Thank you, honey. Thanks for coming."

Unable to speak, I took her hand and squeezed it gently. My own tears had stopped at some point. I must have been in shock.

The officer stepped forward and held out a small rectangle of paper in his hand. "Ma'am, sir, here's my card. I'm assigned to help you through the process of the return of John's remains. I'd like to come back tomorrow to assist you with funeral arrangements."

Mrs. Nagy nodded. "Yes. I'll be here."

Remains. I felt my heart cleave in two. Something in my chest hurt, that's for sure. I stayed the afternoon. When I used the restroom, I didn't recognize myself in the mirror. My eyes mere slits. My lips dry and flaking. I swallowed, and my throat felt dry as sand. When had I last had anything to drink? Hours. My tongue stuck to the roof of my mouth. I needed some water.

Entering the kitchen, I filled a glass at the tap and sipped. Despite my thirst, it was difficult to swallow. John was dead. Why should I quench my thirst?

Chuck sat at the kitchen table. He was pale and shaking.

"Have you checked your sugar?"

He glanced up. "No."

"You have to eat something."

He looked down at the table. I understood his pain and inability to care for himself. I poured him a glass of milk and smeared some peanut butter on a slice of bread. Watching him drink and eat—tiny sips and small bites—I believed he was feeling guilty at being alive. "Dani, if I could change places with him, I would." We both dissolved into tears.

As for me, I didn't know how I could go on living without John.

In the living room, Mr. and Mrs. Nagy paged through an album of family pictures. They sat close to each other and murmured. I didn't want to intrude.

I wandered into John's room and lay on his bed. Sniffed his pillow but couldn't sense him. After all, it had been months since he'd lain there. I opened the closet and caressed every garment hanging on the rod. His beloved yellow 442 t-shirt lay on the floor, in the corner behind his shoes. Snatching it up like a lost treasure, I inhaled his scent. Lime, musk, and cedar from the Jade East he always wore. When I left an hour later, I took the shirt and a half-empty Jade East bottle with me.

When Mom saw me, she covered her mouth with her hand. "Honey, what happened? I thought you were at work. And you're barefoot."

I broke down again. "Jo-John's dead." I set my remembrances on the table and wrapped my arms around her. Paige came in the room with Tim. They stood quietly, faces pale with shock. The personal cost of the war had shattered my life. And destroyed my future.

Sleepwalking my way through the funeral that windy, cloudy day in September, I felt nothing. There was a hollowness in my chest that made me think my heart had disintegrated. I didn't get a last glimpse of my love. The casket was closed. How could I be sure he was really inside?

The flag-draped coffin and the military ceremony at the graveside, where somber young men folded the flag and presented it to Mrs. Nagy, seemed like a movie playing on the screen of my misery. I could replay the movie at will, but I no longer had a will.

Then I retired from life. Quit my job. Didn't bother showing up for the business communication class I'd enrolled in. I slept. I cried. For weeks.

When I did get up, I went to visit Mrs. Nagy. She didn't bake anymore. She lost weight and couldn't seem to settle, getting up every few minutes, staring blankly. We weren't much help to each other, but at some level, there was comfort in each other's presence.

We sat at the kitchen table with cups of tea gone cold.

"*Lánya*, I never talk about this, but I lost a baby sixteen years ago. A boy. How I wish he had lived. I can't stop thinking about that baby now."

I picked up the teacups, poured them out, and put on the kettle. We sat in silence until the kettle shrieked. What could I say to that? Too much loss. My visits became less frequent.

Much of that fall was a blur. In October, I got a letter from John, telling me he'd be home soon. But John was already home, buried under six feet of Illinois soil. My letters to him were returned, stamped "K I A." Each one piercing my chest in the place my heart used to be, bringing a fresh pain.

I woke screaming from nightmares. In those horrific visions, I opened his casket and found a stranger, or bloody body parts. Not once did I see John's face, and maybe that was a good thing.

Sometimes, I had beautiful dreams. About him teaching me to drive, Christmas celebrations, summer kisses. I dreamed about our wedding. How he looked at me as I walked down the aisle in my white empire organza gown. My sheer sleeves banded with lace that matched the illusion neckline. Hair in an up-do, a headpiece of lace medallions attached to the sheer veil that came to my mid-back. Then I woke. And I remembered. No wedding. No dress. When I had the good dreams, being asleep was better than being awake.

One day in December, as I trudged past Mom's room to the bathroom, I overheard her and Paige talking.

"We've got to do something to help her," Paige said. "She's lost it. Totally lost it. When's the last time she combed her hair? Or washed it? Or showered?"

Mom said, "She wears the same pajamas for days, until I force her to change. And that bathrobe. She must have scrounged it from the clothes I put aside to give to charity. Threadbare chenille. But she wears it like a uniform. I thought she'd bounce, but she hasn't. Any ideas?"

I stood in the hallway, listening. Clearing my throat, I said, "I can hear you, you know."

"Good. It's time you heard this." Paige got up from the chair and put her arm around me. Her words were firm, but her touch was gentle.

Mom looked as if she were about to cry. I could give her lessons in crying. "Honey, we want to help you. What can we do?"

"Nothing. There isn't anything anyone can do."

Mom's brow creased. "You can't go on like this. You're nineteen years old. Your whole life is ahead of you."

"Ahead of me? No! My whole life is *over*. Killed in action. Damn war!" I surprised myself with my vehemence. Perhaps there *was* life in me.

"Tell you what," Paige said in an upbeat voice. "Take a shower and get dressed. We'll go for pizza. Vito and Nick's. Right, Mom?"

"Great idea. How about it, Dani?" Mom's bright smile looked forced.

My mouth watered. Vito and Nick's. I hadn't been hungry for weeks. "Okay. Sounds good."

As I headed to the bathroom, I heard Paige say, "Signs of life."

And I did have signs of life. I got up, showered, and dressed almost every day. I registered for Business Communications for the winter quarter. At Ford City Mall, I convinced Lerner's to give me my job back. Although I wasn't living life to the fullest, I was picking up the pieces.

Just before Christmas, I visited Mrs. Nagy, trying to tamp down the guilt I felt for abandoning her. I brought her a Hungarian pastry from the Smakosz Bakery. And a bottle of Evening in Paris cologne. She thanked me and hugged me tightly. Her body, a wisp of her former self. We had tea and nibbled at the pastry, which was adequate, but not up to her former standards. She said, "I worry so about my Chuck. His eyes. I worry about his eyes."

I didn't stay long. The house rang with loss.

I don't recall much about Christmas that year, but I'm sure my family celebrated. Too busy wallowing in misery, my room became my refuge, and I didn't make an appearance. The contrast with past holidays would have been unbearable.

Chapter Six

OFF THE RAILS 1972

Chuck phoned me in February. "Dani, can you come for dinner Sunday? We have some news."

How could I not accept? But as I hung up the phone, a sick feeling of dread crept over me.

Bearing a bouquet of carnations, I knocked on the door I used to walk through with John.

Mr. Nagy opened the door and waved me in. "Good to see you, little grease-monkey girl." His lips turned up, but the smile didn't touch his eyes. My smile, the same.

The temperature was oppressive. Like a hothouse. The aroma of roasting meat hung in the air.

Mrs. Nagy rushed in from the kitchen, her face flushed with exertion. She had gained a little weight back. "Oh, what beautiful flowers. Thank you, *Lánya*."

Her pet name for me. I used to love it. Now it just hurt, but I couldn't let her see that.

Chuck was wearing thick glasses. He'd lost weight and moved like an old man. I had an inkling about the news.

We ate at the kitchen table. The dining room was full of packing materials. Why? I knew I had to make an effort to eat. The roast beef with sour cream gravy served over noodles would match anyone's idea of comfort food. Comfort and solace were beyond my capabilities.

Mr. Nagy passed the bread. "I got a letter from Noah. He's stateside. The entire 101st will be home by the end of March."

I dropped my fork on the floor. Drank some water. Mrs. Nagy had remembered I always had water with my meals. "What else did he say? Was he with John when—"

"No, he was at the firebase." Mr. Nagy's lips trembled. "He did get to see him before...before John...came home."

Mrs. Nagy patted my hand. "Chuck, will you get Dani another fork?"

"Sure."

Forks and roast beef were the farthest things from my mind.

Mr. Nagy broke off a piece of bread and slathered it with butter. Recovering from his emotional lapse, he spoke, "Noah told us a little about the operation the 101st was on. They called it Jefferson Glenn. I have no idea why. It ended last October 8th, about two months too late for John."

His words echoed in my mind. Two months too late. Too late for John. Too late.

"They were patrolling to the west of a city called Huế. The area of operations was called the rocket belt. Crawling with those commie bastards firing rockets at our troops."

Chuck added, "Noah is no fan of the ARVN. Says the South Vietnamese don't have the will to fight. The 101st couldn't depend on them."

Mr. Nagy frowned. "John lost his life trying to support them. Died in a place called Thừa Thiên Province. Might as well be the moon. I used to support the war, but with what I'm reading in the papers these days, I'm not so sure."

"No kidding," Chuck said. "Even the soldiers are refusing to follow orders. When that story broke about Firebase Pace, that's when Nixon announced our troops were only playing defense. He said the ARVN was in charge of offensive operations. If what Noah says is true, the Viet Cong will win after all."

Did John die for nothing? What did it matter? Dead was dead.

Pushing the food around my plate, I asked Chuck about his new glasses.

Silence descended. Mrs. Nagy got up and left the table. I heard a door in the hallway close.

Chuck shrugged. "My vision is worse. In fact, I'm legally blind at this point."

I gasped. "Oh, no! I'm so sorry."

Mr. Nagy rose, and said, "I'm gonna check on Sonia."

I glanced at Chuck. His resemblance to John was not as strong as it used to be. "What's going to happen? Why are there boxes in the dining room? Are you—"

"We're going back to Tennessee. Dad can't handle the garage on his own. He's so stubborn and paranoid. He won't hire someone he hasn't known his entire life to help him. The business is sold, and so is the house. We leave in a couple of weeks."

Mr. and Mrs. Nagy drifted back to the kitchen. Her eyes were swollen, and she clutched a handkerchief. Mr. Nagy's lips were set in a grim line.

As I cleared the dishes, Mrs. Nagy brought a platter of freshly baked kolaches to the table, the kind with the flaky crust. She'd gone all out with the fillings, walnut, poppy seed, apricot, and raspberry. My mother adored these. I'd have to take some home.

"Should I make some coffee?" Mrs. Nagy's voice, thick with tears, cut through my self-centered pain.

"Let me help you." I rushed to her and gave her a hug. "Chuck told me your news. I understand, but I'm sorry to lose you."

"Honey, you will never lose us. Please keep in touch. Perhaps you will visit us."

Maybe I would, someday. John had wanted me to see Tennessee. I entered his room for the last time. Someone had packed up his belongings. I stood at the door looking at the bare mattress on the bed frame. The room held nothing of him.

The Nagys moved on a Saturday. They'd sold the house to a family with four little children. I would never walk through the door again. Couldn't visit anymore. John's room would belong to someone else. The moving van left in a puff of diesel fumes. I hugged all three of them. Made promises to stay in touch I'd probably never keep. As I watched them drive away out of my life, I remembered that August day when John helped me round up Sheba. The day I fell in love. Closing my eyes, I saw him smiling that lopsided smile. I shivered.

I walked straight home and back to bed. My body had wrung out its last tear. I believed I'd used my lifetime allotment. Lying in bed, dry-eyed, I stared at the ceiling, studying the perforations in the acoustic tile, finding animal shapes and faces—ugly faces with screaming mouths.

The next morning, Paige came in and plopped down on the bed. "Rise and shine!"

I flicked my eyes to her, then away. "Nope." Went back to studying the ceiling.

"I have something to show you."

Now I was irritated. I glared at her. "I don't give a shit."

"Ooh, potty mouth." Paige pushed her blond curls behind her ear. "You're not doing this again, Dani. Mom and I are not letting you give up." To demonstrate her resolve, she yanked on my arm, pulling me to a sitting position.

This was too much. "For God's sake, just leave me alone."

"Nope. Come downstairs and have some breakfast. I made a special trip to the bakery. Saved you a chocolate éclair."

I used to love chocolate éclairs. I used to arm wrestle Paige for the last one. "All right. Let me get dressed, and I'll be down."

When I walked in the kitchen, Mom brought me a cup of coffee, and I sat at the place setting with the éclair. "What do you have to show me, Paige?"

Mom and Paige grinned at each other. My sister handed me the newspaper with an ad circled in red ink.

I read it and frowned. "So? What's this got to do with me?"

"Are you kidding me? You'd be perfect," Paige said.

Mom nodded in agreement. "You've always been thin, but since...you know...you're *model* thin. This is a wonderful opportunity. I took the liberty of talking to the modeling agency head, Margo Fontella."

I rolled my eyes. "God, Mom. Did you really? What am I—seven?"

"You have an appointment tomorrow at nine a.m." With a look of satisfaction, Mom bit into a glazed donut.

Paige sat at the table and selected a pastry. "I'll pick out an outfit for you, but I won't be able to do your hair. Got to get to my job."

The next morning, I surprised myself by getting up before the alarm went off. Putting on makeup, I smiled at my image. My face felt funny. I couldn't remember the last time I'd smiled. Paige had selected a purple long-sleeved mini dress with a smocked bodice. Excellent choice. I stepped into chunky heels, grabbed my purse and jacket, and hurried downstairs.

Mom sat at the kitchen table dressed for work, smoking as usual. She was trying to cut down and had a new habit—she smoked a cigarette halfway, stubbed it out, and saved it for later. When she lit up a "halfsie," the reek was appalling. She was working on a fresh one this morning. I bent to give her a hug and said, "I'm off. Wish me luck."

Mom blew smoke away from my face. "You don't need it, honey."

Margo Fontella's office was in Evergreen Park, near the shopping center. I took the elevator to the third floor. The waiting room contained three young women, all thin, all with long hair parted in the middle. I fit right in. The receptionist smiled and asked for my name. "It will be a few minutes, Miss Marek. Have a seat."

I picked up *Glamour* magazine from February. Cheryl Tiegs was on the cover. She reminded me of Paige with her wavy blond hair and blue eyes, although Paige was too curvy to model. Flipping through the pages, I found an article I wanted to read: "How to Find Your New Self-Image." I certainly needed the advice. Before I was halfway through, my name was called.

A woman with her chestnut hair in a French Twist and wearing a crimson suit with a bowed blouse motioned me forward. "Come this way, Miss Marek." She turned smartly and tapped down the tile hallway in her high heels. I felt like a puppy tagging along in her wake.

With a wave of her hand, she motioned me into her office and indicated a chair. Obediently, I sat. She stood at her desk. "You have the look I'm after. Let me watch you walk." She gestured toward a wooden runway in the center of the room. Glad it was only about ten feet long, I complied.

"Turn and walk back."

I did so.

She pointed at a chair. "Sit." She seated herself behind the desk and studied me.

As her narrowed brown eyes bored into me, I felt like a bug under a microscope. I waited, hands folded in my lap, willing myself to remain still.

"Miss Marek, Dani, you have potential. I'll take you on, but you can't lose any weight. We do bridal shows. Our clients are not all thin. They don't want to see a skeleton parading on the runway."

"Okay."

Miss Fontella's lips twisted. "You don't know how to walk. We can work on that."

We did. By the time I left, I knew how to walk and had a folder with clearly written instructions outlining what I would need to bring to each bridal show. Next Sunday, I would observe, and the Sunday after that, I would be on the runway.

Paige made me her project. First, the modeling, then a social life. She had always been a party girl, and that had not diminished. Tim, a party boy in his own right, always knew who was having a blowout. Together they double-teamed me to join them. Worn out by the unrelenting invitations, I agreed to attend a party at Tim's older cousin's place. Michael lived in an old warehouse on the North Side.

The brick façade was draped in dozens of vertical strings of white lights, like an electric waterfall. We entered a vast space with concrete floors, brick walls, and a black ceiling with exposed metal ducts. A kaleidoscopic light show projected on the one white wall. Pulse-pounding rock from a band on a low stage. Huge amps, the size of a mattress. The band was fantastic, playing everything from the Stones to Van Morrison, then seamlessly morphing into a soul review. Great dance music. I felt the bass and drums in my chest, found myself consumed by the beat.

The smoke in the air wasn't from cigarettes. The pungent, earthy, almost piney scent left no doubt in my mind about what was being smoked. I thought about Three Dog Night singing "Mama Told Me Not to Come," and laughed out loud. It *was* the craziest party I'd ever seen, but I liked it. Totally out of my experience, and that was a good thing.

Paige shouted over the band. "Let me introduce you to Michael." She grabbed my hand and led me over to a guy who looked a lot like Tim. Black Irish my mother always termed those dark-haired folk.

Michael brought me over to the bar, handed me a vodka tonic, and offered me his joint. I shook my head—I'd never even flirted with the idea of pot—and watched him inhale like it was life-saving oxygen, holding in the smoke for several moments. Then he pulled me close and kissed me, releasing the smoke into my mouth. Stunned, I took a step back, but then dove in for another, smokeless kiss. What had gotten into me? This was the most alive I'd felt since August 14th.

We downed our drinks, finished the joint, and laughed together. He stood close, backed me up to the brick wall, and kissed me silly. Memories of the only make-out party I'd attended came to my mind, unbidden. Resolutely barring thoughts of the past, I closed my eyes and lived in this moment, with this man. There would be plenty of time to beat myself up for enjoying life while John was dead.

The band began a bass-thumping version of "Dance to the Music." Michael put his arm around me and scooted me to the center of the room, where several people were dancing. We stayed on the dance floor for "Till You Get Enough" by Charles Wright and the Watts 103rd Street Rhythm Band, one of the favorites of my high school graduating class. By that time, I was breathless and thirsty.

Back at the bar, I got the eye from several men. I didn't bother to learn their names, just danced and kissed my way through the evening. The band was so loud, it was impossible to have a conversation, but talk was the last thing on my mind. When the band took a break, Michael blasted more rock—Janis Joplin, The Doors, and Jimi Hendrix. As I recalled the trio of drug-related deaths, I felt a pang of guilt for smoking the pot.

Paige found me in a clinch with Michael about three a.m. "We're splitting."

I gave Michael one more kiss and followed her and Tim out to Tim's 1963 Corvair.

"You looked like you had a good time there, sis." Paige grinned and nudged me in the ribs.

"Michael was having himself a good time too. And several of the other guys. Man, who woulda thought it?" Tim threw back his head to laugh and almost lost his balance.

I felt my face burning. My joy evaporated. "Are you two *judging* me? I thought the whole point was to get me out in circulation and to have some fucking fun."

Paige put her hands up. "Whoa! Lighten up. We're glad you enjoyed yourself. No judgment here."

Mollified, I asked, "Where can I get a really good fake ID? Some of the girls I model with have them and talk about the bars on Rush Street all the time. I think it might be just what I need."

"Going uptown? Wow. I'll see what I can come up with. Tim, any ideas?"

"I might be able to put my hands on a driver's license for you. When are they going to change the drinking age in this Neanderthal state? Twenty-one to drink, eighteen to die for your country." He opened the car door and stopped, possibly realizing what he'd said.

I started sobbing. Paige put her arm around me. "Real sensitive, asshole."

"Oh shit, Dani. I'm sorry. Wasn't thinking. Still a little bit drunk, or high, or both."

Paige came through the next week. I was in business. Someone was missing their driver's license, someone who was a fairly good match for me: five-foot seven, a little shorter than me, and outweighing me by a few pounds. Brown hair, brown eyes—I had hazel eyes—but close enough in the darkness of the clubs on Rush Street. The bouncers wouldn't look too closely, I hoped.

On Friday nights, I ventured to the bars on Rush and Division Streets: Faces, She-nannigans, Bombay Bicycle Club, Butch McGuire's, and my personal favorite, Mother's. The dimly lit basement room featured live bands, and I loved to dance. When we entered a club, my modeling buddies and I caught the eye of every red-blooded male. None of us were twenty-one, but our IDs worked. Suzanne, Cynthia, and Liz were all tall and knew how to walk, dress, and wear makeup. I fit right in.

On Saturdays, if grief and loneliness began to throb in my mind, and the need to forget overwhelmed me, I'd hit the bars on the Southside. Erik the Red was the best. When I wore jeans, I'd even take the slide down from the second floor to the first, usually without spilling my drink. It was a different crowd than Rush Street, but I felt at home there.

I liked the way men chased me, but I wasn't looking to get caught. My flirtations were just that—flirtations. Hot make-out sessions in a secluded booth. Fun for a few hours. None of my nocturnal conquests came close to John, and I promised myself, never would.

Funny thing, Paige and Tim seemed to be bonded for life, and now *I* had a kissing list and was searching for a pair of lips that could help me forget, even for an hour. When I scrutinized myself in the mirror in the ladies' rooms of those bars, applying more blush, my vodka-fueled thoughts revolved around the next victim. My heart was closed for business. Did I even possess one any longer?

The pain from losing John did not diminish with time like everyone said it would. I veered off track. I went off the rails. Each mini seduction was a one-time thing. Choosing from a catalog of fake names to use for the evening and scrawling fake phone numbers on cocktail napkins became routine. I lurched from one encounter to the next without remorse or conscience. If I ever spotted one of my admirers again, I left the bar immediately.

Men fell at my feet. I liked it. I stepped on them for sport. My new favorite sport.

On a Friday night in June, my plan was to meet Rocky, the drummer for The Compadres from Albuquerque, New Mexico, who were booked for the month at Mother's. I'd met him the previous Friday night during a break. He was cute and exotic to a girl from the Southside. Was he twenty-one? Sure didn't look it. About six feet, skinny, with riotously curly, long, black hair. A fascinating, enticing, and glamourous combination—Native American and Mexican, I concluded. Drummers have a rep as wild and crazy, like Keith Moon, but Rocky was sweet and shy.

We'd flirted and made out between sets. He asked me to stay after closing at four a.m., and I couldn't say no. We made out in the back room until the sun came up and agreed to meet again.

The next week, while I waited for the band to take a break so I could spend a few minutes with Rocky, I got bored and glanced around the room. I noticed a guy lounging against one of the pillars in the basement of Mother's, watching the action. He was tall, and I was darned sick of all the cocky little vertically challenged men who pestered me all night. His long black hair was glossy. He had a great body, looked athletic. Tall, dark, not handsome, but tall. Earlier, Suzanne had challenged me to ask a guy to dance and bet me one dollar I wouldn't do it. I never should have taken the bait, but I hated to lose—anything. I'd lost enough. So, I tapped the tall guy on the arm and asked him to dance, trying to get away from the pudgy little gnome who was following me. The Compadres were rocking—"Brown Sugar" by the Stones—and tall guy nodded and followed me onto the dance floor. I didn't look at him once. When I danced, men were props. Men were props, period. I was alone with the beat and the joy of movement. After the music ended, I turned to walk away, and tall guy grabbed my wrist, like he was drowning, and I could save him. I looked back at him, then at my arm. He released me and said, "Now it's my turn to ask you to dance. Luke."

"Dani."

A rare slow dance, a sappy love song by Bread—whom I despised—lasted for four long minutes. Luke couldn't dance; he stepped on my toes more than once, but his tall body felt good.

That night, I stood up Rocky and went for a walk with Luke. We wandered all over the Gold Coast, stopping at a school playground on a whim. Luke pushed me on a swing until I begged for mercy. He lifted me out of the swing and carried me to the merry-go-round. He grabbed the rail and ran in circles, getting it up to speed, then jumped on—the merry-go-round—and me. The sensations of the warm summer wind and the kisses were intoxicating. Eyes closed, I pretended I was kissing John, and it felt wonderful.

When he asked for my phone number, I gave him the real one.

My modeling buddies were waiting for me at my car. I think the only reason they waited was they were stranded because the buses stopped running.

They asked about my date with Rocky, and I told them I'd moved on, which made them laugh. They were used to me moving on.

I had a gig at a bridal show on Sunday, so I stayed in Saturday night and went to bed early, surprised Luke didn't call. I had to wonder why I cared and why I'd given him my real number. Was I seriously thinking of dating him? I didn't date.

The phone rang Sunday night. I told Paige to answer, and if it was a guy, tell him I was out. She rolled her eyes as she always did but complied. Actually, she laid it on pretty thick. I stood there and listened.

"Dani? Sorry, she's out. Who's this?"

She covered the receiver and mouthed, "Luke."

"Who? Never heard of you." Paige earned a thumbs up.

She twirled the cord in her fingers. "I don't know where she went. I can't keep track of all her boyfriends, that'd be a full-time job. Luke, you said?"

She covered the receiver again and giggled. "He sounds desperate."

I smiled.

"Okay, I can take a message. L-U-K-E. Got it."

As she was hanging up, a loud squawk came out of the receiver. Paige took pity on him. "I'm still here." She listened for a moment. "You want to leave your number? Oh, no, no, I don't think so. She never calls anybody back. It's best if you try again." She slammed the receiver back in the cradle, then burst out laughing. "You owe me for that one."

I had classes at DePaul Tuesday and Thursday mornings, and I worked as many hours as I could at Lerner's in the afternoon and evenings. I was rarely home. Weekends were reserved for clubbing. My pattern was Rush Street on Friday, then the Southside bars on Saturday. I'd grab a few hours of sleep, so I'd look dewy fresh and bride-like for my modeling jobs on Sunday.

All week, I played Luke like a fish. He called every night, and Paige told him I was out. She steadfastly refused to take his number; God bless her. I'd have to do something nice for her. On Friday, I answered the phone myself. Time to reel him in.

"Hello," I intoned in what I hoped was a voice full of sultriness and mystery.

"Dani?" His voice was nice and deep, reminding me of John, without the Southern drawl.

"Yes, this is Dani. Who's this?"

"Luke."

"Who?" I looked at my nails and decided to change the color of my polish.

"Luke. We met last Friday at Mother's. You asked me to dance."

"I did?" Thought I did a decent job of infusing disbelief into my question.

"Yeah, and we went for a walk, and I pushed you on the swings at the playground—"

"Oh, yes, yes. You're tall and have black hair. I remember." I pulled the phone cord to its full length, so I could get a glass of water at the sink.

"You're hard to get hold of. I've been trying all week."

Silence.

"Dani? Are you there?"

"Yes. Did you ask me a question?" I sipped the water, pacing.

"No, I was just saying you're hard to get hold of."

"Point taken. Anything else or is that what you called about?" I could feel my laughter sputtering up and struggled to suppress it. I'd either hooked him, or he spit out the lure. Either option was fine with me. Like Paige used to say before she chose Tim Finnegan, there were plenty of fish in the sea. Then I admitted to myself I was interested in this particular fish for some odd reason.

He stuttered as he replied, and I knew he was hooked. "I-I would like to take you out to-to dinner sometime."

"Sometime?"

"Are you free tomorrow?"

"Uh, no." Did he actually think I would accept a date with a day's notice?

"What about next Saturday?"

I heard him breathing on the line and waited a few more seconds before replying. "Hmm. I'm not busy. Where should we meet?"

"Can I pick you up?"

"No." Short and not so sweet.

"Oh. Okay. Do you know Romeo's? It's on the corner of Rush and Oak. Outdoor café. About seven?"

"All right. A week from tomorrow. See you then." I hung up even though he was still talking.

I decided to ditch Rush Street and go to the bars in Mount Greenwood that night just in case Luke went out. Couldn't take a chance on running into him. Erik the Red's was hopping, and I scored some nice weed from a cop when we made out in his smoke-filled car.

The next week flew past with school and work, and I forgot about my date with Luke until Paige mentioned it Saturday afternoon while we were folding our laundry.

I groaned. "Ugh! I'm not sure I want to go. Faces was a bust last night, yet I stayed way too late. And I've got an early bridal show tomorrow." I sat on the bed and picked up a peasant top. Too cute.

Paige turned to me. "Oh, come on. I can't face all the pathetic phone calls I'll have to answer if you ditch him. You know he'll keep calling. Just go. Make it an early night if you have to."

"I guess." Heaving a great sigh, I continued, "I do have that new halter dress I'd like to show off. And he is tall."

As I drove to Rush Street, vaguely surprised I was keeping the date, my mind drifted to the Saturday morning last summer when I learned about John's death. My current life was a relentless quest to distract myself from the fact I'd never see him again. No one could replace the love of my life. My heart had turned to stone, and I couldn't conceive of a way to revive it. There was no Prince Charming in my future, I was certain. What did I think I was doing with all these men? Wreaking revenge on strangers for the tragedy that left me numb? Maybe. That was enough self-examination for me. I turned on the radio. Creedence Clearwater Revival's "Sweet Hitchhiker" blasted through the speakers. Great driving tune. Then the double play, "Fortunate Son," brought tears to my eyes. John went down to war and was not fortunate. Gasping and willing the tears not to fall, I switched off the radio. I had to navigate the Kennedy to the Ohio Street exit and needed my full attention on the road.

I lucked out finding a parking space a block away from Romeo's. Only twenty minutes late. As I approached the restaurant, I spotted Luke craning his neck, looking up and down the street. When he turned my way, I waved, and his face broke out in a smile. He rushed to me and held his arms out. I stepped back and held my straw clutch two-handed at waist level. Shut that down fast.

His smile faded, and he cleared his throat. "You look beautiful. Love the dress."

"Thanks, Luke." I glanced at the crowd. "Popular place. Is the wait long?"

The hostess's voice blared over the loudspeaker, "Table for two for Luke."

He put his arm around me, just grazing my waist, and we made our way to the hostess stand. "Great timing."

A waiter nodded a greeting and led us to the table. The young man held my chair, placed the menus in front of us, and promised to return with water.

Luke couldn't take his eyes off me. I felt like a juicy steak. No problem. I was used to it. Ever since I reached my height at age thirteen, developed cheekbones and a lean physique, I'd dealt with the gaping. Now that I modeled and knew how to walk, I attracted even more notice.

When Luke asked if he could order for me, I laughed. "No, thanks. I'm perfectly capable of choosing and speaking."

His mouth fell open. Not a good look.

I perused the menu and chose a summer salad with chicken and grapes. He ordered a steak. No surprise.

While we waited for the meal, he chatted about the University of Wisconsin and his first job in Madison. Boring. I stifled a yawn and glanced around the restaurant. Yikes! Tony, a guy I encountered at the Back Room once, about a month ago, was staring at me. His date had noticed, and she wasn't pleased. I averted my eyes. Luke continued his soliloquy about his career, triumphantly announcing he'd recently been promoted at the pharmaceutical company, the job that brought him to Chicago. I pretended to listen, nodded, and oohed and aahed. He preened. Good Grief!

At last, the waiter appeared with our food. Luke ordered a bottle of Mateus, shooting me a glance, probably to see if I was impressed. I was not. Already, I regretted keeping this date. Thought about having to get up at seven a.m.

He dug into his food as if he hadn't eaten in a week. I picked at my salad.

When he finally came up for air, he tuned into the fact I hadn't eaten much. "Don't you like your salad? I can send it back."

Send it back? Was he one of those assholes? "It's fine. I eat light in the evening."

"Oh."

"I've got a modeling job tomorrow."

His attention pivoted from his baked potato with all the trimmings to me. "You model?"

"It's a side job. I do bridal shows on Sunday."

"So, you're not famous? Not in any magazines?"

"Nope." This fool set my teeth on edge.

Luke returned to the potato. I pushed my salad around, planning how to end this date fast. Because it was only 9:00, I told myself to chill out and made a mental tally sheet. On the positive side, I was impressed with his sophistication. Luke was six years older, a college graduate, and had a hotshot corporate job with a Fortune 500 pharmaceutical company. He'd traveled. I'd never left Illinois except for family vacations to the Wisconsin Dells. I listened, enthralled with his description of the beaches of Mexico and Jamaica. Would I ever see them? He painted a fairly good word picture, for a guy. On the other hand, the only thing of interest to him regarding me was my looks.

Luke wiped his mouth with his napkin and tossed it on his empty plate. He picked up a pack of Winston's and offered me one. I shook my head. He lit a cigarette, took a deep drag, and leaned back.

I sipped the rosé wine.

"Would you like a nightcap? My apartment is right down the street."

"No." I didn't frown although I wanted to.

He stubbed out the cigarette and raised his hand to signal for the check. I'd seen that imperious gesture in movies, but never in real life. By this point, the negative side of the tally sheet had more entries, including loutish table manners and self-involvement to the point of abrasiveness.

When the check arrived, he asked the waiter, "Do you take American Express?"

Romeo's did not. Luke scowled and made a show of selecting another credit card, shooting me a glance to see if I was impressed. Nope.

The waiter returned with the tab which Luke signed with a dramatic flourish. He stood and assisted me out of my chair. One point earned.

As we walked out of the café, two soldiers in uniform walked by. I made eye contact and smiled. They nodded to me.

Luke noticed the exchange and said, "Suckers. I got a 330 in the lottery. Call me lucky." His heartless attitude and smug face enraged me.

I stopped cold and swung to face him. "Call you lucky? I'll call you an arrogant asshole." Spinning on my heel, I bolted to my car. Luke was lucky, all right. Lucky I didn't scratch the smugness off his face and gouge his eyes out.

"Dani, wait!"

Of course, I did not. Opening the door of the 442, I saw Luke striding toward me. I slipped behind the wheel and plunged the key into the ignition. The full-throated sound of the well-tuned engine comforted me and made me feel close to John. Shoving the gearshift into reverse and turning the wheels, I spotted a clear shot to Oak Street, so I found first gear and gunned it. Luke stood in the street gaping after me.

By the time I arrived home, I'd cooled off. The night was a waste of time and gas. The phone was ringing, and I let it. I wasn't about to answer. Paige was out. Mom was asleep. She could sleep through anything, so the phone didn't wake her. I took it off the hook, waited until the squawk stopped, and retreated to my room. As always, I was grateful I didn't have to share a room with Paige. She was still a freaking slob. I wasn't.

I organized all my gear for the next day because I had to leave the house by 8:30 to be on time for my gig in the northwest suburbs. While washing up, I muttered to myself. "Why couldn't John get a 330?" But I knew he would have enlisted if it weren't for me. Sure, we were all raised patriotic children of patriotic veterans, but many of us questioned and protested the war when it came too close. By the time John died, the war was raging as fiercely at home as it was in Vietnam. Luke's smugness, while thousands of American boys were dying in a faraway jungle, made me ill.

That night I dreamed I picked John up at the airport after his discharge. He was so handsome in his uniform, striding proudly past all the people in the airport lobby with my hand in his. Half of the throng cheered. Half cursed him. We ignored them all. Just as I kissed him, the alarm blared. I closed my eyes, wanting to finish the dream, wanting to *live* in the dream.

Dragging myself out of bed, I dressed and trudged downstairs with my gear. Paige got up from the kitchen table and tagged after me as I carried my bag out to the car. I told her about the disastrous date, and she promised to hang up if Luke called.

"There's no way in hell I'll ever speak to that jerk again."

She gave me a one-armed hug and said, "Amen to that."

Luke called, and each time, Paige or I slammed the phone back on the hook. Eventually, the calls stopped. I forgot about him. My life was busy with school and work. Taking a single class each quarter, I might earn my degree in a couple of decades, but it was all I could afford. Marketing, particularly fashion marketing, excited me, and I thought it was a brilliant career choice for a woman. I remembered how glamorous Doris Day was in *Lover Come Back*. How I yearned to be one of those women who lunched at Sardi's and drank dry martinis while landing the big account.

My job at Lerner's kept me in gas money, and the modeling money helped. Life chugged along. For the time being, to avoid running into Luke, I stuck to the bars in Mount Greenwood.

Then, about a month later, the deliveries started. Flowers, jewelry, books, chocolates. All from Luke. All with the same apology note: *What did I do wrong? Let me make it up to you.*

I wondered how he tracked me down knowing only my first name. He started calling again. According to Paige and my mother, the phone rang first thing in the morning, all hours of the afternoon, and in the evening. Paige knew the drill and hung up on him, but my mother chatted with him.

"Luke sounds like a nice young man. Why don't you call him? He left his number."

I narrowed my eyes. "Traitor! He's a jerk. I want nothing to do with him or his flipping gifts."

"Do you mind if I eat the Frango mints? Marshall Field's. Nice."

"Go for it." I stalked out of the kitchen. At the foot of the stairs, I called over my shoulder. "When he calls again, and he will, hang up for Christ's sake."

The next Sunday, when I opened the door ready to leave for my gig, Luke stood in the driveway. I dropped my bag. My mouth fell open. "What are you doing here? How did you find me?"

He held a bouquet of roses. There had to be three dozen white and yellow blooms. "Don't be mad. I can't forget you. I hired a private eye to find you. Got your license plate number off that hot rod you drive."

"You've got some nerve. Well, you wasted your money. Not interested."

I picked up my bag, stormed past him, and opened the car door. He approached. I spun around and raised my hand as if I were directing traffic. "Back off, bud. My dad's a cop."

"What'd I do wrong? I can't figure out why you bailed on me."

"Are you serious?" I peered at him with disbelief.

His mouth drooped. "I wouldn't be here if I wasn't. Why won't you give me a chance?"

I tossed my bag in the front seat and got in the car. "You're so clueless! Let me fill you in. Do you remember those soldiers when we were leaving the restaurant? You called them 'suckers,' you prick. Mr. 330." I wanted to smack him but couldn't reach him from the bucket seat. "My fiancé got a twenty-three. He died in the jungle while you were congratulating yourself on your so-called luck. Now get out of my sight."

His brow creased, and he glanced away, hanging his head. Red-faced and shame faced.

Could this bozo feel shame?

"I'm so sorry. I was an ass. Won't you let me make it up to you?"

"No."

"Please. Let me take you to dinner. One date, and if I'm not a perfect gentleman, I'll go away. Promise."

Why did I cave? Why? Getting out of the car, I snatched the flowers from him. My mother was in the kitchen, watching out the window. I strode to the door and handed them to her. "I'm late, Mom. Can you put these in water for me, please?"

"Sure. Is that Luke? Are you giving him another chance? He looks like a nice young man. And wow, he drives a Mercedes."

I rolled my eyes. "One date. He's very persistent, and that's not necessarily a bad thing."

We lingered over dinner at Chez Paul's, sharing a bottle of *Pouilly-Fuissé*. I kept the cork, but then again, I kept similar trophies from others. My box of treasures was packed with silk ties, perfume bottles, and assorted memorabilia. And one t-shirt. John's yellow 442 t-shirt.

I had to give Luke points for trying. He didn't attempt to order for me, ate a little slower, asked me if he could smoke—all in all, a much-improved date.

My mind wandered as I checked out the other patrons. I doubted anyone else in the room came from the Southside. Well, maybe the staff.

Then he said, "Pass me one of them rolls."

Horrified, I dredged up my mental tally sheet and made an entry in the negative column: bad grammar. How could he advance in the cutthroat corporate world with that flaw? I passed him the basket of rolls.

Luke raised his eyes from his plate. "Tell me about school. DePaul, right? What's your major?"

So, he *had* listened on our first date. Maybe he wasn't as self-centered as I thought, although his private detective might have filled him in. I was still cynical about him; Luke had a long way to go to redeem himself in my eyes.

"Yes. I'm interested in marketing. But it's slow going, taking one course at a time."

He leaned forward, as if eager to hear about me. I noted he talked less about himself on this date. "Why one course?"

I stared right at him. "Money."

He put down his fork. Amazingly, this far into the meal, there was still some *coq au vin* on his plate. "That's tough. Let me help." His face was the picture of concern and sincerity. What a change from the first date.

My early warning system was going off. Too much, too soon. There was an air of neediness about him, which I found revolting. Was he genuinely concerned about my education and not just interested in my looks?

"You barely know me. Why would you pay for my schooling?" I frowned, then immediately relaxed my facial muscles. No wrinkles. Serene face. At almost twenty, I was getting a little old for the bridal show game. I hadn't been discovered by a New York modeling agency and knew I never would be. That money would dry up, and I'd need to provide for myself. The two examples from my own life never left my consciousness. Since the divorce, my mom was stuck in a stultifying job with no future. I thought about Sandy's mom, Mrs. Wilkins, who was now a vice president at the bank. Good lesson.

He patted his mouth with his napkin. "Oh, sorry. Didn't mean to overstep. You sure have some firm boundaries. Different from most chicks."

"Chicks? Do you by any chance mean women?"

Darned if he didn't blush. That's why I agreed to see him again.

When he walked me to my car, I allowed a kiss. Not too bad, but no thrill like with John.

Sunday morning, I woke to the smell of coffee and bacon, a rare occurrence these days. I wandered into the kitchen. With no bridal show scheduled, I had a luxurious day to myself.

Paige was at the stove, frying bacon and scrambling eggs. Mom made cinnamon toast and brought it to the table. I poured a cup of coffee and sat beside Mom.

"What's the occasion? I didn't know you could cook, Paige."

She put her hand on her hip. "There's so much you don't know about me. Anyway, I knew you were fresh off a hot date Mom and I are dying to hear about. We thought we'd ambush you to get the scoop."

Mom lavishly buttered a slice of toast and handed it to me. I screwed up my face. "Butter? Have you met me?"

She laughed and took it back. I grabbed an unbuttered slice. At the stove, I spooned a tiny portion of egg onto my plate and added a single slice of bacon.

Paige pulled out a chair and set her full plate on the table. "Are you going to dish, or do we have to torture you?" She pinched the back of my hand to reinforce her threat.

"Ouch! No need for violence. What do you want to know?" I tore a corner off my toast and nibbled.

Mom giggled. "Everything. Besides John, Luke is the first young man you've dated more than once. Something's going on."

I swallowed my dry toast, resisting the urge to dab some butter on it. "He wasn't *awful*. Not like on the first date. I have mixed feelings. He gets points for trying. But he's over eager. I find it off-putting."

Paige laughed. "Sounds like you have the upper hand, and that's always a good thing."

My sister surprised me at times with her comments about relationships. After graduating high school by the skin of her teeth, I didn't think she had much ambition, but she set about trying to break into the comedy scene. To my amazement, she was making progress toward her goal. Tim

Finnegan, who snagged a job in the ensemble cast at Second City, got her hired on as a go-fer.

Her kissing list had been retired for almost three years. I was still adding to mine.

For the rest of the summer and fall, Luke and I dated every Saturday night. I enjoyed the restaurants and shows we attended but rarely thought about him the rest of the week. After two months, the inevitable sex occurred. That was the perfect way to describe it—an occurrence, like a dental appointment or going to the dry cleaners—routine, mundane, not unpleasant, but not pleasurable, for me at least. After the anticlimactic event, he grunted, rolled over, and fell asleep. Not even a "thank you, ma'am." I lay there staring into space, disappointed and dissatisfied. My only basis for comparison lay under six feet of dirt in Holy Sepulchre Cemetery. A sob escaped as guilt poured over me for never visiting John's grave. Did he know or care about my neglect? Did he understand why I couldn't? Luke snorted like a wild boar, mumbled something about church, then settled. Eventually, I fell asleep wondering why Luke was dreaming about church.

Luke traveled for his job and was usually gone during the workweek, which was fine with me. Despite my studies and work schedule, I got restless at night and started hitting the clubs on Tuesday and Friday. I thought it prudent to divide my time between the Southside and Rush Street. Because the downtown clubs often were filled with men in town on business who would fly home out of O'Hare on Friday, I usually went to Rush Street on Tuesday. I thought it best to avoid entanglements and minimize the chance of seeing the same man again. If I couldn't get Suzanne, Cynthia, or Liz to join me, I went alone. No biggie.

I met an interesting array of men, one the heir to a bra fortune, who had the type of obsession one might guess.

"Have you ever thought about modeling?" he asked.

"Not only have I thought of it, but I've also done it. Bridal shows." I softened the words with a smile.

He took a big mouthful of his martini and nearly choked. When he stopped sputtering, he mopped his face with a bar napkin. "I mean lingerie."

"No, thanks." I walked away. It took all I had not to roll my eyes. The club was new and aptly named "The Meet-Market," but I had yet to meet anyone I cared to add to my kissing list.

My eyes locked with those of a man at the bar. *Zing!* I looked away first and felt myself blush. He wasn't my usual type. He had sandy hair. I'd always been a sucker for dark hair. Direct gaze. A very kissable mouth.

He got off his barstool and approached. I stood still, waiting. For me, the connection came through the eyes. Only a man who could maintain eye contact had a chance with me. Mr. sandy-hair's eyes crinkled in the corners as a slow smile spread across those lips. A frisson of anticipation made me shiver. This was unexpected. I wondered if he was in town for business, or a local. Luke who?

"Hi there, beautiful. I noticed you made that other guy incapable of swallowing. So, I gotta ask, what're you gonna do to me?"

I laughed outright. This guy had game. I decided to forgive the "Hi there, beautiful" and give him a chance. "Hmm. I haven't decided yet. Still weighing my options."

He chuckled. "What are you drinking?"

"Club soda with lime." I had given up vodka tonics on weeknights.

"That's no fun."

"Fun enough. I do have to drive home."

"That's a shame."

"That's reality."

We stood there for several moments, gazing into each other's eyes. It was pretty darn apparent we both liked what we saw.

He leaned in and took my empty glass. I suppressed a gasp at his approach, thinking he was going to kiss me. He didn't. Yes, he had game. "Be right back with your drink." His eyebrows rose. "Who am I plying with club soda?"

"Dani."

"Dani." He tasted my name. "I like it. Suits you."

I felt my shoulders relax as he walked away. That was intense.

By the time he returned with my drink, I'd gathered my wits. "Thanks. I-I didn't get your name." So much for my composure. I felt like a flustered high school girl.

"Robert. Not Bob, not Rob, and for God's sake, not Bobby. Robert."

"Hmm, Robert, not Bob, not Rob and for God's sake, not Bobby, that's an exceptionally long name. How about I call you Robert?" I grinned at him as he chuckled. Good, he didn't take himself too seriously. "Sounds like you've had some issues there, Robert." I sipped my club soda.

He ran his hand through his hair. "Sorry. Shades of the past. My dad goes by 'Bobby,' a grown man." Robert shook his head and his long hair fell in his eyes again. "Can't help but cringe when someone makes a diminutive of my name."

"Someone?" What color were his eyes?

"Women." He moved a little closer.

Another thrill tickled my senses. "I see."

After a moment, he asked, "Would you like to go somewhere quieter?"

I braced myself for an invitation to his hotel room—which would not happen—but he surprised me. "There's a little bar I like just down the street. Nice and quiet."

"Let's go." I turned away to hide my smile.

We talked for hours. Telling him about my studies and professional ambitions, I listened to his life story. Robert's job brought him to Chicago for business every two weeks. He was in line to take over his father's tool and die company in Des Moines when old Bobby decided to retire. That day could come soon because Bobby became a father for the first and only time at the age of forty.

Rashly, I agreed to meet him for dinner that Saturday despite my standing date with Luke. Funny, I didn't feel the least bit guilty about blowing him off. There was something about Robert that kindled feelings I hadn't felt in months. And pitiably, never with Luke.

***

As I was getting ready for my date, Paige wandered into the bathroom to chat. She sat on the edge of the tub. "Where's Luke taking you tonight? The Bakery? Ireland's? Gene and Georgetti's? Yum, better stop, I'm making myself hungry. Thank God, Tim is bringing a pizza over. Nothing fancy for us."

"I'm not going out with Luke." I applied coral lipstick to complete my look. Abstract Orange by Revlon would complement my pale peach maxi halter dress.

Paige drew in a breath and let it out. "Really. Moving on, hmm. Who's the lucky guy?"

I met her eyes in the mirror. "Robert. We had drinks on Tuesday at that new place, the Meet-Market, and I can't stop thinking about him. I haven't felt anything like this since…John."

Paige's eyes nearly popped out of her skull. "Wow. Bummer for Luke. I never much liked him anyway. He's so arrogant."

Nodding, I agreed. "Yes, he is. But I'm not writing him off—yet. He'd be a good provider and already has offered to pay for my tuition."

"I can't believe I'm hearing the words 'good provider' coming from your lips." Paige frowned. "Sounds so…so calculated. And mature. What about love?"

"What about it? I had love. Once in a lifetime love."

Paige stood and patted me on the shoulder as she moved to the door. "You don't know that."

"Yes, I do. Now I'm gonna meet Robert who is hot as a firecracker and the best kisser I've met in a while. When Luke calls, tell him I'm too sick to come to the phone."

Paige gave me her classic eye roll. "Come on, really?"

"Please?"

"All right, but you owe me." She left in a swirl of her tiered skirt and a cloud of Jōvan Musk. Sure beat the hell out of the patchouli oil she used to drench herself in, but, whew, the musk was strong. I hoped it didn't stick to my clothes because it sure clashed with the Arpège I snitched from Mom.

Robert took me to Maxim's. He must have had clout to get us reservations for the same week. The restaurant was a replica of the Paris café, with red velvet banquettes and mahogany woodwork. Walking down the stairs was a thrill. I recalled my mother gushing about the stars that had graced the room, Audrey Hepburn among them.

The meal was exquisite, although I barely tasted my stuffed sole with crawfish mousse because of the man sitting beside me. Not that we were chatty; there was a lot of hand-holding and deep gazes. Little quivers of anticipation kept running through me. I didn't want the evening to end, so we lingered over dessert, an excellent fruit tart.

Robert placed his empty coffee cup in the saucer. "Dani, I stayed over for this date. I was due back in Des Moines last night."

Our eye lock led to a lip lock. When I pulled away, I asked, "And?"

"And I've got a confession to make."

My stomach sank. Just my luck, he was too good to be true. "Okay, confess."

Robert looked over my shoulder. "I'm engaged." He met my eyes. "But I had to see you again."

"Wow. You seemed so...unencumbered on Tuesday." I felt a twinge of guilt given my own entanglement but being engaged was a lot more serious than whatever I had with Luke. I'd been engaged once upon a time. Never did I waver from fidelity to John. At some level, I had to know what a hypocrite I was, but that night I didn't. Struggling to keep my face serene, I asked, "How long have you been engaged?"

He winced as he said, "Two years. Wedding's in December. She's pregnant."

I stood and said, "Adios, motherfucker." Grabbing my wrap and bag, I stormed off.

From the staircase, I glanced back, just couldn't help it. Robert looked like he'd been slapped upside the head. Good. How did he think I'd react to his revelation? Was I supposed to help extricate him from his upcoming nuptials and fatherhood? Well, my ability to judge men was certainly off. Did that apply to Luke too? After this disaster, maybe I should cut him some slack. He *was* trying.

As I drove home, I rationalized my dating other men. Luke might think we were exclusive, but I sure didn't. My psychology class gave me some unwanted insight I worked hard to bury. Who didn't indulge in a little denial or self-deception from time to time? Was that so bad?

Although I no longer went to church, my deeply ingrained Catholicism, installed by the Sisters of Saint Joseph, who excelled at etching young psyches with their tenets and guilt, had me toying with the idea of going to confession. But since John's death, I hadn't set foot inside St. Bede's.

Luke accepted the lie Paige told for me. He never found out about any of my...flirtations. No harm, no foul.

That Christmas was joyless. I told Luke I had strep throat and couldn't see him. Mom and Ken hosted. The rib roast looked and smelled heavenly, but I had no appetite. Gifts were exchanged; it was all meaningless to me without John.

After the boys, Paige, and Tim left, my mother handed me a Christmas card. "This came for you. I didn't want to give it to you in front of everyone."

I studied her, then the red envelope. The return address was Knoxville, Tennessee. My eyes burned, and I choked off a sob. "It's from John's family."

"I know," Mom said. She put her arm around me, and we sat at the kitchen table.

When I opened the envelope, tears made little wet circles on the paper. I read the card, then the handwritten message. "*Lánya*, we remember our past Christmas joy with you and our John. We hope you are well and will someday visit us."

Shoving back my chair, I got up and grabbed my coat. "I'm going for a walk."

On autopilot, I headed to John's house; I couldn't stop myself. There were new curtains in the living room window and a child's sled in the front yard beside what was left of a melting snowman.

I trudged home and put on my new Christmas pajamas. Flannel, "so practical," I told my mother when I opened the gift. I brushed away tears, reached under my bed, and pulled out my box of treasures. After adding the Nagy's card to my collection, I pressed John's 442 t-shirt to my face and took a deep sniff. Nothing. His scent had faded. I needed to buy another bottle of Jade East. My eyes filled, the pain of my loss full, poignant, and strong as ever. No one could ever compare with John.

Should I continue to see Luke? What was the point? Something about him was off. I knew he wore Aramis. Was it as simple as his cologne choice? He just didn't smell right.

Chapter Seven

LET'S MAKE A DEAL 1973

In late January, Luke summoned me to his apartment on a Wednesday—a school night—but he promised me it would be worth the drive. Because the weather was an unexpectedly balmy 56 degrees, I agreed. It would be good to take a break from my studies. He was in town for a week of corporate meetings which culminated in the company anniversary party, an event I dreaded after attending one cocktail party with his co-workers. I'd never seen so many arrogant people gathered in one room.

I parked and took the elevator up to Luke's twenty-second floor condo. The building was impressive with its private parking, gym, and pool. The apartment itself was stunning: three bedrooms, two bathrooms, state-of-the-art kitchen, and a killer view of Lake Michigan and the Chicago skyline. He told me he had a surprise. I couldn't imagine what.

Before I could turn the key in the lock, Luke threw open the door and drew me inside. He was dressed in a tuxedo. I wore jeans and a sweater. Mismatched—in so many ways. He smiled—exposing all his dental work, including the gold crown—and grasped my hand. He got down on one knee, extracted a jeweler's box from his jacket pocket, and opened it. "Will you marry me?"

When I saw the size of the diamond, I covered my mouth with my free hand. What should I do? I almost felt sorry for him as his big toothy grin started to fade. I didn't love him. My heart was taken once. The first cut was the deepest and—in my case—only cut. Did Luke love me? Perhaps as much as he was capable of loving anyone. If I said yes, I'd be making a deal with open eyes.

"Well?"

"I need to think about it." I turned, flung open the door, and ran to the elevator.

"Dani, what the fuck?" he yelled. Then he was beside me in the hallway. Why was the elevator so darned slow? He grabbed my shoulders, got right in my face. "Think about it? Think about *what*?"

I willed my face to remain tranquil. He was scaring me with his...I guess it was passion. I hadn't ever seen him worked up like that before. Was it possible he did care for me?

Luke's face twisted in misery. "Please, don't do this. I picked up food, chilled Champagne, dressed up in this monkey suit. Come back inside. Please."

I let him take my hand. "You took me by surprise. I didn't know what to say."

"Say yes!"

Back in his condo, he begged me to try on the ring. It was too large and needed resizing.

After a dinner he served on his finest Royal Doulton and a second bottle of bubbly, I accepted Luke's proposal. What made me do it? I had a feeling I'd ponder that question for the rest of my life. Sure, I was tired of the bar scene, especially after that appalling Robert fiasco. And I was so short on money, it would take years to finish school. I had some cogent reasons, so I caved. He dazzled me; I had to admit it. No, to be honest, his money dazzled me. I saw an opportunity for a cushy existence and took it. Did I feel anything for him? Certainly not love—maybe gratitude. Annoyance at times. Would I be able to live with mediocre sex? Those thoughts and others clattered through my mind as he took me to bed for another unsatisfying—and brief—interlude.

I had to break the news to Mom and Paige, so I invited them to dinner at Banana's Steak House, a Southside favorite. Luke had given me a credit card, so there were no worries about paying the tab.

Even though I was almost twenty-one and didn't think I'd be carded, I decided not to antagonize Mom and order a cocktail. Paige wisely didn't flash her fake ID and ask for one either. Mom had her usual Grasshopper. Like dessert before dinner. Yuck.

Mom took a sip of the mint-green confection and dabbed her lips. "You sure were mysterious about this dinner. What's the deal?"

Paige narrowed her eyes and surveyed me. I think she had her suspicions because I continued to see Luke despite the rocky start to our dating—and my secret extracurricular activities. Before meeting him, I'd never seen a man twice—until the Robert debacle.

I sipped my ice water and waited a beat. "Luke proposed."

Mom let out a whoop that earned us the scrutiny of our more genteel fellow diners. "Oh, my God! You're going to be a bride. I can't wait to shop for our dresses." She peered at my left hand. "Where's the ring?"

"Getting resized. The diamond is gigantic."

Paige blurted, "Please don't tell me you love him."

Whoa. Blunt as ever. "No, I don't love him. My heart is granite. No one can get in. Not after John."

Mom moaned and patted my hand. "Now, honey, you don't mean that."

"Yeah, Mom, I do."

Paige buttered a dinner roll. "Why marry him? Just hang out and enjoy his cash."

The waitress placed her tray on the stand next to the table. Two steak dinners and one broiled chicken breast with a salad.

Mom beamed at her steak and inhaled. "Smells delicious." She asked the waitress for more butter. I laughed out loud, remembering my old nickname for her—Bunch-o-butter.

As I ate my salad with no dressing, I thought about what Paige said. She had a point. Luke was fond of throwing his money around in an effort to impress, and I was a willing beneficiary. But he'd asked me to marry him, and that was flattering in a way. "Call me traditional. I'm saying yes to the ring and all it entails."

Mom put down her fork and clapped her hands. "When are you getting the ring back?"

"Oh, Luke said next week. It really is something. A four-carat princess cut with little round diamonds surrounding it and down the sides of the band. And, yeah, it made me feel like a princess."

Mom and Paige never refused dessert. Paige asked the waitress, "What kind of pie do you have?"

"Banana cream and lemon meringue."

Paige licked her lips. "Banana cream, please."

"One of each, and another Grasshopper for me. Thanks!" Mom lit a Viceroy and puffed a cloud of smoke across the table. "I'm celebrating not only Dani's engagement, but the abolishment of the draft. My boys are safe!"

On the drive home, I held back tears for the boy that wasn't safe.

I quit my job at Lerner's and moved into Luke's Gold Coast condo. My mom wasn't thrilled, but what could she say, given her affair with Ken? For God's sake, we were all living in sin, and I was glad Mom wasn't so hypocritical that she'd fault me. Our relationship was better than it had been when I was a child.

With my new address, the commute to school was much shorter. I continued to power my way through DePaul's business classes. Dean's list and magna cum laude would look great on my resume.

My modeling gigs were less frequent these days, but I still worked the occasional Sunday bridal show. Luke loved to brag to his business acquaintances and co-workers about my modeling and would be disappointed if I quit. When I envisioned my forthcoming wedding, I did not see myself in one of the frothy confections I modeled. Neither did I imagine a church ceremony or a large audience.

I knew Luke made a good living, although he never told me how much he made as a regional sales manager for the pharmaceutical company. He also bragged about how much money he made in the stock market. His ambition was a palpable force; he was obsessed with becoming a vice president and totally confident his star was in its ascendancy.

At times, the veneer of confidence cracked, and I witnessed him crippled by self-doubt, usually when he was drinking. Scotch was his drink. Chivas Regal. I found the odor repulsive. On the occasions he overindulged, he wallowed in the mud of self-pity, completely absorbed with his shortcomings: he hadn't gone to an Ivy League school, he hadn't summered in the Hamptons, he hadn't belonged to a fraternity. Fairly sickening. I helped by correcting his grammar. "Could have went," was the phrase that made me cross my eyes in disgust. Why did he continue to use it?

All I knew was he would cough up tuition so I could finish my marketing degree at DePaul. We set a date for June, right after my quarter ended. Civil ceremony, then a two-week honeymoon in Jamaica. The prospect of my first plane ride and the sandy beaches of Jamaica was much more enticing than being married.

The sex was pedestrian at best. No one could live up to John. My fantasy—that I was kissing my lost love the night I met Luke—hadn't endured past the interlude on the merry-go-round. Reality crept in, and Luke's lips lost their allure. Although I had no basis for comparison besides John, Luke was deadly boring as a lover. His self-obsession carried from the business world into the bedroom. Sex was all about him, and he always won, finishing first as if we were in a race. He didn't seem to care I never made it to the finish line. Did he even know women had orgasms? Because he worked sixty, seventy hours a week and traveled, I wouldn't be imposed upon very often. I could live with that.

He insisted I meet his widowed mother and his sister. His brother lived in New Jersey, so I'd be spared meeting those prospective in-laws. At first, I was surprised Luke had a family. He seemed alone in the world. Before he proposed, he'd never mentioned them.

I needed to know what I'd be dealing with and readily agreed.

Luke grew up in Milwaukee, so one Saturday we got in his new MGB—of course it was a convertible, what else would he drive—and headed out on the expressway. Thank God, it was too cold to lower the top. He concentrated on driving, blasting the radio, and playing around with the gears, downshifting to rev the engine for no apparent reason. Like a child playing with a toy.

Because Luke was so tight-lipped about his past, I used this opportunity to gather some facts. I switched off the radio. "When was the last time you visited your mother?"

"Last year."

They weren't close. Good. "What'd she say when you told her we're getting married?"

"Not much." No clue there.

"What's your sister's name?"

He took his eyes off the road to glance at me. "Cathy."

"Tell me a little about her."

He sighed. "She's twelve years older than me. I was eight when she got married, so she wasn't much on my radar. Now she's got five or six ankle-biters. Way too many brats." He grimaced. "I'm glad the kids won't be there today." He reached over and switched on the radio, blasting out some Grand Funk Railroad.

He didn't care to talk about his family. Noted. And he didn't like children. No surprise there. Too self-centered. Given the few syllables Luke spilled, I figured the Baumanns wouldn't impinge on my life. Very reassuring.

Once we left the northern suburbs, we raced past farms, crossed into Wisconsin, and passed more fallow fields until we approached Milwaukee. In the distance, the ground changed elevation, small swells that really couldn't be called hills. I leaned against the window and dreamed of the hills of Tennessee I had never seen.

Luke rolled down the window, letting in the frigid March air, and said, "Welcome to Brew City—home to Miller, Schlitz, Pabst, and Blatz. Take a great big whiff of that." His tone was sarcastic, bitter.

There was no escape from the stench. The aroma was somewhere between hot soggy grain and malt gone bad. "Smells like putrid hot cereal."

"That's the smell of my childhood. I hate it—reminds me of my dad."

"Your dad?"

"He's dead. That's all you need to know." His lips formed a grim line.

The anger came off him in waves—the strongest emotion I'd ever seen him display, so I shut up. A few minutes later, he pulled up to a drab, green-shingled bungalow. "This is it," he said.

Luke parked his MGB in the drive and locked it. "Getting even sketchier around here. I'm gonna have to keep an eye on my baby."

Baby? Luke did seem to care more for inanimate objects than people, so that made sense in a perverse way. I looked at the shabby homes, junk cars, and over-filled garbage cans. "Why does your mother live here? Can't she move?"

He shrugged. "That's her business. Besides, Cathy lives two miles from here. Mother wouldn't move away from her grandkids."

Mother? "You call her 'Mother'? Wow."

"Don't start. Don't make me regret this trip."

Stunned, I couldn't think of a reply.

As we walked up the cracked concrete path, the front door opened and a tall, broad, gray-haired woman with a care-worn face greeted us. There were no hugs, no kisses, no physical contact.

Cold.

She narrowed her ice-blue eyes as she looked me over. "You must be Danielle."

I nodded and tried a smile. Unreturned. Fumbled for words in this awkward situation. "Nice to meet you, Mrs. Baumann. I go by Dani."

She snorted and said, "Dinner's ready." She glanced at Luke. "You're late."

I followed her and Luke through a tatty living room with a fusty orange tweed sofa and faded brocade chairs draped with crocheted doilies. We entered a cramped dining room. The smell of boiled cabbage and potatoes almost made me gag. I swallowed and coughed to hide my discomfort. A wooden table covered with a lace tablecloth and surrounded by six chairs filled the space. Sitting at one end was Cathy, a blondish, middle-aged woman with pink glitter cat's eye eyeglasses. The way she assessed me through the thick lenses did nothing to make me feel welcome.

A gray-haired man with wire-rimmed glasses rose halfway from his chair, clutching his paper napkin so it didn't fall. "Hello. I'm Victor, Cathy's husband." At least his lips could turn up.

We feasted on dry, stringy pork chops, overcooked green beans, cold, lumpy mashed potatoes mixed with wads of cabbage, and hard-as-a-rock biscuits. Luke shoveled the food in like a starving trucker, as did his kin.

The origin of his habit of inhaling his food became clear. If he wanted to climb the corporate ladder, he'd better work on his manners. I spent the meal trying to saw off a piece of the pork and pushing the other delectable foodstuffs around my plate.

Luke nudged me in the side and said, "Pass me them rolls." I complied, inwardly cringing at his grammar. Whenever I corrected him, he got angry. Now, in front of his family, wasn't the time to mention it, but if he wanted that promotion, he needed to work on his grammar.

Cathy said, "You didn't eat much." Her magnified eyes ogled me with intense curiosity, as if I were a subject in a lab. "Are you on a diet? You're already too thin."

"I had a big breakfast," I lied. She should worry more about her own food intake. Unable to remain sitting there under her baleful gaze, I stood and started clearing the dishes.

Victor pushed his chair back. "Let me give you a hand."

I smiled and thanked him. I shuttled the plates and bowls into the kitchen. Victor scraped and rinsed the dishes and placed them in a pan of soapy water. There was no dishwasher. I couldn't help but think Luke could spring for one for his mother, even though she was a soulless grump.

Mrs. Baumann clomped into the kitchen and opened the refrigerator. She didn't acknowledge us as she hefted a large bowl of chocolate pudding, grunting as she lugged it back to the dining room. Glancing at my watch, I couldn't believe we'd only been there twenty-five minutes. How much longer would this visit last? How much longer would *I* last?

Victor wiped his hands on a dishtowel. "Dessert time."

I ran several excuses for leaving through my mind but rejected them all, knowing I should learn as much about Luke's family as possible. Information was power, and I was acutely aware of my lack of power in this relationship. I'd need all the scoop I could gather.

Joining them in the dining room, I accepted a small portion of lumpy chocolate pudding.

Cathy took a second helping of the glop and remarked, "I saw Melody at the Jewel last week."

Luke put down his spoon and glared at her. Victor cleared his throat.

Mrs. Baumann snapped, "Why bring that up?"

Lifting another spoon of pudding to her smirking mouth, Cathy didn't answer.

I stared at Luke, who pushed back from the table and stood. "I'm outta here. Thanks for dinner, Mother." He yanked my chair out, grabbed my hand, and marched me to the door.

Pulling away to retrieve my purse and coat, I muttered, "Jesus, Luke, let me get my things."

He snarled, "Come on. Let's go."

Luke's face was set in angry lines. Totally unapproachable, but I sure as hell wanted to know the Melody story. And the father story. I'd have to be careful about how to drag the information from him. Maybe I'd ply him with scotch to loosen his lips.

The ride back to Chicago was silent. Luke didn't even turn on the radio.

To my mother's immense and everlasting regret, Luke and I got married at City Hall. No white bridal gown for me. I wore an aqua chiffon strapless mini dress with a darling sheer halter that tied in a bow under the empire bodice. Not the typical choice, but I'd be able to wear this confection out to dinner all summer.

Paige and her boyfriend Tim were the witnesses. My sister toned down the hippie look for the event, wearing a simple jacket dress she must have borrowed from my mother. Tim wore a sport coat and khakis, and although he yanked at his collar and claimed the tie was choking him, he made it through the ceremony. Luke booked dinner for the four of us at Le Perroquet, the trendiest restaurant in town. We were checked in by a large man—probably an off-duty cop—who patrolled the tiny lobby and, once satisfied we had a reservation and having scrutinized our suitability, directed us into the fabric-lined private elevator. Paige practically swooned on the slow ride to the third-floor restaurant. "Holy crap. Fancy-schman-cy."

Luke looked scandalized. "Paige, simmer down. This is a high-class place, and the chef is notorious for kicking out loud, disruptive people. For Christ's sake, don't embarrass me."

Tim poked his finger into Luke's chest. "*You* simmer down, bub. Don't talk to Paige like that."

Stepping back, Luke held up his hands in surrender. "All right, all right, no need to get physical."

The elevator door opened to a quiet and beautifully lit dining room. Le Perroquet obviously was French for parrot, and the décor reflected that in a tasteful, understated manner.

The service was attentive. As soon as we were seated, our waiter, Armand, poured Mountain Valley still water and a few seconds later placed on the table with a flourish a plate of tiny little bite-sized appetizers.

"Thank you, but we didn't order anything yet." Luke gaped at the plate and then at the waiter.

"Our compliments. *Amuse-bouche.*"

Paige kicked me under the table and whispered, "Luke is *so* high class. A real sophisticate."

I drank some water, so I didn't burst out laughing.

After a selection of *les terrines et pâtés*, the waiter whisked away our plates and seconds later appeared with miniature cups of sorbet.

When Luke looked in consternation at the waiter, Armand bent his head and murmured, "Grapefruit sorbet. To cleanse the palate."

Tim finished off his sorbet and sat back. "This is some tasty food. French, huh? Don't know what I ate, but I like it."

Paige said, "It sure is delicious, but such tiny portions. I'm still hungry."

"We still have the main course and dessert, but you can order a pizza when you get home," I teased. That earned me another kick under the table.

Luke said very little during dinner. Perhaps the elevator incident affected him. I took pity on him and asked—even though I knew—what time our flight would be leaving in the morning. He perked up at the thought of Jamaica. "Flight's at 8:55 a.m. I've ordered a car for seven sharp."

Tim slung his arm around Paige's neck and pulled her close, kissing her cheek. "Babe, one of these days we'll get ourselves down to the Caribbean. Count on it."

In his element, Luke relaxed and held forth on the best beaches in Jamaica. He regaled us with the itinerary he'd spent hours planning. "We're staying outside Montego Bay at the new Rose Hall to build our base tans. That way, we'll show up at Ocho Rios looking good. We'll stay there for five nights and finally end the honeymoon in Negril for another five nights."

Tim waxed magnanimous. "Got to hand it to you, Luke. Sounds like a great trip."

Paige swiveled in her chair. "Where *is* that entrée?"

A few minutes later, our main dish arrived. *Quenelles de homard Nantua* for me and Luke. Paige and Tim chose the *poulet le vinaigre*. The perfect meal and lovely atmosphere of Le Perroquet impressed me, and I delighted in sharing it with my sister.

Jamaica was as advertised in the brochures. Luke concentrated more on his tan than on me. I wondered why he was so desperate to get married. Then it came to me—career advancement. Climbing the corporate ladder often required a good, strong woman pushing from behind.

Thinking back to the cocktail parties and corporate dinners Luke dragged me to, I cringed at his comments when introducing me—always leading with my modeling, always exaggerating. How he chuckled when talking about my college classes, like a doting father relating his quixotic daughter's wish for a corporate job, as if that were an unobtainable goal for a woman. The men in the room seemed to agree with Luke's implied assessment. To a man, they had what I called professional wives; none of them worked outside the home for money. They didn't work *inside* the home, either. The wives had help; their principal topics of conversation were the help and their charitable efforts. This committee, that charity, this school fundraiser, ad nauseam. They made it clear I did not fit into their world. To me, they were a wealthier, snootier version of the coffee klatsch moms in my childhood neighborhood.

Luke treated me like a possession and as if my looks were his achievement.

Lying in bed on the third night of our honeymoon, relieved at Luke's lack of interest in sex, I couldn't help but wonder what my honeymoon with John would have been like. Comparing John's passion at Rainbow

Beach to Luke's indifference on the tropical beaches of Jamaica brought tears to my eyes. Trying to drown out Luke's snoring, I clutched the pillow to my ears. Ashamed of myself for entering into this fake marriage, I remembered the joy and love John and I shared. I fell asleep imagining making love to John.

On the tenth day of our honeymoon, at the Negril hotel, Luke grabbed his suntan oil and headed to the pool right after he inhaled breakfast. I lingered in the room, taking my time. Choosing a stunning white bikini, I admired the way it showed off my deep tan. My hair was a little dry from all the sun and seawater, so I made an appointment for a conditioning treatment at the spa.

Down at the pool, Luke was working on his tan. I stood over him and asked him to put suntan oil on my back.

"Oh, hell, I just got settled."

"Fine. I'll ask someone else." I took pleasure in watching his eyes pop open and in how fast he sat up.

He growled, "Hell no, you won't. Sit." He oiled my back, lingering at the bikini line. Possessive, letting me know he owned me.

It didn't bode well for our future I was having such negative thoughts about my new husband. At some level, I realized how cold and calculating I was to agree to this union. We were using each other. My heart was coming back to life—it wasn't happy. My conscience was flaring up, making me uncomfortable. Right then, on my Jamaican honeymoon, I decided I would leave Luke once I got my degree and found a job. This callous manipulation wasn't good for either of us.

When I looked into Luke's eyes—and I didn't do it often—they were solid umber, impenetrable, like staring into a bottomless pit. No light or sparkle. I yearned to be looking into John's warm, gingerbread-brown eyes—irises with gold flecks, filled with love. When John had gazed at me, he saw my soul and I saw his.

Luke focused inwardly—on his ego. He sure didn't see me.

On the return flight, just as we were landing at O'Hare, the plane's engines screamed, and the pilot pulled up in a steep climb. Several passengers cried out. I was one of them. Luke sneered. "For God's sake, calm down. Shit happens. We're fine."

We did land safely several long minutes later, but Luke's lack of compassion reinforced my decision to leave him.

I settled into my new life. School was first and foremost; I doubled up on classes, driven to finish my degree. Luke was gone from pre-dawn on Monday until late Friday night, so I had the luxury of being able to study in peace. Microeconomics, macroeconomics, money and banking, and management had to be endured before I could take marketing classes. I looked forward to my market research classes in the winter quarter. In the spring, I hoped to get an internship at the Merchandise Mart.

One way I paid for Luke's largesse was to act as a car service. I got up early nearly every Monday and drove him to O'Hare. The drive was fast. And silent. The Kennedy Expressway wasn't jammed up at that hour. Then I had five days to myself. Occasionally, he didn't have to go out of town, and I dreaded having him home.

Picking him up on Friday night was a real hassle, with traffic both ways on the Kennedy, but I performed this duty as part of the deal. I found out later Luke charged his company for a livery service each week, padding his expense account. Tacky, but par for the course. He was of two minds about money, sometimes skimping on petty things, then splurging on other, unnecessary luxuries. As long as my tuition was paid and I had money for books and parking, I was content.

That December, there was a large company function at the 96th floor of the John Hancock Building. Luke took me shopping; he insisted on choosing my clothes for these events. He wanted to go to Bonwit Teller, but I'd seen a gorgeous dress in an I. Magnin ad and insisted on that store. For once, I got my way. He agreed with my selection of a deep v-back scarlet sheath for the company gathering, and for the small dinner party at his boss's house the next week, he chose a black velvet strapless dress. He spent way too much.

The party at the Hancock was dull. After Luke introduced me with his usual fanfare, he dismissed me while he huddled with his fellow managers and his boss, currying favor, and no doubt, kissing ass. Left alone to drift through the party, I stood on the periphery of the room, enthralled by the glittering views of Lake Shore Drive and the Chicago skyline, a different perspective than from our condo. Wandering into the ladies' room, I primped at the mirror and met the eyes of a well-dressed woman in her forties.

Luke's boss's wife, who would be our hostess for the dinner party, was applying lipstick. "Dani isn't it?" she asked with a saccharine smile.

"Yes, Mrs. Andretti. Luke and I are looking forward to next Saturday."

"Call me Joan, dear. Dinner will be served promptly at seven, so don't be fashionably late." Her eyes flicked to the back of my dress, then the hemline. "Quite the dress. What there is of it." With that, she flounced out the door.

After that confrontation, I remained in the restroom for about an hour, in no mood to face the bitchiness of the professional wives. There was a seating area, and I parked myself on the plush lilac settee, contemplating the turn my life had taken. I'd never fit in with the corporate wives, and as far as I could see, our social life would revolve around those people. Another reason to leave Luke as soon as possible, as if I needed any more reasons.

When I felt up to facing the ogling men and their petty wives, I stood, held my head high and pushed through the door. I stopped short, stunned to see a man I'd flirted with at Bombay Bicycle Club on Division Street last year. He didn't see me. I watched him stride up to a dowdy woman, who was dressed in a housewifely evening gown, and take her elbow. The jerk was married. I'm glad I didn't add him to my kissing list. Still, I didn't want to make eye contact or have Luke notice our acquaintanceship. The man had been quite drunk, so maybe he wouldn't remember. For a moment, I worried my weeknight social activities while Luke and I were dating might be exposed, and something like guilt tickled the back of my neck with icy fingers. I shivered. Averting my face, I walked past the couple and found Luke. Because of his height, he was easy to find in a crowd.

"There you are," he said in an upbeat voice, then directed a frown at me the other men in the group didn't see. My lengthy disappearing act obviously displeased him, not that I cared. "I want you to meet Joel Edison, VP of International Strategy. Joel, this beautiful thing is my wife, Danielle."

Thing. Inside, I was fuming. Outside, I smiled graciously and offered my hand to Joel, who took my hand between his. Yuck, he had sweaty palms, and he stroked my hands until I felt like I needed to shower. Gently, I pulled away and recoiled at his leer. I glanced at Luke out of the corner of my eye and saw he was gloating. Excusing myself, I turned away to head back to my refuge in the ladies' lounge, but Luke grabbed my arm. "Stay," he growled.

I stayed until he was ready to leave. Normally, I drank club soda at these events, but that night I downed three vodka tonics. My head was a little shimmery, and I found myself entranced with the Christmas lights, feeling a little woozy.

At last, Luke said his goodbyes. We took the stomach-dropping elevator down to the parking garage and found the MGB.

When Luke opened the car door for me, I was surprised. He never did that. Had he suddenly become a gentleman? No. He piled in on top of me. Something poked me in the back, and I shoved him away.

"Stop, you jerk! I'm getting impaled on the gearshift." I sat up.

Leaning over me, he tried to kiss me, sticking his scotch tongue in my mouth, and I almost gagged. He reached under my skirt, and I clamped my knees together. Pulling my mouth away, I cursed him again. "Sweet Jesus, wait 'til we get home. It isn't that long a drive." I hoped by the time we arrived, his usual indifference would kick in, and he'd leave me alone.

He wiped his mouth with the back of his hand, clambered out of the car, and stood. "So, I'm feeling a little frisky. Sue me." His lips formed a pout, like a spoiled child refused a treat. He got in the driver's side and started the engine. He revved the car and squealed the tires as he accelerated up the garage ramp.

I gazed out the window, doing my best to pretend he wasn't in my life. But he wouldn't shut up about how all the men were so envious of his gorgeous wife, his beautiful thing.

"I tell ya, Andretti wants to fuck you so bad. You could see it on his face. His wife is an old dried-up prune. She's got to be forty-five if she's a day."

"I saw her in the restroom. She didn't like my dress."

"The bitch is jealous. She probably noticed how Andretti was licking his lips when he checked you out."

"Gee, I can't wait to dine with them next week." My sarcasm went right over Luke's head.

"Yeah, oughta be great. I think Andretti is getting kicked up the ladder soon. That leaves a great big juicy opening for me, for the vice-presidency. I'm the natural choice to take his spot."

"Really?" I tried to keep the skepticism out of my voice and sound supportive, but doubted I was successful. My heart just wasn't in it. My heart.

"And Joel Edison. Man, he was blown away when he saw you. He probably came in his pants when you offered him your hand." Luke was almost manic recounting all the compliments he had received about his choice of wife, as if I were a prize he'd won in a game show. My stomach churned as he preened and grabbed my thigh, reaching under my skirt and trying to penetrate me with his finger. "Andretti and Edison want to fuck you so bad. All of 'em do." I bent back his thumb until he stopped, then moved as close as I could to the passenger door.

"Hey that hurt!" Luke roared.

"Control yourself. It's disgusting how you get off on how other men react to me."

When we got home, I headed straight into the bathroom and started the shower. I left the dress in a scarlet puddle on the floor. Luke opened the door and picked up the dress. "Jesus, Dani, that thing cost a mint." He took it to the closet to hang it.

"Sorry," I mumbled. I wanted, needed to wash the creepiness of the evening off my body. If I stayed in the shower long enough, he might fall asleep. Still angry about him attacking me in the car, I was in no mood to deal with his so-called lovemaking. After drying off, I returned to our room to grab a nightgown. Luke was lying down with his eyes closed, and I hoped he'd leave me alone.

"When're you coming to bed? I almost fell asleep." Luke's grumbling grated on my ears.

Resigned to the unpleasantness, I returned to the bathroom and inserted my diaphragm. This was one of the times I wished I were on the Pill, but my Catholic teaching about conception stuck with me, and I put up with the inconvenience. When I got under the covers, his eyes opened, and he was all over me. He hadn't even brushed his teeth, and the reek of stale scotch repulsed me. I kept my mouth clamped shut, and he gave up trying to kiss me. Good.

Unhappily for me, he got it up. I lay there for the few moments, the very few moments, of his thrusting. Sure enough, he grunted, and the crush of his weight, like a side of beef, squashed me. Over before it started. I shoved him, and he rolled onto his side. I rose to clean myself. By the time I climbed back in bed, he was snoring.

Christmas 1973, my first married Christmas, was not what I'd envisioned when I was planning to marry John. There was no competition to split time between two families and not much festivity. Luke had no plans to see his family for the holidays. My mom and Ken planned a subdued dinner with Luke, me, and Joe in attendance. Paige spent the day with the Finnegans, and Phil celebrated with his girlfriend, Mary Ellen Garrity. They'd been together for three years. I realized that when they started dating, John was still alive. When you're stuck in grief, time passed quickly. Not wanting to ruin the evening, I shoved the memories to a corner of my mind.

When we entered the kitchen door, Luke headed for the liquor, and Mom handed me a card from the Nagys. I slipped it in my purse. Ashamed I hadn't answered their card last year, receiving another flooded me with guilt.

"We can talk later if you want, honey."

Mom's concern touched me, but I shook my head and went to hang up my coat.

At thirteen, Joe still hadn't gotten his growth spurt, but it was obvious he'd matured. Gone were the Hot Wheels. The only thing he could talk about was rock music: Led Zeppelin, Lynyrd Skynyrd, and Aerosmith. At least he had good taste in music.

Ken served another sumptuous meal. Rib roast done to perfection, scalloped potatoes, glazed carrots, and a Bibb lettuce salad. He even baked the dinner rolls from scratch. My mom had found a keeper.

As I ate—lightly, of course—I considered how distant my relationship with my family had become since I moved in with Luke. With my school schedule, I rarely made the drive to the Southside. Paige and Tim visited me at the condo occasionally now they were living near Second City in Old Towne. I'd all but lost touch with my brothers. Phil had his driver's license. Joe was a teenager. How had that happened? I was at such a different place in life than they were. Not being close was a shame, but the divorce had drawn up battle lines, and the boys had made their loyalty to Dad clear from the start. I couldn't understand their choice, but at least they were always polite to Mom.

"Ken, you could be a chef at one of those fancy restaurants." Mom took a roll and passed the basket.

Not bothering to wait for her to ask, I passed her the butter.

Ken flushed with pleasure. "Thanks, honey. It's my pleasure to cook for my family."

So, Ken considered us his family. He was a good man.

Luke dove into the meal. He barely came up for air and then had seconds and thirds.

Joe nearly kept pace with him. One of these days, he'd gain some height, or he'd weigh 300 pounds. "Man, I can't wait until Led Zep comes back. Their concert this summer was righteous!"

I asked, "You went? You're kidding me."

"Yeah, I did, with Phil and Mary Ellen. Zep's sound system is radical. Our seats sucked, but next time I'm getting in line the night before they open ticket sales. Or maybe Dad can pull some strings."

Mom frowned. She wouldn't have let the boys go if they were living with her, I was sure. "If that's how you want to spend the money from your paper route, I guess it's up to you."

Joe grinned. "Yeah, it is."

To my amazement, Mom let it go. Did she take Miltown any longer? I glanced at the open shelf next to the kitchen sink and didn't see the bottle. Could it be with the pressures of raising kids and an unhappy marriage in the past, she no longer needed the pharmaceutical help?

I watched Luke inhale his food, head down, fork in constant movement, and sighed. Did he even taste the beef? Conversation faltered despite the best efforts of Ken with his kind inquiries about my classes, Luke's job, and Joe's latest album purchase.

After dessert, Ken's carrot cake with cream cheese frosting, and coffee, we proceeded to the living room to open presents. Seeing the gifts under the tree brought memories of past Christmases with John. I excused myself and ran upstairs to the bathroom before tears spilled. I tilted my head back to prevent a makeup disaster. Taking a few deep breaths, I ran cold water, soaked a washcloth, and applied it to the back of my neck. I shuddered and pictured a large box covered with silver snowflake wrapping paper, the box I had believed contained my future.

Chapter Eight

BEST LAID PLANS 1974-1975

In March, Luke came home with a bottle of Chivas Regal and a big toothy grin. "Great news! They transferred me to the international division. I get to travel internationally! I'm so fucking pumped."

"What does that mean?" I hadn't seen Luke that animated since the nasty incident at the Christmas party last year. My face must have betrayed my distaste at the memory because Luke noticed.

"Why the grouchy face? Aren't you happy for me?"

Putting on a smile, I answered, "Sure I am, but just what is the new job?"

"Who cares? I'll find out when I start going to Europe and Asia. Maybe even Australia. This is what I always wanted. The international division is high profile, and most of senior management spent time there. I'm on my way!" He strode into the kitchen. "Let's have a toast. Where do you keep the glasses?"

Of course, he knew where I kept them. His question was a subtle nudge for me to serve him. I took two glasses from the cabinet, refraining from asking him how he could be so helpless. Luke was the kind of person who expended minimal effort—in all things physical. He didn't stand if he could sit, and he didn't sit if he could lie down. I decided to be agreeable and accepted a glass of the stinking golden fluid.

"Here's to my soon-to-be vice-presidency!" Utterly confident and smug.

We clicked glasses, and I pretended to drink. How could Luke be oblivious to the fact that I hated scotch? I'd told him a hundred times. He didn't see anyone but himself.

"Tell me a little about the job. Will you travel more?" I wrinkled my brow to convey unhappiness with the thought of him gone for longer periods, although my spirits soared.

He took a healthy slug of his scotch and poured another hefty portion. "Well, sure. And I won't be home on the weekends sometimes."

"Oh, no!" Did I sound artificial? I didn't care. In fact, I couldn't wait for his first overseas trip.

I maxed out my course load in the summer sessions. Aced everything except one class, but I sure put in the effort. Working like a didactic machine, I absorbed the material in my classes and spat it out on tests and in papers. The only class I had trouble with was an elective—Comparative Religion. I had signed up for it because someone told me it was an easy A. I couldn't escape having been raised Catholic, although I'd distanced myself from the Church after one of the priests at St. Bede's quit the priesthood and ran off with a lay teacher at the school. Add to that memories of the nuns smacking innocent children and their attitude toward the public-school kids who came to catechism on Wednesday afternoons. Then the ultimate schism—my disillusionment with the concept of God after John died—and it was no wonder I balked at the course content. As turned off as I was by Catholicism—despite its tentacles set deep in my psyche—I wasn't the least bit curious about how others were indoctrinated in their particular brand of dogma. That class was the only B I received. It galled me that my perfect 4.0 was sullied, but when I was working for one of the big advertising agencies, I doubted the subject would come up.

With Luke's international travel schedule, I was called on less frequently to ferry him to and from O'Hare, and that pleased me. No doubt he continued to pad his expense account. I still had no clue regarding our finances and didn't much care. Luke set up a household checking account for me to pay the utility bills, groceries, and school expenses. The amount was quite generous, and I lacked for nothing. As far as I was concerned, he could take care of the rest. I was a short timer now. Graduation was in sight—next May—mere months to my release date. I couldn't wait to land a job and bid him goodbye.

As I'd anticipated, Luke was absent a lot. When he was home, I felt inconvenienced and did my best to hide it, not wanting to antagonize him. I retreated to the desk I'd set up in the guestroom to study. Our conversations were about his dry cleaning and travel schedule. We never went out anymore. On the one occasion I broached the subject of eating out, he made me regret it.

"The last thing I wanna do is go out to a restaurant. I've been dining out all three meals every day for two weeks."

"I haven't."

"Too damn bad. Go out when I'm gone if it's so important to you."

I took him up on that advice. My clubbing evenings began again. Dusting off my kissing list, I started hitting the bars on Rush and Division Streets, conveniently located two blocks from our condo. I was lonely, and I needed some human interaction besides that of my professors and classmates.

My modeling days ended a while ago, and I'd lost touch with my friends. I didn't miss parading up and down a runway in bridal gowns. Marriage wasn't my favorite topic, and seeing the eager, happy faces at those events just made me sad. How many of them would end up with a lousy man? Then I had to remind myself I'd gone into my deal with eyes wide open.

I hit the clubs alone, drinking only club soda and checking out the men. The makeup of the crowd hadn't changed in the past year. Mostly businessmen during the week looking for a little action, as was I—not that I intended to sleep with anyone. A little flirting and making out did me good. No exchange of phone numbers. I used a different alias depending on my mood. Dagmar was my favorite, although I didn't know why. I alternated that name with Natalie, Heather, and Candice, but drew the line at using Farrah.

A couple of times a week, I'd get home and see the answering machine light blinking. Luke called during the hours I was at school and left brief messages.

"Can't talk long. Paris is fabulous. Too bad you can't see it. Got to go." *Click.*

"Berlin is freezing and ugly. But I found some good German restaurants." *Click.*

"Tokyo. What a long flight, even from L.A. Can't even read a damn street sign. The company assigned me a guide, or I'd be lost. Dinner in a few. I can't use chopsticks. Remind me I need to bring a spoon and fork next time." *Click.*

When Luke came home, I pretended to be interested in his boring tales of the sky lounge on the 747.

"I tell you, I felt like James Bond. Man, so cool to get up from my seat and go upstairs to the bar while flying over the Pacific."

"How nice for you." He didn't look up at my flat tone. I grabbed my textbook on the principles of advertising—my new Bible—and headed to my office.

I glanced back and observed him go to the cabinet where he kept his state-of-the-art component stereo system. He prided himself on the Maranz receiver, JBL speakers, and Pioneer turntable. On the rare occasions he was home, he played Cat Stevens and Bob Dylan albums, drank scotch, and ate. I was counting the days until graduation.

Paige and I talked on the phone every week. She and Tim came by with a pizza one Friday night in July. They were always good company. Tim was having some success at Second City. He landed his first onstage speaking role and was in high spirits. I was happy for him.

"We'd love it if you could come see the show, Dani," Paige wheedled.

I pointed at my pile of textbooks. "I just can't. You don't know how hard it is to maintain my GPA with the course load I'm taking. Graduation is so close, I can taste it. May! Then I'm free."

Paige glanced at Tim, then at me. "Free? Of what?"

I gulped. No use keeping this a secret. "Of Luke."

Paige's mouth fell open. "You're serious? What happened?"

"Nothing happened. You said it yourself when I told you I accepted his proposal. 'Don't tell me you love him.' Remember?"

"Yeah, well, I guess you gotta do what you gotta do."

Tim swallowed his mouthful of pepperoni and said, "I never liked that guy. He's a pompous asshole. Where is he anyway?"

"Luke transferred to the international division, and he travels non-stop. He's gone for two or three weeks at a time. I rarely see him, so I don't have to put up with a lot."

Paige patted my hand. "Your life is sad. At least, it makes me sad. I know you said you'd never love another man after John, but I hope you find someone, someday."

"I'm not counting on it. The quality of love I had with John doesn't come along more than once in a lifetime."

Paige's lips twisted. "You sure have yourself convinced of that. Too bad."

Tim stood and brushed his hands on his jeans. "Have to hit the head."

After he left the room, Paige asked, "How's the sex? Is that the problem?"

My eyes widened, and I felt myself blush. "One of many problems. The sex is lousy. He's too self-involved to realize there's another person in the room. I can count on one hand the number of times we've had sex in the past six months."

"Wow! That sucks."

"Not really. In fact, I prefer it. And that's pathetic."

Sharing even this small confidence with my sister was a release. I'd have to disclose more about my miserable life to Paige, but not then.

Tim returned and asked if anyone wanted another beer. As Tim well knew, I never drank beer. When they visited, I insisted they bring their own six-pack, which they always finished.

Changing the subject to positive news, I told them about the internship I landed at the Merchandise Mart in the spring. I was ecstatic about it.

"This position is vital to landing a job with a big advertising firm next year. I have my eyes on J. Walter Thompson. They actually have women in management positions."

"Sounds like you've got it all figured out. Hope you get what you want." Paige seemed genuinely supportive.

"Thanks, and thanks for the pizza. I'll try to make it to your show one of these days."

After they said their goodbyes, I wrapped the leftover pizza and put it in the fridge. Then I took a shower, letting the water cascade over my tears. Would I burn in hell for being so cutthroat and calculating?

***

The nation was shaken to its core when President Nixon resigned in August. The Watergate scandal had filled the front pages of the newspapers for two years. Gerald Ford was sworn in and within a month pardoned Nixon. To me, it didn't matter. I would never pardon him for killing John.

My focus was on my future and my escape. I was grateful to Luke for the opportunity to fulfill my dream of a marketing career, but how relieved I'd be when I could stop living a lie. After I landed my dream job, I might consider paying back the tuition money—the prospect of my jailbreak made me generous.

It never occurred to me to wonder what Luke might be doing when he was out of town, probably because I didn't care. In mid-August, after returning from Italy, he was especially frisky.

"Did you miss me?" he asked as he pawed me.

"Didn't have time." I stiffened at his touch, revolted by the reek of stale scotch.

"What kind of answer is that? You hurt my feelings," he mumbled into my neck.

I shivered, tamping down my revulsion.

Apparently, he took that as a shiver of delight and pulled my top over my head. "Come on," he urged, dragging me to the bedroom.

"Let me get my diaphragm."

"No. Not now. I'm good to go." He dropped his pants, and he was.

"It'll just take a sec."

"I said no! Come on." He pushed me onto the bed and fell on top of me. The air left my lungs with a grunt.

Striking him with my fists made him laugh. "I know you missed me. Did you miss this?" He entered me and began to thrust. The pain made me groan.

He laughed. "I guess you did."

Then as fast as it started, it was over. He rolled off me, and I jumped from the bed and into the shower. After I cleansed every trace of him from my body, I returned to find him sound asleep and snoring, still in his shirt and tie. I left him there and slept in the guest bed. I attributed his actions to jet lag and scotch and hoped he'd be leaving again on Monday.

Three weeks later, I missed my period. Certain it was from the trauma of the unwanted sexual encounter and the stress from school, I thought nothing of it. I'd missed a period before.

Then I missed a second month. And I knew. Thinking back to that miserable, loveless night, it was shocking to think a new human life would be the result. I didn't tell him, knowing how he felt about children. He'd find out all too soon, and I dreaded his reaction.

To my surprise, Cathy invited us to Thanksgiving. When I suggested we go to my mom's instead, Luke shook his head. "Nope, you and me are going to Milwaukee." He stomped away, giving no reason. I'd given up on correcting his grammar. A minute later, over Cat Stevens' crooning, he bellowed, "Bring a dessert."

I told Mom I felt obligated to go because it was the first overture from the Baumanns and promised we'd be at her house for Christmas. My morning queasiness hadn't progressed to full-blown morning sickness, and for that I was grateful. I wasn't looking forward to the meal, but I'd get to meet Cathy and Victor's kids for the first time. Being pregnant made me curious about children and eager to be around them.

Luke blasted the radio all the way to Milwaukee, and I sat silently, lost in thought, wondering what was happening in my womb. The store-bought pumpkin pie rested in my lap. I thought back to high school biology. Mendel's theory of genetics. What would my little girl or boy look like? I prayed Hungarian genes were stronger than German ones, but I didn't know. Would it be a boy or a girl? I hoped it was a girl and prayed she would take after me.

Luke rolled down the window as we approached Cathy's house. "Welcome to Milwaukee!" That must be a thing he did each time he visited. Was it some sort of back-handed, bitter tribute to his father who had worked at the Blatz brewery?

"Please roll up the window. It's freezing."

He never did tell me why he despised his father, but I believed his hatred of the man would make him a lousy father. One more reason to flee. My getaway was put on hold by the pregnancy, and I hated that. I was careful to do nothing to antagonize him. There was another life to worry about now; I couldn't afford to bring down his wrath.

Cathy and Victor lived in a dreary split-level home. I'd never been in one and wondered who came up with the idea of putting two sets of steps in the foyer. Confusing. I heard kids downstairs and took a step down, but Luke snatched at my elbow and said, "Upstairs." I put the pie on the dining room sideboard and went to greet Luke's mother.

Ursula sat on the royal blue tweed couch; her pinched face didn't change expression as we entered the living room.

"Mother." Luke nodded.

"Hello, Mrs. Baumann." I almost curtsied.

"Ha, you're Mrs. Baumann too," my mother-in-law responded.

What an odd greeting. I regretted accepting Cathy's invitation. It was going to be a long day. Unsure of what to say to this strange woman, I excused myself. I needed the bathroom. After I peed, I stepped into the kitchen to offer Cathy a hand. She was rushing around, breathing hard, and she seemed grateful for my help.

"Can you put together the green bean casserole? The turkey's coming out in a few, and while it rests, the casseroles will have time to cook."

"Sure thing." The cooking smells made my stomach roil, but I managed to make it through the preparation.

Cathy grabbed my sleeve and pulled. "Get the cranberries and relish tray out of the fridge and put them on the table, will ya?"

I looked at the grease mark she left on my chiffon blouse and bit my tongue.

After I made the casserole and brought the cold dishes to the table, the oven buzzed and in a matter of seconds, Victor entered the kitchen. "Turkey time?"

Cathy yapped at him. "Yeah. Take it out and put in the other rack so I can get the casseroles in."

"You got it!" How Victor remained jovial in the face of his wife's prickly nature was beyond my understanding, and I dubbed him "Saint Victor." He kissed Cathy's cheek and patted her butt. "I'll be back in thirty minutes to carve the bird." He returned downstairs to monitor the kids.

After I put the green beans and sweet potato casserole in the oven, I asked, "Anything else I can do to help?"

"Open the gravy and heat it up."

No homemade gravy? I opened the two jars and poured them into a small pot.

Cathy was furiously whipping potatoes. "How's married life?"

I was astonished at the personal question. The Baumanns seemed so impersonal. "Luke travels a lot, so I don't see him much. He really loves his job." Was that a sufficient answer?

"I wondered if you'd go through with it." Her frantic activity and sweat made her glasses slide down her nose. She shoved them up to the bridge of her nose, leaving a dollop of potato on her face.

I didn't tell her.

Then I remembered Melody. This was my chance to get the story, and I engaged. "What do you mean?"

Cathy smirked. "I bet Luke never told you about Melody."

"No, he didn't."

She began to whip the potatoes again. "I suppose it's only right that you know. That witch left him at the altar. Literally. All that money her parents spent on the wedding and reception, and when it came time to walk down the aisle, she took off her bridal gown, put on her jeans, and scooted out the side door of the church. 'Here Comes the Bride' was playing, and the bride didn't come and didn't come, so one of the bridesmaids went back to the dressing room and Melody was gone." She slammed the bowl of potatoes on the counter to punctuate the tale.

"Goodness! I wonder why." I hoped she'd keep talking. Maybe she thought this story would hurt me, but little did she know it wouldn't.

Her lips pursed. "Well, I'm not positive, but I think it may have had something to do with sex."

My eyebrows shot up. I'd never expected to hear the word "sex" cross her lips. However, she must have had it at least five times because she had five children. Or was it six? Luke wasn't sure. I'd be finding out soon. "Really?" I infused my voice with disbelief and hoped she bought it.

Cathy studied me with narrowed eyes.

I gave her nothing. "Do the rolls need to go into the oven?"

Cathy tore her eyes away from me and gritted her teeth. "I knew I forgot something. Yeah, put 'em in." She plopped the potatoes into a serving bowl and began rifling through the cabinets.

After a moment, I decided to ask the question that piqued my curiosity. "What's the story with your father? Luke never talks about him."

Cathy whirled to face me. "That's a very touchy subject in the Baumann family."

"I'm a Baumann." Of course, I didn't mean it.

She tilted her head and took a deep breath. "Helmut Baumann, who departed this world with no tears shed for him by *anyone*, never believed Luke was his."

"That's terrible!"

Cathy nodded. "And it's a sore point, as you can imagine. Don't let on I told you."

"I won't." In a burst of generosity, I said, "Oh, you've got a little smidgen of potato on your cheek."

She wiped her face. Her eyes bored into me, probably wondering how long it had been there.

Victor appeared right on time. A little blond girl about four years old followed him to the stove. She hid behind her father but peeked at me, blue eyes wide. With her thumb in her mouth, she gripped Victor's trouser leg as if it were a security blanket.

I bent down to get eye level with her and almost fainted. I caught myself before I keeled over. Victor looked a question at me. "I didn't have breakfast." It wasn't a lie, but it wasn't the reason for my lightheadedness. "What's your name, sweetie?"

She popped her thumb out of her mouth and whispered, "Honey."

"Your name is Honey?" I was utterly charmed. She was a beautiful little girl.

After Victor carved the turkey and all the side dishes were on the table, Cathy leaned down the stairwell and bellowed, "Dinner!"

A thundering of feet, a cacophony of cheers, and shouts of "finally," preceded the arrival of five stair steps of humanity. The tallest, a bespectacled girl, introduced herself as Sarah, then presented Martin, Peter, Jeff, and Connie, who looked to be about seven. That made six, a number I wouldn't forget, although Luke had. The kids welcomed Luke in a muted fashion. It was obvious they had no relationship with him. When they greeted me with enthusiasm, I was touched. I glanced at Luke, but he was already seated at the foot of the table, ignoring everyone and everything but the food in front of him.

A small hand touched mine. I looked down at Honey and smiled.

"Will you sit next to me, Miss Dani?"

"Of course I will."

After the awful meal I'd had at the other Mrs. Baumann's house, Cathy's dinner was better than I expected. The turkey was moist, and the other dishes were decent. Yet I couldn't eat much, given my condition.

Cathy peered at me; her eyes magnified behind those thick lenses. "You look pale. You're not sick, are you? I don't want my kids to catch anything. They go back to school on Monday."

"I'm fine. Just a little tired. My quarter ends next week, and I stayed up late studying."

Cathy persisted in her dissection of my appearance. "You look like you've gained a little weight."

"Do I?" I left it at that and searched for a change of topic.

But Luke tuned in to Cathy's remark. His lip curled as he assessed me. "Gaining weight? You. Better. Not."

All eyes turned to Luke after that statement, perhaps as taken aback by his vehemence as I.

I didn't tell Luke about the pregnancy. I did tell Paige. One Saturday night in early December, we were giving each other manicures at her place.

I simply spit it out. "I'm pregnant."

Paige's jaw dropped. "Holy crap! I thought you used a diaphragm."

As I related the circumstances of the night I got pregnant, her face crumpled, and she looked like she wanted to cry. "Now I understand why you want to leave him. When are you due?"

"May."

"Wow! You're not even showing. Whatever you want to do, I'm here for you."

In a hormone-driven surge of anger, I snapped. "What do you mean? I'm having this baby. I'd *never* consider an abortion."

"Oh my God! I wasn't suggesting—"

"That's good." I stared a hole in her while blowing on my fingertips to hurry the drying process.

"When are you telling Luke?"

"When it's obvious. Not until then."

That Christmas, Luke went on a junket to play golf in the Bahamas. No complaint from me, although I was surprised he found other men willing to leave their families over the holiday. Did he belong to a club of narcissists?

I spent Christmas day with my family. Paige and Tim joined us for a quiet dinner. Dad and Ginger were taking Phil and Joe out to the superb and expensive buffet at The Drake. I wondered what my mom thought about that; Dad had never taken her there.

Ken's excellent cooking filled the house with wonderful aromas, but I felt queasy and couldn't eat much. After dinner, Ken opened champagne, and I refused it. Paige and Tim glanced knowingly at me.

Mom raised her eyebrows. "Not even a tiny glass for a toast?"

"Can't." I bit my lip to try to stop my confession, then blurted, "I'm pregnant."

"Oh, my God!" Mom shrieked. She stood up so fast her chair fell over. Kneeling beside me, she hugged me. "A baby! Oh Dani, a baby! When are you due?"

"May. I don't know whether the baby or graduation will come first."

The four of them made toast after toast to the baby.

"Luke must be thrilled!" Mom gushed.

I burst out crying. "I haven't told him. He hates children."

Paige said, "He doesn't even care enough to spend Christmas with Dani. I predict he won't be winning 'father of the year.'"

The mood changed from celebratory to somber in a heartbeat.

Ever the diplomat, Ken clapped his hands together. "Let's open presents." He, Tim, and Paige left the table.

Mom sat beside me and held my hand. "The Nagys sent you another card. I'll put it next to your purse."

"Thanks, Mom." I vowed to respond to them this year. It would be a struggle to figure out what to say to them. I doubted they'd want to know I was married. If I told them I was having a baby, it would only make them think of the grandchild John and I never gave them. But I knew in my heart, I should make the effort to get in touch.

Mom stood and pulled me up from where I slumped at the table. "Let's open our presents!"

The emotional tailspin from the revelation of my pregnancy and planning what I'd write to John's family left me perplexed and tearful. Then I felt my baby move. And I smiled.

Because Luke was in the Bahamas, we missed the company Christmas party. I was relieved because I knew my growing belly wouldn't fit into any of the sexy dresses Luke bought for me. After Luke returned from his golf trip with a killer tan, he took me shopping for a dress for the corporate anniversary party, a dull affair held in late January. He dragged me to Bonwit Teller's, where I tried on several non-form-fitting dresses, but Luke didn't like any of them. He brought me a slim sheath with a daring slit up the side to try on, and I shook my head. Size four.

"I don't wear a four, Luke."

"You got a closet full of size fours." His face shone with pugnacity. Ugly. He pinched my waist. "You've gained weight. You know how I feel about that." He shook his head in disgust. "And you used to model. Now look at you. You have two weeks to lose it. I don't care how you do it, just do it." He didn't raise his voice, just growled his insults close to my face. It would have been even worse if the other shoppers heard his abusive remarks.

"I'm pregnant."

He stepped back. "Liar."

How could he? "No. It's true. I'm due in May."

"Your problem. Get rid of it."

Despite knowing he would react that way, his words hurt. "No! I'm five months. I can't. I *won't* and wouldn't even if I were only one day pregnant."

"Like I said, it's your problem." He frowned. "You sure it's mine?"

Stunned, I stared. Feeling pummeled by his accusations and cruelty, I reached for the wall to support myself.

With clenched fists, he leaned toward me. "When did this happen? How?"

Recovering a bit from the psychic blows, I shot back in a fierce whisper. "How? Really? When? I know exactly when it happened. Back in August, when you returned from Italy. Remember? You wouldn't let me have a damn minute to put in my diaphragm." I was so angry I almost levitated. Luckily, we were alone in the dress department.

Luke looked at the ceiling as if he could find answers there. "Jesus Christ. You're the one having it, so have fun taking care of it."

That year, Luke attended the company anniversary party alone. He made up some story about me caring for a sick relative. I was not appropriate for public consumption or viewing. As if I cared.

When he left for the festivities, I took out my box of treasures and re-read the three Christmas cards from the Nagys I had never answered.

Sonia's note this year felt different. In addition to the family news, she wrote extensively about John's childhood friend. "Noah sends his best. He is in his first year of medical school. I'm so proud of him, almost like my son. He studies so hard. It's a shame he has no room for romance in his life. I hope that changes someday."

Why tell me? I'd forgotten about Noah, having never met him. Our only contact occurred when I answered the phone the night of the draft lottery, the night we were all in shock, the night that sealed John's fate—and mine. I sniffed the yellow t-shirt and sprayed it with Jade East. With a heavy heart, I scrounged up some stationery, sat at my desk, and began to write. "Dear Sonia, Miklos, and Chuck..." Stuck for the right words, I wandered into the kitchen to make a cup of tea and thought about the affection I still felt for them.

Back in my office, I reflected on our history, and I left out my sham marriage and pregnancy from the letter. Focusing on college and future job prospects, I kept the letter light and chatty. I almost tore it up. I wanted to write about my granite heart and how I would never love another man like I loved John. Should I tell them how I sprayed Jade East on his t-shirt and closed my eyes while I inhaled, trying to see him in my mind's eye? Would it be right to let them know I thought about getting pregnant back in 1970 so John wouldn't be drafted? Should I beg forgiveness that I hadn't kidnapped my patriotic love and taken him to Canada? I dared not reveal how I married a callous man—not for love—but for money, and how I feared his reaction when our baby was born. No. They lived with their own pain, and those confessions would only add to their grief. Besides, I didn't want them to know what I'd become. I left off my return address. Let them think I still lived at home.

I got a few sideways glances at the Mart during that spring quarter. They didn't see many pregnant interns. At school, there were plenty of raised eyebrows from my professors and fellow students. I ignored them all. Although my escape plan had suffered a setback with my pregnancy, I was still determined to execute it.

When Saigon fell in April 1975, I wept for John and all the young men—and women—who lost their lives in that conflict. Communism emerged the victor. When you fight like that, by any means necessary, without scruples or pity, you win. Sad. Watching the South Vietnamese clinging to helicopter rudders and overloading boats to flee the repression, was sickening. And the loss of my one true love—all for nothing.

The Nagys wrote back congratulating me about school. They were thrilled to tell me Chuck had married, and his new wife was expecting. The unwelcome news: Chuck was now completely blind, but he was learning Braille. Noah was at the top of his class in medical school. No girlfriend yet. Noah sent his regards and congratulations on the Dean's List. As I read their news, I knew I had to come clean about my circumstances, at least partially.

I clutched my belly as my child kicked me under my heart. Yes, my heart was back in business, and soon I'd have someone to love again. I wrote back to tell them I was having a baby too but gave minimal information about Luke. This time, I wrote my return address on the envelope.

Because I was eight-and-a-half months pregnant, I didn't attend graduation. I didn't know if they made maternity graduation gowns and didn't bother to ask. Besides, I was consumed with preparations for the birth of my child.

Luke was in Spain when my daughter was born, but I wasn't alone. Paige and Mom were present at her birth. They gave me the spinal a little too late, so I had some pain, but the result was exquisite. I named her Lorelei, the prettiest name I'd ever heard. Her name came to me in a vision: I closed my eyes, and a meadow appeared, with tall grass and wildflowers bending in a gentle breeze. In the streams of sunlight, butterflies danced, and I believed I caught sight of the wings of a fairy. Then I heard a whisper: Lorelei.

My daughter was beautiful. A cherub with a fuzzy blond head and wide, innocent blue eyes. I couldn't see a trace of Luke in her, but I did see Paige.

Even though Luke and I were dark-haired, we had blond siblings and blond parents, so the one-in-four chance of a fair child came to be.

Lorelei was perfect. She was long, at twenty-two inches, but slight, at six pounds four ounces. She nursed easily and didn't fuss much. I held my daughter as much as possible. I made a ritual of kissing her tiny fingers and toes, couldn't get enough of her.

When I was discharged from the hospital, Paige and Mom came to stay the first week.

My dad, Tim, Ken, and my brothers all visited me and Lorelei at the condo. Dad came without Ginger, which I appreciated. He started a college fund for Lorelei and presented me with the bank book. Nice. Ken brought casseroles and flowers. Peonies. As I inhaled their sweet fragrance, I cried, remembering the peonies John brought my mother the first time they met.

Tim and Paige gave me the most darling baby dresses. Phil and Joe were proud to be uncles at the age of eighteen and fifteen. Hard to believe Phil was headed to college in a few weeks. He received a baseball scholarship to the University of Illinois in Champaign. Joe finally had grown a bit, but he'd never be as tall as Phil. He recently bought a used drum set and formed a band with some classmates. They called themselves "Sledgehammer." I congratulated him and told him what a fantastic name he chose.

"Actually, Ginger thought of it."

So, Ginger was still in the picture.

Dad and my brothers stayed for a brief face-to-face with my daughter. "She looks so much like Paige when she was a baby." My dad's eyes teared up, and my heart forgave him a little for destroying our family.

After they left, I took my daughter to my room to nurse her.

The week passed quickly. I felt a little spoiled with Mom and Paige waiting on me. How would I manage when they left?

On their last day, while Mom was heating up some soup for lunch, Paige entered my room and sat on the bed. Lorelei was asleep on my chest. "You're glowing. Pure happiness. I'm envious."

I smiled. "One day, you'll have a child. Then you'll glow."

Paige shrugged. "Eventually, I guess, but not for a while."

Reaching out for her hand, I squeezed it and asked, "Is Tim the one? You've been together quite a while."

"Yeah, he's the one. I've never met anyone who understands me like he does."

"I'm glad. You know I've always liked him."

When I raised my arms to stretch, Lorelei opened her eyes and blew a bubble on her sweet lips. When it popped, she jumped, and Paige and I cracked up. My baby's lip quivered, then she started to cry. Our loud laughter must have startled her.

Holding her close, I sat up. "Better get up and put her in the bassinette. Tell Mom I'll be there in a minute." Lorelei settled and stopped crying.

We sat in the dining room and ate Campbell's chicken noodle soup. Comfort food, and gentle on the stomach. The doorbell rang, and Paige got up to answer. She soon appeared with a package.

"It's from Tennessee. Guess it's from John's family."

Hearing his name said aloud took my breath away. Tears sprang to my eyes. After a moment, I managed to croak, "Oh! How nice."

I opened the package and held up an embroidered ivory christening gown.

"So pretty!" Paige said.

Mom gasped. "It's gorgeous. Read the card."

The Nagy's gesture broke my heart a little, and I brushed the tears from my eyes. The card read: "*Lánya*, Miklos and I are so happy for you. God bless your child. God bless you. Your husband must be so happy. Noah also sends his greetings."

Mom and Paige exchanged a look. My sister asked, "Who's Noah?"

I tossed the card on the table. "John's best friend from childhood in Tennessee. They served together in Vietnam."

"I've never heard you mention him." Mom folded the christening gown, patting it as if it were a puppy.

"Well, I've never met him, only heard his voice once on the phone—the night they both got those awful draft numbers."

"Oh. When is the christening?" Mom was all about the Holy Roman Catholic Apostolic Church. I would have to find a nearby venue for the christening. I wasn't about to hold it at St. Bede's. Too much residual pain from the wedding that never happened, and I didn't need to reignite the fading memories of sitting beside John on Sunday mornings.

"After I recover. Give me a month." All I could think about was how I wished John were Lorelei's father.

Mom patted my hand. "Your soup is getting cold. You need to eat. By the way, when is Luke due back?"

I dropped my spoon. "Oh, shit! Tonight. And I won't be there to pick him up."

"He expects you to pick him up when you just had a baby?" Mom's look of indignation was worthy of an Academy Award.

"He doesn't know I had her."

Paige pushed her chair back. "What? Wait, when's the last time he called?"

"He left a couple of messages last week, or the week before. Then I went to the hospital, and he hasn't called since I've been home."

"Humph. His Excellency, Mr. Baumann, will call when no one picks him up at the airport." Mom sniffed, her face set in disapproval.

"Either he'll grab a taxi and come home, or he'll call here all angry. Don't much care. I'm worried about how he'll treat Lorelei. When I told him I was pregnant, he asked me if I was sure he was the father."

Mom tossed her napkin on the table and exploded. "And to think I encouraged you to date him. My God, Danielle!"

Paige broke in. "Mom, Dani is biding her time until she can leave him. Her timeline is screwed, what with the baby, but she has her degree now, and she'll get out when she can."

"Maybe when he sees that beautiful baby, he'll have a change of heart," Mom said in a hopeful tone.

I rolled my eyes. "Heart? Have you met him? He doesn't know how many nieces and nephews he has. By the way, it's six. I'm sure he couldn't even name two of them. He doesn't like children. I have no expectations. When I told him I was pregnant, he said, 'Get rid of it.' I deliberately hid it until I couldn't because I knew how he'd react."

Mom's hand flew to her mouth and her eyes filled with tears. "Oh, honey. I had no idea. I know you had your doubts about him, said you didn't love him. Why did you marry him?"

I gave her a direct stare. "Purely selfish reasons. Financial motive. I have a grudging admiration for his work ethic but look at the cost. Although I do enjoy the fruits of his labor." I waved my hand at the expensive furnishings in the condo.

Paige spoke up. "You've paid a price for this life. Maybe too high."

Everyone was asleep at 1:15 a.m., when Luke arrived home. He turned on the lights, and judging from the noise, flung his luggage across the foyer. He bellowed, "Dani! Where the fuck are you?"

Lorelei whimpered, then began to wail. I wondered what Mom and Paige must think. If they were smart, they'd stay in the guest room.

"What the hell?" Luke stomped into our room. I was just sitting up. He turned on the overhead light and stalked up to the bassinette. "So, it's arrived."

It? He didn't even ask if his child was a boy or girl, or what I named the baby. Despite expecting his coldness, tears sprang to my eyes at his indifference. He left the room, and I heard the clatter of crystal coming from the kitchen. Apparently, he remembered where the glasses were. He never forgot where the scotch was.

During my pregnancy, I gained very little weight. I went from 114 pounds to 129. Still, Luke averted his eyes from my body once he learned of my condition. I had a reprieve from his unwanted attention for the last four months of pregnancy and the first three months of Lorelei's life as I got back in shape. I'd have been happy if he never touched me again. My waistline no longer measured twenty-three inches, but I was back in a size four in record time.

Luke ignored Lorelei as much as possible. The business travel continued. I was relieved. When he was home, he seemed jealous of the time dedicated to my baby's care.

Then, in August, he took a week off, the first time since our honeymoon. He left the house each morning and came home every evening to be fed, if for no other reason. I hadn't a clue how he spent his days and didn't care enough to ask.

One afternoon, he came home in high spirits. "You won't believe what I did today."

He was probably right. "Okay, I'll bite. What did you do today?"

"I bought a Greystone."

I turned from the stove where I was heating up baby cereal. Lorelei had started to take her first solid food. "Why?"

"Why? Because I can. So, I did. It's a Potter Palmer and has the original wood staircase and mosaic tile foyer. Ceilings are fifteen fucking feet high! I want you to see the place." Luke was immensely pleased with himself. He lit up a Winston and blew a cloud of smoke not two feet from Lorelei.

I shrieked, "Don't smoke near the baby!"

Luke squinted through the smoke, the cigarette hanging off his lip. "Take it down a notch, will ya? Don't worry, I don't want to be anywhere near that baby." He grabbed a glass from the cabinet and walked away.

Lorelei's wide eyes followed him. I vowed to step up my job search so we could escape.

I could predict his next moves. Open the liquor cabinet, pour some scotch, put a record on the turntable. Soon, Bob Dylan could be heard whining his way through "Tangled up in Blue." I could identify.

The next morning, Luke shook me awake. "Get up! I'm meeting the realtor at the Greystone."

Slowly, I sat up, tired from nursing at two a.m. and six a.m. "What time is it?"

"Eight-thirty. We're meeting her at nine." He clapped his hands. "Start moving!" He yanked the covers off and threw them on the floor.

"I have to take care of Lorelei. It'll take me at least half an hour to get ready. I was up during the night."

"That's why I sleep in the guest room. I don't need my rest interrupted with all that baby bullshit. You're gonna have to speed it up. I suppose you'll have to bring it with?"

I wanted to strangle him. At that moment, I would cheerfully have become a murderess. "Lorelei is not an 'it.'" I bit my tongue, so I didn't curse him.

"Lorelei? I guess it's a girl. Where the hell did you come up with such a stupid name?" He turned and entered the closet. A minute later, he emerged, carried his clothes into the bathroom, and slammed the door.

Silently, I got up and approached the bassinette, peeked at my little cherub. Relieved that Lorelei slept through the noise, I dressed quickly and used the hall bath to brush my teeth and wash my face. I skipped a shower because I didn't want to provoke Luke by being late.

By the time Luke came out of the shower and dressed, I'd managed to nurse Lorelei a little and dress her for outdoors.

"We're walking. It's around the corner, a block and a half down. Can you carry i—her that far?"

"Yes, I have a carrier." I found it in the hall closet, put it on, and placed the drowsy baby inside. I prayed she wouldn't annoy Luke on the tour.

We met Mimi, the perky blond realtor, in front of an imposing Greystone. It was literally a mansion.

Mimi gestured like a game show hostess and said, "Mrs. Baumann, what we have here is a Potter Palmer Greystone. This stately lady has 3365 square feet under roof. There are five bedrooms and six bathrooms."

Luke grinned from ear to ear. "She's a beauty. And she's mine!"

Beauty? Sure, beauty was in the eye of the beholder, but I didn't see whatever he saw.

My jaw dropped. "It's huge. Way too big."

Luke scoffed. "Hardly. It's the perfect showcase for entertaining. And I expect to do a lot of entertaining."

Mimi led us up the wide stairs and turned the key in the lock. The creaking of the huge wooden door as it opened sounded ominous, like a haunted house. The ruins inside were revealed by the light streaming in the large bay window.

I gasped. "It's a wreck."

Mimi said, "This splendid home has the original leaded glass windows and plaster moldings."

"What's left of them," I mumbled, earning a frown from Luke, and raised eyebrows from Mimi.

"Let's continue through the first floor. There are three floors and a basement, a partial basement. We're right around the corner from Goudy Park, which you'll love for your little girl."

At least Mimi recognized Lorelei was a girl.

"Is there a patio or garden?"

"Not exactly. On the second floor, there's a small terrace on the side of the house, but nothing at ground level. There's always the park." I knew that park, the site of the merry-go-round ride on the first night I met Luke. I couldn't imagine frequenting the place of one of the greatest mistakes in my life with my baby.

When I saw what Mimi had so grandly called a terrace was merely a small rectangle of metal grating beside the creepy fire stairs, my interest, what little I had, waned. The tiny flame of curiosity was extinguished entirely in the dank, crumbling basement. It would take a fortune to fix the place, but perhaps Luke had a fortune.

Luke thanked Mimi for her assistance and accepted the keys. She got in her car and left, squealing her tires in her haste. I bet she was gloating all the way to the bank at foisting off this disaster on Luke.

"Is there parking?"

Luke looked everywhere but at me. "Nope."

"Great." I imagined lugging in groceries and baby gear, but then realized I would probably never have to. It would take months, if not years, to make this dump habitable. Lorelei and I would be long gone by then. At that happy thought, I broke out in a smile.

When he saw my face, Luke cheered up. "I knew you'd like it."

I kept my mouth shut. Then Lorelei woke and whimpered.

"Jesus, stop that racket."

Luke had a grand vision I didn't share. All I saw was work, misery, and dollar signs. I had never insinuated myself into his financial affairs, and he liked it that way. Now was not the time to start.

He gestured grandly at the ruin in front of us. "It needs a little work, but I lined up a contractor. He's finishing a job and should be able to start demolition next week."

Demolition. I had already done a fairly decent job of demolishing my life.

I didn't bring up the subject of what I'd come to call "the second residence" and Luke didn't, either. In my opinion, he was so certain he was getting the vice-presidency he rolled the dice and bought the Greystone. Busy as I was taking care of Lorelei and combing the want ads in the *Trib* and *Sun Times* looking for a job, I had no time to worry about what I had no control over.

Ever since Luke's callous, glacial reaction to our—no—my child, I started to skim a little cash from my household account. Luke never noticed a few hundred here and there. I didn't feel the least bit guilty. There was no compunction for taking room and board and tuition, either. I figured I'd earned it with the taxi service, sexual favors, such as they were, and the many, many unappreciated meals. Remembering my spurt of generosity before Lorelei was conceived, in planning to pay back my school costs when I left, I shook my head. No, I now had no intention of repaying him.

Paige was a doll about babysitting. She and Tim shared a house on North Park Avenue with a group of Second City actors. They worked mostly in the evening, so I had built-in babysitting during the day.

I bought a suit at Mark Shale, although I'd rather be shopping at My Sister's Circus—loved the name and the clothes. Fun things, but not business wear, and I had to present as business-like at my interview in three days' time at J. Walter Thompson.

After about a hundred attempts on the typewriter, I produced an error-free resume emphasizing my retail experience at Lerner's. Doubting my ability to repeat this success, I planned to stop at a Kinko's copy shop and order several photocopies in case I needed them.

The morning of the interview, I dressed in the navy-blue suit, tied the bow of the blouse, and stepped into low heels. My handbag was slim and professional. I also carried a portfolio, meticulously crafted during my design internship at the Mart, containing my resume and work samples.

I couldn't carry my bags, Lorelei, and all her gear at once. With my heart in my mouth, I left her in the condo, took everything non-human down in one trip, and loaded the car. Right after Lorelei was born, Mom and Ken had installed a Bobbi-Mac baby-seat in the 442. I was so grateful.

My heart raced as I waited for the elevator to take me back up to the twenty-second floor where my baby was alone. It seemed like hours but was merely minutes until I held her in my arms. All this before eight a.m.

When I pulled up in front of Paige's apartment, I had a moment of panic. I was leaving Lorelei in a strange environment. And, if the interview went well, and the job was mine, I'd be leaving my daughter in this place five days a week. Paige's flat would become as familiar to Lorelei as her home.

I lifted her out of the car seat and rang the bell. After two long minutes, Paige, yawning, opened the door. She held out her arms for her niece.

"Sorry it's so early. I'll be right back with her stuff." After I unloaded all the baby gear and gave Paige a treatise on Lorelei's care, I kissed my sleeping baby's sweet head and clattered down the stairs, calling over my shoulder, "Got to run. I'll be back as soon as humanly possible."

Paige waved. "Don't worry. See you later."

The door closed, and my stomach sank. How did working mothers do it? I felt so bad.

J. Walter Thompson's offices were in the Mart, a place I adored. It was huge and bustling, teeming with people and churning out money. The epitome of commerce. The last time I'd been inside, a year and a half ago, I'd been a pregnant student intern. Now I was on my way to a career in advertising, I hoped.

My appointment was with a woman named Charlotte. Her Southern drawl took me by surprise. I learned she was from Texas. Despite her feminine exterior, she was made of steel and asked pointed questions. I'd subscribed to *Advertising Age* two years ago and devoured everything I could about the company and their clients, so I was well versed in the firm's activities.

"I especially like your new Oscar Mayer campaign with that darling little boy singing about his bologna."

That tidbit impressed her. I got the job. Six hundred dollars a month. I had three thousand plus in skimmings. Not enough to make my move, although I had enough for first and last month's rent and a security deposit. I still needed a cushion, but with my salary, I'd be accumulating at a faster pace. As I realized I'd be able to leave Luke soon, my hands started to shake. I could almost taste my freedom.

When I told Luke about the job, he smirked. "Whatever. Big career woman. Are you forgetting about the kid? It's on you to take care of her. Not a penny from me. In fact, I'm cutting your household budget since you don't have school costs anymore."

Meek, eyes downcast so he didn't see my glee, I replied, "I understand." Then I realized I'd need more than one business suit. I'd be heading back to Mark Shale to do some damage to his credit card. "One thing, Luke. I won't be able to take you to the airport on Mondays."

"Yeah, I figured that out all by myself. I can manage. Make sure you're available to pick me up when I get back in."

"Sure, as long as it's not during working hours."

He didn't even ask how much I'd make—that's how inconsequential my achievement was to him. Taking his disdain as tacit approval to keep my salary for myself, I did so.

I loved my job and the atmosphere of creative energy in our space. The people I worked with were upbeat and driven. The large open room where I sat with the other copywriters buzzed with activity. Those in management were the only ones with enclosed offices. As I had read, there were several women among them. Most were single, and none had a child. They had no other obligations, and I knew I'd have to work hard to compete with them.

My Christmas card from the Nagys came to the condo this year. I was happy to learn that Chuck and his wife had a baby boy. They named him Michael John. Sonia was beside herself with joy. Due to the loss of Chuck's eyesight, the couple lived with her and Miklos, which she counted as a blessing. Sonia told me Noah was acing all his classes in med school and how proud she was of him. They seemed to be close. Still no serious girlfriend in the picture because Noah was so busy with school. Sonia seemed overly concerned about Noah's love life, but I remembered John had said he and Noah were like brothers growing up. I wonder if Noah missed John as much as I did.

Lorelei's first Christmas was a little like old times. Luke was in town—no golf outing this year—and we drove to Mom's in my car because it had the car seat. I was still driving the 442. It was a beast. Nine years old, but it still ran like a champ. Every time I drove it, I felt close to John. He'd been gone more than four years. My life was completely different from what I'd envisioned as his wife. Resolutely, I turned my mind to celebrating my daughter's first Christmas, struggling to push aside the memories of the years with my lost love.

All four of us kids came to celebrate at Mom's. Ken cooked an immense turkey with sage and sausage stuffing. Paige and Tim brought a yummy sweet potato casserole. I didn't bring anything; Mom told me not to worry about making a dish.

Phil introduced us to his new girlfriend Clare Madsen. I felt a twinge of sadness for Mary Ellen Garrity; she'd been crazy about Phil, but young love never seemed to last—for one reason or another. He met Clare at college. She was from Peoria and seemed quite taken with my brother.

Joe's hair was longer than mine. He was seriously into music. Hard as it was to picture my baby brother behind a drum set, his band Sledgehammer performed at teen dance clubs, birthdays, and Bar and Bat Mitzvahs. He'd really come out of his shell. "Man, I'm still on a high from The Who concert this month. I can't explain."

Turning to Joe, I chuckled. "'I Can't Explain?' Clever. They're still doing that song? An oldie, 1965, if I remember right. It still holds up."

Mom appeared scandalized. "High?"

Joe grinned. "High on music, Mom. Chill out."

Everyone laughed except Luke, who had his face about three inches from his plate, the better to gulp down his food.

Lorelei slept in her traveling crib. I had called Paige twice to remind her to bring it. My baby didn't make a peep during dinner. After feeding her, I brought her into the living room for the exchange of gifts. She had lost her baby peach fuzz and her hair was coming in golden blonde. Her wide blue eyes sought the lights on the Christmas tree, and her hand reached out to touch the tinsel.

Since Mom had been with Ken—six years now—he'd bought a Douglas Fir instead of the traditional Scotch Pine every Christmas and decorated it worthy of the cover of *Better Homes and Gardens*. He'd sold his bungalow and moved in with Mom this past summer. The house never looked so good. Besides his full-time job, Ken cooked, cleaned, gardened, and maintained the house—an amazing man.

We settled on the couch, chairs, or the floor. Phil organized the piles of gifts and acted as master of ceremonies, making sure we all had a gift to open.

Ken came in from the kitchen, wiping his hands on a dishtowel. "Wait for me." He ran back to the kitchen and returned with a small, foil-wrapped present. He got down on one knee and presented it to my mother. "Will you marry me, Ellen?"

Mom's hands flew to her face; she appeared genuinely surprised. The room was silent except for a little cooing from Lorelei. With tears tracking down her smiling cheeks, Mom said, "Yes, yes, yes." Clapping and whistles broke out. She made the rounds, showing off a beautiful round diamond solitaire. Classic.

I looked around for Luke. He stood in the doorway to the hall, frowning, with a glass in hand. He must have been getting a fresh scotch.

I gazed at his sour face and closed my eyes, preferring to see John's lopsided smile and his funny little two-fingered salute.

Chapter Nine

KARMA BITES 1976

In February 1976, I hit the nadir of loneliness. Luke ignored me and Lorelei on the infrequent weekends he was home. Truthfully, I didn't want his attention. Besides a rare, truncated fumble between the sheets, he left me alone. As long as dinner was on the table at seven when he was in town, and there was a supply of Chivas Regal, he was satisfied. I thought about buying ear plugs, so I didn't have to listen to Bob Dylan and Cat Stevens, but I needed to hear Lorelei, and refrained.

It amazed me he didn't show the slightest interest in my daughter. He never asked me a thing about her, never suggested we take her to meet her grandmother, aunt, uncle, or cousins. There was no way in hell I'd bring up a visit to them. But this omission made me certain he didn't believe Lorelei was his. Not a surprise given his family history, but I'd grown numb to his repudiation of my daughter.

My next-door neighbor in the condo, Mrs. Grendell, often stopped me in the hallway to admire Lorelei. She was widowed and had grandchildren in Arizona whom she seldom saw. She offered to babysit in the evening. Rather than have me lug all the baby equipment down the hall to her place, she agreed to come to us to watch Lorelei. Grateful for this respite, I wondered at her motive, if she knew how miserable my marriage was. Although we never discussed it, she must have noticed I was always alone with my child when we encountered each other.

At loose ends and in need of validation, I returned to the bar scene. Although I knew it was wrong, and despite the shame and guilt, I resumed my evenings out. Still drinking club soda, still checking out men. A little flirtatious banter, a few compliments, and I felt better. No matter how horny I was, my boundaries remained firm at kissing. To a certain extent, the teachings of the nuns and Holy Roman Catholic Apostolic Church had penetrated to my marrow. But, according to the Sisters of Saint Joseph, much of how I conducted my life—pre-marital sex, going to a "condemned" movie like *Carrie*, and using birth control—marked my soul with indelible black marks. What would Sister Saint Lucy have to say about my flirtations?

Once or twice a week, I'd ask Mrs. Grendell to come by for a few hours. I always had Lorelei fed, bathed, and ready for bed when she arrived and made sure I was home by eleven. My kissing list had evolved—no longer did I keep a paper with names. The list took the form of matchbooks and cocktail napkins. Bombay Bicycle Club, Zebra Lounge, Butch McGuire's, She-nannigans, Faces, the Back Room. I rotated among them. If I was short on time, I went to the Hangge Uppe, the most active of the meet-markets. Because it reminded me of the colossal mistake I'd made there in 1972, I avoided Mother's. My matchbooks were stored in my box of treasures. Besides containing matchbooks, the box was filled with perfume bottles, silk ties, wine corks, and four cards from the Nagys.

And one t-shirt and an empty bottle of Jade East.

Did the men use their real names? I sure didn't. Dagmar was resurrected, and she looked darned good for someone's mother. I hadn't lost my touch—or my allure. Eager men approached me. I never left with anyone. Some mild flirtation and a few kisses felt good. I had no admiration or affection in my life, and I needed it. In my heart, I knew what I was doing was selfish and foolish but couldn't stop.

I promptly forgot each man at the end of the evening until one night in The Lodge. There was a fairly light crowd, so the peanut shells on the floor weren't too deep. Paul Simon was on the sound system, crooning "50 Ways to Leave your Lover." There was no escape from that song; it was everywhere.

There was a man who didn't quite fit in with all the gray and charcoal three-piece suits. From the back, he reminded me of Robert. Robert of the tool and die company headquartered in Iowa. The man who almost made me throw over Luke. That flirtation blew up in my face. What a stupid mistake. Robert promised passion and stability but delivered duplicity and deceit. Although, if he had been for real, I couldn't envision myself languishing away in Des Moines, not after I worked so hard for my career.

And I wouldn't have Lorelei. The thought of my daughter filled me with shame. There I was, the mother of an infant, standing in a bar, looking for a few crumbs of attention. I was the queen of duplicity and deceit and hadn't the right to judge others.

As I was about to slink home, the Robert look-alike turned from the bar and locked eyes with me. My feet froze to the crunchy floor. He approached, and I stared, transfixed. He wore jeans and a thick fisherman's sweater. Lean, but what a set of shoulders. Shock of sandy hair, long on top, short on the sides. He stopped in front of me and grinned. "Hello there."

I smiled back. "Hello yourself."

"Can I buy you a drink?"

"Sure. Club soda with lime." So much for my plans to leave. What was it about this man that made me forget the recrimination I'd just leveled at myself?

"You got it." He put his beer down on a tabletop and pulled a stool out for me.

While I waited, I gave him points for not commenting on my drink choice. The new tune by Roxy Music blasted from the speakers around the bar. "Love is the Drug." Sexy song. Compelling beat. Compelling idea.

He strode back to the table and put my drink in front of me. He stood close, not taking the seat across from me as I expected. "Name's Daniel."

Without thinking, I let slip my real name. "Danielle." He smelled like pine and spices. He smelled fresh. I inhaled deeply. "Kind of funny."

"Not so funny. Maybe fateful." His grin was dazzling.

Why did I give him my real name? What had gotten into me?

"What do you do, Danielle?"

"I work for J. Walter Thompson. It's an advertising agency. One of the best. I write copy for several accounts, you know, slogans and advertising material. I've only been there a few months, but I love it. How about you?"

"I restore old houses. Learned the trades from my dad. He and my brothers still run their business in Des Plaines."

Good grammar. How refreshing. "You don't work with them anymore?"

"Nope. Saw an opportunity in the city, so I set up my own shop, found some good workers in the trades. I'm making a go of it."

His hands were huge. Rough-looking. I flashed on Luke applying hand lotion and almost cracked up. Luke couldn't change a light bulb with his soft, supple hands. Then, one of Daniel's rough hands cupped my cheek, and he planted a great big kiss on my lips. My toes curled. My belly flipped. It had been a long, long time since I'd been kissed like that. And it wasn't by Luke. Given the unwanted thoughts of him popping into my head, I must be feeling guilty. I broke away, but not before Daniel knew how he'd affected me. How could he not feel the way I melted into him and returned the kiss with conviction?

This could be dangerous. As lonely and vulnerable as I was, there was a significant chance I'd abandon my morals and sleep with him, given the silent dance in my lower abdomen. It couldn't happen. Composing my face, I said, "I've got to go." Daniel looked aghast and reached out for me, but I was too fast. The Eagles were harmonizing on "Take it to the Limit" as I dashed from the bar and hurried home. I cooled it on the singles' bars for a few weeks. No way could I afford a complication like Daniel.

Life limped on. I was biding my time until I could support myself and Lorelei. How I longed to ditch Luke. Sure, I chose to marry him without loving him. I doubted he loved me. No, I knew he didn't.

Luke showed me off at corporate functions. I detested those snore fests. He preened every time someone complimented my looks, as if my appearance were his personal doing. And my looks were all anyone ever commented on. I was a face and body. No one cared that I graduated college, had a career. Irrelevant and ignored by Luke and his corporate cronies.

One Sunday evening, I was preparing dinner and feeding Lorelei when Luke stomped into the kitchen, waving a sheaf of papers.

"Stop what you're doing. I need you to listen to my speech." Self-involved and blind to anyone else's needs.

"Give me a sec."

Luke stalked to the highchair and dragged me away from Lorelei, who began to wail.

"Shut her up."

"Jesus. Take it easy. Let me change her and put her in bed. Then you'll have my undivided attention." Self-control, I told myself. I wanted to scratch his eyes out for the way he treated Lorelei.

"Make it fast."

I turned off the stove and oven. Let dinner dissolve into an inedible mess. Wouldn't be the first time, but Luke would eat anything.

As I comforted Lorelei, I reminded myself one day we'd escape. I kissed my little girl, holding her and rocking her until she calmed. I placed her in the crib and returned to face a boring speech delivered by a boring, grammatically challenged man.

Luke stood in the living room, glass of scotch in hand, glowering. "About time."

Dropping onto the couch, I said, "Let's hear it."

He cleared his throat and began to drone. I tuned out, not bothering to correct his grammar, but maintaining an attentive posture.

When he finished his oration about sales figures and the reorganization of his division, he spread his arms. "So, what do ya think?"

"I can't comment on the numbers, but it flowed. Good delivery, no flubs. I'd say you've got it down."

Luke nodded and rubbed his chin. "Yeah, I think I do. What's for dinner?"

"Whatever I can salvage." I stood and walked into the kitchen.

Three days later, Luke's arrival home was announced by a door slam and a thud as he drop-kicked his briefcase down the hall. "Argh! I screwed up royally."

He stormed into the kitchen. "I froze. Fucking froze. In front of God and the entire board of directors. Hope I didn't blow my chance at the vice-presidency." He ran his hands through his hair. Pacing with his head down, he was the picture of dejection.

I didn't feel a thing for him. I'd probably be more sympathetic to a stranger. After all, I knew him now. The awareness that I'd hitched my wagon to the wrong star was always on my mind.

My job prospects, as opposed to his, were looking up. I'd already been given a raise and was bringing in a cool seven hundred a month. Knowing Luke would be less than generous in a divorce settlement, I told him most of my salary went to childcare. He snorted and walked away. "Ha, I knew it. Hope it was worth all the effort, to make a few bucks. Very few."

Paige was a godsend caring for Lorelei. She refused to take money, and I would have to think of a way to compensate her. Someday. I always worried our arrangement might end and had no clue what I'd do if that happened. She and Tim still worked at Second City, he more than she. Paige worked behind the scenes, doing the scut work, running errands, painting scenery, whatever was called for. She had ambitions to get onstage, like Tim. No doubt in my mind, she'd succeed.

My job brought in enough money that I could add to my escape fund. I stopped buying new clothes, except for Lorelei, to speed up the process. In a few months, when Luke was away on one of his extended trips, I'd make my move.

While the world of marketing had not proven to be as glamorous as I had envisioned, I held hope for advancement. Writing copy, most of which was never used, generating ideas that were tossed in the circular file, was demotivating, but I knew the future would bring more opportunities.

When I picked up Luke from O'Hare on his return from Korea, I stupidly asked him about the Greystone. I hadn't been to the place since my initial tour. I didn't plan to live there ever, so it wasn't on my list of priorities.

"Don't worry about it. I've got it handled." Abrupt, rude, par for the course.

"I'm not worried, just making conversation." Why did I bother?

"Actually, the work is progressing great. In a month or so, we'll be ready for city inspections. I'll have to ask someone at work who to bribe."

"Bribe? Are you kidding?" I wanted to glare at him but would never take my eyes off the road with Lorelei in the car.

Luke smirked. "Grow up. That's just reality."

The North Avenue exit zipped by, and I had to maneuver quickly to take the exit on Division Street. I signaled and barely made it.

"But I'm glad you brought it up. I'll have to put the condo on the market soon, but first I want my contractor to give me an estimate for redoing the hall bath."

"Tearing out the bathroom? That'll be inconvenient."

"Too bad. You'll just have to suck it up. I'll let you know when he can swing by."

After I parked and carried Lorelei up to the condo, got her settled, and hurried back to the garage to bring in her things and my purse, I saw Luke at the liquor cabinet, pouring a scotch. He picked up his glass and walked past me without a word. Soon I heard *Blood on the Tracks* featuring Bob Dylan's nasal whine going on and on and on about "Idiot Wind."

Who was the bigger idiot—Luke or me?

In early June, Luke had a week of meetings in town. Ugh! I resigned myself to his presence. I'd have to fit in an extra trip to the grocery store and plan meals. What an inconvenience. But he was paying the bills. I hoped he'd leave me alone in bed.

That week, Luke dressed in a different gray suit every day. He agonized over his tie choice each morning. By Friday, I was dragging from the stress of having him home. When he was out of town, I usually had a can of soup or a salad for dinner. In addition to working and performing the baby shuttle, I had to prepare a full meal for him.

While I was struggling to dress for work and pack Lorelei's things and mine, Luke announced the contractor would be bringing by some drawings and taking a look at the hall bath that afternoon.

Annoyed, I put my hand on my hip and said, "I have work."

"And I gotta a late dinner after the conference. I'll tell him to come at six. You oughta be home by then."

"Fine." I'd never make it to Paige's during rush hour to pick up Lorelei and be home by six, but I wasn't about to explain that fact to the self-involved blob of protoplasm standing in front of me.

Then the blob shoved two ties in my face. "Which one?"

I swatted the ties away. "I don't know. They're both blue. Both have stripes. Either one is fine."

"I don't need fine. I need perfect." He dragged me into his closet and waved at the vast display of silk. "Which one is perfect? Which one will guarantee me the vice-presidency?" He was serious.

To save time, I played along. "That one," I said, pointing to another blue tie with stripes.

"Hmm. I think you're right." He plucked the tie from the rack.

"Got to get Lori to Pa—the sitter." I made my escape with his words following me down the hall.

"Wish me luck. Actually, I don't need it. I got this." He was supremely confident that when they announced promotions, his name would be front and center.

When I dropped Lorelei off at Paige's, I told her about the contractor appointment and that I'd be late. She shrugged, "No biggie. I'd keep her forever if you let me."

"Not a chance."

As soon as I arrived home, I changed into a loose blouse and palazzo pants. Nice to take off the pantyhose and suit. I was pulling my hair into a topknot when the bell rang. Letting my hair fall, I put down the brush and answered the door.

Daniel stood there, looking uncomfortable, a little dusty. He had a roll of blueprints under his arm.

Instantly, things clicked. I gasped.

"Oh, my God." He blushed and stared with wide eyes. "Danielle?"

I knew my face was as red as his. My voice cracked. "C-come in."

I stood back to let him enter. He hesitated a few seconds and then strode in. His work boots, covered with construction dust, left little puffs of powder on the black marble floor with each step. He noticed the mess he made and took off his boots. "Sorry about that."

"Don't worry about it. Here, let me take the drawings."

I tossed them on the dining room table and came back.

"Aren't you going to look at them? It's the finishing detail."

"No. I don't plan to live there. Ever. You've met the reason why."

"Yes, I have. I thought some society ice queen would open the door. I wondered why his wife never came to the site." He rubbed his neck and looked around. "Nice place. I guess I need to look at the bathroom."

"Follow me."

"I'd follow you anywhere," he murmured.

Was I meant to hear that? The attraction was still there. Very strong. Irresistible. I showed him the bathroom door. He didn't enter. He stepped within an inch of my body. My body. He tilted my chin and kissed me.

I was lost.

I came up gasping, grabbed his hand, and led him into my bedroom. Into my bed. We kissed again. And again. My heart swelled, along with my nether regions. The sensation of wanting him inside me was almost painful.

Poised over me, he raised an eyebrow, and I nodded. It was everything I'd been missing since 1970.

Spent, I tried to catch my breath after a luscious interlude with a magnificent man. Daniel turned on his side and smiled, drawing his finger down my arm.

"Wow."

I returned his smile. "I agree."

A scraping sound at the front door alarmed me, then I heard the door open. *Luke?*

Daniel's eyes popped. "What the hell. You expecting someone?"

"No."

Luke scuffed into the room, dropped his briefcase, and gaped at us. "What the ever-loving fuck!" he shouted.

Clutching the sheet to my breasts, I saw his red eyes, tear-streaked face, disheveled hair and clothes, smelled the reek of scotch, and knew something bad had happened—before this *mise-en-scène*, this betrayal.

He never came home this early when he was in town. Had someone died?

Daniel backed out of the bed, picked up his clothes, and left the room. Brushing past Luke, he muttered, "Sorry, man." My husband didn't acknowledge him or watch him leave. A minute later, the front door closed. I pictured Daniel with unzipped jeans, juggling his shirt and boots while waiting for the elevator. I wanted to go with him.

Luke stared a hole in me. "Get out! Get the fuck out!" The veins stood out in his neck. I thought he might have a stroke. "Pack your things. I'll give you thirty minutes. Don't be here when I get back, you fucking slut. I lost my fucking job today, and now I lost my fucking wife." He slammed the bedroom door on his way out. I heard him scream, "Fucking wife. Yeah, she was fucking all right. Bitch!"

Then I heard the condo door slam with a force that sent something ceramic crashing to the floor. He was gone. I jumped into action, pulling on my discarded clothing.

First, I drew my box of treasures from its hiding place, under a pile of dirty clothes in my hamper. Then, I packed as many of my clothes as I could, makeup bag, all my jewelry. Took my accumulated cash. Then I packed Lorelei's tiny clothes and some toys. I used every suitcase in the place and made three trips to the car. I kept looking at my watch. Sweating, breathing heavily. Desperate to be gone before he returned.

Shaking, I locked the door behind me and took the elevator to the garage. His MGB wasn't there, and I breathed a sigh of relief. Thirty-five minutes.

Crying and shivering, I drove to Paige's place. I stalled the 442 three times because of the tremors in my legs. The residual adrenalin-flush made my limbs tingle. I felt weightless, insubstantial, unreal. My emotions had whipsawed from blissful afterglow to shock, panic, and fear in a split second, and that, combined with my furious packing activity, left me a wreck. Then there was the Catholic guilt. Although I no longer attended Mass, the training from the nuns in grades one through eight haunted me, especially when I was in a moral crisis. At least I knew I was in a moral crisis.

Luckily, there was a spot in front of Paige's place big enough so I didn't have to parallel park. When Paige opened the door and saw my face, her own face crumpled. "Oh, Dani. What happened?" I started blubbering, and she put her arm around me, drawing me inside her home.

Lorelei was standing up in the playpen, wobbly but determined. "Mama?" Paige had put her few strands of hair in a bow.

I rushed to my daughter and picked her up, holding her tight. "Mama's here, my love. My Lorelei."

Paige took a bottle of vodka out of the freezer and brought it, with a bottle of tonic, to the living room. She filled two glasses halfway with the liquor and topped it off with the soda. I chugged the glass down and asked for another. Paige didn't comment, just poured.

Since it was Friday, I had the weekend to get squared away before I had to work again.

I told my sister everything. She was stunned I'd cheated on Luke, but then again, so was I. The act was surreal, but I'd been starved for love for years, and my appetite took over. Did I feel guilty? Yes and no. I knew I'd have to put this into some sort of perspective eventually, but my focus was on finding a place to live—by Sunday.

Lorelei had eaten her dinner, but she needed a bath and then bed. Paige and I tended to her needs and placed her in the traveling crib.

We returned to the living room. Paige ordered a pizza. "You have to eat, Dani. Can't live on vodka tonics."

Feeling like a deflated balloon, I collapsed onto the couch. "What am I going to do? My marriage is over. Not that it was ever much of one. Not that I wasn't planning to end it, but still..."

"You can stay here. One of the guys moved out. Howie got on at 'NBC's Saturday Night.' Moved to the Big Apple. Awesome for him. You can have his room. It's totally cool."

"Thanks so much. I have my stash, so I'll look for something nearby. Promise I won't impose on you for long."

"Impose? You won't be."

The pizza arrived, and it smelled so good my stomach grumbled. Hadn't had a thing since breakfast. Besides, I needed something to absorb all the vodka. I ate two slices. After we finished, Paige and I unloaded the car. We carried the bags upstairs, and she helped me make up the bed in my new room.

"I'm going to call him and apologize. I have to."

"Tonight? Are you sure? Give him some time to cool off. His big fat ego just took a licking. Give it until morning. He might call you."

I attempted a smile. Not capable at the moment. "Oh, believe me, I know all about his ego. Still, I need to do this for my soul."

"Getting all metaphysical, are ya? Well, okay, go for it."

The phone rang eight times, then the machine picked up. My message was brief. "I'm so sorry, Luke. I'm staying with Paige. You have the number."

The next morning, I had a screamer of a headache. The vodka. I drank black coffee and downed four aspirin. Then my stomach revolted. A fitting punishment for my treachery. Luke hadn't returned my call. Over Paige's objections, I tried again. "Luke, I'm sorry. I know you won't forgive me, but we have to talk at some point. Please call me back."

I settled into my new room. This place would be a blessing. With no more morning drop-offs and evening pickups, I'd have more time with Lorelei. Bustling around the space, I set up a changing station on the dresser and put our clothes away. Luke didn't call, and by the afternoon, I was worried. Even if he cursed me, I needed to speak to him.

I carried Lorelei downstairs to fix her dinner. Paige bustled around the kitchen, opening cans, and stirring something in a massive bowl.

After I settled Lorelei in the highchair, I joined Paige at the counter. "Shades of childhood. Tuna casserole. Don't think I've had any since 1969."

Paige looked up from her work. "Don't knock it. It's cheap. And filling. Tim loves it."

"All righty then. Are you serving it over noodles, rice, or Mom's specialty—those canned, crunchy chow mein noodles?"

"Oh my God! La Choy. I haven't had those in years. Remind me to pick some up for the next time I make this." Paige put the dish in the oven and washed her hands.

"Sure. Listen, I'm going to run by the condo. Luke hasn't returned my calls, and I'm concerned. I think he'd at least use the opportunity to cuss me out."

"Want me to go with you?"

"Would you? Let me feed Lori, and then the three of us can go. Thanks, sis."

"No problem. I'll leave a note for Tim. He's going to run home for dinner in a few. He's got a show tonight."

After tucking sleepy, well-fed Lorelei into her car seat, I drove to the condo. Both parking spots were empty. "His car isn't here."

"Maybe he went on a little vacation. Or perhaps he's holed up in a hotel room with a hooker. Oh, I know, he moved back home with his mother." That was Paige, always coming up with imaginative options.

I glanced at her but said nothing. Anything was possible.

Paige took Lorelei out of the car and carried her to the elevator. I brought two empty suitcases to fill with the rest of my things and as much as I could pack of the baby's.

In the hallway, I put my ear to the door. Nothing. Unlocked the door and pushed it open. The broken vase was right where it fell when Luke slammed the door as he stormed out. Dust from Daniel's boots still powdered the black floor. The entry looked exactly as I left it less than twenty-four hours ago. There was no way to tell if Luke had come back. The air was still and stale.

Paige carried Lorelei to her room and put her in the bassinette, and I brought her a suitcase. It was a shame we couldn't take the baby's crib and changing table, but I could make arrangements for that once I got in touch with Luke. He had no use for them.

I shoved all my shoes and purses and the rest of my lingerie in the suitcase and took three hanging garment bags for my suits and dresses. The only things I left behind were outfits I didn't care for, mostly those Luke had chosen for me. He could donate them to charity or give them to another size four if he found one foolish enough.

It took two trips, but we got it all in the 442. When we got back to Paige's place, Tim and the other housemates—Eric and Jill—were eating the tuna casserole. Someone had made rice. I wasn't hungry.

Sunday morning, I woke with a feeling of dread. My empty stomach rumbled, and I had a dull headache. Lorelei was still asleep, so I grabbed my clothes, ran to the bathroom, and quickly dressed. By the time I got back, she was standing in her crib looking around the room. I changed her and tiptoed to the kitchen to feed her. It was still early, and everyone else was asleep. I made coffee. With Lorelei in her playpen, I sat down in the living room with a cup to contemplate a plan.

Living with Paige gave me a reprieve, but I couldn't see us staying with her and her roomies indefinitely. Eric and Jill were pleasant and accepting, but I was certain they'd choose a solo adult in place of a mother and child. I had to get in touch with Luke. It would be ugly—really ugly. Unfortunately, I had no clue how divorce worked. Would I get alimony? Would he pay child support, or would he use my affair to avoid it? So many questions only an attorney could answer. Given my new reliance on my salary, I hoped there was a law firm in the Merchandise Mart so I wouldn't have to lose a day of work to find one. There went my bankroll.

I needed to eat something. Toast might work. Yet, I couldn't even get up.

After a time, footsteps on the stairs dragged me from my reverie. Paige and Tim plodded into the room. Tim was not a morning person, but Paige was becoming one since she'd been caring for Lorelei. Now she had a hard time staying awake to see Tim after a show. She must nap when my baby did. Then it struck me, Lorelei wasn't a baby anymore. She had taken her first faltering steps and soon would be walking on her own, which meant childproofing. Especially the stairs.

"Morning, Dani." Paige took Lorelei from my arms. "How's the bestest, cutest baby in the world?"

Lorelei gurgled and giggled. She loved Paige.

Tim brought two mugs of coffee into the living room and sat on the couch. "Paige says you're gonna stay with us, at least for a while. We're here for you. Let me know if you need anything."

"I hate to ask, but I'm getting really worried about Luke. Will you come with me to the Greystone? I can't think of anywhere else to look."

Tim pursed his lips. "No word from him?"

"Nothing. I can't imagine where he is. We should stop back at the condo too."

"Ya know, I think he needs a little time to cool off, but if you're that concerned, I'll do it. Let's have some breakfast, then we'll go."

"Thanks. I appreciate it."

"Hey, can I drive? I love that muscle car of yours."

"Sure, Tim."

Paige handed Lorelei to me. "I'm making pancakes. Follow me to where the magic happens."

Tim laughed. "I thought the magic happens upstairs in our room."

I was astonished to see Paige blush. While my sister cooked, I changed Lorelei, then brought her back to the kitchen. She loved being in the center of things in her highchair, watching every move we made. I picked at my food. Living on coffee, vodka tonics, and pizza was not healthy, but I had no appetite. My sense of shame was overwhelming. Starved for love and attention, I'd betrayed my morals and ethics. The phrase "situational ethics" skittered through my mind. It was something I heard in one of my classes. I didn't believe in it. Ethics were immutable to me, and I'd flouted them. Catholic guilt poured over me in waves, good old-fashioned guilt too. My stomach felt hollow; my core felt hollow, as if I'd lost a piece of myself. No wonder I couldn't eat.

I kissed Lorelei goodbye. Her eyelids were drooping.

Paige said, "Maybe I'll take a little nap while she does." She whisked my daughter upstairs. As Tim closed the door, I heard them laughing.

I handed Tim the keys and got in the passenger side. The Greystone was only about a mile away, but it was worlds apart in socio-economic status. Because there was no parking at the second residence, when we were two blocks away, I began to scan the street for a spot.

"There's Luke's car!"

"Where?" Tim asked.

"We just passed it. Look, there's a space on the right."

Tim maneuvered the car into the slot. He was an excellent parallel parker. Anyone who lived in the city had to be.

"Okay, where is this palace Luke bought?"

"Around the corner. I haven't been there since he bought it. It was a disaster. From what Luke says, the restoration is almost finished. I don't have a key. I hope he'll let me in."

Then I pictured Daniel, and my emotions tumbled. I wanted to see him again, and that desire brought a hefty dose of guilt. I wallowed in it for a moment. The memory of our lovemaking surfaced, and I felt my face get warm. He wouldn't be there on a Sunday, but I was about to see the result of his labors.

We approached the Greystone. The only evidence of the work going on inside was a neat pile of wood under a metal ladder on the porch. The exterior looked the same as when I first saw the place.

Tim held his arm out at the top of the stairs. "Wait, the door's open a crack. Did someone break in?" He listened a moment. "Don't hear anything." Picking up a length of wood from the porch, he said, "Okay, I'm going in. Stay behind me." He pushed the door open. The hinges squealed.

Then I screamed.

Luke hung by the neck from the banister on the second-floor balcony overlooking the foyer.

"Jesus, Mary, and Joseph, and all the Saints!" Tim dropped the piece of wood and dashed up the stairs. "Don't look, Dani." He felt for a pulse, but from the stinking puddles on the mosaic tile floor and the deep purple/blue of his bloated features, there was no doubt Luke was dead.

"What can I use to cut him down? Shit, shit, shit." Tim dashed out of sight into the upstairs rooms, rushed out again. "I can't find a fucking...anything!"

"Tim, I don't think you should touch...the b-b-body. We have to call for help."

"Is there a working phone here?" Tim plodded down the stairs.

"I don't know. I'm going next door for help."

"Okay. I'll stay here." He bent over and vomited.

Thankful I hadn't eaten much, I managed not to follow suit. I hurried out the door, stumbled down the stairs, and ran to the next-door neighbor. Pounded on the door, leaned into the bell. It seemed to take several minutes for someone to answer. An elderly man, supported by a cane, opened the door. I babbled. "We need an ambulance. The police. He's dead."

"My goodness. Please, come in." He graciously ushered me inside and pointed to a phone on the hallway table. My shaking finger didn't make it all the way around the dial from zero for the operator—an instruction I remembered from my childhood. On the second try, I completed the call.

"Miss, can I get you a glass of water? You look a little wobbly."

I shook my head. "I better go wait for the police. Thank you." In a daze, I clomped back to the second residence and joined Tim on the porch. Already, sirens pierced the Sunday quiet. Three squad cars screeched to a halt in the street. With guns drawn, a team entered the house.

A tall, black male officer led me to his cruiser and helped me into the back seat. He was in his fifties with a name tag that identified him as "Weston."

Glancing out the rear window, I watched a chubby, red-headed police-woman talking to Tim on the sidewalk. His color had returned, but his face reflected the horror of what he'd seen. Tim shrugged and shook his head as he answered questions. He glanced at me and raised his chin in a gesture I took to be solidarity.

Officer Weston asked me to relate every moment since arriving at the house. I did my best, then he peppered me with questions.

"Mrs. Baumann, what led you to come to this address today?"

Mrs. Baumann? Was I still Mrs. Baumann? Had I ever been? "I had a fight with my husband on Friday night and went to stay at my sister's. That night I called him...to a-apologize...and he didn't call me back..." I trailed off.

"Then what?" The officer was all business.

"I called again Saturday and Paige—she's my sister—and I drove to our condo, but he wasn't there. I was sure he'd call today, but he didn't, so I asked Tim to bring me here."

"How did you know he was here?"

I looked up at the sharp tone in his voice. "I didn't but couldn't think of where else he could be, so Tim drove me here. We saw his car on the street and then... the door was open...and I s-s-saw him..." The mental picture of Luke's protruding tongue and purple/blue face was so horrifying, I lost it. Bending at the waist, I wailed at the image, the last sight of the man I married.

My mind searched for a different, happier picture to replace the revolting scene, but failed. Our history scrolled through my head, but all I could recall was his search for the perfect tan on our honeymoon, the hours spent on the Kennedy to and from O'Hare, Bob Dylan on the stereo, a bottle of Chivas Regal, and how Lorelei annoyed him.

It was over. My escape was here. But the mess of what was to come made my head spin.

The officer's voice broke through my sobs. "Ma'am, ma'am. Calm down."

Trying to pull myself together, I dug through my purse for a tissue. I couldn't put my finger on why I'd broken down in tears. After all, I never loved him. Most likely, it was the stress and the unpleasantness that lay ahead. Or the guilt.

Officer Weston paged back in his notebook. He narrowed his eyes. "What did you fight about?"

That question made my heart pound. Should I admit my infidelity? Should I lie? If I didn't tell Weston about the affair and Tim did, how would that look? Shame made my entire body flush. Shame for the affair and shame I would consider lying.

"Mrs. Baumann?"

I gulped and looked down as I whispered, "He found me in bed with another man."

"I see." He closed his notebook, picked up the radio. "I'm inbound with a witness. Need a detective."

I should have kept my big fat mouth shut. "Wait! What's happening? I want to go to my sister's. My baby is there. Are you *arresting* me? Do I—"

"Settle down. Let me call back and tell them to meet us at your sister's place. And no, you're not under arrest." He shook his head, picked up the transmitter, and relayed the change of plan.

My vision grayed, and I must have blacked out because the next thing I remember is Weston patting my face and calling my name.

Tim and the female officer stood next to the squad car.

"We're taking her to her sister's. The detective will meet us there," Officer Weston told them.

I sat up. My limbs felt limp and weak, like noodles. "Thank you. I need to see my baby."

The short silent drive gave me a minute to pull myself together. Tim parked the 442, rushed back to the police car, and helped me up the steps to the front door.

Paige opened the door, and when she saw the double-parked squad and the police officers, her hands flew to cover her mouth. With wide eyes, she asked, "What happened?"

Officer Weston told her.

Paige's mouth formed a perfect circle. "Oh, no! Come into the living room. Can I get you some coffee?"

They accepted, and she withdrew to the kitchen. Tim trailed her and, judging from her face when she brought the coffee to them, no doubt filled her in on the details. Lorelei was still napping, and I told the officers I needed to check on her.

Paige followed me up the stairs. "Oh my God, Dani. I'm so sorry. This is the worst...the most..." She ran out of words. I had too.

I hugged her. What could I say?

Paige patted my shoulder. "I'm making you some cinnamon toast." She returned downstairs to the kitchen.

Lorelei was sleeping, oblivious. I hoped she'd stay that way a while. I doubted she would have any memory of the man who provided half of the genetic material to create her. That would normally be a sad thing, but not in this case. I tiptoed out of the room and trudged downstairs.

In the living room, the two officers sipped coffee. Paige brought in a plate of toast for me. "Eat!"

I did. My stomach settled, but the sense of unreality remained. My emotions ping-ponged between elation at my release and the horror of what Luke had done. A thick coating of Catholic guilt congealed on the day's events.

Why did he end his life? I wondered if losing his job was the causative factor, or if my infidelity pushed him over the edge. The police didn't find a note or message, so I would never know for sure. My best guess was Luke hung himself because of the loss of status and prestige when he lost his job. I had no illusion I meant more to him than any other ornament or possession. My cheating was just the icing on the cake.

A few minutes later, the bell rang, and the officers got up to answer the door. They stood on the porch with the detective for several minutes, filling him in, I guessed. The detective, a man in his thirties in a wrinkled suit and pale, unshaven face, entered alone.

Paige sat at my side. She stayed there through the entire interview. I held nothing back from the detective. He asked Paige and Tim questions too.

Just as I was thinking I'd answered the same questions four or five times, he slapped his notebook shut and stood. "Here's my card, Mrs. Baumann. If you think of anything else, give me a call. My condolences on your loss."

"Can I ask...what will happen to his, to Luke's body?"

"He'll go to the morgue. We'll let you know when he can be released for the funeral."

"Oh." I hadn't thought that far ahead. Truthfully, I hadn't thought much at all—I was stunned. All I wanted was to hold Lorelei, take a bath, lie in bed, and forget what I'd seen.

After the door closed, I asked Tim, "What do I do now? I know nothing of Luke's finances, if he had a will. What do I do?"

Tim offered to call his cousin who was a divorce attorney. "I'm sure he'd be happy to help."

"I don't think so, but thanks. Luke kept all his papers in his office in the condo. I suppose I'll have to go through them and figure it out from there."

"I'll call Mom and let her know," Paige said.

"Thanks, I think." What could my mother do? Did I want her involved? "Wait! Don't tell her about Daniel."

I was a widow at twenty-four—with a baby.

Chapter Ten

AFTERMATH 1976-1977

The next morning, I drove to the condo. Usually, I thought the elevator ride too slow, but that day, the car arrived on the twenty-second floor in an eye blink. I hesitated at the door, taking several deep breaths before entering. The stillness and silence were absolute. Thinking of how to dispose of Luke's possessions made me sick. I would donate all the clothes. Didn't know what I'd do with the MGB. I thought Paige and Tim might like his stereo equipment—minus the Bob Dylan and Cat Stevens records.

Was Luke's entire life reduced to things? All that remained was a closetful of three-piece suits, a massive tie collection, and some electronics. He had spent most of his time on his career, and when he lost that, he lost everything that made life worth living to him. Would he have felt such despair if he had loved me and Lorelei? Would it have made a difference if I had loved him? I should have made more of an effort, but the knowledge I'd planned to leave him from the start left me feeling lower than the underside of the sidewalk.

I knew I'd live with the guilt—and the image of his dead body hanging from the banister—for the rest of my life.

In the third bedroom where Luke kept an office, I drew open the drapes and stared at his live-edge walnut slab of a desk. The top was bare except for a leather-edged pad, matching leather accessories, and a phone. There were no drawers in the desk. The marble-topped credenza must be where he stored his secret financial papers. I opened a drawer and rifled through a neat, carefully labeled, alphabetized array of folders. I removed the one designated last will and testament and sat down to read.

From what I could tell, I was the sole beneficiary. Although the document was dated after her birth, there was no mention of Lorelei. That infuriated me. A token $500.00 to his mother, sister, and brother. What a cheapskate! I snatched up the receiver and dialed the number for the attorney that appeared on the letterhead.

When I informed Mr. Preston that Luke had committed suicide and I had a copy of the will, there was silence on the other end of the line, followed by throat-clearing, and at last, words assuring me the firm would handle everything.

I let them.

JWT was supportive when I called to ask for a leave of absence, very understanding. They gave me four weeks to settle my affairs—ouch—that word stung. My job would be there when I returned.

Luke left instructions that his body be cremated, and the urn of ashes given to his wife. He didn't want a ceremony of any kind. That was a relief. I didn't want the remains, but there was no rational excuse I could offer to refuse them. To ease my mind, I decided to give them to his mother.

Mr. Preston was as good as his word; the firm handled all the details I couldn't bear to think about. Three weeks after Luke's death, I felt able to sit down with the attorney and learn where I stood financially. My mother and Ken insisted on coming with me. At first, I objected, then I thought about it and accepted their support. I'd be needing their help in a big way soon.

The attorney looked nothing like I expected. I had imagined a tall, gray-haired, solemn man. Mr. Preston was short, blond, and jolly. He ushered us into his lushly carpeted and paneled office on Dearborn Street, where I introduced him to Mom and Ken. Preston offered us coffee.

I took a seat in a deep leather chair. "No thanks."

Mom and Ken sank into matching chairs on either side of me. They accepted his offer, both caffeine fans.

After coffee was served, Preston got down to business. "Let's get right to it. Luke's net worth comes mainly from his investment portfolio. He did quite well in the stock market. A good deal of those profits went into the real estate holdings."

My mother interrupted, "Holdings? What do you mean?"

Mr. Preston glanced at me. "Do you want your parents privy to this discussion?"

I nodded and didn't bother to correct the attorney about Ken's relationship to me. "Yes, I do."

Preston leaned back in his tall chair and continued. "Mr. Baumann had two real estate assets. He owned the condominium outright. There is a small mortgage on the Greystone, but with the appreciation since he purchased it, well, the amount is negligible."

Ken leaned forward. "Have you had the properties appraised?"

Mr. Preston held out a slim folder. "Here are the reports."

Mom, Ken, and I looked at the numbers and then at each other. I was rich.

Preston studied our joint reaction. "I spoke to the contractor, and he intends to finish the job on the Greystone. It should take about three weeks."

"Okay." I wished I'd paid more attention in accounting class. After things were settled, I'd ask Mr. Preston to recommend a financial advisor.

"Mrs. Baumann, you'll be able to choose which residence to live in. Perhaps you'll want to rent out or sell the other."

There was that name again. I'd never thought of myself as Mrs. Baumann. Could I take my maiden name back even though I was no longer a maiden? But what about Lorelei? Not wanting to get sidetracked, I pushed that debate from my mind.

"I don't want to live in either of them," I blurted. "Just sell them."

Raised eyebrows. "Whatever you say, Mrs. Baumann. There was a life insurance policy. A big one. Despite the suicide, the insurer will pay out given that Mr. Baumann purchased the policy more than three years ago."

Then he handed me another paper. "Here is a copy of the death certificate." Jumping out at me were the words, "manner of death, suicide," and location "other, second residence."

I left the office in a daze. At twenty-four, I was a rich widow with a baby.

Fall arrived, and with it, my return to work. I had paid my dues with a year of writing copy for lunchmeat, cleaning products, and cosmetics—most of which never saw the light of day—and was ready for more. Charlotte assigned me to a new product team, and I was eager to start.

Lorelei and I still lived with Paige and Tim, but as my daughter became more vocal and active during the day, the housemates became less supportive.

Financially, I was golden. The condo sold in a week. I kept only Lorelei's baby gear and sold the place furnished. The Greystone was still under construction. Three weeks to finish turned out to be optimistic. When week five came, I decided to check on the progress.

After I finally wedged the 442 into a parking spot, I walked to the Greystone and climbed the steps. The door was partially open. My heart rate climbed. I raised my shaking hand to push open the door. I realized I was holding my breath and exhaled. The odor of paint, rather than death, wafted out the door. Inside, someone was playing a radio. "Magic Man," by Heart.

I entered and three painters stopped rolling their rollers and stared. I raised my voice, so I'd be heard over the radio. "Is Daniel here?" The lyrics about a magic man resonated, and I rebuked myself for even thinking about our destructive liaison.

One of the men turned off the radio and yelled, "Hey, Daniel. Someone to see ya."

"Be right there." His voice made me shiver.

Work boots sounded on the hardwood floor. I saw his feet approach, then raised my eyes. Still gorgeous. Determined to be all business, I announced to the air over his shoulder, "I came to check on the work. The completion date has come and gone. I want to put it on the market as soon as possible."

His face was pink. I knew mine must be as well. Our eyes locked.

"Sorry for the delay. The tile for the bathrooms was damaged in transit, and I had to order more. Now the tiling is done, and as you can see, we're painting. Should have everything wrapped up by next week. Can I show you around?"

Torn, I thought for a moment. Recalling what a disaster the place had been when Luke bought it, I wondered if it was habitable. And salable. "Sure. Thank you." Formal and distant, but in my heart, I wanted a few more minutes near him.

My eyes searched the mosaic tile floor in the entry for any trace of the tragedy that had stained the foyer. Although I couldn't detect anything, the image of the floor that day would remain with me. I made a wide berth around the area where Luke's body fluids had pooled and followed Daniel upstairs, wondering who had cleaned up the mess.

After viewing the three floors and basement, I had to admit Daniel was a craftsman. The place was beautiful, fresh, and clean. The selection of tile, carpet, paint, cabinetry, subdued and lovely. I tried to picture living in this splendor and couldn't. Who would buy it? Someone rich, who had a lot of money to furnish the huge place. Would the real estate agent need to disclose Luke's suicide? Then I realized the efficient and able Mr. Preston would deal with those details. Of course, if I had asked, he would have checked on the reason for the delay. I admitted to myself the only reason I came was to see Daniel one last time.

Returning to the foyer, I prepared to leave. "Thanks for the tour."

"Let me walk you out," Daniel said. He glanced at the idle painters and made a motion for them to start working.

Once we were on the sidewalk, Daniel asked, "Where's your car?"

Avoiding his gaze, I said, "No need."

He took a step forward. "Danielle, I'm so sorry."

I got up the nerve to look him in the eyes. "So am I." Then I walked away and didn't look back.

Once Mr. Preston tallied up the proceeds from the condo and the Greystone, the brokerage accounts, the retirement account, and the life insurance, I stared at the astronomic sum. I knew I would be able to take care of my daughter, but why not do something for Mrs. Baumann?

When I told Paige my plan, she thought I was suffering from guilt. "You don't owe that old bitch anything. And, if you're passing out money, write me a check."

I frowned at my sister. "You didn't see her house. Luke was such a skinflint he never even bought her a dishwasher. She raised him, no matter how poorly. I'm going to do something for her. When I called to say I was coming, her muted response was, 'All right.' No pleasantries, no chit-chat, no nothing. She never mentioned Lorelei. I can't believe she's never seen her granddaughter."

"Like I said, you don't owe her anything."

On a Sunday afternoon, I drove the MGB to Milwaukee. I went alone, except for the urn in the passenger seat.

Once I parked in the driveway and got out of the car with my burden, the malty smell of the breweries overpowered me. Mrs. Baumann—the real Mrs. Baumann—must have been watching for me. She opened the door and stood there like a Colossus—still, stolid, implacable.

I gulped. Returning her stare, I entered the house.

We sat in the parlor. I, on the uncomfortable, scratchy orange tweed couch; she on the doily-covered gold brocade chair. Silence. No greeting. No offer of coffee. I held the urn out to her. The thing weighed twenty pounds. It was top of the line, cast bronze with a verdigris patina finish.

She leaned over and took my burden. "Why don't you want Luke's remains?"

I lied. "He wanted you to have them."

"Then thank you."

"You're welcome." I opened my purse and took out an envelope. Inside was a check for $50,000, the amount of Luke's severance check from the pharmaceutical firm. I lied again. "He wanted you to have this too."

She frowned at the envelope. I kept holding it, offering it, jiggling it, and she eventually took it. When I rehearsed this visit in my mind, I never imagined she would be this impassive, given the circumstances. Based on what I learned from Cathy, I didn't have to guess what made her this way. No doubt the causative factor was the unmourned Mr. Helmut Baumann.

She drew the paper from the envelope and unfolded the letter I'd typed: "Mother, I want you to buy yourself a nice house in a better neighborhood.

Make sure you get yourself a dishwasher. Love, Luke." As she read, her mouth fell open, and I thought I saw her eyes glisten with tears.

When she was done, she stared right at me. No sign of tears. No sign of emotion. "This isn't from him. It's from you."

I protested. "No, no, it was him. He wanted this for you."

She shook her head, her mouth in a tight line. I knew she didn't believe me, but she said nothing further. I would never understand her, or anyone in her strange family. She didn't ask about Lorelei, and I didn't mention my daughter, either.

I saw myself out and drove off in the MGB. At Christmas, I planned to give the car to Phil. He'd be thrilled. I hoped he knew how to drive stick. Then I'd have to do something nice for Joe, but I'd have to think about what.

Once the Greystone closed and I had the necessary cash, I started looking for places in the area. My mother and Ken came with me. The previous week, I'd thrown myself on their mercy, exploiting my pathetic status as a widowed single mother.

"I can't stay with Paige much longer. Their roommates aren't thrilled with having a toddler in the house, not when they work nights. Would you consider moving in with me? Mom, would you quit your job and take care of Lori?" It was a big request, but her response couldn't have been more enthusiastic.

She squealed and clapped her hands. "Quit my job? In a heartbeat! Oh, I'm so happy. Ken, what do you say, honey?"

Ken pursed his lips. "Are you looking on the near north side? If so, I'm in. My commute will be a breeze."

I considered how my relationship with my mother had evolved. My childhood jealousy of Paige frayed the mother-daughter bond. In my teenage years, the intensity of my love for John caused strife. And after I moved out to live with Luke prior to our sham marriage, I rarely saw her. With Lorelei's birth, a new understanding between us mysteriously materialized. Was it the bond of motherhood that changed our dynamic?

"Oh honey, I can't think of anything I'd rather do than take care of Lorelei."

"I can't think of anyone else I'd rather have take care of her—besides Paige of course." I didn't tell my mother about Paige and Tim moving to Los Angeles. Tim had accepted a part in a movie, and they were making their announcement at Christmas. Paige had sworn me to secrecy.

Not wanting even the most remote connection to Luke, I found a real estate agent who specialized in the Gold Coast and wasn't affiliated with Mimi's firm. Leslie was a cool, slim blonde—chic, classy, and knowledgeable. Together with Mom and Ken, we must have looked at thirty places before I found my new home. A high rise didn't fit the bill for several reasons, but mainly because I wanted some green space for Lorelei, which was hard to come by in the city.

Leslie said, "The best option for you is a co-op. But that will require one hundred percent cash and board approval."

Board approval? I'd deal with that hurdle later. Finally, I found a two-story unit in a quiet building on Astor Street.

We all fell in love with the three-bedroom, three-and-a-half bath place. Mom and Ken would have a bedroom suite on the first floor, while Lorelei and I each had space upstairs. Ideal. The shared first-floor interior courtyard was a boon. Only four units could access the area. It would have been difficult to live on the upper floors with no access to the green space, and I felt blessed at being able to offer this to my family. It would be hard to wait until March to move in.

Ken could barely conceal his delight at the kitchen with its white cabinets and commercial-grade appliances. The soapstone counters and classic black and white tile were something I'd only seen in magazines. Or at displays at the Mart, displays for the carriage trade. I certainly didn't feel like a member of that exalted assembly. I worked for a living. And after I plunked down a huge percentage of my new wealth on the co-op, I needed my job.

Christmas 1976 was the last one at our childhood home. Mom and Ken planned to list the house after the first of the year. The holiday marked several momentous changes. I was a widow. Lorelei was walking and becoming a chatterbox. Mom and Ken were moving in with me.

Phil, a star player on the varsity baseball team at Champaign, was being scouted by the major leagues. He and Clare were still an item, but she joined her family for Christmas in Peoria that year. Joe, a junior in high school, craved a career in music. His girlfriend Joanie was joining us for dessert. My brothers. How much of their lives had I missed in the seven years since the divorce? They were approaching adulthood and had visions for their future and had plans I wasn't part of.

Then there was the big, life-changing announcement from Paige and Tim. How would my mother react? Did Dad know? I hadn't seen my father recently, although he called after Luke's death, expressing sympathy, and informing me the police closed the case as a suicide with no further investigation. As soon as Joe graduated, he and Ginger planned to leave our neighborhood too. They wanted to be closer to the police station.

No one from the Marek family would remain in our neighborhood. My parents had been among the first families to buy on the block, but not the first to leave. As we set the table, Mom caught me up on the neighborhood news. Mrs. Wilkins had remarried and moved to Arizona. Sandy and Beth were still together and had moved to the Northside, near Wrigley Field. Sheba had passed away in her sleep at the age of eleven. When I heard that, a piercing pain struck my heart, taking me back to August 12, 1965. To a tall handsome boy of fifteen, the boy I'd pledged my undying love to. The boy who died.

In agony, I bent over and sobbed.

Mom dropped the rest of the silverware with a clatter. "Dani, what's wrong?"

I raced upstairs to the girls' bathroom and threw myself on the floor, rolling and wailing and sobbing until I was spent.

What had I become after John died? Whatever it was, I hated myself. I acknowledged my callousness as I snubbed men, mocked them, walked away from them. My heartlessness disgusted me, but I didn't own a heart after John died, after my entire future died.

What kind of girl gets married while planning to end it after achieving a selfish goal? How could I take those vows when I did not intend to keep them? I'd been faithful until Daniel, I told myself, but it wasn't true. I was faithless the entire time.

With my eyes finally opened to my lack of character, I sank into a deep sadness. There was only one thing that could bring me back. My child. My Lorelei.

I stood and splashed cold water on my face. My eye makeup was a disaster, but I didn't care. The thought of going downstairs to face my family made me want to curl up into a ball and stay in the bathroom. But I couldn't.

When I opened the door, Paige and my mom came to me and encircled me with their arms and their love.

Mom rubbed small circles on my back. "Oh, honey. That wasn't all about little Sheba, was it?"

I shook my head.

"I love you, sis," Paige whispered. "You needed to let that out. Let's go eat Ken's yummy turkey."

Sniffing, I nodded and followed them downstairs.

"Mama cry?" Lorelei asked from her highchair.

"No, Lori. Mama's fine." I kissed the top of her head and sat at the table where a sumptuous dinner awaited. Everyone smiled, and no one commented on my abrupt flight upstairs.

"You okay, kid?" Ken whispered as he passed me his sublime mashed potatoes.

"Sure am." And I was. A dam had broken, and a gush of pent-up emotion erupted from what remained of my soul. Catharsis—and perhaps the start of healing. As I cut up turkey into tiny pieces for the other love of my life, I felt able to face the future.

Once we piled our plates high and took those first luscious bites, the talk turned to music.

Joe went on and on about how much he hated disco. "What's happening to music? I can barely listen to the radio anymore. All you hear is the Bee Gees screeching about dancing. Or that band who wants you to shake your bootie. Disgusting."

Phil laughed. "Are you stuck on AM, bud? Check out the FM dial. XRT is cool. There's still some good rock out there. AC/DC, Aerosmith, The Stones, and Led Zeppelin all released albums this year. Have you heard Bob Seger's new album? It's amazing. And it's your Christmas gift. Listen to 'Rock and Roll Never Forgets.' It'll make you feel all better."

Paige and Tim shared sidelong looks throughout the meal. I thought they would have dropped their news by now, but they seemed nervous.

I took matters into my own hands. "Anything new in the world of comedy, Tim?"

Tim gulped and reached for his beer. "Um. Yeah. I've got some news."

Paige put down her fork and grasped his hand. "Big news." She turned to Mom and said, "I hope you'll be happy for us."

Mom broke out in a dazzling smile. "A baby? Are you pregnant?" I imagined visions of more grandchildren danced in her head.

"No!" Paige and Tim exclaimed in unison.

Tim grinned and ducked his head. "I've had an offer to do a movie. L. A. here we come!"

"Holy crap!" Phil shouted.

Joe chimed in, "That's so cool."

Mom's hands covered her mouth, her blue eyes shining with tears, but not tears of happiness. Sobbing, she pushed back from the table and fled the room.

Ken called after her. "Ellen, honey, come back."

Paige's face was distraught. "I thought she'd be happy for us."

Ken shrugged and stood. "I guess it's the hormones. She's pregnant."

Five shocked faces stared at Ken as he raced up the stairs after his wife.

When I was expecting, I'd read about pregnancy in older women. "I did the math. Mom's forty-three. High risk." My new sibling would be younger than my child. Crazy!

Tim gulped his beer.

"Well, that blows my mind," Paige said. "Did she even hear our news?"

Phil grinned. "So, they're still getting it on at their age? Cool."

"I'm glad we got that out of the way before Joanie got here." Joe's face flushed. "Let's not mention it, okay?"

Tim, Phil, and Joe cleared the table while Paige made coffee. Lorelei held her arms up to be released from her highchair, and I picked her up. While we waited for Mom and Ken to reappear, we adjourned to the living room to give Lorelei her presents. She wasn't able to open them herself, so her uncles sat on the floor and helped. They were good with her. My daughter fell in love with her Snoopy stuffed toy. She said, "dog-dog" over and over. Was a love of dogs genetic? Someday I would give my girl a real dog. She barely looked at her busy box and rainbow stacker. I had to hand it to my family, all the gifts were well chosen for a toddler. No tiny pieces.

The doorbell rang, and Joe rushed to answer. "Please don't say anything to embarrass me."

Paige and I cracked up.

Ken returned and said, "Your mom will be down shortly. I'll get dessert. Homemade cheesecake and chocolate pecan pie."

Joanie, a petite, pretty girl with black hair down to her butt and long bangs, walked into the room glued to Joe's side. She wore jeans and a Led Zeppelin t-shirt, same as Joe. He gripped her hand as if she were about to bolt. Joanie smiled and nodded as Joe introduced us.

As we headed back to the kitchen for dessert, Joanie said, "What a cute little girl! Those blond curls are gorgeous. And Lorelei is such a pretty name." I liked her already.

Mom called from the bottom of the stairs, "Paige, Dani, I need to see you."

Handing Lorelei to Joanie, Paige and I went to our mother, who was standing in the shadows in the downstairs hall, wringing her hands. "Girls, you may not know I had a miscarriage between Paige and Phil. That's why I broke down. I'm scared, and Paige won't be here to help me."

My sister put her arms around Mom. "So that's why there's four years between me and Phil. Oh, Mom, I'll come back for visits. As much as I can."

"You'll be living with me," I reminded her. "Ken and I will be there for you. I'll find you the best OB in town."

Mom patted her eyes with a tissue. "My emotions are on a hair trigger. And I quit smoking as soon as I found out. Not easy stopping cold turkey, but I'm doing my best to have a healthy baby."

I put my arm around her shoulders. "You quit smoking? Mom, I'm so proud of you. I knew something was different, but I couldn't put my finger on it."

"Now, I want to meet Joe's girl and have some dessert. I'm eating for two."

Concerned faces looked up when we entered the kitchen. Ken rose and pulled out Mom's chair. He rubbed his hands together. "Who wants cheesecake?"

We all did.

While we ate, Tim told us about the movie he would soon be filming. As expected, it was a comedy. Most of the actors were relatively unknown, but he was excited at having the opportunity.

I put Lorelei down for a nap while the rest of us opened presents. I handed Phil an envelope with the title and keys to the MGB. "A car? You kidding me? I'm so stoked."

"Can you drive stick?"

"Duh!" Phil hugged me and lifted me off the floor. "Dani, this is the best present I ever got. My clunker is about ten miles away from going to the junk heap."

The joy of giving made me flush with pleasure, made me feel like I was human again. "If you need help with the insurance, let me know."

Another hug left me breathless and smiling.

After consulting with Mom and Ken, I ponied up two thousand dollars for a gift certificate so Joe could buy a Ludwig drum kit like the one John Bonham used. When he opened the envelope he shouted, "Holy shit! Should I get the green or silver sparkle?" Joe was in heaven, and he didn't even need a stairway to get there.

Paige and Tim received bathing suits, suntan oil, and sunglasses. A note in my card informed them I was saving my real present for their going-away party. I didn't want them to feel slighted.

February—and Tim and Paige's farewell party—arrived in a flash. The Finnegan clan knew how to throw a shindig. They rented Scottsdale Park

Field House and invited over a hundred people. The place was packed with Paige and Tim's friends and the extended Finnegan family. I was apprehensive about seeing Tim's cousin Michael, remembering our encounter five years earlier, but Tim assured me Michael had settled down.

"He's married and has two kids and another on the way. His party days are o-ver."

When I walked in, Joe's band Sledgehammer was onstage doing a great rendition of "Sweet Jane," the Velvet Underground version. My brother looked fabulous sitting behind his green sparkle kit. The music and laughter overcame me like an ocean wave. This was a party.

Tim's eight brothers and their wives, live-ins, and dates provided a buffet of appetizers: mini quiches, pigs in a blanket, rumaki, Swedish meatballs, stuffed mushrooms, deviled eggs, and cheese balls of every description—rolled in parsley, covered in pecans, decorated with pimento. Tubs of potato chips and vats of French onion dip, buckets of pretzels, and bowls of cocktail nuts dotted the long table. The calories, incalculable. I was glad no one dared bring a fondue—too messy. The sheer quantity was daunting, but with the horde of people in attendance, I doubted there would be many leftovers.

Sledgehammer rocked their way through a set of Bob Seger. The contagious beat drew part of the crowd onto the dance floor, making it possible to navigate the periphery of the large hall. I found Paige and Tim holding court in the kitchenette and hugged them both.

Ken drove the minivan I bought Paige and Tim to the field house. He stayed only a few minutes because he wanted to return to Mom, who was fatigued and nauseous from her pregnancy.

I presented Tim and Paige with the title and the keys. Paige's yelp of surprise came in a break between songs and drew the attention of the crowd. Tim rushed to the stage and grabbed the microphone off the stand.

"Don't worry, no one's hurt. That yowl was Paige." He grinned and shook his head. "I wasn't gonna make a speech, but we just got a gift that blew me away! Paige's sister Dani bought us a brand-new Chevy minivan. I'll tell you, the thought of driving my cranky old Corvair to L.A. freaked me out. Thank you, Dani. We really appreciate it."

Claps, whistles, foot stomps, and hooting greeted the announcement. Then, the throng quickly returned to the dance floor for "Walk This Way," an Aerosmith tune.

Beer was the main beverage that night, keg after keg. There was also a bar with liquor and mixes. Michael was tending bar, and I almost walked away, then realized that was silly.

I kept my voice cool. "Hey, barkeep, can I get a vodka tonic?"

Turning to face me, Michael's eyes widened. "Hey, yourself, Dani. Coming right up." As he handed me the drink, he asked, "How've you been? I mean, I heard about your husband. My sympathies."

"I'm doing well. Work helps. And my daughter. She's almost two."

He pulled out his wallet and showed me pictures of two little black-haired, dark-eyed boys. "Wife's due in June. She's hoping for a girl but with our family history, she may be out of luck."

I toasted him. "To a healthy baby. Thanks for the drink." I strolled away, sipping the drink. Heavy on the vodka.

"Wanna dance?" a deep voice rumbled.

I looked up at another specimen of the Finnegan family. No idea if he was one of Tim's brothers, or a cousin. After I downed my vodka tonic, I followed him to the dance floor. Looking around at the other couples, it was apparent all the Finnegans could really get down. I had a blast—it had been years since I danced like that.

The party wound down around two a.m. The guests of honor were still partying when I left. They were driving out to Los Angeles in a few days.

The Garrity's youngest was babysitting Lorelei, and I needed to pick her up. That night, I was staying over for the last time in my old room.

Lorelei barely roused as I bundled her in her snowsuit for the short walk to Mom's. She snuggled against me as I carried her upstairs to bed. When I settled her in her traveling crib, she stirred and said, "Mama."

"Sleep well, sweet girl."

As I lay in my childhood bed, the bed where John and I shared our love and passion, I cried myself to sleep. I was a rich widow with a baby. And a ghost.

Make that two.

Chapter Eleven

A STRICKEN HEART 1977

Mom's house sold in early March, and the moving van was scheduled to pick up their bedroom set, clothes, and several boxes of keepsakes. Ken planned a garage sale to dispose of the rest of the furniture.

I'd bought new furniture for the living room and dining room at Walter E. Smithe. On an impulse, I splurged a bit on bedroom sets for me and Lorelei. A fresh start.

With the chaos of the move over, the family life I created with Mom and Ken was working. The co-op was set up perfectly for shared space, with our private rooms on different floors. Grateful that her nausea let up in her third trimester, Mom was counting the days until her due date. For her age, she'd had an uneventful and healthy pregnancy.

Ken continued to work as a buyer for Sears and insisted on paying half the expenses. Because real estate taxes were quite high, I accepted his offer. Besides paying all cash for the co-op, I spent lavishly on Christmas gifts and furnishing my new home. Even though I hadn't hired a financial advisor, I knew from my bank balance I needed to conserve cash.

Lorelei would be two in a few weeks and so excited there would be a new baby in the house. She kissed Mom's belly every chance she got, and when they sat on the couch reading, she kept her hand on Mom's bump and giggled each time the baby kicked. She carried dog-dog with her wherever she went. When I put her toy in the wash for the first time,

I had to deal with a trembling lip and tears while she stood in front of the washing machine until dog-dog was clean, then her terror as her constant companion took a ride in the dryer. But I learned from my blunder; I purchased several more of the stuffed Snoopys, so there wouldn't be a repeat of that near-tragic laundry day.

On a beautiful April morning, a rare spring day in Chicago, I couldn't wait to get to work; I had a big morning ahead. My team had a presentation to a new client. Charlotte had assigned me to head the project. The junior staffer Andrea was content to follow my lead. She was a recent hire and knew she had to work her way up. The other team member was another story. Alan didn't like to take direction from a woman; he made that clear the first day we met at orientation. We were in a death match for a promotion. Only one account manager position would be awarded this year, and I'd be darned if I let Alan weasel his way into it. JWT had been good to me. Although I had yet to reach my goal of management, I was on the fast track from all indications. If I landed the Luxe Candy account, I'd be golden.

"Love you, Lori," I said as I bent to hug her. When I kissed my little girl goodbye, I got a sticky, pancake syrup kiss in return.

I picked up my briefcase and purse. "Mom, I might be late. After the presentation, I have to return to the office. I'll call and let you know."

"Okay, honey. Miss Lorelei will help me make some cookies later."

Lorelei, blond curls askew, tackled Mom's legs. "Can we, can we, can we cookies?"

"You bet, princess."

And Lorelei was a princess, beautiful and bright. I couldn't see a trace of Luke—or his dour relatives—in her sweet face. I knew his genes were in there somewhere but hoped the only genetic contribution was his mother's blond, blue-eyed genes. Ursula's lack of interest in her grandchild still rankled, but I had made peace with her disregard.

On the other hand, my mom was the best grandma one could imagine. She was eight months pregnant and doing well. Her daily walks with Lorelei gave her the right amount of exercise. When Ken came into her life, some of his cooking skills rubbed off on her. She no longer burnt, overcooked, or undercooked food. Her crowning achievement was her cookie baking, and Lorelei was her number one fan.

As I was leaving, I heard Mom say, "Let's get dog-dog and you can read it to me. Okay?"

"'Kay Gamma."

If I hadn't had such a perfect situation for Lorelei's care, I wondered how I could possibly work full time. The only other woman at JWT who had a child had nightmare tales to tell of shuttling her baby to and from childcare. Her guilt was palpable. I had guilt too, but nothing was going to stop me from having a career.

Andrea, the junior staffer, had been trying to fix me up with her brother for weeks. Luke had been gone almost a year, and while I wasn't mourning, it felt unseemly to date so soon. That didn't stop me from the occasional evening in the bars. I always made sure to read to Lorelei and settle her for the night before I left. Her favorite books besides *Go Dog Go,* were *Scuppers the Sailor Dog* and anything by Dr. Seuss.

A little flirtation and a few kisses were harmless. One evening in early May, Mom gave me the stink-eye as I was leaving for a couple hours on Division Street. Whenever I ventured out, I could count on words of disapproval.

"Don't you have to work tomorrow, Danielle?" Mom, hands on her hips and frowning, transported me back to my teenage years.

"Yes, I do. I'll only be down the street and back by eleven." My mother trying to guilt-trip me about having a little fun was the only downside of living in the same house, and I did feel like an overgrown adolescent at times.

Ken walked me to the door. He whispered, "Dani, I think your mom is ready to go into labor any day now. Her due date is two weeks away, but I think she'll go sooner. I've got her bag packed and keep the car gassed up, but I confess I'm nervous. My first child at age forty-five. My head is spinning."

I patted his shoulder. "Mom's a pro. She'll recognize the signs of labor. Relax a little."

The night was balmy, and the breeze off the lake refreshing as I walked to Division Street. For old time's sake, I went to Mother's, dismissing the bad karma as foolish. I hadn't been there in years, avoiding the bar because that was where I met Luke. Maybe I wanted closure; God knows I needed it. The narrow, poorly lit steps down to the dance floor were as I remembered. When the bouncer carded me, I flushed with pleasure. The band was on a break, so the only noises were the clank of the air hockey and foosball tables and the low rumble of flirtation. I almost gagged on the smoke. When I got home, I'd have to wash my hair. As soon as I entered the bar area, a man approached me.

"Hey, darling, can I buy you a drink?" He had a nice smile and made good eye contact.

I smiled back and agreed. We found a table in the corner against the wall and hopped up on the tall stools. I sipped my club soda, and he told me his story. Actually, I could have recited it for him: in town on business, loved Mother's, great band, how pretty he thought I was, want to dance, want to go to my hotel. Then the band came back and played "Life in the Fast Lane." I froze. What the hell did I think I was doing? Should a twenty-four-year-old mother be living in the fast lane? All at once, the guy was all over me, shoving me against the wall, nibbling my neck, licking my ear, and mauling my breasts.

My knee made contact with his groin.

"Oof! You bitch," he growled as he bent over to cradle himself.

I elbowed him in the side and made my getaway. The incident didn't garner so much as a raised eyebrow in the dim, smoky room. Taking the stairs two at a time, I didn't breathe until I was out on Division Street. I rushed home, vowing never to go to the singles' bars again. I'd made that pledge before, but I always backtracked, always returned. One day, I'd have to examine my life, wouldn't I?

Ken was right, Mom's baby came three days later. I bought Paige an airline ticket, and she arrived two days after the baby was born. Mom had an easy birth and named her boy Andrew. He weighed in at a healthy nine pounds and measured twenty-one inches long. Mom came home wreathed in smiles. Andrew was a sleepy baby. He ate well and slept during the day.

Nights were another story. Ken took two weeks of vacation to help acclimate to fatherhood. He was a doting, loving, but sleep-deprived father.

Paige arrived with a dash of Hollywood glamour. I almost didn't recognize her with her straightened white-blond hair and Goldie Hawn sunglasses. Gone was any vestige of her hippie days. Yes, Paige had gone Hollywood. It had been only four months since Lorelei saw her, but she reacted as if Paige were a stranger. After the sunglasses came off and Paige spoke, my daughter recognized her aunt.

Paige was full of news about "the industry." Mom couldn't get enough of her stories about the stars she met, saw at parties, and rubbed elbows with at the studio.

"I had a walk-on in Tim's movie." Paige said. "Got my SAG card."

Mom squealed in delight. She was still fascinated by TV and movie stars.

Paige stayed with us for three days; it just seemed longer, especially after the private chat she insisted on having. On my sister's last night, after Lorelei was settled in bed, Paige corralled me in the living room. We sat on the couch and sipped the green tea she brought from California. I doctored mine with honey and lemon, but Paige drank hers plain.

"Dani, I have to tell you. I should've been born a California girl."

"You sure look like one. So, you really like it out there?"

"Babe, I love it. But I want to talk about you. I'm in such a good place, and I think I can help you. Have you ever heard of est?"

"Est? Are those initials? An acronym?"

"I guess. It stands for Erhard Seminars Training. Amazing stuff. Tim and I both took the training—"

"Training?"

Paige shook her head and her platinum hair shimmered in the light. "It's life-changing. Almost transcendent."

Getting a little impatient, I prodded her. "High praise. What the heck is it?"

"It's sort of like self-awareness training. It's a sixty-hour course, two weekends. About two hundred and fifty people take the instruction together. It starts with the students entering into agreements with the trainers, like you can't talk to the other participants, can't go to the bathroom, or leave the room except on scheduled breaks—"

"Uh, you're kidding. No potty breaks? I'm in the camp of when you gotta go, you gotta go. It sounds stupid. Kind of like a cult."

Paige frowned and huffed. "Open your mind, sis. With all the trauma you've had in your life, you might benefit from the process."

"Air my dirty laundry in front of two hundred and fifty people? No thanks."

Paige hopped up from the couch and gestured dramatically, her arms wide. "You're so closed off. Expand your consciousness and listen for a minute."

I held my hands up in surrender. "All right. I'll listen."

"Consider the self. There are three aspects of self. One is the concept of self. Two is the self as experience. And most important, the self as self."

I burst out laughing. "Tell me you're joking. It's a skit, right? Satire?"

She flounced back to the couch and sat sideways, making intense eye contact. "I think the therapy could help you. When you were only nineteen, you lost John. You said you'd never love another man, then you set out to *prove* it. You married Luke for money and that ended in tragedy. Those two events have affected you in ways you don't know or can't admit. Est helps you come to grips with your experience." She leaned forward and grasped my hand. "They're having the training right here in Chi-town. Let's call and get you signed up."

"Two weekends? Paige, weekends are my time to be with Lorelei and to recuperate after the work week. I just can't see it."

"I get it. Really, I do. At least read *The Book of est* by Luke Rhinehart. The man himself, Werner Erhard, wrote a forward, so he approves. I brought you a copy."

I knew if I argued or made more objections, she'd never let up. "Okay. Thanks, Paige."

My sister glowed with inner happiness at my agreement. Hmm. Now that I thought about it, she did seem a little more centered. Maybe I would read the book, but I wasn't about to waste two weekends for some trendy California fad.

Lorelei adored the baby, whom she dubbed "Dew." We all hoped that name wouldn't stick. Andrew slept in his parents' room, but when he got older, we'd have to rethink our living arrangements. I figured I had at least a year to work out a solution. Trading my unit for a four bedroom in the co-op was a possibility, although there would be the same hassle of moving in any scenario.

In a rare moment of clarity, I was taken aback by this train of thought. Was I unable to envision a different future other than the life I was living? Was I stuck? Would I live with my mother forever? Would I haunt the bars on Rush Street until I needed dentures? As usual, when I began to examine my situation, I immediately shut that down.

My little girl adjusted to having the baby in the house—a little too well. She said, "Lori wanna baby," over and over. There was nothing for me to do but make a trip to Toys R Us. Critical error—I took Lorelei with me. We spent hours searching for the perfect baby. After what seemed like days, we narrowed the choice down to Baby Tenderlove and Baby Brother Tenderlove. After much vacillation, Lorelei turned her little nose up at the boy doll and chose the girl version with blond curls and blue eyes. The doll bore a striking resemblance to her. Would dog-dog take a backseat to the baby doll? No, I was assured, her baby loved dog-dog as much as she did.

Mom was back to full health and energy in a few weeks. Ken returned to work, and the daily routine was reestablished.

My team was successful in landing the Luxe Candy account. I had high hopes for getting the account manager job. My hopes and ego were shattered when Alan received the promotion instead. His own project for snack chips won the day for him. I tried not to be bitter, but it was hard. Now, he was the lead on both accounts, and I had to report to him. I was steamed and decided to speak to Charlotte.

I knocked on her open door and strode right in. Probably made a mistake when I launched at her. "I'd like to transfer to another team, Charlotte."

She rose and came around her desk, eyebrows raised. "Good morning, Dani."

"Is it?" With arms folded across my chest, I planted my feet.

Charlotte sighed. "Come over here and have a seat." We settled on the rose-colored leather tub chairs, facing each other.

My eyes burned, and my throat was dry.

"I assume this is about the manager's position. I want you to know it was a difficult choice. Although I advocated for you strongly, the executive committee voted, and Alan prevailed." She crossed her legs and appraised me.

"Oh." I felt foolish. "Thank you." So small and petty of me to doubt Charlotte. It was childish to ask to move to another team. Had I blown any future chance at promotion with my petulance?

Charlotte's face softened. "Think very carefully, Dani. Think about how it would look to the executive committee if you were unable to work with Alan. My advice to you is to stay where you are and put your best work forward."

I frowned at my lap, then looked her in the eye. "You're right. I love my job, and the company has been good to me. So stupid to let my disappointment cloud my thinking." I stood and forced a smile. "Thanks for hearing me out."

Walking back to my desk, I decided to give it six months, and if things didn't work out, I would move on. I didn't want to leave JWT, but I couldn't understand how Alan had won advancement over me. With J. Walter Thompson's history of promoting women, I must have failed in some way.

I thought about quitting but couldn't live off the balance of my inheritance for long. The taxes, utilities, food, and insurance added up. Soon there would be school expenses for Lorelei. I needed to work. I wanted to work. But a part of me wanted to stay home with my daughter. Finally, I could admit that to myself.

Ever since I reestablished communication with the Nagys during my pregnancy, we corresponded regularly. After Luke's suicide, I feared their reaction, but informed them anyway. Sonia couldn't have been kinder.

Comparing her to Ursula brought on another bout of self-pity and regret. Would I ever stop contrasting everything in my life with how it could have been? How it should have been? Yes, I was mired in the past, and I didn't know how to escape.

Because of the chaos of the move to the co-op, Mom's pregnancy, and Paige relocating to California, I neglected to notify the Nagys of my change of address. When I received an envelope forwarded from the condo, I realized my omission.

I carried the thick envelope up to my room. Sonia shared pictures of her grandson Michael John. Seeing the dark-haired, dark-eyed boy, filled me with sorrow for my loss. Would my child with John have looked like this baby?

All the news from Knoxville was positive. The garage was doing well. Chuck's wife did the books, and he stayed home with the baby. The couple was expecting another child around Christmas. Noah had stopped by and asked about me. He was in his last year of medical school. Sonia added her phone number to the bottom of the letter.

"I want to hear your voice again, *Lánya*," she wrote.

My mind insisted on some introspection, something I avoided. Usually, I concentrated on the very busy present. Working and having a toddler filled my days. Whenever I dwelled on the past, my emotions became unruly and had to be put back in the box—the box of treasures. If I had a bad day, I reached under my bed and dragged out my source of consolation, my pacifier. Less often than a year ago, but at least once a week.

It had been five years since the Nagys moved to Tennessee, almost six since John was killed. My life had had its ups and down in that time. Going off the rails as I did led to the tragedy of Luke. My ambition to succeed in marketing hit a wall, and now I was flailing, looking for direction. When I was thirteen, I had been so certain of what my life would be. For six years, I was close to John's family, then I threw them away. How could it have taken me two years to answer their Christmas cards? Had I forgotten what they meant to me? Sonia, who still called me her daughter, Miklos, with his accepting heart under his gruff exterior, and earnest, hard-working Chuck. I'd been closer to them than my own family. Not wasting another minute, I picked up the phone and dialed. I wanted to hear Sonia's voice too.

She answered after three rings. "Hello?"

Her voice sent chills down my arms. "Sonia, it's Dani."

"*Lánya*, so happy you called. How are you, sweetheart?"

I could hear the smile in her voice. Daughter? No, that had never happened. Sweetheart? No, if she knew my checkered history, she would be appalled.

"I'm doing well, Sonia," I lied.

Our conversation lasted only a few minutes. We exchanged anecdotes about Lorelei, Michael John, and Andrew. She was amazed my mother had a baby at age forty-three. After promising to send pictures of Lorelei, I gave her my phone number and told her the best time to call was in the evening.

Her last bit of news surprised me. "Noah wants to come visit you."

Andrea, my staffer, wouldn't let up on trying to fix me up with her brother. "You won't regret it, Danielle." She rhapsodized about his fine qualities so often and so heartily, I finally gave in. Besides, I was lonely. And horny as hell. Whenever I thought back to that fateful encounter with Daniel, my desire bloomed. It had been over a year since I slept with him. I reminded myself I lived with infrequent, mediocre sex for three years with Luke, but Daniel had reawakened those yearnings. Despite my lust for him, I knew I could never get in touch, not after Luke's suicide. But I still thought about how he made me feel in those stolen minutes.

Once a week, the singles in the office went out for drinks after work. Because of Lorelei, I rarely joined them. After the incident at Mother's, I doubted I would go back to the singles' bars. Besides, the music had changed. We were in a strange musical era: disco was everywhere. I loved to dance, but I always danced solo, freestyle. I couldn't master the twirling and flinging, the fast pace of disco. At twenty-five, I felt old. With a brief flash of insight, I realized I'd become proficient at beating myself up. Should I read Paige's self-help book? Could it help?

I had to wonder why the bars played their siren song for me. Was I that much in need of validation? Did I need the admiration of men to feel good about myself? Whoa, lately I was spending way too much time analyzing my life. That had to stop.

I agreed to meet Andrea's brother Paul for dinner at Eli's Place for Steak. It was a few blocks from the co-op, and if I hated Paul, I could make a quick getaway. Lorelei watched me dress and do my hair and makeup. She sat on the bed with her baby doll, whom she'd named Pookie, and dog-dog. In between her chatter with them, she followed my movements with solemn intensity.

"Mama pretty."

"Why, thank you, Lori."

"Mama go bye-bye?"

"Yes, honey. I'll have Ken or Grandma read you a story tonight. Want to pick out a book?"

I helped her and her family down from the bed, and we walked to her room.

"*Go dog-dog go*," she stated firmly. The choice that wasn't really a choice.

We walked downstairs, and I kissed her goodbye. Mom and Ken sat together in the living room. Andrew was quiet; his evening distress yet to come. Ken picked up Lorelei and settled her on the couch between them with Pookie, dog-dog, and her book.

I grabbed my handbag and a light wrap and hailed a cab.

A tall man in a navy-blue suit was pacing in front of the canopy at Eli's. He looked nervous. I alit from the cab and approached him with a smile.

"Paul?"

He spun and smiled in return. "Danielle, I presume?"

We entered through the revolving door and were soon escorted to a table for two in a softly lit corner of the room. The aroma of sizzling steak made my stomach growl. I hoped he didn't hear.

The young waiter poured water, presented us with menus, and recited a list of specials. Paul ordered a vodka tonic and so did I. One point for him; he hadn't ordered a scotch. I had an aversion to men who drank scotch. Too many bad memories centered on the peaty drink.

"Andrea tells me you've been at J. Walter Thompson for a couple of years. She's thrilled to be on your team."

"And I'm glad to have her. She's bright and focused. I think she'll do well. She tells me you're a patent attorney." I had no idea what a patent attorney did, beyond the obvious. It sounded deadly dull.

"Guilty as charged." He laughed. "Sorry about the law humor. I work for the oldest law firm in Chicago—Fitch, Even, Tabin, and Luedeka. Quite a mouthful, isn't it?"

Our drinks arrived. A welcome distraction.

I studied his face. He was good-looking, with thick dark hair and deep brown eyes. My type. But I wasn't feeling attraction, no zing, no belly flip. Was I dead inside? "Tell me about a typical day in your world."

He jawed away, telling me things I forgot as soon as he uttered the words. I nodded and oohed and aahed at what I figured were the correct places. Then he stopped speaking and put his hand over mine.

I jumped a little but didn't remove my hand. A man's touch, how I missed it. Meeting his eyes, I reconsidered. Paul had to be in his thirties, maybe as much as ten years older than I. Stable, good career, attractive. Why was I turning my nose up at him? Then there was his touch.

"You're not really listening, are you?" Paul's voice held no recrimination and a touch of amusement.

I laughed. "That obvious?"

"Kinda. I'll admit the patent attorney world isn't as sexy as the world of marketing and advertising."

I removed my hand from under his and picked up my drink. "Another topic?"

He nodded, sipped his drink, and set it down.

The waiter came to take our order. We were both carnivores and ordered steaks. Paul asked for a recommendation for a red wine. After the waiter left, we began to speak at the same time. We laughed. I loosened up, and he appeared to relax too.

"What do you do for fun, Paul?"

"Photography. I have a Canon F1 SLR—I mean single lens reflex. Take a lot of landscapes and wildlife photos. I've even set up a rudimentary darkroom."

"Sounds like you're really into it."

"Yeah. I've started to teach my son. He's eight."

"Did Andrea tell you I have a daughter? She's two and a half. Lorelei."

"That's a beautiful name. Unusual."

"It's the prettiest name I ever heard. It suits my little beauty. What's your son's name?"

"Paul. Real original, huh?"

I shrugged. "Your kid, your choice."

The sommelier brought the wine and went through the routine of opening, pouring, and waiting for approval.

I finished my vodka tonic and folded my hands in my lap, telling myself to let the wine breathe and to go easy. Because I rarely drank anymore, the vodka went to my head quickly.

Silence fell. Was I deliberately sabotaging this date? Why hadn't Andrea told me he had a child? Is that why she thought we'd get along? Because we were both single parents?

Our steaks arrived, accompanied by loaded baked potatoes and asparagus spears. What was I thinking? I'd never finish this meal.

While we ate, conversation was minimal, mostly about the food. Paul finished everything on his plate. I asked for a doggie bag.

"You didn't eat much."

I shook my head. "The steak was huge. I'll have enough for another meal tomorrow. It was delicious."

Paul tilted his head. "Here we are talking about the food. We might as well be talking about the weather."

"Yeah. I'm not very scintillating tonight." I didn't know how to end the evening. My history with men was so strange. Six years of devotion to a man who then died in a war. After that, my personal vendetta against men—lethal flirtation-rejection—until I committed the cardinal sin of marrying a man I didn't love. How do I interact with a sincere, kind man who was interested in me? I felt like a fool.

Paul leaned forward. "I'd like to see you again, Danielle, but I'm not sure you feel the same." He impressed me with his candor. Not a game player.

I stammered. "I-I-I don't know how I feel."

"Do I have a chance?"

I wrung the life out of my cloth napkin. Why was I having such a hard time? I shrugged and glanced away. "Sure. We could go on another date," I said, not certain if I meant it.

Paul exhaled and leaned back in his chair. "Great! Hey, I have an idea. How about we take the kids to the zoo?"

That suggestion made me think he wanted a mother for his child. "Is Paul's mother in the picture?"

His eyes widened, and he drew in a breath. "Didn't Andrea tell you? My wife died two years ago."

I gasped. "No, she didn't. I'm so sorry. Sure stepped in it."

Paul shook his head. "*Andrea* stepped in it. Apparently, she told me all about you but neglected to tell you about me."

"So, you know about my...Luke?" I gulped.

"I know you're a widow."

"Yes, I am." When I saw Andrea next week, I'd have some questions for her. In the meantime, there was no need to give Paul details about the circumstances of Luke's death. Then I realized Andrea had been hired after the fact, and she missed the drama at the office. After a moment, I almost laughed at my naiveté. Such a juicy story was fine fodder for office gossip, and I guessed all the staff at JWT knew about the suicide, including Andrea.

Paul suggested coffee, and I agreed. We found some common ground after all, planning our outing to the Lincoln Park Zoo on Sunday. Lorelei would be thrilled.

After he paid the check, he hailed me a cab. He opened the door and leaned in for a kiss. Nice, but it didn't have the effect I desired.

I made the mistake of telling Lorelei about our trip to the zoo a day in advance. "When we going zoo?" she asked every five minutes or so. By the time Sunday arrived, she had a pile of toys and books in her room that had to "go zoo," probably half her belongings. I didn't think I'd be able to convince her to leave her books and stuffed animals at home. While I found her enthusiasm charming, I worried we'd never be ready when Paul and his son arrived to pick us up. Sure enough, the bell rang while I was still dressing.

Lorelei, arms full of toys and books, rushed out of her room calling, "Ready!" Ken met her on the stairs and corralled her and her things. I surveyed myself in the mirror, wondering if ivory pants were a wise choice for a day with children. Too late now. At least my patterned blouse should hide stains. I brushed my hair and left the bathroom. Ken was talking softly to Lorelei, convincing her to leave the bulk of her toys at home. I had to admire the way he handled her. He would need those skills with Andrew soon enough.

"Dani, I let Paul and his little boy in. He seems like a nice guy. The boy looks just like him. I said you'd be down in a minute or two."

"Thanks, Ken. Can you help Lorelei downstairs? I have to grab a few things." In reality, my nerves needed settling. Closing the door to the bathroom behind me, I stared at myself in the mirror. Apparently, vamping my way through Chicago's bars, never at a loss for banter came naturally, but when faced with a normal date or family outing, I dissolved into a pile of goo. I placed a cold washcloth on the back of my neck. A few minutes later, I descended the stairs. Mom and Ken chatted with Paul and his son. My mother turned to me with a hope-filled face, and I wondered if she pitied me.

Young Paul did look like his father. He was tall for his age and well-mannered. I thought I saw sadness in his eyes. What must it be like to lose your mother at age six? Lorelei was fascinated by the "big boy" and enthusiastically introduced him to Pookie and dog-dog. She was adamant her baby and dog-dog were going to the zoo. There was no point in arguing. I tucked my tiny purse in the voluminous diaper bag and helped Paul fold the stroller so we could stow it in the trunk of his Cadillac. The logistics finally taken care of, we headed to Lincoln Park.

Lorelei wanted to see the dogs, and I explained the zoo didn't have them. Young Paul was kind to my daughter and patiently told her about each exhibit. The click and whir of Paul's camera provided the backdrop to our tour. He carried a shoulder bag and had to stop several times to change rolls of film or lenses. Quite the production, but it was apparent he knew what he was doing.

After several stops to let Lorelei out of the stroller, I gave up and let her walk. She was at the age where she resisted the constraint. Because the big boy was on foot, she wanted to be as well.

As I pushed the stroller with Pookie, dog-dog, and the diaper bag behind the two children, Paul and I had time to chat.

"I didn't know how Paul would react to such a little girl. He has cousins, but they're all older."

"He's wonderful with her. Tolerant. Kind. Does he get that from you?"

Paul shrugged. "I don't know. He and I are close since his mother died. But she was a soft-spoken, gentle woman."

Why did I ask him that leading question? Conversation about dead spouses wasn't a recommended dating strategy, I chided myself.

"Looks like Paul has spotted the popcorn concession. Better get my wallet out."

I laughed. "You're right. We better catch up."

The kids enjoyed the Children's Zoo and the Farm at the Zoo. Lorelei said, "Like Ol' MacDonald." She sang "E I E I O" to the point of embarrassment.

We ate lunch at Cafe Brauer. I used the restroom to change Lorelei's diaper, wishing some sort of table were available. So awkward. The rigors of potty-training were ahead and, at times like this, I couldn't wait.

The walking and fresh air had a calming effect on Lorelei. Two hours after lunch, her eyelids started drooping, and she willingly sat in the stroller. Time to leave.

"Paul, I think we better head home."

"Sure. It was a wonderful day, wasn't it, big guy?" Paul asked his son with a grin.

Young Paul nodded solemnly. "I liked the polar bear best. Lorelei liked everything."

After we unloaded our gear, the two Pauls walked us to the door. A kiss didn't seem appropriate in front of the children, so we just said goodbye.

"I'll call you." Paul waved as he retreated backward down the walkway. He put his arm around his son's shoulder as they left.

I sighed. He was a good man, but was he for me?

My job lost its luster. I had to drag myself to the office each day. Gone were the days when I was excited and exhilarated to walk through the doors of JWT. I even doubted my future in the marketing and advertising field. Perhaps I should have become an accountant. It would be boring, but at least I wouldn't be subject to the ups and downs of my current position.

I asked Andrea to lunch. She accepted as if I'd offered her a winning lottery ticket. I was getting so jaded I found her endless enthusiasm annoying. My ulterior motive was to find out if Paul had talked with her about leaving out the details of his history when she fixed us up, or if he had talked about me at all.

After ordering the soup and salad, she leaned forward in her seat. "Thanks for asking me to lunch!"

Take it down a notch, girl. "Have you spoken to Paul recently?"

Her face fell. "Oh, is that why you invited me?"

Now I was irked. "No, Andrea. I invited you because we're colleagues and friends," I lied.

"Oh, cool!" She glanced around to see if other JWT interns were in the room.

The waitress returned with our tomato bisque and chef salads. Andrea spiked the greens with her fork and froze.

"Oh my God, Charlotte just walked in."

"I guess she's hungry. It happens." My flat tone got her attention.

"Ha! Of course." She smiled and revealed a big piece of lettuce stuck between her teeth.

I couldn't take her anywhere. Showing my teeth, I gestured at my mouth. She picked up on my message and clamped her lips. Good Lord, I was regretting my invitation and the remark about being friends. She acted as if she were still in high school. I picked up my spoon and returned to the soup, deciding this ploy to get information about Paul was a failure. Might as well eat.

Andrea wiped her mouth with her napkin, drank some water, and then flashed her teeth. "Gone?"

I nodded and hurriedly finished my meal. The waitress brought the check, and I paid. As I was getting up, Andrea blurted, "Paul was so pissed I didn't tell you he was a widower and had a kid. Are you mad too?"

"No. But it would have been nice to know in advance." I shrugged, figuring Paul wouldn't confide in his younger sister about our dates.

"Thanks for lunch, Danielle. I think Paul really likes you."

"Great." I didn't want to say more. We took the elevator back to our office and went our separate ways.

I wondered why I hadn't heard from Paul. Not certain of my feelings, I made a pro and con chart about him. Comparing the positives and negatives could help clear things up, but would it even matter if he never called again?

Positives: Tall, decent job, good-looking, kind, familiar with children. Negatives: Hmm. What *were* the negatives? Then I pictured Paul in a cardigan, sitting beside the fire, pipe in hand, feet on an ottoman, while I begged him to go out dancing.

I reached a détente with Alan. Since his promotion, he was a lot easier to work with, probably because he didn't have to follow a woman's lead. But that was his problem and would no doubt bite him in the ass someday. Taking Charlotte's advice, I worked hard, brainstorming new packaging ideas for the Luxe candy account. Alan expressed appreciation for my efforts and magnanimously gave me credit. My attitude did a one-eighty.

Two weeks after our zoo excursion, Paul called. I'd given up on hearing from him.

"Danielle, I've got the pictures from the zoo. When can we get together so I can show you?"

Was that why he hadn't called? Waiting on photos? I had to admit, my ego was a bit bruised.

"What sort of get-together do you have in mind?" I lobbed the ball into his court. After my two-week wait, I wasn't going to make things easy for him. Did he want another family outing, or was he interested in me romantically? My female intuition had deserted me. I wasn't about to fall all over him. And still, I hadn't a clue whether we had chemistry.

"How about lunch on Saturday?"

Lunch? "Tell me more."

"I make a mean chile con carne, and with the cold front we're supposed to get, I thought it sounded good."

"Your place? What about your son?"

"He'll be here. Bring Lorelei if you'd like."

That cleared things up. "Thanks for the invitation, but I have plans." I hung up. Abrupt? So what, I just didn't care. No romance in the cards for me. Well, there were always the bars—even though I'd sworn off Rush Street.

I'd won the love lottery at age thirteen. Then John died, and my luck ran out.

That fall I returned to the bars—despite my vow and the disco music—and resumed collecting scalps in my war against men. I started jogging and enrolled in a yoga class. I'd never been more fit. Those activities filled the time outside of work and raising Lorelei. If I stopped for a minute, the loneliness and horniness overcame me.

How was I able to rationalize my behavior?

Denial.

As Christmas approached, Mom made a startling suggestion at dinner one night. She wanted to invite the entire family for the holiday, including Dad and Ginger. I almost choked on the surprisingly moist meatloaf. What on earth? Did she want to show off her husband and her baby, let Dad know she was still sexually active?

"Are you sure, Mom? When's the last time anyone besides Joe has talked to Dad?" I glanced at Ken to see his reaction.

"I think that's a great idea, honey." Ken patted Mom's hand.

Mom turned to me with a slight frown. "We talk from time to time. About the boys. And you girls."

I hoped Dad and Ginger wouldn't come. But they did.

Garlands and red ribbons decked the halls of the co-op. Lorelei, fascinated by the Nativity scene, lay on her belly talking to the ceramic figures. Pookie and dog-dog loved baby Jesus, she assured me. The last time I was in a church was her christening. Mom and Ken attended services every Sunday at nearby Immaculate Conception. They suggested Lorelei attend with them. I was ambivalent, as I was about everything these days, so I let Lorelei decide. My little girl loved getting dressed up, and she readily agreed to accompany them. I felt a twinge of regret allowing Lorelei to get indoctrinated, but that quiet hour-and-a-half on Sunday morning was blissful.

Ken toiled all day roasting a stuffed turkey and a standing rib roast. The aroma of garlic-crusted beef competed with roasted bird. Mom, Ken, and I had prepared the side dishes as much as possible in advance, and the double ovens were in constant use.

When the bell rang, I hurried to the door. My brothers and their girls entered, shaking off the bitter cold. Lorelei ran to the entry hall, then stopped short in front of the quartet, suddenly shy. Moving my daughter back from the frigid air, I called to Mom. "Can you come get Lori? Traffic jam in the hallway."

Mom rushed in and helped with the heavy coats and scarves, then directed Lorelei back to the kitchen.

"Wait!" Clare called. Pulling off her gloves, she held out her left hand. "We're engaged!" With her bright smile and rosy cheeks, she radiated happiness.

Mom grasped Clare's hand and inspected the tiny diamond, then hugged her. "I'm so happy for you, dear."

"What about me?" Phil asked. He grabbed Mom in a bear hug and lifted her off her feet. "I've got some news to share, but I'm waiting until Dad gets here."

Dressed alike in Bob Seger t-shirts and black jeans, Joe and Joanie related the news their band had cut a demo single, and it was getting a little airplay. Joe said, "We've been playing a few gigs around town. Last week, we opened for Buddy Guy at Kingston Mines."

"Isn't that a blues club?" I asked.

"It is. But we've been getting into the blues," Joanie said.

"Yeah, Joanie's voice was made for the blues. One of the guitarists in the house band called it 'a sultry contralto.'" Joe pushed his long hair back and bumped hips with Joanie.

"I'm proud of you two." Mom beamed at them. "You're going after your dream."

Clutching his skinny waist, Joe said, "Man, the food smells incredible. I'm starving!"

"Ken can use a few extra hands in the kitchen," Mom said. "Come on, Clare and Joanie." The three of them left to help with the last-minute preparations.

This year, the family had decided to bring gifts only for the children. I turned to my brothers. "Guys, you can put the kids' gifts under the tree in the living room. Dad and Paige should be here soon. At least I hope so. I'm going to set the table. Help yourselves to the bar. And let everyone in when they get here, will you?"

Lorelei tiptoed into the living room. "Presents? From Santa?"

"Why don't you ask Phil and Joe to read you a story?"

"Go, dog-dog, go. Okay?"

My brothers laughed. "Sure, Lori. Bring me your book," Phil said.

Joe plopped himself on the couch and patted the cushion beside him. "Over here, kiddo."

I took the opportunity to head to the dining room. As I set the table for eleven, my spirits plummeted. Mom, Paige, Phil, Joe, and Dad were all paired. I had no one. Sure, I had my child and my family, but there was no romance, no lover. Tears filled my eyes, and the pity party commenced. Letting the silverware fall to the table with a clatter, I covered my face with my hands and thundered upstairs to my room. I had an overwhelming urge to smell John's t-shirt, to be transported back in time to the only man I had ever loved. And the only man who had ever loved me. Was I tainted somehow and no longer worthy of a man's love? Faintly ashamed, I felt like a lovelorn teenager as I inhaled the Jade East.

Something had to change for me. I needed to live in the present. The ghost of Christmas past lurked just out of my vision—his face becoming less distinct in my memory. I reached into the box of treasures and found the last picture of him—the one Paige took on John's leave before deployment. "There you are, my love."

"Dani?" Mom knocked on my door. Shoving the picture back in the box, I kicked it under the bed. "C-come in."

"What's wrong? What's that yellow rag you're holding?" She sniffed the air. "And what's that smell? Do you have a new cologne? I think you put on too much."

I broke down and told her about my ritual. She sat beside me on the bed, held me, and let me cry. "Oh, honey. I never knew. I wish you'd confided in me. John is gone. Gone! You have to move on."

I blubbered. "How? Look at how I screwed up with Luke! I married a man I didn't love, and now I'll have guilt for the rest of my life at...how he, how it ended."

She gripped my shoulders and turned me to face her. "Maybe you could try therapy. What do you think?"

I got up and grabbed a box of tissue from my bathroom and remained standing. "No. Absolutely not. I will not sit on a couch and whine to a shrink."

"Honey, it's not whining. Just think about it." She stood and walked to the door, then turned to me with another thought. "Come to church with us. They have a young people's group."

Avoiding an answer, I sniffled and wiped my eyes. "Let me fix my makeup. I need to finish setting the table."

"Already done. Paige and Tim finally got here. Your dad and Ginger too. Come down when you're ready. We're putting the side dishes out, and we'll eat in a few."

"Okay." She left, and I wondered if I would ever be ready to face my family. It was hard enough to face myself.

When I entered the living room, I stopped short. Who was that in the strawberry-blond Afro? Paige turned to face me, and I had to admit, she brought it off. Tim and Paige's deep suntans contrasted with the winter pallor of the rest of us. Paige's tan clashed with her reddish hair, a surprising lapse of fashion sense. She squealed and hugged me until I was breathless.

Envisioning Ginger, the peroxide-blonde with dark roots, in my mind, I stared at the brunette sitting next to Dad. Ginger had changed. She wore a subdued sweater set that would have looked appropriate on a librarian. And sensible shoes. Skirt below the knees. Dad looked well. His hair now silver, he was coming up on twenty years with the Chicago police and planned to retire next year. An ex-cop had offered him a job at his security firm. He held Andrew on one knee and Lorelei on the other. He beamed at the little ones.

Mom hustled into the room. "Dinner is served." She whisked Andrew from Dad's lap. "Dew needs a nap."

"Mom, you promised never to call him that!" I didn't want Andrew to be saddled with that silly name.

As we walked into the dining room, I held Lorelei's hand. She pulled away and moved her booster seat to a chair between Paige and Joanie. I was a teeny bit jealous. Lorelei seemed to be enamored both with Paige's red hair and the sleek black curtain falling down Joanie's back. She touched her own yellow curls and said, "Pretty hair," as her gaze alternated between the two women.

Ken carried in the turkey and Mom brought in the rib roast. The side dishes crowded on the long table, filling the space. I should have had a buffet. Plates were passed and, in assembly-line fashion, portions of mashed potatoes, stuffing, sweet potatoes, broccoli, green bean casserole, and cranberries were laded. Mom had thoughtfully prepared three gravy boats with turkey gravy and two of beef au jus.

I usually sat next to Lorelei to help her, but Paige cut her food into bite-sized pieces.

"More juice, please!" Lorelei held up her empty sippy cup. Joanie leapt to her feet to fill it for her.

I relaxed. The meal was perfect. Ginger complimented Ken. "I've never had such a delicious meal, Ken. And Ellen, thank you for the invitation."

Mom smiled. "We're glad to have you. More wine?"

I turned to Phil. "You said you had some news you were saving. Spill."

"Dad, everybody, I got called to go to spring training with the White Sox in Sarasota."

My dad threw down his napkin, jumped to his feet, and rounded the table to clap Phil on the shoulder. "I knew you'd make it, son. By God, I'm so proud of you!"

Phil ducked his head. "Doesn't mean I'll make the bigs. More likely their farm team."

Returning to his seat, Dad said, "Don't sell yourself short."

When we were kids, there was no escape from baseball in our house—until the divorce.

Looking around at the happy faces at the table, I thought about forgiveness and redemption. My shattered family, gathered in harmony, made me take stock. If Mom could forgive Dad, could I forgive myself?

Baby Andrew slept through dinner. Mom wisely got him up for present opening, hoping he would sleep through the night. He'd been doing better lately. I was glad I didn't hear him during his nocturnal wailing, but I often saw a bleary-eyed Ken at breakfast after a night of broken sleep.

In keeping with the spirit of the season, Mom and I had taken Lorelei shopping for presents for all our guests—a good lesson in giving. We shopped at Woolworths. While Lorelei wanted to select all the gifts from the toy section, we convinced her to look in the clothing and toiletry departments for her adult relatives.

The men all received ties. Lorelei chose bubble bath for Paige, Ginger, Clare, and Joanie. My little girl surprised me by wanting to buy her baby uncle a Snoopy toy. "Baby Andy wanna dog-dog." On our way to the checkout, she realized she hadn't bought anything for her grandma or me. We grabbed two more bubble baths, or we wouldn't have been able to leave the store.

After checking out, she asked, "Where is Lori's present?"

Putting a happy note in my voice to cushion my words, I said, "Honey, people don't buy presents for themselves."

She didn't agree. Her lip trembled, and a tear fell.

"When we get home, you can have a cookie. How about that?" I smiled at my sweet girl.

Her tears stopped. "Okay, Mama."

As I watched my extended family enjoying Lorelei opening her gifts, I thought about future Christmases. What was in the cards? Would I ever find a man to exorcise my ghosts?

Chapter Twelve

NOAH 1978

After my Christmas of self-pity, I threw myself into work, determined to be the best copywriter J. Walter Thompson had ever seen. I would concentrate on my career and my daughter and forget about romance. Love wasn't in my future. Probably cosmic payback for Luke and Daniel.

I swallowed my pride and accepted my role in Alan's group. An undeclared truce made the situation palatable—that is, if I didn't think too hard.

One afternoon in March, Alan appeared at my workspace. I looked up from the scribbles on my writing pad, a few discarded ideas for a new campaign for an old face soap.

"Come to my office and let me see what you've got," he ordered.

Valiantly maintaining a pleasant look on my face, I answered, "Sure, be right there."

He turned and stalked away.

I had nothing. Not a decent phrase, not a decent word. Just couldn't produce anything fresh. Trudging to his office, I realized I used that very soap. Why didn't I use my personal experience?

Alan removed his feet from the windowsill where he'd been watching boat traffic on the Chicago River. Not only had he won the manager job over me, but he also snagged a premier river-view office. He swiveled his leather armchair around to face me.

"Whatcha got?"

I lifted my lips, but they failed to stay in a smile. "I don't know if you know this, but I use this soap personally."

"How would I know what soap you use?" His scathing tone grated, but I kept my cool.

I summoned a chuckle. "Oh, ha, you're right. I meant my own experience is useful in creating copy."

"So, whatcha got?" He put his hands behind his head and spun his chair to face the window. Insufferable.

"Clean you can feel."

"Okay. What else?" He turned his chair back to face me.

"Quality and purity for your precious skin. Or the skin you're in."

"Acceptable. Like the second one better. Anything else?"

I picked up my pad and stood. "I'm working on a few more ideas. Should have them by Friday."

"Thursday."

"Sure thing." I hustled out of his august presence and went to lunch.

That spring I ran through two bottles of Jade East. John's 442 t-shirt had faded from the color of a school bus to the paleness of a lemon chiffon cake. I resisted the idea of returning to the single's bars. Because of the vicious cold and snow last winter, I didn't make the effort to trek outdoors to have a night out. How many months had it been since I ventured to those dark clubs? The kick I got from those meaningless flirtations didn't appeal any longer. And after all, I was the mother of a three-year-old.

In May, Lorelei and I were looking through the Sears catalog, perusing the toy section from last Christmas. It was one of our favorite pastimes after dinner. Mom and Ken tucked Andrew in his stroller and left for an evening walk. Andy, as he was called by everyone, including Lorelei, had grown out of his wakefulness at night and now slept through. He was able to stand, and Mom thought he'd be walking before his first birthday, which was coming soon.

Lorelei was determined to find him a present. She pointed to a picture of a miniature cowboy. The six-gun and holster my daughter selected weren't the ideal first birthday gift.

"I bet Andy would like to be a cowboy, but not until he's older."

The phone rang. I hopped to my feet and picked up the living room extension.

"Danielle?" A male voice with a hint of a Tennessee drawl.

"Yes?" I shivered at the sound of the voice. The memory of another such voice swept over me. Familiar—yet different.

"It's Noah."

My voice rose. "Noah? From Tennessee?" Sonia told me he often talked about me, but I never thought we'd connect. Did I want it to happen? What would John think?

A low laugh. "One and the same. Do you know many Noahs?"

"Actually, I don't know you, even though I used to feel like I did."

"Is that right?"

"How are you? Sonia told me you're in medical school."

"Finished last month, as a matter of fact. Waitin' on my residency assignment." His voice made me think he was smiling.

"You don't get to pick where you go?"

"No, ma'am. Uncle Sam keeps that decision for his ownself. I'll go where I'm sent, and I'll like it." He chuckled. "That's a little army humor."

Charmed by his manner and his drawl, I fiddled with my hair. "I'm glad you're able to find humor in the army."

"I find humor everywhere, darlin.' Just the way I am."

Silence. I couldn't think of a thing to say. Would it be rude to ask him why he called? My curiosity was piqued.

"The reason I called—"

Lorelei stood and dragged the thick catalog to where I was standing. "Truck. Get a truck!" she shouted.

"Lorelei, give me a minute..."

"What's that about a truck? Is that your little girl?"

"Yes, sorry. We're trying to pick out a birthday present for her uncle."

"A truck is quite the present. Is your daughter independently wealthy?"

I laughed. "Her uncle is a one-year-old baby. Long story. It's a toy truck, although it does have all the bells and whistles."

"Well, you tell Lorelei a truck is a fine present."

My daughter tugged at my slacks. "Hungry. Need a snack, Mama." She knew when Mama was distracted and didn't like it.

"Noah, Lori's hungry." For some reason, I didn't want to ask him to call back later, needed to keep the connection going. "Would you give me a minute to get her a snack and some juice? Be right back."

"Sure thing."

Putting the phone down, I rushed to the kitchen, my daughter at my heels. Why was I beside myself with excitement? What was going on? I poured juice and dabbed peanut butter on crackers. Lorelei followed me back to the living room, and she sat at my feet with her plate and cup. After taking a deep, calming breath, I picked up the receiver.

"Still there?"

"Sure am. Got all the patience in the world. Been in the army for seven years and lookin' at four more."

"More army humor?"

"Yes, ma'am."

Certain he could hear the smile in my voice, I said, "You were going to tell me why you called."

"Yes, I was."

"Very funny. I'm on tenterhooks. Don't keep me waiting any longer."

"I'm in town at a medical conference and wondered if you'd like to go to dinner."

Almost before he stopped speaking, "Yes," popped out of my mouth.

"Great. Wow. How 'bout tomorrow night? Can I come by at seven to pick you up?"

Work night. I'll leave early. "Sounds great!" I was glad he couldn't see me through the phone cord, with my cheeks stretched from a huge grin.

"I don't have your address."

I gave it to him. After I hung up, I shimmied, sort of like a celebration dance.

Lorelei tugged at my pants leg and asked, "Mama happy?"

I was. "Mama's got a date!"

"Oh," she said wisely. "Truck?"

I gave in and called Sears, enunciating each number and letter of the item listing to the clerk. When the order came in, I'd pick it up at the Sears on State on my lunch hour.

I hadn't dressed with such care since my modeling days. No, I wasn't wearing a sweet frothy confection of tulle and lace. I'd gone to Bonwit's at lunch and picked out a stunning black sheath with spaghetti straps. So what if it was a little daring? I felt daring.

Mom brought Lorelei to my room as I was putting the finishing touches on my look. "You're glowing. I haven't seen you excited like this—in forever."

"I know." A little arrow of pain shot through me at the thought. Forever never happened.

"Let me put your hair up." Channeling Audrey Hepburn, Mom fashioned my hair in an updo. She stepped back and appraised me. "I'd say Holly Golightly but without the call girl connotation."

"No kidding? Thanks!"

Before I could stop her, Lorelei grabbed my lipstick and started applying it to her face. Without the benefit of a mirror, she painted herself bright red from her eyebrows to her chin.

I gently pried the nearly empty tube of Revlon "Playing with Fire" from her hand. "Can you get her cleaned up? Noah will be here any minute, and I'd like him to meet her."

"Sure thing. Come here, little glamour girl. Let's go to my room and get your lips back where they belong."

As I spritzed some Opium on my wrists and the back of my neck, the doorbell rang. Male voices carried up the stairs; it sounded like Ken answered the door. I froze, then smiled at myself in the mirror. Lucky thing I did, I had lipstick on my teeth—like a clown. I repaired the damage and slipped into my favorite pair of black heels by Charles Jourdan. Although the master designer had died, his shoes lived on.

More than a little nervous, I tucked my evening bag under my arm and pranced down the stairs. I stopped on the landing, hyperventilating. I'd never even seen a picture of Noah. What if his looks repelled me? My yoga teacher's voice whispered to me, "Visualize your breath. Breathe from the soles of your feet. Take slow, deep breaths." I did so. My pulse was throbbing in my neck. I could feel my heart beating. Worked up like a teenager. A teenager. It was true; I hadn't felt this level of hyperawareness and anticipation since those days.

I continued down to the living room at a more sedate pace. Mom and Ken edged past me, discreetly leaving the three of us. Mom mouthed, "I like him." Ken gave me a subtle thumbs-up.

My first glimpse of Noah was in profile. He was kneeling beside Lorelei, admiring dog-dog and Pookie. He glanced up and saw me. A dazzling smile. Sandy hair, short on the sides, but longer on top. Was he tall?

He stood, and I moved forward to greet him.

In my three-inch heels, we were eye to eye, so Noah had to be at least six feet. When our eyes met, I felt like I knew him, and we were old friends. His direct gaze, with his eyes crinkled in the corners, captivated me. Windows of the soul, indeed. I couldn't determine his eye color. Chameleon-like, they appeared green at first, then gray, then hazel. Yes, I stared. My mouth dried, and my composure crumbled.

I held out my hand, and he stepped back.

"Handshake?" He came close and hugged me as if we were long-lost friends.

So many things flashed through my mind—images of rolling hills, helicopters, jungle, hospitals, a flag-draped casket, a lopsided smile, and Noah's amazing eyes. Tears threatened. I pulled away but kept hold of his hand for a moment. Speechless.

Noah's eyes widened. "Did I overstep?"

I heard, "Did Ah overstep?" The sound of his voice transported me, but it wasn't only the memory of John. I couldn't deny the attraction. Ever since Sonia had told me about Noah's desire to meet me, the idea must have been floating in the inner recesses of my mind. Now my imagination fired. I counseled myself to slow down, way down.

I glanced away. "No."

He moved so he could find my gaze. Reaching out his hand, he tilted my chin. "Danielle?"

Lorelei broke the spell. "Noah? Noah?" She came to my side.

Noah and I cracked up, and the tension dissipated. "Yes, Miss Lorelei?"

"Mama going out? Can I come? Me too?"

Noah said, "Not tonight. You need to take care of Pookie and dog-dog."

Lorelei solemnly nodded, clutching the toys to her chest.

Mom and Ken must have been hovering in the hall. They entered the living room. "Lori, let's go pick out a book to read to Pookie," Mom said.

I bent to kiss my daughter goodnight. "See you in the morning, princess."

Mom took Lorelei's hand. Ken shook hands with Noah. "Nice to meet you."

As she was ushered from the room, Lorelei looked back. Dog-dog waved at us.

"Your little girl *is* a princess. Nice family. I like your parents."

"Oh, Ken isn't my father. I'll fill you in at the restaurant."

"I've made reservations at Gene and Georgetti. The local fellas at the conference recommended it. That all right?"

"Perfect." My composure hadn't quite returned.

As we walked to the door, Noah put his hand low on my back. It felt wonderful.

"I'm remiss in not telling you how lovely you look, like you stepped out of a Hollywood movie."

"Flatterer." But inside, I soared.

We snared a cab right away and on the ride to the restaurant, a Chicago icon, I pointed out some of the sights.

"I feel like a rube lookin' at all the tall buildings. This city is massive."

"Where'd you go to medical school?"

"Fort Sam."

"Where's that?"

"Pardon me. Fort Sam Houston in San Antonio, Texas. We have a few tall buildings, but nothin' like y'all have. But I spent some time at other army hospitals; right now, I'm at the Eisenhower in Augusta, Georgia. If I had my druthers, that's where I'd choose for my residency. It's not too far from home."

"Texas. Georgia. I've never been."

Eyebrows raised, he turned to me. "Really? We'll have to fix that." He reached for my hand. "That is, if you're so inclined."

I smiled, relishing the warmth of his hand, relishing him. "I'm inclined."

Things couldn't have been going smoother. Already we were easy with each other. I first heard his name way back in 1965, from John's lips. He thought of Noah as his brother. I remembered how John bragged about Noah's intelligence and his ambition to be a doctor, even as a kid. After Noah's dad died in Korea, he and his mom moved in with his aunt and her veterinarian husband. They lived on acreage—just down the road from John's family—where his uncle had his practice and bred Border Terriers. As kids, John and Noah had spent a lot of time playing with the puppies.

The cabbie pulled up to the restaurant. Noah paid the tab and opened the door. He extended his hand to assist me out of the seat. The L clattered overhead.

"I don't know how you city folk live with that racket."

I shrugged. "When you've been raised here, you adapt."

Noah guided me to the entry. The aroma of broiling meat overcame us.

"Whoo-hee, that smells great!" Noah grinned.

We moved across the deep red carpeting to our table. The white-garbed waiter brought menus, water, and a wine list.

I compared the way I felt at my last steak dinner with Paul to how I felt with Noah. No comparison. With Paul there had been no spark, with Noah, I was afraid our spark might ignite a fire right in the restaurant.

Noah ordered the t-bone for two, medium rare. I hoped he was hungry.

"I'd like a nice Italian red. What do you recommend?" Noah asked. At the waiter's summons, the sommelier rushed to the table.

"Ah. The Il Poggiono Brunello di Montalcino 1975. *Magnifico!*" The steward kissed his fingertips.

"You've convinced me."

The sommelier returned with the bottle and went through his routine. Noah and I smiled and gazed at each other. He took my hand and caressed it. Could he see me shiver? We let the wine breathe as suggested. I had to remember to breathe myself.

Alarmed at the tingling his touch caused, I withdrew my hand and sipped some water. "Tell me about growing up in Knoxville."

Noah offered me the basket of bread. I demurred, and he helped himself. "What do you want to know?"

"Start with your childhood. John told me some things, but I'd like to hear it from your lips." He had nice lips.

"My dad died when I was two. I don't remember him at all. The Korean War." The corners of his mouth turned down. He glanced at me and tossed his bread onto his plate.

"Not knowing your dad must have been hard."

"Mr. Nagy and my Aunt Darlene's husband Terence were my surrogate fathers. Between them, I got a fine education about all things male." He smiled faintly as he gazed at me. "John and I were inseparable, that is until the Nagys moved to Chicago. I guess there was some sort of falling out with Miklos and his brother at the garage. But that's history now. They're partners again."

"Sonia writes to me with their news. I've kept up." Boldly, I touched his hand. "I want to hear about you."

Our salads arrived. The waiter bowed and left. I took a sip of the wine. "Hmm, the wine is delicious."

He picked up his glass in a toast. "To the girl I admired in pictures. You're even more beautiful in person."

I gulped. Pictures? Then I realized John must have shown him my photograph. "My! I don't know what to say." And I didn't.

With a rueful grin, Noah said, "I have a confession to make."

My heart stopped beating. I knew he was too good to be true. Thinking back to the cad Robert and his confession, I girded myself to hear about his wife, fiancé, or girlfriend. I took a healthy swallow of wine, then rasped, "Confession?"

His eyes widened. "You look all stove up. It's nothing bad. At least, I hope you won't think ill of me."

Making my face blank, I shrugged, but inside I was anything but sanguine.

His brow furrowed in earnestness. "I'm a little embarrassed, but here it is." After a beat, he continued, "I've kept a picture of you with me since Nam."

I gasped.

"John had so many pictures of you. After he was killed, I made sure all his belongings were packed up and sent to the Nagys, except for that one photograph." He looked down but kept talking, finishing his declaration. "Your picture hung on my wall all through college and med school. Having a part of you got me through."

"Oh." Chills tingled my bare arms.

He met my gaze. "Will you forgive me?"

I sat back and wrung the life from the red cloth napkin in my lap. After a few moments, I blurted. "Forgive?" In my ears, my voice was high and tight, as if my vocal cords were frozen. "There's nothing to forgive. I'm flattered."

I thought back to the cards and letters Sonia had sent me over the last few years. Taken together, her words provided more than a slight clue about Noah's interest in me. It should have penetrated my thick skull. Why hadn't I seen it? It might have saved me a few years of loneliness. Yes, I was there already. Noah was the cure I'd been seeking. I knew it in my bones—and in my heart. At last, for the first time since August 14, 1971, I felt something beyond lust for a man. I felt my heart open.

Noah exhaled, wiped his brow, and laughed. "You can't know how relieved I am. I was sweatin' it, let me tell you."

I twisted my lips in amusement. "All for nothing. Now eat your salad. It looks great."

He picked up his fork and speared some lettuce. "Yes, ma'am."

We heard and smelled the t-bone before it arrived. The waiter placed the sizzling platter and two plates on the table.

"Just a small portion for me."

"As you wish." The waiter was courtly.

Noah beamed. "I'll take the rest!"

While we ate the delicious meat, Noah told me a little more about his Knoxville childhood. He had always been a good student, excelling in math and science. Because of his love for animals, he considered becoming a veterinarian, but ultimately decided to treat people.

"My residency will be in Pediatrics."

"You're a pediatrician? No wonder you were so at ease with Lorelei." I dabbed my lips with my napkin. "This meal was fantastic. Thank you."

"Hang on a minute. Don't tell me the evening is ending already." His mouth drooped.

"No! I just wanted to say thanks. Should we get coffee?"

"Decaf for me. Still have tomorrow morning at the conference."

Our attentive waiter whisked away the plates and brought the coffee and a dessert menu.

"Nothing for me." Since I had my daughter, my waist no longer measured twenty-three inches, but I still watched what I ate.

Noah pursed his lips. "Will you have a bite of my tiramisu?"

I smiled. "One bite." Although I did think about nibbling his lip. Maybe later.

Noah explained the commitment he'd made to the army in return for a debt-free medical education. He owed them four years at an Army hospital.

"Will you spend all four years at the same place?"

"Most likely, but things could change. I could get deployed, although we aren't in a shootin' war right now."

"War..." My entire body shuddered. My eyes burned.

Noah scooted his chair close and encircled me with his arm. I sank into his shoulder. Words weren't necessary. After a minute, I straightened.

"You know, Dani, I miss him too. Guess I always will."

How selfish of me not to realize Noah also lost his best friend. "I'd better get home. Work in the morning."

"I don't want the night to end." He spoke those words slowly and emphatically.

Noah wasn't a game player. I liked that about him. I liked a lot of things about him. Could it be this easy? Not in my world. Was I grasping at Noah because of the John connection? It didn't feel that way to me. My mind was all over the place. I regretted the wine. If I was going to figure this out,

I needed a clear head. Then I realized I wouldn't solve this puzzle in one evening.

Noah paid the check. I noticed he tipped lavishly and recalled how cheap Luke was in that regard. Ugh. I didn't want negative thoughts about Luke to intrude on this blissful night. For a moment, I panicked as I realized I would have to share that story with Noah. He'd probably hate me after he learned how I had behaved—how venal I was. I really needed to get home. Tomorrow I'd be a zombie if I didn't get a few hours of sleep. Even though I had a feeling I wouldn't be getting much sleep tonight, I knew I'd be dreaming. Dreaming about having a man, a good man, in my life.

We sat close on the cab ride home. Could I climb inside his clothes? We kissed, and it happened. That unique and unmistakable feeling of superb chemistry. That thrill deep in my belly.

All too soon, we arrived at my co-op.

"I don't want the night to end either," I confessed. Why not put it on the table?

His face broke out in a grin.

"But I have to say good night, Noah."

He groaned in a good-natured way. "I'm flyin' out tomorrow afternoon. Took all my nerve to call you yesterday. Should've given you a ring the first day I got here." He shook his head in regret.

I leaned in and kissed him. Added a gentle nibble. "Call me." As I opened the door, I had a fleeting hope he'd kidnap me and take me with him. Laughing at my schoolgirl foolishness, I waved to him as the cab drove away. Something happened this evening. I'd need time to figure out what it was.

The next morning, I popped out of bed at the first buzz from the alarm clock. Surprisingly, I'd slept well. After my shower, I woke Lorelei. She came to my room while I dressed, and we chatted. Pookie and dog-dog liked Noah. Did Mama have to go to work today?

We walked downstairs and found Ken and Mom in the kitchen. The aroma of coffee and toast wafted through the air.

Lorelei raced ahead of me, scrambled onto a chair, then across to the chair that held her booster seat. "Juice, Gramma? Please."

Mom appraised me and raised an eyebrow. "Well?"

I felt my face get warm. I couldn't stop grinning. "It was a wonderful evening."

"That's it?" She parked her hand on her hip. "Oh no, you don't. Spill."

I indicated Lorelei. "I'll call you later. Got to jet."

My mind wandered all day at work. First to the kiss in the cab, then to our dinner, then Noah's amazing eyes and my imaginings of what Tennessee and Georgia were like.

Alan tapped me on the shoulder, and I jumped a foot. "Where the hell are you? I called your name three times."

Irritated, I lied, "Deep in thought about Luxe packaging for the holidays."

"Charlotte is giving us a week to finalize our pitch. Meeting in my office in ten." He strolled away, king of all he surveyed.

Grumbling to myself about having to work when life was starting to happen, I rushed to the restroom to freshen up before grabbing my notebook and sketches and entering Mordor.

Through the meeting, I was merely occupying my seat, not tracking the content Alan called vital. When it was my turn to present, I faked a confident stride to the white board and wrote: "Love notes."

When I turned back to the assembled staff, half of them were frowning and the other half wore an expression that conveyed their puzzlement.

From his leather executive chair, Alan asked in a sardonic tone, "Care to amplify on that?"

"Certainly. Imagine opening a delicious Luxe candy bar and finding a lace-edged note with a message."

"Lace? A message?" Alan's delivery was dripping with skepticism.

Andrea interrupted, "I get it. A love note. Like 'Be mine' or 'Always,' like you see on those candy Valentine hearts."

"That's corny. And probably expensive," Alan objected.

A buzz rose from the team. Alan looked around the room, astonished the team was taking the idea and running with it. But Alan wasn't stupid, and he realized my idea—a serendipitous whimsy based on mooning over Noah—had merit. I was as astonished as he was.

Alan stood, rubbing his chin. "Meeting's over. Bring me your ideas of how to implement this without bankrupting Luxe, and we'll convene again. Remember, our presentation is only a week away, people!"

The team filed out, chattering about my idea. I nodded at Alan. "I'm going to lunch."

I grabbed a sandwich from a lunch cart and headed to the bank of telephones. After I found an empty booth, I dialed home.

Mom answered.

"Hi, Mom. How's my princess?"

"Perfect. Of course, you knew that. We had a lovely morning outside in the garden. We planted some marigolds Ken picked up to put among his vegetables. Something about keeping bugs away. Lori helped me. Don't worry, she's cleaned up nicely. Don't keep me in suspense. Tell me about your date. Do you like him?"

"Sure do."

"Danielle, don't make me pull the words from you. Because you know I will..."

"Good Lord, Mom! Okay, I *really* like him. In fact, I haven't felt like this about a man in a good long time."

"Fantastic! Did you invite him here for dinner?"

"No, he's on his way back to Augusta. He should learn where he'll spend his residency soon. He'd like to be assigned to Eisenhower, in Augusta, but he could go anywhere."

"Aren't you going to see him again?" Mom sounded so disappointed. Did she expect me to plan the wedding already?

Shocked at the direction of my thinking, I placated her. "Noah's promised to call and then we'll figure out if this is going anywhere. I'll have to wait and see." After a single date, it would be foolish to express my giddy hope for a future with Noah.

"All right. See you tonight."

At dinner, the doorbell rang. A rare occurrence. Ken answered and led Noah into the dining room.

I stood, realized my mouth was hanging open, and clamped it shut.

Noah's brow was furrowed, his face red. "I didn't mean to interrupt your dinner. I'll come back." He took a step toward the hall.

Lorelei, Mom, and Ken's heads swiveled between me and Noah as if they were watching a tennis match. Andy was busy shoving pasta into his mouth with both hands.

I lunged forward. "No! Join us. I'll get another plate."

Noah sat with us and ate Ken's spaghetti Bolognese with gusto. "When I got to O'Hare, I couldn't get on the plane. Changed my flight to Sunday."

After we finished eating, I led Noah out to the patio where we could speak privately.

The evening was balmy. We brought glasses of lemonade and sat on the wrought-iron chairs. As usual, no one from the other units was in the courtyard.

Overcome by shyness, the two of us stammered and blushed, stealing glances at each other. Were we in high school? I recalled Sonia's letters that implied Noah was reserved, even shy, with women. However, last night's kiss was anything but shy.

We sat in silence for several minutes. Eventually, I spoke. "I'm glad you stayed."

He met my eyes briefly, then returned his gaze to his glass. "Couldn't make my legs walk to the gate. I had to come back."

More silence. Ice clinked in our glasses as we sipped and contemplated what was happening.

"Danielle?"

"Yes."

Our eyes locked.

"Would you come to Augusta? To see if it's someplace you'd consider living?"

"I thought you didn't know where your residency would be." We blew right past whether we would see each other again.

"My C. O.—that's commanding officer to you civilians—called the hotel this morning. I've been assigned to Eisenhower."

"I'm happy you got the assignment you wanted."

"I am too. But you didn't answer. Will you come visit me?"

"I'm not big on flying."

"You won't have to fly. The jet will." He grinned.

I burst out laughing. Such a silly joke and so effective in overcoming my ridiculous timidity.

He stood, took my lemonade glass out of my hand, set it down, pulled me to my feet, and enveloped me in his arms. We didn't kiss, just held each other. I turned my head slightly and saw a little nose pressed against the patio door. Lorelei. My daughter who had never known a father.

I pulled away slowly and said, "Don't look now, but we have an audience. A small one."

"Lorelei?"

"Uh-huh. Let's go in."

When Noah opened the patio door, my daughter flung herself at me, wrapping her arms around my legs. Pookie and dog-dog fell to the ground. She needed reassurance, and I knelt to hold her close.

I picked up her toys and handed them back. "Let's go inside. Where's Grandma?"

"Andy has bedtime."

"Is Ken washing dishes?"

Lorelei nodded.

Noah sat on the couch. "Why don't you come sit here, Lorelei?"

She hustled over and handed Pookie and dog-dog to Noah. "Please hold my babies." I was surprised and happy she trusted Noah enough to hold her toys. Then she pulled herself up and retrieved her doll and Snoopy. I sat beside her and contemplated the tableau we made. A mother, a child, and a father just like in picture books. This wouldn't be a mere romance. This would be constructing a family.

Noah smiled and held out his hand to Lorelei. "Can you tell me about dog-dog?"

She giggled. "Dog-dog isn't a real dog. He wanna a real dog." She turned her head to make sure I heard.

"So, you like real dogs?" Noah asked.

"I love doggies."

Noah glanced at me. "Would you have one?"

"Hold that thought." I guided Lorelei to the kitchen where Mom waited to give her a snack. "Eat your snack and then it's bedtime."

"Okay, Mama."

Returning to the living room, I kicked off my shoes and settled beside Noah. "Where were we?"

"I think Lorelei would say 'real dog' is the topic at hand."

Tears sprang to my eyes. "I'd love to have a dog. When I was a kid, I begged my parents, but Mom said no. I rely on her to care for Lori and the house, so I don't think it's in the cards."

"I don't want to brag, but I've got connections. My aunt and her husband still raise Border Terriers."

"What're they like? The dogs I mean."

"Border Terriers are the best. They come from the Cheviot Hills, where England borders Scotland, hence the name. Tough little guys—small, hardy, active. The English used them for fox hunting."

"How are they with children?"

"They're great with kids. I'm speakin' from personal experience. When I was a boy, I had one, named him Fred. From the time I was three until he passed, he was my shadow. He died from venerable old age, dozin' in the sun—the way all dogs should." Noah's eyes blazed green with unshed tears. He looked away for a moment. "I haven't been in a position to have a dog since I was drafted. But I will someday soon."

Watching Noah and Lorelei together led me to fantasies of us forming a family. White picket fence, the whole thing. I sighed. "It's something to think about—for the future. Right now, I've got to get Lori to bed."

Mom and Lorelei stepped into the living room. Lorelei ran to me. "Can I get a doggie?" Her blue eyes were immense. "A real dog, Mama. Please!"

Hard to brush aside that sweet plea. I smiled and said, "I'll think about it."

"Dog? What's that about?" Mom stared at me.

"I'll tell you later."

"Okay. I'll walk Lori upstairs so you can have a minute with Noah."

"Thanks, Mom. I'll be up in a bit."

I walked Noah to the door, and in the privacy of the entry, we kissed. That somersaulting sensation rose from my core. Pulling away, I met his eyes, and I could tell he was feeling it too.

Brushing back my hair, I exhaled. "I'm a little apprehensive how fast this is going."

Noah smiled. "I'm not. I've waited a long time for love. To tell the truth, I think a little piece of me fell in love with you when I first saw your picture. Can't say I was jealous of John, but I sure wished I'd moved to Chicago instead of him."

Startled by the mention of the ghost we shared, I took a breath. "John. Will he always be a part of this, of us? I have to confess I worry my attraction to you is because of that connection."

"Hmm, never crossed my mind. You might need some time to cogitate on this. But I don't."

Again, I marveled at his honesty and integrity. A good man. I'd better not try to sabotage this.

After making plans to go to the Art Institute and lunch the next day, I meandered upstairs to Lorelei's room. We read her favorite story, and I tucked her in.

Nine o'clock in Chicago meant it was seven p.m. in L.A. Not too late to call Paige. Through the years, our relationship had grown closer. I remembered with shame how jealous I was of her as a child. Had I actually cut off her blond curls? Yes, I did. The rivalry over my mother's affection was manufactured on my part. Paige and Mom had an effortless, uncomplicated love, while I was reserved and suffered from self-inflicted misery. Sometime during our teenage years, after I realized I was the only one participating, I gave up the competition with Paige.

She answered on the second ring.

"Hey, Paige. Got some news. I've finally met Noah."

"Noah? Oh yeah, that other guy from Tennessee, the one the Nagys wrote to you about. And?"

I inhaled deeply before I answered. "I may be falling for him."

"Wow!"

"Am I crazy? Is this too fast? Am—"

"Chill out, Dani. Slow down and tell me every last detail."

First, I gave her the stats. About six feet but seemed taller. Military bearing. Sandy hair longer on top but white walls on the sides. His startling chameleon eyes, his sense of humor. Then I related our intimate dinner and his surprise visit today after he couldn't leave town without seeing me again. About how good he was with Lorelei.

"He sounds picture perfect to me. Speaking of pictures, send me one. I've gotta get a look at this Adonis. And since when do you like blond men?"

I sighed. "No picture, but I'll have a chance to get one this weekend. And yes, I usually go for dark men, but there have been two notable exceptions." Robert and Daniel's images danced through my mind.

"Hmm. I never knew."

"Immaterial." I paused. "There's just one thing."

"Uh-oh."

Twisting the phone cord around my finger, I said, "It's not bad. It's sad. John."

Paige sounded perplexed. "John? What do you mean?"

"Am I chasing John's ghost? Is that all this is?"

"Oh, I don't think so. Not after how you described Noah and the way you felt when he kissed you. That's not spectral—it's real."

We chatted a while longer. Tim was up for another role in a comedy. In between her waitress job, Paige showed up for every casting call she could possibly fill. Their life was humming along. Even though they didn't have a lot of money, they were both doing what they loved. I wished them well. When we were teenagers, I couldn't have imagined she would still be with Tim, or in California.

Noah and I spent Saturday at the Art Institute, viewing the Impressionist exhibit featuring the works of Renoir, Monet, Degas, Cassatt, and the iconic "A Sunday on La Grande Jatte" by Seurat. Since I was a kid, I had enjoyed the Ancient Egyptian exhibits, and we spent some time in that section of the vast museum too. There was so much to see, it would have taken weeks to delve into all the prized collections.

We ate a light lunch at the café, then returned to the second floor to continue our perusal of Modern American art. I marveled at the way Edward Hopper captured light in his masterpiece, "Nighthawks."

I insisted we visit the Thorne Gallery, with its sixty-eight painstakingly crafted miniature rooms from historic eras ranging from the French Revolution to American Colonial times and beyond.

Noah tagged behind me as I peered at each room. I spent an inordinate amount of time studying the French and English Boudoirs.

Sighing, Noah said, "To tell the truth, I liked that full-size room of the Chicago Stock Exchange more than these little bitty things. But I bet Lorelei would love these."

Surprised and pleased he was thinking of my daughter, I dragged myself away from the French Library exhibit of the Louis XV period and laid a big kiss on his luscious lips.

To the consternation of the sedate group of older women in the hall, he responded with enthusiasm. I didn't care. A moment later, we were startled when the museum's loudspeaker announced the exhibits were closing. Amazed the day was gone, we strolled up Michigan Avenue holding hands and stopping to kiss every few feet. We caught a cab at the bridge over the Chicago River but didn't get home until after Lorelei had eaten and been bathed.

Mommy-guilt covered me from head to toe. My conscience informed me I was short-changing Lorelei, so I planned a family lunch at home on Sunday. Promptly at noon, Noah arrived in a cab. Since he'd checked out of the hotel, he had his suitcase and garment bag with him. After lunch, he'd call another taxi to take him to O'Hare.

When we opened the door, the first thing out of Lorelei's mouth was, "Where is the doggie?"

Noah told her there was no real dog hidden in the suitcase, and her lower lip trembled. I knew I'd have to give in soon.

Ken went all out, making his famous chicken salad. The deboned chicken was marinated overnight in French dressing, then drained and tossed with artichoke hearts, mushrooms, celery, and green olives. Once assembled, he dressed the concoction with mayonnaise and refrigerated it for four hours. With the fresh-baked baguette and kiwi sorbet, it was a wonderful menu. Because it was a sunny day, we planned to eat on the patio.

Noah helped Mom set the table and then returned to the kitchen to bring out the bread and iced tea. Ken followed with the immense bowl of his delicious chicken salad.

Lorelei dragged Pookie and dog-dog to the table. "Mama, please hold my babies?"

I gently pried them from her grip and explained that the babies would take a nap on the chaise lounge while we ate.

Mom poured iced tea.

"Is it sweet or unsweet?" Noah asked.

Setting the pitcher on the table, Mom said, "I've never heard that before, 'unsweet.'"

Noah answered, "I think it's a Southernism, if that's a word."

"I like it," Mom said. "It's unsweet."

Lunch conversation revolved around Noah's future as a pediatrician. Mom flattered him shamelessly. Ken was respectful. I was enamored. Lorelei gazed at him with wonder. She said, "Noah is a doctor? Say ah. Shot in the butt." I chuckled at what was going through her mind.

I picked out all the green olives, celery, and mushrooms from Lorelei's salad and cut the rest into minute pieces.

"I forgot the butter," Mom said and hurried away to get it.

Ken and I shared a glance and then burst into laughter. We laughed until we cried.

Noah looked at us and said, "Let me in on the joke."

When I could speak, I sputtered, "B-b-butter. It's always about the butter. Mom can't get enough. I call her 'Bunch-o-butter.'"

Ken slapped the table. Lorelei started giggling. Noah's laughter was deep and genuine.

When she rushed back clutching the vital condiment to her bosom, Mom looked confused by the hilarity for a moment. Then she grinned, "I get it. You told Noah about my love affair with the yellow stuff."

After lunch, we carried our plates inside. I put Lorelei down for a nap and returned to the kitchen. Mom brought in Andy and fed him. Refusing Noah's offer to help clean the kitchen, Ken said, "You kids relax. I know

Noah has to leave for the airport soon." Once again, Ken demonstrated his sensitivity.

I took Noah's hand and led him back out to the patio, so we could have some time alone.

After we were seated, he spoke. "Words can't express how you've made me feel." He leaned forward and took my hands. "This was a wonderful...no...a magical weekend. Dani, you're an amazing woman. A man couldn't ask for more."

"Why, thank you. You ain't so bad yourself. I had a great time too."

"Have you thought about comin' to Augusta?"

"Yes."

He scooted his chair closer to me. "Yes, you've thought about it or yes, you will?"

"I will."

His face broke out into a grin. "When?"

I hedged. Things were intense at work. "Probably not until after the first of the year."

Noah's face fell. "That's six months away. No sooner?"

I shook my head. "Sorry. Work is busy this time of year. Then there are the holidays."

Even though he looked disappointed, Noah nodded. "Okay, that will give me time to get settled. I'll have my schedule, and I can fly back here when I have a three-day stretch off-duty." He kissed my hand. "I'll be countin' every minute, darlin.'"

Standing on the sidewalk, I waved at the cab until it was out of sight. Then I plodded upstairs, threw myself on the bed, and bawled my eyes out. Why? Tension release or terror? Happiness or guilt? Fear or hope? What would Noah think of me if he knew my history with Luke? I knew I had to tell him but dreaded it.

Noah called when he could. Odd hours. Sometimes I was at work, and he chatted with Mom or Lorelei. With my daughter, there was one topic of conversation—real dog.

Charlotte gave me a new assignment at work. I was heading a team to find a name for a new perfume. If we prevailed over Foote, Cone, and Belding's nomination, we'd launch a full-blown campaign. I bid farewell to Alan with so much enthusiasm he seemed miffed. Too darn bad.

Andrea, Patrice, and a new hire, Ted, were my team members. It seemed like I couldn't escape Andrea. Ted was quiet and self-effacing, as befit a new hire. But I'd seen how the mild and meek Alan transformed into a tyrant. Would that happen to Ted? I sure hoped it wouldn't. Although I hadn't worked with Patrice before, I knew she had experience at another agency with cosmetics. I was happy to have her.

I led my team to the conference room and wrote on the whiteboard: "Today's woman."

Holding the marker so I could use it to hammer home my points, I challenged them. "Stream of consciousness, describe today's woman." I couldn't wait to hear what twenty-two-year-old, skinny, bespectacled Ted had to say. A fleeting thought about asking Charlotte to trade him for a more seasoned team member, preferably a woman, was discarded as quickly as it came. She would refuse and demand I carry on with what I had. So, I did.

"Independent!" shouted Andrea.

I gestured for her to lower her voice. No points for loudness.

"Self-sufficient?" Ted quavered.

Turning to him, I asked, "What else?"

His voice getting stronger, Ted added, "Educated. Sophisticated. Stylish."

"Good." I turned and wrote those words on the board.

"Patrice?"

She flipped her long honey-colored hair over her shoulder and breathed, "Sexy, thrilling, dazzling."

I added those adjectives to the list. "Let's look at one of the most successful recent perfume releases. I'm talking about 'Charlie' by Revlon. I can still see Shelley Hack breezing down the street. So confident. So carefree." To the amazement of my team, I burst into song, "Kinda young, kinda now, Charlie! Kinda free, kinda wow! Charlie!"

Boy, that got their attention. Andrea and Ted sat with gaping mouths. Patrice threw her head back and laughed. All three started to clap, and I burst out laughing.

"No applause required. I want you to think about what went into that successful ad campaign in 1973." I tapped the marker in my open palm. "Here we are in 1978, five years later, and I want new. I want different. I want contemporary. We'll start with a name for the fragrance, but we won't stop there. I want sketches, suggestions for a face, slogans, songs, bottle design, package proposal, the whole nine yards. We're going to come up with the winning name. Foote, Cone and Belding won't stand a chance of landing this account. And I want to hit the ground running when we do."

From their reaction, my speech lit a fire under them. They left the conference room with heads together, chatting, radiating enthusiasm.

Andy was walking and speaking a few basic words. He followed Lorelei as if he were attached by an invisible cord. "Lolo. Lolo."

For her part, Lorelei now called him—and Pookie—"Andy." She was kind to both the doll and the real thing. To be honest, it was a little confusing at times.

Mom took the kids for long walks every day. In the spring, I'd have to look into a pre-school for Lorelei. Some places started kids at three, but I thought it better to wait until she was four.

Noah couldn't finagle a three-day weekend until September. By that time, I had begun to wonder if his first visit was real or if I had merely conjured a perfect man. Luckily, the perfume campaign kept me focused on work, a blessed distraction.

After he arrived and checked in at the Ambassador East, a few blocks from home, he called me. "Darlin,' I'm unpacked, and I'll be over for dinner in a few minutes."

Ken's homemade sweet Italian sausage lasagna smelled delicious, but I was too nervous to eat. Noah's appetite seemed dampened as well. We exchanged quick glances and secret smiles. I anticipated we'd be making love for the first time, and I knew Noah did too. We acted like shy teenagers. No one seemed to notice as they enjoyed Ken's cooking.

After the meal, Noah cleared the table and joined Ken in the kitchen while Mom and I bathed our little ones. Noah came upstairs to help me tuck Lorelei into bed and read her favorite book.

I kissed her forehead. "Sweetie, I'm going on a trip. I won't be here tomorrow, but I'll be back on Sunday."

Lorelei thought a moment. "Okay, Mama. Give Andy and dog-dog a kiss."

She gazed at Noah, "Real dog?"

Noah looked a question at me.

I sighed. "Someday, Lori."

On the short walk to the Ambassador East, I chattered like someone released from prolonged social isolation. Noah was silent, nodding at my conversational gambits. As we rode the elevator up to his room, my hands were clammy, and my right eye twitched. There was so much riding on our sexual compatibility. Going by our limited encounters, all the signs were positive, but I was still a nervous wreck. My mind swirled with images of my teenage years with John, the misery of lousy sex with Luke, and the fatal-after-the-fact encounter with Daniel. Quite the variety. I knew I needed to cleanse my mind of those memories.

With his hands clenched at his sides, one white-knuckled hand clutching my overnight case, Noah stared at the floor indicator as if he were absorbed in our ascension.

At last, we reached the tenth floor, and he ushered me into the hall with his hand on my back. Could he tell how tense I was?

Noah opened the door and placed my bag on the floor. He pulled me close. "I'm nervous too, honey."

I turned up my face for his kiss. The tummy twirl was there. I'd be good to go. We put away our coats and sat on the bed. I waited for him to start. And waited.

He bent forward and put his face in his hands. "Let's have a cocktail," he mumbled through his fingers.

"Vodka tonic, please." I grasped his shoulders and nudged him upright. "I'm going to unpack and run a bath. Care to join me?"

He reddened even as he grinned. "Sounds good."

We had never discussed our sexual history. I had no interest in doing so, and I figured Noah was too much of a Southern gentleman to start a discussion. Obviously, Noah knew about John and that I had a child. But I was starting to wonder if Noah had any experience at all. Of course, I was aware he was ready and willing from our kissing sessions. How many lovers had he had? He was twenty-eight, and I was fairly sure he wasn't a virgin. Please God, don't let him be a virgin, I prayed.

I carried my toiletry bag into the bathroom and turned on the tap in the oversized tub. I poured lavender-scented bath crystals into the water and undressed, washed off my makeup, put my hair in a ponytail and pinned it up. Wrapped in a towel, I slipped back to the bedroom. Noah had undressed and donned one of the plush hotel robes. He must have gone out for ice. Handing me a vodka tonic, he clicked my glass with his.

"To us." His throat moved as he swallowed his drink in one go.

I took a sip of my drink and grasped his hand. "Bath's ready."

We moved to the bathroom, and I turned off the overhead light, letting the illumination from the bedside lamp provide an ambient glow. I let my towel fall. All at once, Noah lost his reticence—and his robe. He picked me up and placed me in the enormous tub. He joined me and picked up a bar of soap. When our activities sloshed water over the side of the bath, he stood and held out his hand. I saw I had been worrying for nothing.

Noah helped me up and dried me slowly and thoroughly with a towel. Then I returned the favor. In the bedroom, I lay back on the luxurious linens. Noah turned off the lamp.

We kissed. Oh, how we kissed. As he moved over me, my body responded. I called his name, and he found my mouth again.

Later, we held each other.

"I love you, Dani," Noah whispered, then he brushed his lips across my forehead.

Tears ran down my face, blending with the sweat along my hairline. They were tears of joy. But for some reason, I couldn't tell him I loved him.

Because of his work schedule, I didn't see Noah again for two months; he had a three-day weekend every eight weeks. When he called to confirm our early November visit, I asked him about the holidays, and he said he managed to trade his Thanksgiving holiday for Christmas and would be able to be with us again in December.

On our November weekend, I stayed with him again at the Ambassador East. The awkwardness of our first sexual encounter was gone. We meshed perfectly. This time, after our reunion lovemaking session, I said the words I withheld in September, words I hadn't said aloud since 1970. "I love you," came unbidden from my lips as we lay entwined and satisfied.

Although we spent many delicious and productive hours in bed, my mommy-guilt ensured that we spent time with family. We ate several meals at the co-op. Noah suggested we take Lorelei to her first movie, *Mickey Mouse's Birthday Party Show*. Again, I marveled at his kindness and consideration toward my daughter. She was enchanted with the old cartoons and the Mouseketeers who performed in the compilation.

After Noah left for Augusta, I dreamed about John for the first time in years. My lost love no longer haunted my dreams as he once did. In my vision, John walked in on me and Noah in bed, saluted, and disappeared, his lopsided smile hanging in the air like the Cheshire Cat. I woke gasping, threw off the covers, and turned on the light to dispel the image. What did the dream mean? Did I have John's blessing? The next morning, I couldn't shake the apparition of my first love. Doubt and worry invaded my new happiness. Should I confide in Mom or Paige? No, I couldn't bear to be judged. Instead, I medicated myself with the 442 t-shirt but found the bottle of Jade East empty. And I cried.

I had yet to plan my trip to Augusta. Noah was giving me space. He didn't press me to make reservations. Reservations—I had plenty—about flying.

I shuddered as I recalled my white-knuckled first flight to Jamaica and the aborted landing on our return to O'Hare. I would worry about that when the time came.

Noah was far away and busy, and I was glad I had work to concentrate on. We won the perfume account. Charlotte adored the name, "Emancipation," thought it brilliant. The launch campaign went off without a hitch. It turned out I was worried for nothing; the client was fully onboard. They loved the asymmetrical bottle, and called our take on the red, white, and blue packaging unexpected and stunning. But if sales fell short, I could kiss the next promotion goodbye. Another disappointment would be devastating.

That Christmas, there were ten of us: four couples and the two children. Mom wanted to invite Dad and Ginger again this year. That was fine with me. Paige and I had softened toward Dad with the passage of time. Nine years since the divorce. I reflected on my life in that time span: death, marriage, birth, suicide, career, and maybe, just maybe, a happy ending for me.

Phil and Clare were spending the holiday in Peoria with her family. They hadn't set a date for their wedding yet. Joe and Joanie were on tour in Texas, playing whatever gigs came their way. When last heard from, they were in Austin.

For the first time, Noah was staying at the co-op. This weekend, I planned to tell him about my history with Luke. I needed to confess before things progressed further.

Noah arrived two days before the others. "Man, it's cold," he said as he took off his camelhair coat.

"Merry Christmas, honey." Throwing my arms around his neck, I held on tight. I kissed him with passion, trying to push my upcoming confession from my consciousness.

He returned the kiss. "Wow. I missed you too!"

Lorelei came running in, eyes searching the entry. "Is there a doggie?"

Kneeling in front of her, I said, "Not this time."

"Maybe Santa will bring me a doggie."

Which was worse: giving her false hope or ruining her Christmas? "Maybe."

With my daughter on his heels, Noah carried his suitcase and garment bag upstairs. I followed them to monitor her questions. And I was afraid she would go through his bags looking for a real dog—despite telling her there wasn't one.

The four of us, Noah, Mom, Ken, and I, spent the following day cooking. Ken was organized. He had printed a menu and our assignments on note cards. He reserved the turkey, stuffing, and rolls for himself, delegated the ham to Mom, and split the side dishes between Noah and me.

Paige and Tim were arriving the next day and staying at the Drake. I couldn't wait to see her latest hairstyle.

The next afternoon, the doorbell rang, and Lorelei ran to answer. Andrew stumbled after her. He walked well but hadn't mastered running. I was hot on their heels.

The blast of frigid air forced the children back from the door.

Paige hurried in, wearing a parka with a hood, Tim close behind.

"I sure don't miss the cold, but I don't think it's as cold as last year. No white Christmas. Not that I'm hoping for a blizzard." Tim said.

Paige shrugged off her coat, and tawny blond waves cascaded around her face. The Afro was history.

Mom came in, wiping her hands on a kitchen towel. "My God, is that Julie Christie?"

"Hi, Mom." Paige beamed and hugged Mom with exuberance.

"I notice you didn't confuse me with Warren Beatty," Tim groused.

"Always with the one-liners. I bet they love you on the set." Mom pulled them aside, eager for tidbits of insider Hollywood gossip.

Lorelei threw her arms around Paige's legs. "Annie Paige. Give Andy and dog-dog a kiss!"

"Where's Pookie?"

"Not Pookie. This is Andy," Lorelei insisted as she held up her blond baby girl doll.

I stood back, watching the interaction. Lorelei looked more like Paige's daughter than mine. I blinked away that sentiment; she belonged to me.

Tim bent down to Andrew. "Hi there, buddy."

Andrew's blue eyes grew big as he regarded first Tim, then Paige. I wondered what he was thinking; he was seven months old the last time they met. After a moment, he broke out in a smile, revealing his baby teeth covered with teething drool.

Mom offered drinks, and the kids tagged along as we all moved to the living room. The tree gleamed with lights and ornaments. Lorelei and Andy spent a lot of time sitting before it in wonder. My daughter, fascinated by the Nativity, helpfully explained about baby Jesus to Andy, who nodded in cadence with his niece's voice. His blond curls had not been submitted to his first haircut; Mom was more than reluctant. Ken complained that when he took Andy to the store, the women cooed over his cute little granddaughter. "I'm tired of telling everybody I meet he's a boy who hasn't had his first haircut. And that I'm the dad. Grandfather? Do I look that old? Is it the gray hair?"

"Darling, your gray hair is distinguished. I swear you could be a stand-in for Gregory Peck!"

Noah entered the room. He shook hands with Tim. Paige assessed him, then grinned and hugged him.

"At last, we meet the famous Noah!"

"Famous? Not me. But I hear Tim is a movie star."

Tim ducked his head, self-deprecating as always. "I wouldn't say 'star,' but I'm working and paying the bills. That's a victory in Hollywood."

Baking bread, roasting turkey, and honey-glazed ham filled the house with delicious mouth-watering aromas.

"Dinner soon?" Lorelei begged, holding her tummy.

"As soon as Stan and Ginger get here," I assured her. In my mind, Ken was Lorelei's grandfather and deserved the title—although she called him Ken—so my father was "Stan" to her. And Ginger was not getting the honorific of grandmother, in any form. Although I had softened toward my father, rancor occasionally emerged from its hiding place.

The phone rang, and I picked up.

"Dani, Ginger and I are running late. We're heading out the door now. Should be there in thirty minutes."

I rushed to the kitchen to tell Mom and Ken about the delay.

Mom's mouth formed a tight line, but Ken put his arm around her and said, "No problem."

Dad must have sped through the city. He and Ginger arrived twenty-five minutes later. While the kitchen crew hustled to put all the dishes on the table, I hung up their coats. "We're ready to eat."

Ginger handed me a bottle of champagne, and Dad placed the presents for the children under the tree. Our family continued the new tradition of providing presents only for the little ones.

Noah approached with his hand extended in greeting. I introduced him to the couple. He and Dad shook. Noah nodded to Ginger. "Pleased to meet you, ma'am." She still had her natural dark hair and librarian fashion sense. So, it wasn't an aberration last year. I wondered what had prompted the change in her but didn't dwell on it.

Tim herded the kids to the dining room, and everyone found seats around the table. Lorelei sat between Paige and me.

Ken, at the head of the table, passed the rolls. "Butter, Ellen?" he asked. Everyone but Ginger laughed.

Andrew, in his strategically placed highchair between his parents, was a hearty eater. Mom cut up turkey, ham, and squash into finely minced morsels.

"This squash is wonderful. I'd love to have the recipe," Ginger said.

Ken smiled. "I'll write it down for you after dinner. It's not that difficult. The basic ingredients are lemon, butter, and maple syrup."

"It's so delicious, Ken," Ginger, sedate and gracious, amazed me. Gone were the cigarettes and chewing gum.

Dad addressed Noah, who sat at the foot of the table. "I hear you're a doctor."

"I'm still in my residency in pediatrics. And I have about three and a half years I still owe Uncle Sam."

"Pediatrics?" Dad's brow furrowed. "Why'd you choose to work with kids?"

Noah shrugged. "I started out wanting to practice emergency medicine, but after the war, I-I lost the desire. When I had my pediatric rotation, I knew I'd found my calling."

"Yeah, I bet you saw some terrible things in Nam."

I turned to my father and glared at him. One of those terrible things was John's dead body, a subject I determinedly banished from my mind.

Mom noticed my reaction to Dad's statement and quickly got back on topic. "I think it's wonderful you work with children," Mom said.

I unclenched my fists and jaw and picked up my fork.

The sound of silverware clinking on plates and soft conversation was soothing. Everyone appeared to appreciate the fine meal. Ken, modest as always about his culinary prowess, redirected the many compliments on the food to Mom, Noah, and me. "You have to give credit for the honey mustard glaze on the ham to Ellen. And Dani and Noah did the mashed potatoes, cauliflower gratin, the green beans, and the sweet potato casserole."

Second helpings were underway when Andrew turned blue and began to wheeze.

Lorelei's hands cupped her face. "Oh no! Baby Andy."

Before Mom or Ken could react, Noah charged to Andy and picked him up. On one knee, Noah placed the little boy on his thigh and smacked him on the back. After the third blow, a piece of turkey flew from Andy's mouth, and he began to wail. His color changed from sickly blue to bright red.

Noah handed off the crying toddler to Mom. "I'll be right back."

He returned with his stethoscope, listened to Andy's chest, and pronounced his lungs clear.

"You're a handy guy to have around." Dad looked and sounded impressed.

Ken and Mom held Andrew between them, lavishing him with kisses.

Mom's tear-streaked face and her shaking hands revealed how upset she was. I knew she'd blame herself. It was what moms did. Her voice shook. "Noah, I don't know how to thank you."

Noah ducked his head in humility. "No thanks necessary, Ellen."

As if she were at a performance, Paige stood and clapped. "Bravo!" I guess it came with the Hollywood address.

Mom and Ken retreated to their room with Andy.

Tim took over host duties. "Let's clear the table and start clean up. We can have dessert when Ken and Ellen come back."

Six people were too many in the kitchen. I asked my father and Ginger to take Lorelei to the living room. "There's a pile of storybooks in a basket next to the couch."

Dad smiled. "I'd be happy to read Lorelei a story or two." Ginger nodded. She was quiet this evening.

The four of us made quick work of clearing the table and taking care of the leftovers. Paige regaled us with anecdotes of whom she seated in her restaurant at lunch. "I've been promoted to hostess. No more waitressing for me. You won't believe who I met this week...John Travolta!" With her dazzling smile, curvy figure, and stylish hair, there was no doubt she was an asset to the trendy restaurant. She had occasional work on the set of a daytime drama, or as I liked to say, soap opera. Mom would kick herself for missing this, but I was sure Paige would share her stories later. Their fascination with the stars was a mystery to me.

Tim's first movie was a minor success. He was working on another comedy and had a callback for a television role in a medical drama. "Hey, Noah, if I get it, can I call you for pointers?"

Noah grinned. "Sure thing."

Ken joined us in the kitchen. "Andy's in bed. Ellen is resting. When he's asleep, she'll come back to the festivities." He glanced at the cleared counters and said, "Thanks for the help. Let me get dessert. I have the traditional pumpkin pie, but this year I tried something new. I found the recipe in a magazine while we were waiting at the pediatrician. Italian Cream Cake. I'd never heard of it. I think it's a Southern thing."

Noah said, "Yes, sir, it is. And it's one of my favorites."

I carried the dessert plates into the dining room, and Ken and Paige brought the cake and pie. With Dad and Ginger trailing her, Lorelei ran to her seat. "Yummy pie. Yummy cake!"

Ken sliced and served the desserts. "Let me check on Ellen."

After a few minutes, they returned to the table. Mom smiled wanly, and I could tell she was still worried about Andy.

Dad exulted over Phil's success with the White Sox farm team. I remembered how there was no escape from baseball when I was a kid. My dad taught me to pitch and catch and hit, but when Phil came along, he left me on the bench, forgotten. In our childhood home, dinnertime conversation centered on White Sox baseball. The sport was inextricably woven into the fabric of my formative years. It became a habit to pick up the players' names and their stats, almost by osmosis. After I met John, those things went by the wayside and gradually out of my consciousness. The wave of nostalgia at those memories took me by surprise, and I reached out for Noah's hand.

"I'm so damn proud of Phil," Dad proclaimed. "He made Triple-A. The Iowa Oaks. I'm gonna get to as many games as possible. He's still hoping to be called up to the bigs. I hope he makes it."

"How's Clare?" Paige asked.

"Fine." With that dismissive one-word answer, Dad continued to expound on the charms of America's pastime, reminding me of our failed family dynamic.

Paige rolled her eyes at me. I hid my smirk.

After coffee and dessert, Mom followed us to the living room. "Noah, could you look in on Andy?"

"Certainly. I'll listen again." He grabbed his stethoscope and left the room. When he returned, he was carrying the toddler. "This little guy wants his presents."

Andy agreed. "Pesents. Pesents. Lolo said."

Mom and Ken glanced at each other, relief written on their faces.

Fisher-Price and Little Tikes were well represented under the tree. Noah gave Lorelei a copy of *Mister Dog*. "This is the closest story I could find about a Border Terrier, the kind of dog I had as a boy. Crispin's Crispian belongs to himself, but I bet I can find a puppy who might consider belonging to a little girl."

Lorelei gazed at Noah with wide eyes. "A border doggie. I can have a real dog?"

My heart went out to her, and I vowed to make her dream come true.

Andy was enamored with his sit-on riding scooter. He barely looked at anything else.

That night, after Lorelei was tucked in, Noah drew me to my bedroom and got down on one knee for a different reason. "Will you do me the honor of becoming my wife?"

My hands clapped over my mouth. My eyes watered. After the first rush of joy, my checkered past flitted through my mind, and I dropped my hands. Avoiding Noah's eyes, I felt my cheeks burn. "I don't know if you'll want to marry me after I tell you what I have to tell you." With my nerves ratcheting up, I didn't recognize my voice.

Noah rose. With his eyes narrowed in thought, he took my hand and walked me over to the bed. We sat.

"What on earth are you talkin' about? Are you a fugitive from justice? In witness protection? A foreign agent?" Noah's chuckle died, his attempt at levity falling flat.

I flicked my eyes to his face then looked at my lap. "I need a tissue."

Noah reached over to the bedside table and placed the box of tissues beside me. "Here you go." He put his arm around me and drew me to his side. "Tell me, sweetheart. I can't imagine anything you'd say would change my mind."

A sob escaped. "God, I hope you're right."

His arm tightened around my shoulder. I leaned into him. Taking in a deep breath, I began.

"You know Lori's father committed suicide."

Noah's brow furrowed. "Ye-es."

I turned to him, threw my arms around his neck, and we fell back on the bed. Burrowing into his chest, I clung to him like I was drowning, then began my confession. "I was a different person then. The truth is...I never loved Luke. I married him for financial security, so he would pay for my college tuition. As soon as I graduated and got a job, I planned to divorce him. Then Lori happened. That was an accident, and the circumstances were...ugly. My plan was delayed. Luke lost his job—and me—then he killed himself." I whispered, "Do you hate me?"

Noah leaned back and tipped my chin to meet his eyes. I watched for disgust, a turning away, but it never came. He drew me close again.

"Honey, that's a straight-up tragedy. I can't imagine. Your heart broke when John died, and people with broken hearts do things they normally wouldn't."

"Oh, Noah, I was so stupid. I never should have married him. I did it for all the wrong reasons."

"Hush now. Yes, your motives were wrong, but you are *not* responsible for the person Luke was. For a man to take his life, there are deep, underlying problems." He stroked my hair, held me tight.

The relief of telling Noah the worst thing I'd ever done, and having him accept me despite it, was a turning point for me. I knew right then my instincts about his decency and integrity were correct.

After a few minutes of cuddling, Noah blurted, "Hey, you didn't answer my question."

I rolled over on top of him, took his face in my hands, and kissed him. "Does that answer your question?"

His smile was everything.

Chapter Thirteen

A HEALING HEART 1979

The next morning, we entered the kitchen with our hands entwined and big grins on our faces. Ken laid out coffee cups, and my mother stood at the stove, flipping pancakes.

Noah took the spatula from Mom, who looked confused. "I'll return this after our big announcement. Ellen, your daughter has accepted my proposal of marriage."

Mom threw her hands in the air. "Oh, my God! That's wonderful!"

Ken flung open the refrigerator door. "Champagne. We didn't drink it last night." He took four flutes from the cabinet and popped the cork.

I saved it for my box of treasures. The knife of guilt pricked my conscience. Was it right to keep this memento with those of my past?

Lorelei studied the reactions of Mom and Ken and decided it was good news. Her mouth formed an "O," and she clapped her hands, mirroring Mom. At three and a half, she didn't understand the implications. Andy banged his sippy cup on the highchair tray. Mom called Paige's hotel and ordered her and Tim to come running over for pancakes and some big news.

Ken toasted us. "To love."

"Want some too!" Lorelei's lip quivered.

I put my glass down and rummaged in the fridge for a bottle of ginger ale. My daughter's smile returned when I handed her the drink in a champagne flute. No plastic cup for this.

Paige and Tim arrived a few minutes later to raise a glass. We were peppered with hugs and congratulations. And questions, most of which we didn't know the answer to. At least I didn't. Noah expertly navigated the minefield of queries about when and where, saying we still had much to discuss.

As I sipped champagne, a tiny part of me regretted not coming completely clean with Noah. I told him that Luke lost me. He didn't ask how, letting it slide, but had he read between the lines? Maybe he didn't want to know. Without a doubt, I didn't want to tell him. I ignored the tiny prickles from my conscience.

When Noah flew back to Augusta the next day, a piece of my heart went with him. For the last six months, my work and home life maintained their usual rhythm, interrupted by those delightful interludes every eight weeks. I knew we couldn't go on this way forever, and I'd have to make some decisions about our future together and about my job.

No, it was a career.

I was in love—and engaged—but I struggled with what I would have to sacrifice for us to be together.

January 1979 brought the most miserable weather since the Great Snowstorm of 1967. We got a good seven inches of snow on New Year's Eve. That didn't matter because I was staying home. Then it began to snow on the night of January 12th and didn't stop until two a.m. on January 14th. Nineteen inches of the white stuff, stuff the city couldn't manage to plow. The freezing temperatures were the icing on the cake, so to speak.

When Noah called, I told him about the latest Chicago snow scandal. The mayor who took over after Richard M. Daley died wasn't getting the job done.

"O'Hare is closed, it's freezing cold, and we haven't seen a snowplow. This is ridiculous." I related the news story of a snowplow driver going nuts and running over thirty-four cars. One person was killed, but that wasn't the only death blamed on the storm.

"Hmm, it's a balmy fifty-three degrees here. How do y'all stand that weather? Perhaps it's making you yearn for more temperate climes?"

"Maybe." He had a point. We were housebound. Public transportation was sporadic, and garbage sat in the alleyways, overflowing and uncollected.

I wandered downstairs and sat at the kitchen table with Mom. The kids were napping. Bored out of their minds. It was too wretched and frigid to go outdoors.

"Mom, what would you think about moving to Georgia?"

Getting up to put on the tea kettle, Mom was silent for a long minute before answering. "Honey, Ken's job is here. He's got a good twenty years before he retires. I don't think he'd want to start over at his age."

"What do *you* think about moving?" I wanted to hear her thoughts, not Ken's.

As she was gathering tea bags and cups, Mom kept her back to me.

I waited.

She sat down and patted my hand. "I love this city. Lived here my whole life. Not once, even with the terrible weather, have I ever thought of leaving."

"Well, I guess that answers that."

Mom's forehead creased. "So, you're moving to Georgia, just like that? What about your job?"

I sputtered, "I think you mean my *career*."

"Touchy, aren't you?" The tea kettle whistled, and she got up again to pour boiling water into cups and carried them to the table. "Oh, I forgot the sugar."

I stood. "I'll get it."

"Please bring the half-and-half too. And I have fresh lemons. I know how you like them."

When I returned with the additives, I said, "I'm engaged to a man who lives in Georgia, so of course I'm moving."

"Can't Noah transfer here?"

Even though her question annoyed me, I tamped down my feelings. "I don't know, but I do know he doesn't want to." I glanced at her. "You know I've had dreams of going to Tennessee since I was thirteen years old.

Augusta isn't that far from Knoxville. I'd like to meet Noah's family. And see the Nagys again."

"I'll never understand this enmeshment with the Nagys. Sometimes I think you're still in love with John. He's been gone more than, let me count, more than seven years." She stirred her tea, loaded with three spoons of sugar and an ounce of half-and-half. Her eyebrows rose, and she asked, "You don't still have that yellow rag and that overpowering men's cologne, do you? Please tell me you got rid of it."

She might as well have slapped me. I became a statue.

Mom must have seen the look on my face. "Sorry for being blunt, but do you love Noah for himself or because he's John's friend?"

I shoved my chair back and shrieked, "How can you say such a thing?" Racing upstairs, I threw myself on the bed, wondering how my mother sensed my misgivings. Why did I still have them?

A few days later, I called Paige, leading with complaints about the weather.

She laughed. "It's sunny and sixty-two degrees here. Kind of chilly, but I'll take it."

"If it were sixty-two here, I'd strip naked and sprint down Astor Street."

Paige snorted. "I highly doubt it. But thanks for the visual."

"You're very welcome." Sitting on the bed, I pulled the phone next to me so I could lean against the pillows. "I talked to Mom about moving to Georgia."

"Mom moving? Are you kidding me? Don't you think the whole in-law thing would put a damper on your future marriage? Besides, I can't see her leaving Chi-town."

"Well, you're right, she doesn't want to leave. I don't know; it was just a thought."

"If I were you, I'd leave that polar ice cap you live on and get my ass to sunny Georgia as fast as possible. Don't you want to be with Noah?"

"With all my heart! I'm crazy about him. But on some level, I'm scared."

"Scared of what? Getting married, the move, what?" Paige's voice oozed exasperation. I could picture her face—that look she had when she was annoyed and impatient with me.

"Look at my last marriage."

"Sis, that wasn't a marriage, it was a deal with the devil."

"Ouch!"

"You need to get over it."

"Easy for you to say," I muttered.

"Yeah, it is. And it should be easy for you *if* you're in love."

Paige was pushing my buttons. She knew where they were located because she was present when Mom installed them.

"I'm as sure of Noah as I've been of anything since John. But I'm concerned about the connection. And then Mom said...never mind."

"Oh no, you don't. Mom said what?"

"She asked me if I loved Noah for himself or because he's John's friend."

"Wow! Way to go, Mom. But you gotta admit, you've been struggling with that for a while now. You're blocked."

"Then she had the audacity to ask me if I threw away—" I clamped my mouth shut. Why did I decide to play true confessions?

"Threw away what? Come on, tell me what's going on."

"It's nothing. A-a keepsake I have."

"You mean that yellow t-shirt and the Jade East?"

Stunned, I asked, "You know about that?"

Paige sighed. In my mind, I could see her rolling her eyes in her trademark way. "Mom told me, must've been a year ago. So, you're still doing the...whatever thing you do? That's kind of out there, Dani."

"I hate being judged."

"Oh, for God's sake, I'm not judging you. Look, you're engaged! Go with that. Why can't you just accept you've been lucky enough to get a second chance at love?"

My eyes stung. "I'll never forget John—"

"Of course not! I'm not saying you should but get some perspective. John is gone and Noah is living and breathing and quite the hunk. Just take the leap! Get on with your life. That mind of yours is beyond my comprehension."

"What do you mean?"

"I can almost see the wheels turning when you consider something. Your brainpower works against you sometimes. Plan, plan, plan, think, think, think. You need to go with the flow. Embrace life."

"Huh. I'll have to think about that."

Paige's laughter floated through the phone line. "Exactly!"

Things were still a little tense between me and Mom. I knew we had to clear the air and discuss selling the condo and finding them a new place. Conversations about money always put me in a bad frame of mind because they reminded me of how I came to have the money. Luke.

On the way home from work, I picked up some chocolates as a peace offering. We sat in the kitchen sipping coffee.

"Look, Mom, I've made my decision. I'm moving to Augusta as soon as I tie up things here."

She bit into a truffle and swooned with pleasure. "What about the co-op? Ken can't afford the taxes and annual assessment."

"There's no way I can keep this place. I'll have to sell. You and Ken have a nice nest egg from selling both your houses, so you can afford to buy something."

Mom pursed her lips. "You're right. But I love this place, and it's all Andy has ever known."

I shrugged. "Kids are adaptable."

"I guess we'll both find out if that's true. Lorelei's going to be four in a few months, and this has been her home since she was a baby." Mom chose another chocolate. "These are delicious."

Although I expressed outward confidence about the adaptability of my girl, inside I was a mass of conflict. Could she adjust to having a father and moving to a new home away from her extended family? I knew one thing that would help: a real dog.

Despite my inner conflict, the idea of being with Noah in Augusta had taken root. His visits were heavenly, but I needed more. I looked out the window at the snow pressing against the pane. How deep was it? Would it ever go away? Did it snow in Augusta?

It was a struggle to get to work that month. Absenteeism was high with the snow, below- zero temperatures, and frozen L tracks. The bus lines couldn't handle the extra passengers, and some streets were still impassable, requiring detours. I was late several times.

The good news was the launch of "Emancipation" was a resounding success. The sales for Christmas were stellar for a new perfume. I was awarded a promotion to account manager and, with barely concealed glee, moved to my own enclosed office. With a door. After all my effort, I reached the pinnacle of my ambitions—management. But the achievement had lost its luster somewhere along the line. When I thought about it, I could pinpoint the date: Christmas, when Noah proposed.

Sitting in my new high-backed leather executive chair, I spun to face the window overlooking Kinzie. No river view for me. Holding out my hand, I admired the way the sunlight cast rainbows of color from my simple and elegant half-carat round brilliant cut engagement diamond. Was I yearning to be a traditional woman? Could I give up my career? I thought back to the first working woman I knew—Mrs. Wilkins. Her success and Mom's struggles after the divorce were in stark contrast.

I chose Mrs. Wilkins as a role model instead of my mother. But my drive and ambition led me to a sham marriage for the sake of tuition money. Disgraceful. I never discussed Luke with my family, and as an act of self-preservation, I buried his memory in a locked container—certainly not my box of treasures—deep in my subconscious. Rarely did a thought of him intrude into the present. When it did, I acted quickly, shoving him back inside and slamming the lid. I counted myself lucky I never dreamed about him and his bloated purple face. Cold needles pierced the back of my neck, and I changed the subject from the macabre to the practical.

I remembered the feelings that swamped me on the first day of work, when I had palpitations at the thought of leaving Lorelei. If I'd had to place her in the hands of strangers, I knew I wouldn't have done it. There would be no family support in Augusta; I wouldn't know a soul. Was I ready to chuck everything I had worked for and move? Augusta was a small town—50,000 people compared to Chicago's three million—and I doubted they even had an advertising agency. But the worst aspect would be leaving my daughter with a stranger. A vision of Charlotte pulling my feet while Noah and Lorelei pulled my arms in the opposite direction played in my head. Was love or a career more important? When I was in Noah's arms, I chose love. When I was alone, my ghosts and uncertainty held sway.

Noah supported me in my career, and while he expressed polite interest in my projects, I knew he didn't understand my passion. Of course, in comparison with his profession, mine wasn't as vital—except to me.

I needed to talk to Noah about this and not on the phone. He wouldn't be coming to Chicago until the end of February. Plenty of time for me to think and brood.

Charlotte had given me and my team a new assignment. To tell the truth, I was a bit intimidated by the product—a home video game system that featured titles like they had in bars and arcades. My only experience was with the game of "Pong," and that had to be six years ago. Those diversions were not the reason I frequented the bars. Ted would be useful on this project. The team had endured long recitations of his prowess with "Space Invaders." I grabbed the phone and summoned him to my office to pick his brain.

When Noah called the next weekend, I made sure to be upbeat and chatty. He asked again when I was coming out to Georgia.

Deflecting on committing to a date, I said, "Tell me about the flight. How long is it?"

"Well, first you'll fly to Atlanta, then change planes for Augusta."

I gulped, inaudibly I hoped. "That means two take-offs and landings before I even see you."

Noah laughed. "Won't it be worth it?"

"Sure. I'm just nervous. The last time I was in a plane, we had an aborted landing at O'Hare."

"So that's why you're not big on flying. Well sugar, those are pretty rare."

I shivered. "All I know is, I don't want to endure another. But I can't wait to see you—and Augusta—so I'll go ahead and book the flights for March. The snow might be melted by then."

"What's the weather like for next week? Will I have to deal with a blizzard?"

"No. There's still snow on the ground, but nothing in the forecast. We've actually been above freezing during the day."

When Noah arrived the next Friday, I fell into his arms. My shoulders relaxed, and I felt my lips curve into a smile.

"I've missed you so much," I murmured into his neck.

His embrace tightened and the strength and solidity of him reassured me.

We fed the kids early and had a late, adults-only dinner. Mom had done the prep, and I helped her with the cooking. Ken was stuck at work and arrived as Mom was starting to fret the meatloaf would be overdone. Visions of crunchy meatloaf from childhood reminded me of how things had changed—and they were about to change even more.

It was good to focus on grown-up matters. My prospective move to Georgia was never far from my thoughts. The to-do list was daunting: find a new house, plan a move, strategize the wedding—although we still hadn't set a date.

Noah and I had discussed having him adopt Lorelei, but we hadn't had that discussion with her yet. She wasn't quite four. How should I frame the conversation? Should I go with, "How would you like a daddy?" That didn't sound right.

Lorelei had no memory of Luke; it had always been the two of us. But she was observant and had to notice Andy had a mommy and daddy. I should go to the library and look for some books on stepparents or blending families or whatever they were calling it these days.

Noah asked Mom to pass the meatloaf. "I hope you don't mind me taking a second helping, but this is amazingly delicious."

Mom couldn't hide her pleasure. I thought of all those years of her awful cooking when I was growing up. What a contrast!

"More wine?" Ken asked.

One glass was enough for me. "No, but thanks." I felt myself fading and wanted to be conscious for Noah's first night. Kicking off my Ferragamo heels, I reached for his hand and stroked it, then played a little footsie under the table. It had been almost two months since we'd been together, and I wanted him.

Noah declined a second glass as well. He turned to me and smiled that bright smile. He'd also kicked off his shoes, and the game of footsie was heating up. I was too.

Mom stood. "I have chocolate cake for dessert."

Glancing at Noah, I said, "I've got my dessert right here."

He broke out laughing. Ken spit out his wine, and Mom blushed. I didn't care.

"Sorry, but we have some catching up to do." I picked up my shoes and hustled up the stairs. Noah followed me in sock feet.

Our reunion was spectacular. Amazing how horny one could get in eight weeks and how blissful the release. After we made love, Noah turned on the bedside lamp and propped pillows so we could sit.

"Honey, we need to make plans. I'm settled into the hospital, but I don't think you want to live on base. We need to find a house."

"We need to plan a wedding." I admired my engagement ring twinkling in the ambient light.

"That too." He encircled me with his arm and pulled me closer.

I sighed. "So much to do, and I still haven't seen Augusta."

"You'll be out there in a matter of weeks. It's past time we figured things out."

"Like my career."

Noah caressed my arm. "I know how hard you worked to achieve a management position. Will you be all right leaving your job?" He tilted my chin to search my face.

I closed my eyes, not wanting him to see the wheels turning. "I don't know."

"Sweetheart, you're going to have to. Do you want to find a job in Augusta? Would you rather stay at home?" He brushed my hair back. "Don't you think Lori would like a brother or sister?"

Against my will, my eyes popped open. "Oh!" At the moment, that was all I could think to say.

How many times had I been to O'Hare? About a hundred times to drop off or pick up Luke—and the one trip to Jamaica I'd rather forget. I exited the taxi and looked for a porter to help with my bags. There was no doubt I'd overpacked for a week-long trip. Riding the wave of success of the perfume campaign, it was easy to wrangle a week off. Charlotte had reminded me about the deadline for our new project, and I assured her my crack team, led by Ted, was hard at work coming up with a fabulous campaign. Did I believe that? Maybe, but did I care? As I checked my bag, I pondered my shifting focus from work to Noah. Had I made my decision without realizing it? I knew I wanted Noah, but that was about it at this point.

Sitting in the non-smoking section didn't make a difference; my hair would need a shampoo, and my clothes would reek of smoke when I arrived. I took the window seat and a man with a briefcase sat in the aisle seat. No one claimed the middle seat.

When the jet accelerated and finally took off, I prayed like I hadn't since my First Holy Communion. I whispered, "Thank you, God," once we were above the clouds. My seatmate glanced over and tutted at my fear. Dressed in a suit, he was obviously a seasoned business traveler. I ignored him. Spying a *Vogue* magazine in the seat pouch, I fell on it with relief, welcoming the distraction. The stewardess sashayed down the aisle with the drink cart, and I ordered a vodka tonic, not caring it was eleven a.m. Got another sideways glare from the gray-haired businessman, who ordered black coffee. He removed some papers from his briefcase and donned reading glasses.

Peering out the tiny window in wonder, my fear subsided a bit. I knew take-offs and landings were the most dangerous part of flying, so I tried to relax before the next risky event. Growing used to the hum of the engines, I had another vodka tonic. If I were going to die, I might as well be feeling no pain.

The engine noise changed. I started, sat up, and craned my neck to see how the other passengers were reacting to our impending death. No one else seemed alarmed.

The gruff businessman took pity on my confusion and fear. "Trimming the engines to prepare for approach."

"Oh, I forgot that part. Last time I flew, I-I had a horrific experience."

"I take this flight every week. All is well."

"Thank you."

Glasses perched on his nose, he turned back to the papers on his tray table.

Minutes later, the plane landed with a small thump and rolled to a stop. My stomach felt a bit queasy as I made my way off the jet and onto a smaller plane with propellers.

We had to wait for luggage transfer and connecting passengers. With each passing moment, my nervousness grew. I thought back to old movies of air travel in propeller planes. They'd been in use for decades and must be safe. When he visited me, Noah took the same flights. I regretted the two drinks. The numbing effect was wearing off, and a dull headache pressed against my temples.

I wouldn't be at my best to see Noah.

After twenty fraught minutes, the door closed, and the plane rolled for take-off. Only a few seats were taken, which I figured gave the plane a better chance to stay aloft. The take-off was so smooth I didn't feel it. I knew the flight was brief and was mentally prepared for the change in the engine sound when we began our approach to Bush Field. After a skilled landing and a brief taxi, we arrived at the gate. I was about to meet my fiancé in Augusta.

Noah, dressed in scrubs, waited at the gate with flowers, a smile, and a dizzying kiss. He was right. The flights were worth it.

At the baggage carousel, Noah hefted my two full suitcases. I carried my makeup case and purse. We made our way to his car in the lot. A light green Chevy Impala four-door sedan. I never would have guessed. It seemed a bit tame for a young guy.

As we drove into town, Noah acted as a tour guide. He took me out to an early dinner at a little Italian restaurant, then back to his quarters on base. To my surprise, he had a neat little frame bungalow for himself. He parked, grabbed my luggage, and led me up the walk. He stopped on the porch. "Wait here a minute." After he carried in my bags, he picked me up and carried me over the threshold.

"Just practicin,' darlin'."

We raced to the bedroom and practiced some more for our life together. Lying in bed afterward, we talked about our future.

"I'm so glad you're finally here. What do you think so far?"

I nuzzled his neck and giggled. "I think you'll be a very good husband."

Noah chuckled. "I meant Augusta. Could you live here?"

Realizing I *had* made my decision, I said without reservation, "I can live wherever you are, my love. I'm ready to move."

Noah held me tight. Were those tears I felt on his face?

I put on Noah's undershirt and got out of bed. "I need to unpack some clothes for tomorrow and freshen up."

"There's clean towels in the bathroom. I'll join you."

When I opened my luggage and lifted the top layer of clothing, I found dog-dog on top of my blouses. "Oh, no!"

"What?"

"Lorelei packed dog-dog." I glanced at Noah. "I've got to call my mother. Let her know to pull out a spare from my stash."

"That's another thing we have to talk about. Lorelei. You know I want to adopt her."

I sat beside him on the bed, head on his shoulder. "And I want you to. For weeks, I've been struggling with how to bring up the subject of you becoming her father. With her, I mean."

"Don't stress about it, darlin.' Once y'all move here, the situation will evolve naturally."

"I hope you're right."

After I called my mother, Noah and I showered and planned our visit to Knoxville. I was apprehensive about seeing the Nagys after all this time. The prospect of meeting Noah's mother Jocelyn, as well as his aunt and uncle, made my teeth chatter. What if they didn't like me?

The drive took all day, but given the company and the scenery, I didn't mind. Coming from flat Chicago, the mountain vistas were enthralling. Noah entertained me with stories of his boyhood adventures. When he mentioned John, my heart fluttered. Would that reaction ever go away?

We stopped for an early lunch at a tiny BBQ joint on the highway. The food was heavenly.

"Mom and the Bradens are expecting us for dinner. You'll get to see their property and meet a Border Terrier or two."

"I hope your mother likes me." The barbecue sat in my belly like a lump of concrete.

Noah grinned. "She'll love you. Sonia has sung your praises to her."

Why hadn't that occurred to me? Jocelyn and Sonia were friends. They lived near each other and shared the bond of their sons.

On the rest of the drive, my mind wandered back to Chicago. I thought of the last time I saw the Nagys. Seven years had passed. I had changed a lot during that time. Had they?

Noah's aunt and uncle's place sat on the outskirts of Knoxville. The gravel drive ran past the veterinary offices and boarding kennels, then continued for about a quarter mile before reaching their home.

The closer we came to the compound, the faster my pulse raced. They must have heard the car crunching on the drive because when we pulled up to the main house, three people stood on the porch. A blond woman ran down the stairs to the car. Had to be Noah's mother Jocelyn.

We opened our doors and stepped out. The couple descended from the porch and approached, followed by a chubby, slow-moving dog. My first glimpse of a Border Terrier.

Jocelyn threw her arms around me. "So happy to meet you, Dani! This is my sister Darlene and her husband Terence." She released me and hugged Noah.

I could see the family resemblance between the sisters; both were slender and fit. Terence was a tall, lean man with gray hair and horn-rimmed glasses. My nervousness dissipated with their smiling faces and warm welcome. "I'm so happy to finally get to Tennessee and meet you." Then a piercing arrow reminded me of my plans for my first visit to Tennessee—with John. Would he always haunt me?

Darlene smiled. "Come on in. Supper's waitin' on the sideboard."

Lunch was hours ago, and the concrete lump in my belly had dissolved. An insistent, wet nose poked my leg. Someone didn't want to be ignored. I bent to pet the dog. "Who is this? Are all Border Terriers this...chubby?"

Terence answered. "That's Harriet. She's pregnant, due any time with her first litter. The sire Henry is around here somewhere." He whistled, and another dog came running. Henry insisted on his share of attention.

I didn't comment, but I thought Henry looked like a mutt. Nondescript, with brown grizzled fur, a sturdy body, and a neat head sporting a beard. As Noah promised, the terriers were friendly.

We left our luggage in the car. The drive had taken longer than planned, and Noah's family had delayed dinner, or supper as they called it, for us. Darlene had prepared a feast. The sight and smell of the food ignited my appetite. Noah raved about the homemade biscuits—almost as good as Ken's—served with honey butter. The chunky coleslaw, with a tangy twist, impressed me. Between bites of fried chicken—hand-battered, not Kentucky Fried—Noah's family told tales about his childhood at the Braden's property. Many of the stories included mention of John. Jocelyn watched my reaction, and I tried to appear stoic, but each time I heard his name, I dug my fingernails into the palm of my hand in an effort to replace the psychic pain with physical discomfort.

Conversation included several polite questions about my job and family. I pulled a small photo album from my purse and showed them pictures of Lorelei from birth to present.

"She's a beautiful child," Jocelyn said with a smile. She met my eyes. "I can't wait to meet her. Hope you're plannin' to give her several siblings."

Noah put down his fork and addressed his mother. "Already? You're goin' there already?" He shook his head and chuckled. "We're still figurin' out where to have the weddin'!"

Darlene exclaimed, "Here. Have it here!"

Terence looked a bit taken aback, but after a moment agreed. "Sure, we could do that. Long as your guests don't mind dogs."

Noah and I stared at each other. I hadn't even thought about a location for the wedding, but this offer was lovely. It could work. My family was scattered, but Noah's family and the Nagys were here, and Noah told me he would like to move to Knoxville after his commitment to the army was done. The hills of Tennessee had already captured my heart, so I was on board with the idea.

After dinner, Noah brought our luggage to his mom's cottage. We would stay the night in his childhood bedroom decorated with brown plaid bedspreads and matching drapes. Years ago, my brothers had the same ones; this room was a time capsule. Noah pushed the two twin beds together and unpacked.

I wandered around the room, taking in his boyhood treasures: the baseball trophies, the posters of The Stones, Hendrix, and The Who. When I spotted the Dr. No poster, I smiled. Apparently, Noah liked James Bond movies too—or Ursula Andress in her white bikini. Cringing at a mounted bass, I stopped cold, staring at a picture hanging beneath the unfortunate fish.

My hands shook as I picked it up. John and Noah.

"What you got there?" Noah came up behind me and rested his chin on my shoulder.

"Is-is this you and John?"

"Sure is. I remember that day so clearly. Miklos took us to Fort Loudon Lake. We had a blast."

"I can see that."

Noah took the picture from my hands and wrapped his arms around me. "I miss him too. Come on, darlin,' let's get some sleep. Aren't you tired?"

"Yes." Exhausted from the travel and the nerve-wracking pressure of meeting his family, I changed into pajamas and fell into bed. But it took a while for me to fall asleep. My mind swirled with memories of John.

While it was still dark, Noah shook me awake. "Harriet's having her puppies. Let's go!"

He yanked the covers from me and handed me last night's clothes. "Hurry! Throw these on. We don't want to miss this."

His urgency penetrated my sleep-fog. The excitement was contagious. I leapt out of bed, tossed on my clothes, and shoved my feet into shoes.

Noah grabbed a flashlight and led the way to the kennels, which were blazing with light. There, Terence, Darlene, and Jocelyn gathered at the whelping box. Harriet lay on her side, panting. Her body convulsed, and a blob fell from her nether parts.

I gasped. "Is that a puppy? What's wrong with it?"

Terence glanced at me. "Sure enough, that's a puppy in the sac. Just watch."

I did. A miracle. Harriet was a trouper. Even though this was her first litter, her instincts took over, and she managed beautifully, producing four tiny bits of life. She got up to go outside, and we followed. She delivered the placenta, and the dawn light revealed that was all—no more pups.

Harriet trotted back inside and curled up to nurse the newborns. Terence removed the pups one at a time to check their sex and weigh them. Two boys and two girls. All together, they weighed less than two pounds. So much life and potential packed in those tiny bodies.

"I'll take the small male," Noah said. "Dani, what do you think of the name 'Hank?'"

"It's perfect." Thrilled, I didn't think twice about the commitment—or the logistics. "Lorelei will love him, but don't be surprised if she calls him 'real dog.'"

We ate an early breakfast, then returned to the kennel. Henry sat guard outside the pen. Did he understand that the puppies were part of him? Did he miss Harriet, who was otherwise occupied? I would soon be learning a lot about dogs.

We showered and dressed for our luncheon. I had brought presents for the Nagys. Pálinka, an apricot brandy, for Miklos. It was hard to find in the U.S., but I got lucky. I brought Mrs. Nagy a silk scarf. After struggling with what to get Chuck and wife Carrie, I ended up buying a pair of brass candlesticks. Not very imaginative. The kids were easier to buy gifts for—Dr. Seuss books.

The Nagys welcomed us as if we were visiting royalty.

"*Lánya*, I am so happy to see you!" She threw her arms around me, and the years slipped away. Sonia hadn't changed much in the seven years since I saw them. A few gray hairs, a few lines on her brow. I knew what caused those.

Miklos grinned. "Little grease-monkey girl!" His hug left me breathless. He appeared to be thriving now he was back in Tennessee.

Chuck, although blind, was functioning well. Miklos had built a cottage on his property for Chuck's family. The design enabled Chuck to negotiate the rooms and hallways with ease. His wife Carrie worked for Miklos doing the books. Their children, Michael John, four, and Valerie, two, made my heart clutch—the family resemblance made me ache as I again wondered what my children with John would have looked like.

I saw Noah watching me and wondered if he knew what I was thinking. Guilt consumed me: why wasn't I wondering what my kids with Noah would look like? His forlorn face, his body language told me he had concerns. Forcing a smile, I took his hand and squeezed. He looked relieved.

Expecting a Hungarian dinner, I was surprised to see Miklos manning the grill. Hamburgers and hot dogs were on the menu. The one Hungarian treat was Sonia's rétes. Both loaves were poppyseed, John's favorite.

Miklos opened the Pálinka, and we toasted John's memory. The burn of the liquor made my eyes water, or were they watering for another reason?

Sonia blinked away tears. "My biggest regret is that John is buried in Chicago."

I knew then what I had to do.

Chapter Fourteen

BURYING THE PAST 1979

I dreaded giving my notice at J. Walter Thompson. As I rode the elevator, my stomach sank. I faced the fact I'd be abandoning my dreams and ambitions; dreams I'd had for years and worked so hard to achieve. It was a tremendous loss, but I was gaining so much more. At least that's what I told myself, and I was all but convinced.

Despite holding my head high and shoulders back, my feet dragged as I trudged down the corridor to Charlotte's office. As I approached, she was coming out the door. Taking one look at my face, she stopped and waved me in.

"Somethin's got your shorts in a knot. Spit it out."

I gulped several times and opened my mouth, doing a darn good imitation of a fish out of water.

Charlotte folded her arms, leaned against her desk, and said nothing.

I stood before her, my fists clenched, nails digging into my palms. "Charlotte, I am giving my two-week notice. I appreciate everything you and the firm have done for me."

"Don't tell me you're goin' over to the enemy."

I shook my head. "Oh, no. Never. I'm moving to Augusta, Georgia. My fiancé is doing his residency there. I have no career plans at this point."

"I'm sorry to lose you. You've performed well for us." Charlotte's voice was level. I couldn't read anything from her body language.

"Thank you, Charlotte."

"I'll let you know who will be taking on your responsibilities, and you can bring him or her up to speed." That woman was all business, a total professional.

I nodded and fled. At least she hadn't said someone was *replacing* me. My ego was pleased.

When I informed the co-op board of my pending move, they expressed polite regret, and assured me my shares would sell quickly. That was a huge relief.

Mom and Ken used their nest egg to buy a two-flat near where Paige used to live. Ken liked the ease of the commute from the north side, and they'd have an income from renting out the upstairs unit. There was a tenant in place, so the transition would be easy.

Everything was coming together. One last task remained—telling Lorelei. My nerve was failing, but it had to be done. After discussing—with Noah, Mom, and Ken—how to present our new reality to my daughter, I still had no clear idea what I would tell my almost four-year-old.

Our evening ritual of Lorelei's bath and bedtime story was the perfect occasion to broach the subject and at least start to prepare her. I selected *Mister Dog* to read that night. Was it really a choice? We read *Mister Dog* every night. Settling in bed with sweet-smelling, slightly damp Lorelei, I opened the book.

As usual, she sighed and said, "I wanna real dog, Mama. You said soon. When is soon?"

Grateful for this opening, I put my arm around her and snuggled her against my side. "When I was away on my trip, I met a little boy puppy named Hank. He looks a little bit like Crispin's Crispian. Noah will be bringing him home soon."

"Home here?" Lorelei's face was full of hope and longing.

"No, honey, home where Noah lives in Georgia."

Hands clasped, she pleaded with all her heart. "Can I go? Please?"

"Would you like us to live with Noah and Hank? We'd have to move to a new house. Far away."

Her furrowed brow cleared, and a smile spread across her face. She clapped her hands. "Okay. Let's go! I wanna a real dog and a new house."

I hugged her, tears stinging my eyes. "Yes, baby, it is okay."

She pulled back and asked, "Can Noah be my daddy?"

Time stopped as I contemplated how much Lorelei understood. I had sold her short. Thinking I would need moral support, I had planned to have this talk when Noah arrived on Friday for our April interlude. It turned out to be so easy. When I could speak, I asked, "Do you want Noah to be your daddy?"

My little girl nodded, and my heart rejoiced.

On Friday evening, as soon as Noah came through the door, Lorelei threw herself at him and hugged his legs. "A real dog and a new house soon! When is soon?"

Noah met my eyes, and I read joy in his face. His chameleon eyes blazed green with tears. He knelt on the floor and hugged Lorelei. "Very soon, little one."

Lorelei kissed his cheek. "Noah, my daddy." She held his face with her hands and smiled.

Can you feel your heart expand with joy? At that moment, I thought so.

Mom stepped into the hall and announced dinner. "Ken made his famous chicken salad."

During the meal, we chatted about Mom and Ken's new place, Lorelei's first airplane ride, and when Hank would be big enough to leave his mother and come home.

I broke off a piece of Ken's excellent baguette and asked Mom to pass the butter. We laughed.

Mom's breath hitched, and her face crumpled. "I'm going to miss you so much."

I knew there would be pain and regret about the move. Mom would be a mess. With Paige in California, Phil in Iowa, and Joe still on the road, her world was reduced to Ken and Andrew. Andrew didn't seem to understand how his world was changing. He had seen the new house and wanted his room to be an airplane, but Lolo moving away hadn't seemed to penetrate.

Noah ran upstairs to get pictures of Hank from his suitcase. He came back with the photos and showed them to Lorelei. She touched Hank's image as if she were petting him, then kissed the picture. "I love Hank."

***

We woke to the smell of cinnamon rolls and coffee. Noah asked for five more minutes, so I let him sleep. I rose, showered, and dressed. When I peeked in Lorelei's room, it was empty. Mom must have gotten her up to help with breakfast. There wouldn't be many more opportunities. My breath caught. Life was changing.

The co-op shares sold immediately. I was happy with the price and glad the closing was in forty-five days; now I had external motivation to complete the transition. My timeline—for finding a house, coordinating the move, and making wedding plans—compressed. Now that I wasn't working, I was free to fly to Augusta for some serious house hunting. Lorelei would come with me. Noah was picking up Hank in two weeks, so she would be able to meet him.

"Your five minutes are up, mister!" I fell on Noah and embraced him with a fierceness that surprised me.

"Ouch! You don't know your own strength, woman."

"Get up, honey, before the cinnamon rolls are gone."

Two weeks later, I prepared for our house hunting trip. It took an unreasonable amount of time to pack Lorelei's small suitcase. She piled all her books inside the bag, and I removed them. Then her clothes went through the same process. She wanted to cram the entire contents of her room in the bag. I explained we would only be gone a few days, and she needed to take three outfits, one or two books, and one or two toys. There was no question she'd choose *Mister Dog*, and *Go Dog Go*, and Andy and dog-dog. I should have packed for her; the chore took three times as long with her help.

Goodbyes dragged on forever. The waiting taxi's horn blared as Lorelei told Andy for the fifth time she was going in an airplane to see a real dog. I gently urged her to the front door.

Lorelei bounced in the backseat of the taxi. As we approached O'Hare, she craned her neck and pointed at the sky. "Look! Airplane! Lori going up in the sky!" Eyes wide, she turned to me. "Am I, Mama? Going up in the sky?"

I assured her she would indeed go up in the sky, and Noah did it all the time.

The flights were smooth. I maintained a stoic attitude and managed a tense smile, not wanting Lorelei to know how much I disliked flying. I recalled Noah telling me I wouldn't have to fly, the airplane would, and I burst out laughing. Lorelei joined in. "Mama is happy!" And I was. Fascinated with the experience, Lorelei behaved perfectly, handling her first flight like a champ.

Noah picked us up and drove to his bungalow. A latticed wooden baby gate blocked the entrance to the kitchen. Newspapers covered the floor, and a tiny dish of water sat in one corner. But our eyes were drawn to a pile of blankets.

As Lorelei tiptoed to the barrier, she whispered, "Hank is here?"

Noah removed the gate. "Yes, he sure is."

Lorelei stepped forward. A little brown head appeared from under the blankets. Hank's ears pricked up, and he freed himself from his nest. Tail wagging, he scurried to Lorelei and peed at her feet.

"Oops! Hank tinkled." She checked our faces to see if Hank was in trouble.

Noah said, "It's okay, Lori. Hank is still a baby. He'll have to learn to go potty outside."

"Oh. Real dogs go potty outside. Okay."

I expected my daughter to fall to the floor and cradle the puppy in her arms, but she stood there, struck motionless, seemingly in awe of the tiny creature.

"Are you going to pet him?" I asked.

"Can I? Can I hold him?" Lorelei bent to the little dog and said, "Hi, Hank. I am Lori and you are a real dog." She held out her hand, and Hank licked it. Her peals of laughter and beaming face made me tear up.

"Let's take Hank outside to see if he has more potty," Noah said. He picked up the puppy and led the way to the small, fenced yard.

Hank did in fact have more potty. When the puppy was finished, he ambled over to Lorelei. She whispered, "Real dog. Hank is a real dog." She sat on the lawn, and the pup clambered into her lap.

"Honey, can you get your camera?" I asked.

Noah ducked inside, returned with the camera, and took several pictures. "Think I got some good ones."

As expected, Lorelei was besotted with the puppy. She peered up at Noah. "Thank you for Hank. I love him."

Noah knelt beside her. "When I was a little boy, I had a dog like Hank. His name was Fred."

"Where is he?"

"Fred went to heaven a long time ago. I miss him, but I'm so happy to have Hank in our family."

"Me too!"

"Me three!" I scooped up Hank, got nose to nose with him. He licked my face, and I giggled like a child.

The next morning, I had a hard time getting Lorelei to leave the puppy at home while we looked at houses. I understood her reluctance, but the realtor was due to pick us up at any moment.

Not wanting to trigger tears, I kept my voice level, but firm. "Honey, it's too warm to leave Hank in the car while we go in houses. He is still a baby and needs a lot of naps. It's nice and cool here, inside the house. We'll be back soon."

Susan, our realtor, was the wife of one of Noah's fellow residents. An Augusta native, she knew the best areas. I convinced Noah to accept the proceeds from my co-op for our down payment. His masculine pride might have taken a hit, but he agreed. I told him he could pay me back when he made his huge doctor's salary.

During the morning, we toured several houses, but nothing impressed.

As we all piled in the car after another failed showing, Susan sighed. "I've got two more houses for us to view, but I have a feeling you'll really like this next one."

Noah and I exchanged a look. I whispered, "I sure hope so." Lorelei's behavior had been exemplary to this point, but I knew it couldn't last much longer.

The minute we pulled up in front of the red brick Georgian, I knew we'd found our home.

Susan announced, "This fabulous home was built in 1916 and was completely renovated just last year. It's fully fenced. And there's a pool for those hot Georgia summers."

"Speaking of hot, is it always this toasty in May?" I dabbed my upper lip with a tissue.

In her smooth realtor's voice, Susan answered, "It can be."

When we entered through the eight-foot-tall door, the rush of air-conditioned coolness was welcome.

The house was laid out well. A bit formal, but the eat-in kitchen changed my mind. Five bedrooms. I closed my eyes and envisioned those rooms filled with children. Lorelei would love to have a brother or sister.

As we made our way through the house, Noah flipped electrical switches and checked the water pressure in the sinks. From his smiling reaction, I had no doubt he was as impressed and excited as I.

I touched his arm, and he met my eyes. "This is it," he said. "Do you agree?"

"Yes, I love it!" It was too quiet. "Wait, where's Lori?"

"Bet she went back to that pink little girl's room. She was fascinated by the window seat."

"I hope you're right." With Noah close behind, I dashed down the hall, flashing on the thought of the swimming pool. My heart returned to a normal rhythm when I saw my girl kneeling on the cushions covering the window seat, her nose pressed to the glass.

"There you are!" I sat beside her and gave the canopy bed, the pink walls, and the sky-blue ceiling with painted puffy white clouds a closer examination. This was a room fit for a princess.

Lorelei faced me. "Mama, see the swimming pool? Can we go in, can we?"

Noah picked her up and said, "Not today, princess. You'll have to wait until we move in. Okay?"

"When? Soon? Can Hank come?"

Noah and I spoke at the same time. "Yes, yes!"

"I wanna go see Hank," Lorelei insisted. Her lip trembled and a fat tear fell from her eye. She needed lunch and a nap. Noah asked Susan to drive us home and told her we'd be in touch.

When we came through the front door, Hank whimpered. Noah helped Lorelei through the gate. She fell to her knees and hugged the little dog. "Don't cry, baby Hank."

After a peanut butter and jelly sandwich, I tucked her in for a nap.

While Lorelei slept, I told Noah about my plan to bring John's body back to Tennessee.

"When did you decide *this*?"

Stunned at his tone, I recoiled, not expecting that reaction. "When we visited the Nagys."

"So, two months ago. And you didn't bother to tell me?" His folded arms across his chest put a barrier between us.

"Where is this coming from? Are you upset?"

In an icy voice, he asked, "Why didn't you tell me?"

I gulped. "I-I-I...don't know."

"Humph, you don't know. Odd." Noah paced around the living room of the bungalow. "I saw the way you were with Chuck's children. Maybe I'm wrong, but I couldn't help thinkin' you were picturin' the children you would have had with John." He studied me. "Tell me I'm wrong. Tell me you're not in love with a ghost."

First my mother, now Noah. Were they right? "B-but the reburial isn't for me, it's for Sonia."

His face set in stern lines, Noah rasped, "Is it? And I didn't hear a denial."

My world shattered. I didn't know where to look, couldn't stand the expression on Noah's face. Had I done it again, caused irreparable harm to a man? Sabotaged my chance for love? I started to blubber.

Noah rushed to me, grabbed my shoulders, and forced eye contact. "After all this time, you're still wounded. And I don't know how to fix it."

Between sobs, I protested, "But I quit my job. And Lorelei wants you to be her daddy. A few hours ago, we were about to buy a house." I pulled away, disgusted with myself for pleading. Anger flared. "For God's sake, I have to vacate my condo in three weeks! What are you saying?"

Shaking his head, he moved to the front window and rested his forehead against the glass. "I don't know what I'm saying." He smacked the glass and turned to face me. "When are you doing this? Before or after our wedding? By the way, are we goin' to set a date? Hell, are we even gettin' married?"

His words struck me like so many stones. I couldn't speak.

He threw his arms wide. "I know it's irrational to think I'm competin' with a dead man, but that's how I feel. Maybe I was wrong to seek you out. Maybe John is a roadblock rather than a shared memory." He gulped and in a husky voice said, "I need you to be sure of *me*. Of *us*. If there is an us."

I approached him and put my arms around his resistant body. It was like hugging a block of ice. "How can you say that? Of course there is an us. And I am sure. How can I prove it to you?"

He escaped my embrace. "You're gonna have to think on that, Dani." Then he kissed my forehead. "I'm going to stay at a hotel tonight. Be back in the morning to take y'all to the airport."

I watched him drive away. Choking back tears, I dialed the airline to move up our return flight.

***

With our strained parting—polite goodbyes and a perfunctory kiss—the flight back was an ordeal. Lorelei didn't want to leave Hank in Augusta. Over and over, she asked, "When do we go to the new house? Soon? I miss Hank."

On the second leg of the flight, Lorelei fell asleep. I wondered if there would be a new house, if we would ever see Hank again, if I could move in with Mom and Ken until I found another place, if I could beg Charlotte to give me my job back. My mind spun, taking me to horrific, heart-breaking scenarios.

After we arrived at O'Hare and retrieved our luggage, we located Ken's car idling at the curb on the lower level. As he accelerated onto the Kennedy, Linda Ronstadt came on the radio, singing "Just One Look." I buried my face in my hands and begged, "Please turn it off."

By the time we arrived at the condo, I managed to get the lyrics of "Just One Look" out of my head. But hearing that song, so evocative of the night I fell in love with John, was torture, and my emotions still gyrated out of control.

When she saw my tear-stained face and smeared mascara, Mom flinched in dismay. "What happened? Did—"

I shook my head. "Not now." Brushing past her, I picked up my daughter and bounded upstairs.

As I bathed Lorelei and fielded her questions about "when," I brooded. Noah was hurt. How did I fail to show him my heart? He thinks I'm not ready, even after everything I've done. How can I show him I am?

During my vendetta against men, I had rated each kiss on the scale of John. I'd met some good kissers who rated very high, but there was always that benchmark, impossible to meet. When I first kissed Noah, I once again used my rating system. I shouldn't have. It was time I removed the qualifier and admitted to myself I had never felt this way—ever. My love for Noah was something new, different, and real.

As I tucked Lorelei in bed after the thousandth reading of *Go Dog Go*, she was already asleep. I trudged into my bathroom, cringed at my face in the mirror, and started bawling like I'd lost my best friend. Perhaps I had. I washed my face and changed into a soft sweater and pants, then forced myself to go downstairs to talk to my mother.

The next morning, I dragged the phone to the bedroom chair and plopped down, gazing out the window at the courtyard. Glad for the extra-long phone cord, I dialed Paige.

"I thought I'd be calling you for advice about a wedding dress."

"Interesting opening. So, you're not?"

"Nope. And...I'm not even sure I'm getting m-married."

Paige shrieked, "What the hell! I thought you went to Augusta to buy a house. My God, spill."

Letting out a sigh, I said, "I'm burying John."

"Now you're talking crazy. Didn't you already do that, like seven years ago?"

When I didn't reply, Paige asked, "Hey! You there?"

"Give me a moment. I'm a mess. When I told Noah about my plan, he said he didn't think I'm ready to get married."

"Holy shit! Okay. Take your time. What plan?"

"When I visited the Nagys in March, Sonia told me she regretted that John was buried in Chicago. I knew then I had to bring him home."

"Wow, sounds complicated, not to mention insane and expensive."

"Oh, it's complicated and expensive. Not insane, though. I've made all the arrangements with Holy Sepulchre and booked cross-country transport. Had to get the Holy Roman Apostolic Catholic Church involved too. Sonia doesn't know yet. Miklos helped with the logistics in Tennessee."

Paige snorted. "Like I said, it's insane. How does this prove you're ready to marry Noah? Connect the dots for me."

I shivered. "When John's casket is buried at Knoxville National Cemetery, I'm placing a few items in his grave."

"Let me guess. A yellow t-shirt and a bottle of Jade East."

"And a gold bracelet engraved with *John and Dani 4ever*." Tears welled. I rose from the chair, yanked the phone to the bed, and reached for the box of tissues on the nightstand.

"Holy Mother of God! I know you always felt like John was the only one, but I thought you'd gotten over that a long time ago, especially since you got *engaged to be married!*" Paige's voice rose to a crescendo.

"My fiancé doesn't think I have."

"Good grief. You've tortured yourself for years, Dani. It's got to stop. Let John go—all of him."

I covered the receiver for a moment to muffle my sobs.

"Dani?"

Gathering myself, I answered, "I'm going to—really. Maybe my totems are just symbols, but I feel like I'm burying John at last. I've used him as a crutch for far too long."

"Yes, you have. You took self-sabotage to a whole new level. When is this burial plan happening?"

"Next week. I'm flying out alone."

"What about Noah? Is he going to be there?"

"I don't know, but I sure hope so. We haven't talked, and I need to make things right. I can't lose him."

When I booked my flights, I groaned at learning I'd have to change planes in Atlanta. Scenarios of Noah waiting at the gate for me floated through my mind—mere fantasy. He had no way of knowing my plans. The second leg took me to Knoxville's McGhee Tyson Airport, where I rented a car and drove to the Nagy's.

Miklos had invited me to their home before the ceremony. When he told Sonia about what we had arranged, she broke down. She was both devastated and happy. And grateful. The Nagys never would have been able to afford this.

When I walked in the door, Sonia rushed to me. We embraced. "*Lánya*, my darling girl. I can never thank you enough for bringing my son home to me."

Miklos escorted us to his van for the drive to the cemetery.

My gigantic purse was loaded with tissue and makeup for touchups. I expected to cry buckets. In addition, it contained my talismans: a ragged yellow t-shirt, an empty bottle of Jade East, and a gold bracelet.

The day was overcast with the temperature in the seventies. My mind traveled back to that September day in 1971, a day I barely recalled, when John was buried at Holy Sepulchre. Memories, wrapped in gauze and sorrow, floated just out of range. The flag-draped coffin and military ceremony at the graveside in Knoxville seemed familiar, but I couldn't discern whether the scene playing out in front of me was identical to the one from that distant day or something I'd seen in a movie. My sense of unreality was that strong.

Sonia trudged to the coffin and laid a rose on top. I followed her and placed the t-shirt, bottle, and bracelet beside the flower. My eyes sought the golden heart. I couldn't read the inscription but knew it read *Dani and John 4ever*. At that thought, the dam of my grief broke, and I clung to my not-to-be mother-in-law.

"John is finally home in the hills of Tennessee," I whispered to Sonia.

Warm hands clasped my shoulders. Startled, I turned to see Noah.

I patted my eyes. "I-I didn't think you'd come."

Noah glanced at me, then away. "I didn't come for you. John was my brother, and I came for the Nagys."

I hung my head and muttered, "I deserve that."

He tipped up my chin and studied me.

I waited for him to say something, but he didn't, so I accepted this was up to me. "It's so good to see you. I've missed you, missed talking to you."

"Have you?" His lips twisted. "I saw you put something on the casket. Care to tell me what?"

"Just a memento. Nothing that matters anymore."

"Really? Sure seems like it matters." His gaze never left my face.

"When John died, I fought to keep him alive, if only in my memory. I convinced myself I'd never love another man. Then came you. You changed everything. *You* matter. I love you. Only you. Please tell me you believe me." I choked on my tears. "Please, Noah."

My heartbeat ticked down the seconds as I anticipated his response.

He took my left hand. "I see you're wearing your engagement ring."

"I never take it off."

"Why?"

"Because I want to marry you!"

His piercing green eyes studied me.

I waited in agony.

"I believe you." Then Noah swept me into his arms and kissed me with conviction. When he caught his breath, he said, "Let's plan that weddin'!"

As we walked back to his car, I pondered the men I have loved—or married. At last, here was a man I could love *and* marry—this good man, Noah Grant.

My total immersion in love at thirteen was exceptional. I believe with all my heart it was true love and would have lasted. When John died, my equilibrium was knocked sideways. Losing him brought lingering consequences. His handsome face and gentleness will remain etched in my soul. Yes, our bond would have lasted, but it wasn't meant to be.

John taught me about love. I learned the lesson, then forgot it when I lost him. At age nineteen, my coping mechanisms were lousy. The withdrawal from life—renouncing school, work, and family—took a toll. Paige and Mom nurtured me through my grief; their love brought me back to life—but as a monster, a walking, talking, vengeful bitch determined to hurt men. I broke a lot of hearts—and destroyed one. For all my cataloging of Luke's deficiencies, I never faced my own until years after his suicide. I will never know his full history, but his family was broken. Luke was incapable of love; back then, I was too. The litany of insults I had for myself during that time was long: venal, manipulative, greedy, calculating, conniving, unprincipled, and most of all, dishonest. Dishonest with Luke, but also with myself.

The shame of those years would never leave me, I was certain. How should I partition the blame for Luke's suicide? That task was beyond me. In fact, it was not my job—and now I was able to let it go.

Then came Noah, my salvation, and the light of my life. His compassion and understanding empowered me to forgive myself for my past failings.

At long last, I buried the ghost we shared.

They grow some good men in Knoxville, Tennessee. I have had the great honor of loving, and being loved by, two of them.

The End

Acknowledgments

Just One Look is a true labor of love. The novel is set in the Chicago neighborhood where I grew up, and I hope my affection for the people and the era comes through in my writing. I must make a disclaimer to my childhood friends: this is a work of fiction.

My critique partners at the Kerrville Writers Association contributed many excellent insights as I brought them pages. My beta readers, Daryl Herring, Ann Bishop, Vicki George, Elizabeth Roberts, and Vicki Brower added valuable suggestions and comments. Thank you so much.

Joanne Kukanza Easley

A retired registered nurse with experience in both the cold, clinical operating room and the emotionally fraught world of psychiatric hospitals, Joanne lives on a small ranch in the Texas Hill Country, where she writes fiction about complicated, twentieth-century women. Her multi-award winning debut, *Sweet Jane,* released in March, 2020, was named the adult fiction winner at the Texas Author Project and shortlisted for the Sarton Award and Eric Hoffer Award, among others. *Just One Look*, Joanne's second novel, was a May 2022 Pulpwood Queen Book Club Pick. *I'll Be Seeing You,* her third novel, features characters from *Sweet Jane*. Her prize-winning short stories and poetry have appeared in several anthologies.

Sweet Jane

A drunken mother makes childhood ugly. Jane runs away at sixteen, determined to leave her fraught upbringing in the rearview. Vowing never to return, she hitchhikes to California, right on time for the Summer of Love. Seventeen years later, she looks good on paper: married, grad school, sober, but her carefully constructed life is crumbling. When Mama dies, Jane returns for the funeral, leaving her husband in the dark about her history. Seeing her childhood home and significant people from her youth catapults Jane back to the events that made her the woman she is. She faces down her past and the ghosts that shaped her family. A stunning discovery helps Jane see her problems through a new lens.

I'll Be Seeing You

A saga spanning five decades, *I'll Be Seeing You*, explores one woman's life, with and without alcohol to numb the pain. Young Lauren knows she doesn't want to be a ranch wife in Palo Pinto County, Texas. After she's discovered by a modeling scout at the 1940 Fort Worth Stock Show Parade, she moves to Manhattan to begin her glamourous career. A setback ends her dream, and she drifts into alcohol dependence and promiscuity. By twenty-four, she's been widowed and divorced, and has developed a pattern of fleeing her problems with geographical cures. Lauren's last escape lands her in Austin, where, after ten chaotic years, she achieves lasting sobriety and starts a successful business, but happiness eludes her. Fast forward to 1985. With a history of burning bridges and never looking back, Lauren is stunned when Brett, her third husband, resurfaces, wanting to reconcile after thirty-three years. The losses and regrets of the past engulf her, and she seeks the counsel of Jane, a long-time friend from AA. In the end, the choice is Lauren's.